Meet Me in Virginia

A Far & Away Novel

Elizabeth Camden

This is a work of fiction. Names, characters, incidents, and dialogues are products of the author's imagination and are not to be construed as real. Any resemblance to actual events or persons, living or dead, is entirely coincidental.

Published by Three Magnolias Press

Cover design by Hannah Linder Designs

ISBN (print): 978-1-7332225-6-3
ISBN (digital): 978-1-7332225-7-0

Chapter One

Williamsburg, Virginia

Three months ago, Alice Chadwick had been in love, on the cusp of tenure as a history professor, and had embarked on a dazzling adventure in London. Everyone at the College of William & Mary had been cheering her on, but like Icarus flying too close to the sun, Alice endured a catastrophic fall from grace.

At least she was finally home. The taxi pulled away and she wheeled two suitcases toward her townhouse, grateful nobody was in the parking lot to witness her humiliating return to Williamsburg.

A profusion of lilacs bloomed near her front porch. Normally she would pause to sample their heavenly scent, but the urge to hurry inside, slip beneath the covers, and scrub the last three months from her mind was too strong. Once she recovered from jet lag, she would begin planning for how to salvage her career because maybe it wasn't too late. She was only thirty-two years old and had plenty of time to start over. Life was good, wasn't it? She should be grateful.

She *was* grateful, but her career as a history professor was hanging by a thread, and it would snap if word of what happened in London got out. Everything felt heavy as she trudged up her porch steps, but the sight of some climbing ivy strangling her lilacs couldn't be ignored. She dropped to her knees and tugged the ivy away.

Once free, the lilacs seemed to quiver in relief. "Poor things," she murmured. If she'd been here, she wouldn't have let the ivy get out of control.

She twisted around to sit on the top step, battling the urge to weep. Strange, because she hadn't cried once through all the trauma of the past three months, but the familiar scent of lilacs was so quintessentially American that it triggered a prickle behind her eyes. She needed to get inside before anyone saw her. Mrs. Wieland next door was a terrible gossip and Alice needed a few days before she told anyone she was home. If people at the college knew, they'd want to know why she had returned from her semester of leave so early, and it was the last thing she wanted to discuss.

She couldn't resist a quick inhale of floral sweetness, and sighed at the soothing effect. The head of the chemistry department said that aromatherapy was "bunk" with no scientific grounding, but Alice knew better.

First of all, she would never use a tacky word like *bunk*, and secondly, she didn't need proof. Women had been nurturing gardens for millennia and knew the power of herbal scents to calm a fractured spirit. She smoothed the fabric of her gingham skirt as it pooled around her legs, glad to be home despite the reason for it.

Sixteen hours of travel had left her tired and grubby. Strands of her mahogany-brown hair tugged free in the breeze, and she finger-combed them back behind her ears. A shower and clean hair would feel good, but at the moment, the thought of blow-drying hair that fell almost to her elbows was exhausting.

A clank and a muffled "Shhhhhh" sounded from somewhere nearby.

Alice shot to her feet, glancing about. Aside from the chirp of nearby sparrows, now all was still and silent. The wooden shutters on her bay window were closed, just as she'd left them to protect the antiques in the front room. She cocked her head to listen and observe.

A hint of cigar smoke lingered in the air, and speckles of ash dotted the porch railing. Had someone been smoking on her private front porch? Quite odd. Nobody in this enclave of fine townhouses smoked cigars.

Anxiety prickled across her skin. It sounded like the noise had come from *inside* her townhouse. Maybe it was paranoia, but the last few months taught her to be cautious.

She hurried down the front steps, scanning the parking lot for anything out of place . . . and that was when she spotted it. In a parking lot filled with practical cars, Daisy Tucker's alpine white Lexus looked like a swan among crows.

Daisy was the only person in all of Williamsburg who knew Alice was returning home today. And the cigar scent? Kingsley Tucker, Daisy's father-in-law, was known for smoking fine Cuban cigars. How he managed to get cigars from Cuba despite the American embargo was a mystery, but the Tuckers had their ways.

There was no avoiding this. At least Daisy and Kingsley were friends she could count on not to pry into her humiliating expulsion from London. After a brief chat, she would plead jet lag and ask them to leave. She squared her shoulders and twisted her key in the lock, then pushed the door open.

"Surprise!" The lights flipped on and a spray of confetti flew in the air.

Countless people crammed into her front room, smiling and clapping. Daisy rushed forward to greet her in a cloud of Chanel No. 5.

"Welcome home," Daisy said while delivering a perfect set of air kisses beside both of Alice's cheeks.

"Oh, wow," Alice managed to choke out. "Just . . . *wow*." At least twenty people ringed her living room, all of them smiling, holding teacups of punch and looking at her in expectation. "My goodness, thank you for this homecoming. It's so . . . unexpected."

What a disaster. She wasn't ready to face anyone yet, but people crowded around her. Someone opened the blinds and sunlight flooded the room, illuminating her vintage furniture and walls of shelving filled with well-thumbed books.

"How was the filming?" Kingsley Tucker asked, his grandfatherly voice booming. Chatter in the room came to a halt as everyone turned to listen.

And so it begins. Landing a plum job on a movie set packed with every high-profile British actor imaginable was bound to unleash a torrent of questions. She'd known it would happen, and already had the perfect excuse to evade the scrutiny.

"It was wonderful, but you should see the confidentiality forms I had to sign. No gossiping allowed!"

It wasn't a lie. The attorneys in London unloaded a firestorm of threats against her and she signed dozens of forms, including an iron-clad nondisclosure agreement.

"We're all very proud," Kingsley said. "Once that movie comes out, there won't be any more griping from the History Department about granting tenure to a Jane Austen expert, right?"

Over in the corner, a few of her colleagues from the History Department frowned. Alice specialized in all aspects of nineteenth-century history, although her specialty was the world of Jane Austen.

Why did the study of Jane Austen still invite such contempt from her male colleagues? They instinctively dismissed Austen's heroines as passive, doe-eyed ingénues with limited accomplishments. Alice's doctoral dissertation was a flaming arrow aimed at destroying this condescending attitude. Jane Austen wrote with a sharp quill and acid wit. Her heroines used their intelligence and domestic skills to transform cold houses into havens of beauty and moral order. These women weren't passive; they were on a crusade to tame the harshness of society and soften its sharp edges.

When a British film company embarked on a big-budget adaptation of *Emma*, one of Jane Austen's most celebrated novels, they hired Alice to be the historical consultant on the film. The choice of an American for such a plum appointment had been controversial from the outset. Foolishly, Alice had believed that the high-profile accomplishment would strengthen her case for tenure at William & Mary.

"As I said, I'm not really allowed to talk about anything related to the film."

Kingsley's patrician face softened in concern and he lowered his voice. "Those old dinosaurs in your department aren't going to give you any pushback, are they? A high-profile movie seems more influential than the dry academic articles they obsess over."

Mrs. Wieland, the nosy widow from next door who was completely ignorant of the political infighting around academic tenure, approached holding a platter. "Crab cakes with mango salsa," she proudly announced.

"They look delicious," Alice said, eager to discuss anything other than her fading hope of tenure.

"I made them myself, but I used your recipe," Mrs. Wieland said. "It took me three tries, but I think they're as good as the ones you make."

Alice gamely sampled a crab cake. "They're *better* than the ones I make," she said, causing Mrs. Wieland to beam with pride. It looked like Kingsley wanted to keep talking business, and Alice scrambled for an excuse to disengage.

"I should be helping Daisy with the drinks," she said with a quick squeeze on Kingsley's arm before heading to the kitchen.

She loved this tiny kitchen with its view over the herb garden and overhead rack of dangling copper pans. A butcher-block counter provided plenty of room to cook while demarcating the kitchen from the living area. Daisy was adding sprigs of mint to glasses of iced tea.

"Thank you for all this, but you shouldn't have," Alice said.

"Of course I should have!" Daisy said with a toss of her sleek blond hair. "So tell me ... what was it like working with Sebastian Bell?"

"I can't talk about—"

"I heard about the nondisclosure agreement, but come on. You can tell me."

Sebastian Bell was the reigning heartthrob of British historical movies, and naturally the person everyone would want to know about. He was also at the top of the list of things Alice had been forbidden to discuss in the nondisclosure agreements.

Alice tried to sound at ease as she reached for trays of ice from the freezer. "I promised not to discuss anything on the set."

Daisy rolled her eyes but moved on. "I'm sorry Kyle couldn't come. He's over at the country club working with Jack on the golf course."

"Hmmm," Alice said as she filled a silver bucket with ice cubes. The impending golf course had been debated since the day it was announced. As the largest landowners in the county, the Tuckers had embarked on a controversial decision to convert over a hundred acres of wilderness into an 18-hole golf course, complete with a grandiose new clubhouse. Daisy's husband, Kyle, had been the biggest advocate for the fancy new golf course.

Alice and Daisy had been friends for years, but the golf course was a delicate topic they would never agree upon, and rarely discussed. Alice had been opposed to the golf course from the moment she heard of it. She joined with other professors and students at the college to protest it. They'd picketed, gathered signatures, and appealed to the state to intervene.

None of it worked. The clubhouse was already built, but political wrangling to stop the golf course succeeded in delaying it for a few years. The Tuckers ultimately prevailed and they'd broken ground on the golf course shortly before Alice left for England.

The loss of all that pristine wilderness seemed unbearably sad as Alice slowly refilled the ice trays.

"What's wrong?" Daisy asked. "You look as worn out as a biscuit dunked in gravy."

Alice nodded. "It's after midnight in London."

"Oh my heavens, you poor dear," Daisy gushed. "I didn't think. You go put your feet up, and I'll wind this party down."

It took almost an hour, but Daisy finally managed to gracefully nudge people out of the house. Daisy left soon after for a touch-up appointment to have her roots dyed but left her father-in-law behind to help Alice restore the townhouse to order. Alice had a dishwasher but rarely used it because she'd never put antique Staffordshire porcelain into a dishwasher.

Kingsley rolled up his sleeves to wash and rinse, while Alice dried each piece as it came to her. With luck, they'd finish soon and she could finally collapse into bed.

"Did you hear about what's going on down at the Roost?" Kingsley asked as he handed her another serving dish.

Alice stilled. Her last hope to save her career lay in solving the mysterious origins of the Roost. The derelict building was at least three hundred years old, and its location hidden in the woods left it vulnerable to antique hunters, drunken students, and vandalism.

"What's going on at the Roost?" she asked in a calm voice, although her heart started pounding. The only good thing that came from her time in London was finding another piece of the puzzle about the Roost's enigmatic history. The more she learned, the more fascinating the place became.

"Kyle is letting a fellow named Jack Latimer live in it. Jack is the golf course architect who's been here ever since we broke ground."

"Kyle is letting someone *live* in the Roost?" It was unthinkable, and she nearly dropped the Staffordshire bowl.

Kingsley held up his hands to placate her. "I know, I tried to stop him, but you know Kyle. I delegated management of the family trust to him, and I can't step in to micromanage every decision he makes."

The Roost was one of the last original buildings from the early settlers at Jamestown. Every inch of its weathered oak timbers was laden with history, folklore, and secrets of the past. It was located close to the new golf course, shielded by a hundred yards of ancient sycamore and oak trees. To let anyone live inside the Roost boggled her mind.

"The place isn't even habitable," Alice said. "Nobody has lived in the Roost since the 1930s. It doesn't even have water or electricity."

Kingsley shrugged. "Jack doesn't mind, and Kyle will do anything to keep him happy. A Jack Latimer golf course will add luster to the country club and attract golfers from all over the state. He'll only be living there for a few months, and he's jerry-rigged a generator to get a little electricity. There are some tractors and a run-down trailer parked at the place, too. He put a Baltimore Ravens flag out front."

Alice put a hand to her forehead, refusing to panic yet as she began pacing in the compact kitchen. The Roost was on land that had belonged to the Tucker family since the eighteenth century, when they owned over five thousand acres of tidewater property. The Tuckers were Virginia royalty, their name as prestigious as the Lees, the Jeffersons, and the Washingtons. They could trace their heritage back to the earliest days of American settlement, and the Roost had been their first homestead. They had sold off some of their land over the twentieth century, but they still retained ownership of the land on which the new golf course, the country club, and the Roost were situated.

"Did Kyle formally lease the Roost to this man?" she asked Kingsley. "Was there actually a signed contract?"

"A handshake deal," Kingsley said. "The word of a Tucker is stronger than any flimsy piece of paper."

She'd trust a handshake deal from Kingsley, but not his son. Kyle owned an antique store in town and had a reputation for misleading customers about the value of his offerings. He'd also pocketed a fortune by selling off parcels of family land. When Kyle took over management of the family business, Tucker's Grove was three thousand acres of mostly undeveloped land in the southern portion of the county. The pristine wilderness was a priceless treasure reminiscent of what the earliest English settlers would have seen when they landed on these shores in 1607.

Alice and the other concerned citizens opposing development lost the battle about the clubhouse and the golf course, but the Roost could still be saved.

"Would you mind if I went to have a look at the Roost?" Alice asked Kingsley. "It would be a shame if the person lodging there did something to damage its historic nature."

Kingsley's eyes warmed. "I would be grateful," he said. "I'm incredibly proud of what Daisy and Kyle have accomplished, but they don't share the same veneration for history as you and I. By all means, you have my permission to do whatever you think best to preserve the Roost."

Chapter Two

Alice set off the following morning to investigate the Roost. Her body was still on UK time, so she awoke early enough to wash and blow-dry her hair before styling it into a French twist. She ironed the wrinkles from her blue damask skirt and used spray starch for a crisp white collar on her blouse. Just because she was going into battle didn't mean she shouldn't look feminine. She completed the look with low wedge espadrille sandals and a single strand of pearls around her neck.

Most of the drive out to the Roost was on a lovely road that passed through miles of tall switchgrass rustling in the breeze. She had to avert her gaze while passing the acres of destroyed, scraped-over land that would soon be a golf course. What had once been flat, marshy land was drained and reshaped with rolling hills and ponds. Nothing had been planted yet, just flat, reddish dirt as far as the eye could see.

The battle over the golf course was lost, but the Roost could still be saved. She had so many questions about the place! Everything that was known about the origins of the Roost had been burned in 1698 when a terrible fire destroyed Virginia's statehouse located in Jamestown. So many of the colony's early court records, land grants, and government deeds went up in flames. Historians believed the Roost dated to around 1680, but whoever built it was lost to history thanks to that awful fire. It wasn't until 1705 that another mention of the Roost occurred in an official record. A single line in a courthouse document noted that Reid's Roost, once owned by the late Widow Santos, had been sold at auction to Archibald Tucker.

That was all. Who was the Widow Santos, and who was Reid? Those details had been lost in the fire, but Alice had found some clues to their identity in London and needed time to unravel the mystery.

She slowed her car to turn onto the gravel drive leading to the Roost. What had once been a lovely drive through a tunnel of apple and pear trees had been badly abused. Heavy equipment left gouges in the path and dislodged gravel pinged the undercarriage of her Prius as she drove beneath the scraggly tunnel of overgrown trees. Photos from the late-nineteenth century when people still lived here showed a graceful arch of fruiting trees lining the avenue, welcoming visitors to the homestead.

Those days were long gone. Whatever monstrous vehicles gouged the ruts into the dirt path had also damaged the trees. Some of the branches had been knocked down, while other limbs still clung to the trees, dangling at haphazard angles. They'd probably snap off when the next oversized truck barreled down this path.

The Roost looked grungy and dilapidated beneath the shade of ancient sycamore trees. The two-story building was constructed of half stone and half rough-cut timber. Mismatched gables and a porch across the front gave evidence that the Roost had been expanded and modified many times over the centuries. It was hard to know what the original building had looked like, but she could clearly see Jack Latimer's influence on the place.

A Baltimore Ravens flag mounted on the front post wafted on the weak breeze. A satellite dish was clamped to the top of the chimney. A car with no wheels sat beside a moldering trailer parked in the yard. A pair of crows hopped in and out of a trash can on the front porch, scattering popcorn and empty bags of potato chips.

She clenched the wheel, willing her breath to slow. It was essential to remain poised and respectful if she was to win Jack Latimer's cooperation to vacate the Roost and find somewhere else to live while the golf course was under construction.

She resisted the urge to slam the car door, letting it close with a deliberate click instead, then made her way toward the house. The front door was a massive slab of old walnut that always hurt her knuckles if she tried to knock, so she called out instead.

"Hello? Anyone home?" She wiggled the heavy brass handle to generate a little noise, but no signs of life stirred inside.

She walked to the nearest window. The first-floor windows featured small, diamond-shaped bits of wavy glass soldered into lead panes that were original to the house. Alice squinted to peer through the window. It was dim inside, so it took a while for her eyes to grasp the horror. It looked like vagrants had made themselves at home. Sleeping bags and pizza boxes littered the floor. A clothesline dotted with filthy rags was strung before the yawning pit of the fireplace.

The creak of the front door opening caused Alice to rear away from the window.

A man shuffled outside and yes, he looked like a vagrant ... skinny, weathered, and not particularly clean.

"Are you Sophie?" he asked. His voice wasn't the friendliest Alice had ever heard.

"No, I'm not," she answered. "I'm looking for Jack Latimer."

Relief spread across his leathery skin. "So long as you're not Sophie, you can find Jack down at the golf course. He's working on the waterfall today, so he'll either be there or at the clubhouse."

Alice nodded and turned away, frightening the crow wrestling an empty bag of Cheetos from the trash can. A discarded bag of microwave popcorn had already scattered un-popped kernels across the porch, leaving greasy pockmarks on the weathered boards.

She tamped down frustration as she retrieved the lid of the garbage can. The burden of being compulsively tidy meant she simply couldn't ignore this.

"Covering the can will attract fewer pests," she said apologetically, but why should she apologize? The Roost was a historic treasure; Jack and this homeless man were the ones who ought to be apologetic.

She secured the bungee cords to anchor the garbage can lid in place while the vagrant chuckled. "There's no point," he said. "The raccoons will pull it off tonight to get at whatever is inside."

All the more reason nobody should be living here. The Roost still held secrets, and discovering them was Alice's only hope of resurrecting her moribund career.

Alice returned to her car and drove the half mile to the clubhouse. As much as she disapproved of the golf course, the clubhouse was spectacular. It had opened two years earlier, a Colonial Revival mansion with magnificent white columns supporting porticos and balconies. Every bride within fifty miles wanted to get married at the Tucker's Grove Clubhouse.

A man in khaki shorts and a grubby T-shirt sat on the front steps of the veranda. Sunlight glinted off the golden tones in his unkempt hair. He was a good-looking man, no question—broad shoulders, easy confidence, but ... *was he eating pudding with his fingers?*

She couldn't believe it, but even as she approached and locked gazes with him, he continued scooping chocolate pudding out of a plastic cup with two fingers. Dunking and licking. Her raised eyebrow must've tipped him off, because he chuckled softly.

"I forgot a spoon," he said, shrugging. "Gotta make do."

She smoothed her skirt and assumed a pleasant expression. "I'm looking for Jack Latimer. Is he here?"

"You found him," he said, running his index finger along all four sides and the bottom of the disposable pudding cup for a final clean-up before sucking the last of it off his finger. He stood and tossed the cup into a trash can, then met her gaze with a heart-stopping grin.

"I'd offer to shake your hand, but I don't think you'd accept," he said with a wink.

His easy charm caught her off guard, and she took a step back. "I'm Alice Chadwick. I was surprised to hear you had taken up residence in the Roost."

He made a low noise, a cross between a grunt and a scoff. "Yeah, me too. But hey, it's free so I've got no complaints. Doc and I have been living there since February."

"Doc" must be the man she mistook for a vagrant. She didn't care who he was, she didn't want anyone living in a rare and fragile historic building.

"I have an academic interest in the Roost," Alice said. "The building is at least three hundred years old, and there are well-defined protocols for the preservation of such a property."

His eyes narrowed. "Are you from the state?"

"No."

"The county?"

"No, I'm a history professor at William & Mary, but I've always been fond of the Roost. Any building with such a storied past shouldn't be subjected to the wear and tear it's currently receiving."

Jack set his hands on his hips, probably to show off the corded muscles up and down his arms, but at least he had a hint of sympathy in his expression. "Yeah, sorry about that. I asked the Tuckers for a room in the clubhouse, but something about it not being permitted for residential use won't let them do it. So I'll be at the Roost for the next couple of months."

"It doesn't even have running water, does it?"

"Nope," Jack confirmed. "I set up a porta-potty out back and I use the locker rooms in the clubhouse for a shower. A generator provides electricity if I need to run the microwave or power up my laptop."

He was going to live in squalor for months? "I'm sorry, but this isn't acceptable. Why can't the Tuckers put you up at their hotel? They own a very nice hotel in town and it's quite comfortable for long-term stays."

Jack shrugged. "They're flat broke. I guess they need to squeeze every dime they can get out of the hotel."

"They're not broke! The Tuckers are one of the wealthiest families in the state."

"Maybe they were rich once upon a time, but they don't have enough money to meet their bills."

There were a couple of construction workers fiddling at a nearby pump, and they glanced over, eavesdropping. She took a step closer and lowered her voice. "None of that is true, and you shouldn't start that sort of rumor. It's tacky and damaging to the Tuckers' reputation."

Jack threw up his hands, even though he seemed more amused than threatened. "Fine, have it your way," he said. "The Tuckers are rolling in dough and lied when they begged me to accept a thirty-percent stake in the golf course in exchange for funding the construction. I'm too cheap to pay what they wanted for a room at their overpriced hotel in town, so Kyle is letting me stay at the Roost for free."

A sickening feeling began to grow in Alice's gut. Why would anyone choose to live with no water and only spotty electricity unless what Jack said was true? The Tuckers must have a short-term cash flow issue. Even millionaires and billionaires could have problems accessing immediate cash.

"I don't like seeing that satellite dish on the roof."

"I need internet access," he said. "I'm bringing in another dish next week. A bigger one, so you're going to have to get used to it."

She took a steadying breath. Not everyone respected history and tradition as much as she, and that was okay. It was different skills and interests that made the world so vibrant, but she couldn't avert her gaze while a treasure was in the process of being destroyed.

"I have an academic interest in the Roost," she stated again.

Jack gave a friendly nod. "Come on over and poke around if you like. Take pictures, whatever. I'm probably going to tear the place down pretty soon, so don't wait too long."

"You're going to *what*?" She must have misunderstood.

"The land it's sitting on has great views. I'll tear down the Roost, get rid of those scraggly fruit trees, regrade the land, and put in an amphitheater. Those places can make a mint if managed properly."

She reached for a column to steady herself, struggling to get her breathing under control. First a golf course, now an amphitheater? He kept talking, spinning big dreams about hosting concerts and attracting golf tournaments. The amphitheater would be a huge draw for the PGA, and television rights would be icing on the cake.

All of it would require the demolition of the Roost. Did Daisy and Kyle realize what their golf course architect had planned?

No. It wouldn't happen. She couldn't stand aside while an outsider casually demolished the irreplaceable heritage that belonged to all Virginians. It would be a race against the clock to win legal protection for the Roost, but she intended to do it.

"There are rules about destroying historic landmarks," she said, then took a step back when Jack shot to his feet.

"Whoa, stop right there," he snapped. "That old ruin doesn't have landmark status. Trust me, I already checked."

"Not yet, but that can be remedied," she said. "The Historic Preservation Board takes our heritage seriously, and they *will* protect the Roost."

The blue heat in Jack's gaze turned incendiary, and it was a little disconcerting. Alice turned to leave and felt his glare burning two pinpoints between her shoulder blades until she reached the safety of her car and drove away.

Chapter Three

Historic preservationist busybodies were the bane of Jack's existence. They were strict, joyless, and unyielding when it came to stopping progress on anything that might introduce a bit of fun into the world. He'd spent months working with the local planning commission to be certain he was abiding by all the local rules before he broke ground on the golf course, and there weren't any stumbling blocks surrounding the Roost.

He wouldn't waste time going on bended knee to the Historic Preservation Board. He was going straight to the top, and gave Kyle Tucker a call.

Kyle was just as eager as Jack to get the golf course completed on time, and agreed to meet him at the country club at later that afternoon.

Precisely on time, Kyle's E-class Mercedes rolled to a halt on the circular drop-off at the front of the country club. The parking lot was only a stone's throw away, but nobody would tell Kyle Tucker he couldn't park his snazzy car at the front door.

The forty-something heir of the Tucker family unfolded himself from the sedan, an effortlessly cultured man of the world as he adjusted his white linen sports jacket. He was a good-looking guy, with a preppy haircut and a Robert Redford vibe, but it was hard to look past that monocle clenched over one eye. Kyle claimed it was because his LASIK surgery failed in that eye, though it was probably an affectation. Who else besides the Monopoly guy and Mr. Peanut wore a monocle?

"Thanks for coming," Jack said as Kyle approached the steps. "I don't know where that lady gets the notion she can issue edicts about the Roost. There's no record of it ever having been granted protected status."

"Don't worry; it's not a problem," Kyle said with the confidence of a man used to getting his way.

Jack could never afford to be so nonchalant when it came to historic preservation boards. The old gentlemen and white-haired ladies might look as harmless as kittens napping in the sun, but they could scheme and swarm like angry wasps if you took your eyes off them for a split second.

"She was running her mouth about kicking me out of the Roost."

"Don't worry about Alice," Kyle said. "She's a gem. Just be nice to her and you'll be able to sweet-talk her into anything. Besides, my family owns the Roost lock, stock, and barrel. The historic preservationists can't worm their way in and issue edicts. My wife is a member of the commission and Daisy won't let it get out of hand."

That ought to be reassuring, but he'd spent two years haggling with the locals about this golf course. Before he even arrived in Virginia he was battling petitions, protests, and injunctions. The biggest concern had always been protecting the environment, especially the wetlands that abutted the proposed golf course. The only way to get the environmentalists off his back was to agree to enlarge the protected wetland area and consent to regular testing to ensure no golf course runoff would contaminate the water.

The biggest part of the wetlands was the improbably named Saint Helga's Spring. It was a pretty spot, surrounded by bald cypress and crepe myrtle trees. Most importantly to the environmentalists, it was a sanctuary for endangered waterfowl and migratory birds. Protecting and enlarging the area was a challenge, but it also brought Jack a tax break, so he considered the struggle with the locals a win-win.

"I've already spent a couple thousand dollars taking out trees to clear the view around the amphitheater," he said. "If there's going to be any trouble, I need to know now."

"Daisy won't let the board get out of hand," Kyle reiterated. "Hey, show me the view from the waterfall. I'd like to see these 360-degree views you promised."

Jack grinned. "Follow me."

Jack set off for the 4th hole, which was destined to be the signature hole for the entire course.

Signature holes were important. Done well, they could catapult a golf course onto the cover of sporting magazines and be featured on every golfer's social media page. The course Jack built in Santa Barbara had a 16th hole overlooking a breathtaking cliffside view. In Puerto Rico, he designed the 8th, 9th, and 10th holes to run alongside an old wall built during the days of the Spanish Conquistadors.

In Williamsburg, the 4th hole would feature a sixty-foot waterfall built from boulders imported from a nearby quarry. Half his budget for this course had been spent on excavating and building up the waterfall. Creating the pond, installing pumps, and renting a crane to handle the rock placement had cost a fortune. It took a week to mound the honey-colored boulders into a realistic waterfall, and even without the finishing landscaping touches it already looked spectacular.

Jack pointed to the newly cleared patch of land where he'd cut down eight scraggly apple trees that were nothing but an eyesore. "You can see Saint Helga's Spring through that break in the trees," he said. "The amphitheater will have a terrific view of the spring, the woods, and the waterfall."

"It's going to be fantastic," Kyle breathed, rapture on his face as he took in the view. Some men got excited over a beautiful woman or a pile of riches, but Jack and Kyle were kindred spirits about the sublime perfection of a well-designed golf course.

Jack lifted his hands to frame the view as a television camera would see it. The natural beauty of the course would be irresistible to the PGA. Between broadcast rights, sponsorships, and ticket sales, PGA tournaments could double the revenue of an ordinary golf course.

But only if he could pull off these spectacular views. He'd need to yank down more trees to clear the line of sight all the way to Saint Helga's Spring.

"The students are going to grumble if I keep cutting down those scraggly fruit trees," he said. Many college students hated the idea of any tree being cut down. It didn't matter if the trees were dying or impeded job creation; students had the luxury of not caring about practicality and instinctively sided with Mother Nature.

"Let them complain," Kyle said with a shrug. "In the competition between town and gown, the town will always win. Students cycle through Williamsburg every four years. The faculty last a little longer, but half of them won't get tenure, so they get quietly shuffled out of town, never to be heard from again. The tenured faculty will stick around twenty or thirty years ... but the Tuckers? We've been here for three centuries. It's the First Families of Virginia who make the rules here. The Washingtons, the Lees, the Jeffersons, and the Tuckers. Don't worry, you're on the winning side of this battle."

They walked down the gently rolling swell of land for a better view of the spring. Jack spent weeks grading this soil to the perfect slope to make it both a challenge to the golfers and a thing of beauty to the viewers. A sense of well-being filled him as he strolled down the hill . . . where the soil felt unusually soft. Almost squishy.

That was odd. It hadn't rained in several days and the irrigation system wasn't in operation yet. He cast a worried eye toward the waterfall.

"I need to check something out," he told Kyle, redirecting their path to head up to the waterfall. The pumps and drains strategically hidden throughout the structure directed water up and over the rocks, circulated it within the basin, then propelled it through an artistically designed brook that meandered across a third of the golf course.

The closer he got, the worse the ground felt. It was so spongy it made a sucking sound.

"Something doesn't seem right," Kyle said, and Jack tried to act like it was no big deal.

"One of the drainage pumps probably needs to be recalibrated," he said, trying to hide his annoyance because getting a plumber out on a Friday evening was going to be expensive.

Water dribbled over the rim of the pond and seeped down the slope. It was heading straight toward Saint Helga's Spring. The work crews were already gone for the day, but with luck, this was something Jack could handle himself. He unfastened his watch and handed it to Kyle.

"Hold this, will you? I'll try to get that drainage pump started again."

It was only a thirty-dollar watch. When the Tuckers offered Jack partial ownership in the golf course, he sold his Rolex and invested his entire life savings into this project. It had the potential to be among the most lucrative golf courses in the country, but he had to get it across the finish line first. The Tuckers were out of money and funding everything from his own savings meant Jack's showy Rolex had to go.

It also meant he didn't want to shell out for a plumber on a Friday night. He knelt beside a group of smaller rocks that hid the pumps. He rolled up his sleeve and winced as icy water covered his arm all the way to his shoulder as he reached down to the pump. Flecks of water splashed his face, damp penetrated his shirt, but worst of all was the feel of the pump. There was no sign of life as he splayed his fingers across the suction pipe.

He cursed under his breath and pushed to his feet. He braced his hands on his hips, staring at the water rushing downward toward the wetlands that bordered the golf course. No fertilizer had been laid yet, so the water was clean, but the environmentalists were sure to kick up a fuss anyway. If they got wind of this broken pump, they'd swoop down like harpies to stop development. If a pump could fail before a golf course even opened, they'd start panicking about how it could break in the years to come when there would be pesticides and fertilizers heading for their precious wetlands.

Kyle understood as soon as Jack explained, but didn't seem overly worried. "It's the weekend," he said with a shrug. "County inspectors don't work on the weekends, and the students are gone for the summer. Nobody will know if you let this slide until Monday."

Maybe, but Jack couldn't risk word getting out and needed this solved tonight. Raymond Gannet owned a local hardware store, and Jack had made a point of buying the guy a few beers when he took a group of local contractors and businessmen to a William & Mary football game last fall. Sooner or later being friendly with the locals always paid off.

He scrolled through his phone until he found Raymond's number, then placed the call.

"Hey, Raymond," he said in a jovial tone, as though they'd been friends for years instead of barely knowing each other. "I've got an issue out at the Tucker's Grove course. Is there any way I can get my hands on a utility pump?"

"Does it have to be tonight?" Raymond asked. The sound of laughter and a party could be heard over the phone, and the last thing Raymond probably wanted was to send someone to reopen the hardware store.

"Sorry, but yes. I need it tonight."

Raymond grumbled but agreed. Relief nearly drove Jack to his knees, but he projected easy gratitude over the phone. "Hey, thanks! The next round of beers at the season opener in September are on me. Doc will be over in half an hour to get that pump."

There was a pause on the other end. "Does Doc have a driver's license?"

It wasn't an unreasonable question, but Doc had been dry ever since Jack met him loitering outside the government permitting office, holding a sign promising to work for food.

It happened shortly after Jack arrived in town four months earlier. Panhandlers always claimed they'd be willing to work for food. Jack ought to have ignored him, but nobody with personal experience of being hungry found it easy to overlook someone in need of a meal. Although Jack had plenty of work to offer, most of his jobs required construction certifications or handling heavy machinery. Doc had been so thin it was a wonder he could hold his head up on that skinny neck, but he straightened as Jack approached, a hint of anticipation in his gaze.

"Have you got a driver's license?" Jack asked.

Hope faded from the bum's eyes. "Sorry, no."

Then Jack really didn't have any work for him. Still, this was the first time he ever encountered a panhandler who offered to work for food and actually meant it. The guy took a drag on a cigarette and stared into space as an awkward moment stretched. A faded purple tattoo of a familiar star on the man's bicep was blurry and faded.

"You were in the army?" Jack asked.

The guy blew out a lung of smoke. "Twenty-two years."

Jack didn't have a bleeding heart. Heck, his last girlfriend told him he had a lump of iron for a heart, but too many military vets ended up addicted on the street, and if this guy was willing to work, Jack would find something for him to do.

"Can you dig a trench?"

The man nodded. "If someone gives me a shovel."

That was how he and Doc ended up living together at the Roost. Doc had been an army psychologist, and listening to the woes of suffering veterans had taken its toll. He drank too much, his wife left him, and he ended up on the streets.

Doc had his troubles, but no driving offenses—just old fines for vagrancy that had cost him his driver's license. Jack easily covered the fines and court costs to restore it.

"Doc got his license back a few months ago," Jack said to Raymond over the phone.

There was a long pause before Raymond spoke again. "Look, I know you're new in town, but you need to watch out for Doc Gibson. He's fallen off the wagon before, and usually ends up back on the streets."

Jack didn't have time for this tonight. He knew all about Doc's issues, but Raymond was within his rights to worry about a ten-thousand-dollar piece of equipment in the hands of an alcoholic. "Tell you what ... I'll be down in half an hour, okay?"

"Sounds like a better plan," Raymond said.

An hour later Jack returned to the golf course, wheeling the ungainly pump out to the waterfall. It was a moonless night and they were in the middle of nowhere. Doc held a battery-operated lantern as Jack prepared the area. The two decorative boulders hiding the valves were only about twenty pounds each, and he hoisted them aside to get the pump into position. For tonight, his only goal was to redirect enough water back into the reservoir to keep the environmentalists off his back.

Same with Alice Chadwick. She wanted to impede his progress, and he wouldn't let her . . . even though he kind of liked her prissy fussiness. The way she fiddled with her pearl necklace was strangely appealing.

He respected Alice Chadwick's old-fashioned gentility, but his life savings was invested in this course, and he wouldn't let her meddle with it.

Getting the utility pump hooked up and operating went off without a hitch. Within twenty minutes the temporary patch had the recirculation working in the fountain again, and on Monday he'd call in the professionals.

It wasn't until the clean-up that a major problem hit. Jack was hoisting one of the decorative boulders back into place when he slipped on a wet patch and dropped it on his foot. It didn't hurt that much, but for a hemophiliac, this could quickly become a nightmare.

His string of curses turned the air blue, and Doc looked at him in curiosity. "You okay?"

Jack dropped to the ground and unlaced his work boot, carefully lifting his foot free, then peeled his sock off. No skin had broken, but that didn't mean he was in the clear. There could be damage beneath his skin that could plunge him into dangerous territory.

"Yeah, I'm okay. Hey, can you drive me back to the Roost? I've got something I need to do right away."

Doc looked at the mess of equipment scattered around the fountain. "Should we load up first?"

"Sorry, I need to go now. It's urgent."

Jack was able to live a normal life most of the time, but no hemophiliac could ignore an injury like this. Even now he could be bleeding beneath the skin and his blood's inability to clot could land him in the hospital.

Doc nodded agreeably, and Jack hurried into the passenger seat. As soon as the truck rolled up to the Roost, Jack rushed inside. The mini-fridge was the only appliance Jack kept wired to the generator around the clock, and he needed to get to it immediately. Every pore in his body perspired and nervous energy made him tremble as he grabbed the vials of life-saving clotting factor. It was dark inside the Roost, but he'd been doing these injections three times a week for decades and could perform the task blind-folded.

It took a while to warm the vial to room temperature, rolling it between his palms as he worried.

It would be a day or two before he'd know if he was in the clear. Once when he was a kid, Jack had stumbled on a staircase at school and twisted his ankle. Everything seemed fine until the middle of the night when he awoke, his ankle swollen to twice its normal size and the pain so severe his dad had to carry him to the car. He spent three days in the hospital, strapped to pumps and IV devices, until his ankle joint returned to normal size.

Medical technology had come a long way since then, and tonight's additional infusion would probably ensure that he'd be okay.

To the outside world Jack appeared to be the epitome of vibrant health, but it was an illusion. Hemophilia had caused all manner of strange twists in his life, and he'd learned to live with it by becoming a fighter. No matter what the challenge, Jack planned, strategized, and persevered. Early on, he recognized the futility of sinking into the deceptive comfort of self-pity. He refused to become a victim of his condition and kept his gaze fixed on a singular vision: to become the best golf course designer in the world—a man who would never again be homeless, hungry, or paralyzed by the fear of an unpaid medical bill. That dream became his anchor, rendering him unstoppable, even unreasonable. His relentless drive, sharpened by hardship, transformed every hurdle into fuel for his ambition.

Obstacles became challenges to solve, whether it was hemophilia or a pretty local professor who thought she could interfere with his career.

Once his supplies were cleaned, sterilized, and brought to the proper temperature, Jack pressed the needle into his vein with steady hands, and watched as the clotting factor flowed into his bloodstream.

It was hard to predict how much trouble Alice Chadwick might stir up. She was pretty, smart, and her genteel Southern drawl was the most alluring thing he'd ever heard. She might be the perfect companion over the coming months as he completed the golf course, a challenge who would keep him sharp and inspired through the long months ahead.

But if she tried to throw up roadblocks to his golf course, digging in to protect her slice of Virginia's past? He'd pour everything into winning her over—not just for the course, but because something about Alice Chadwick made him want to prove he was more than just a guy who knew how to build things.

He wanted to be a man who could be worthy of her.

Chapter Four

Alice had to wait until Monday to attend an emergency meeting of the local Historic Preservation Board. The five committee members who served on the HPB were simultaneously the most beloved and most feared members of the community. Properties that fell within their purview could be declared worthy of preservation and benefit from tax incentives and free advice from expert conservators, but those benefits came at a cost. Any property that won historic landmark status had to abide by stringent rules that blocked the owner from altering the outside appearance of the structure. Some of the rules were admittedly nitpicky, such as the prohibition against painting the house a color that did not conform with the historic era. Or in the case of the Roost, by mounting a satellite dish on the roof and a Baltimore Ravens flag on the front porch. The most important issue for Alice, of course, was to stop Jack Latimer from tearing down the Roost to make way for a new golf course.

The board members were mostly civic-minded residents with a passion for history, but not all of them had formal training in historic architecture. While their intentions were good, the board had developed a reputation for an overly generous grants of preservation status to buildings regardless of architectural merit or historical significance. This became a source of frustration for developers and homeowners alike. Enter General Epstein, recently elected to the board on a wave of support from real estate advocates. His mandate was clear: to bring a measure of discipline and common sense to a group that, in his words, treated every drafty attic and sagging porch as sacred ground. He wasn't opposed to preservation—but he believed in balance, and he'd come armed with a mission to question the knee-jerk "no" that had stalled too many projects for too long. Alice was certain General Epstein would be her biggest stumbling block today.

The hastily convened meeting was held at the home of the president of the board. Greg McGarity was a retired real estate agent who loved both history and golf. Though Greg was an enthusiastic supporter of the new golf course, Alice prayed he wouldn't have completely fallen under Jack Latimer's spell and would be willing to protect the Roost.

The McGaritys lived in a charming home that looked like it belonged in Colonial Williamsburg. White wainscoting in the parlor matched perfectly with the muted Wedgwood blue wallpaper. The hardwood floors gleamed beneath a cluster of wingback chairs arranged in a semicircle around the fireplace.

Alice was the first to arrive, which left her alone with Greg after his wife retreated to the kitchen to finish preparing her famous tomato sandwiches. Mrs. McGarity always cut soft white bread using a round cookie cutter so the tomatoes matched the bread to perfection.

"How was England, Professor Chadwick?"

Greg always used her full title, even though it somehow sounded condescending the way he said it. He had zero respect for Jane Austen or anything else he considered frilly, feminine, and useless. He was the sort of old-school Virginian who thought women should never have been admitted to William & Mary, let alone allowed to join the faculty.

It didn't matter. She wasn't here to defend Jane Austen; she had come to save the Roost. "England was wonderful," she said noncommittally, and pretended to admire the framed photos on the family room wall. One was of Scotland at the Old Course at St. Andrews, generally considered to be the birthplace of golf. The other showed Greg shaking hands with Arnold Palmer on the 18th green at Pebble Beach.

"I hope you're not planning on causing trouble for Jack," Greg said with a hint of warning in his tone. "We were lucky to get him as the architect for this project. He's one of the best golf course architects in the business."

Was there actually an entire profession of golf course architecture? From the way Greg described it, golf course architecture was a prestigious career involving civil engineering, agronomy, and a thorough understanding of the game of golf. Jack Latimer had designed golf courses all over the world, Greg told her, and his name brought prestige to any club associated with his designs.

"Greg, I hope you're not boring Alice with talk about every golf course you've ever played," Mrs. McGarity said as she set a platter of tomato sandwiches on the coffee table.

"She needs to understand what's on the line," Greg said. "A Jack Latimer golf course is a thing of beauty. I played the one he built in Ireland, and another in California. I had to twist his arm to get him to come to Virginia because a bunch of Japanese investors have been trying for years to lure him out to do a second course on Honshu."

Greg's craggy face lit with excitement as he described the incredible views of the coming golf course while Alice sat mute. Her knowledge of golf couldn't fill a thimble and she breathed a sigh of relief as Daisy Tucker's familiar voice sounded on the walkway.

"Well, bless my heart, I just love seeing Alice back among us," she announced as she breezed into the room. "It's been tiresome being the only lady on the board."

Daisy rushed over to Alice to exchange air kisses. Daisy was only thirty but already reigned over Williamsburg's social scene with an iron fist. She had a perfectly coiffed blond bob and a double strand of the Tucker antique pearls around her neck.

Daisy was an unabashed snob, but she did everything with such bright good cheer that people instantly adored her, Alice included. Alice had been one of twelve bridesmaids when Daisy married Kyle three years earlier. When Alice received a scathing midcourse tenure review—a critical evaluation halfway through the six-year probationary period during which professors must prove their value to the college—it was a clear warning from the History Department that she was on thin ice and unlikely to earn tenure unless she published something extraordinary. In her moment of despair, it was Daisy she turned to for comfort.

"Who cares if you haven't published any boring articles?" Daisy had said. *"Your Chantilly cake could make the angels weep, and let's be honest, which one matters more?"*

Daisy made serving on the preservation board a joy. The final two members of the board were Arlo Whitworth and General Michael Epstein, Alice's favorite and least favorite members, respectively. Arlo worked in historical art preservation and was famous for wearing cheerful bow ties. Tonight his green-and-gold tie was a nod to William & Mary, his alma mater. Over the years she'd seen Arlo at pool parties, church, even a 10K race. He always wore a bow tie regardless of the venue.

General Epstein was a Marine who was spending his retirement writing a definitive history of the U.S. Marines in the Far East. Alice often encountered him at the college library, where his growly voice always seemed out of place in the tweedy world of academia.

He frowned while Daisy chattered about the upcoming Kentucky Derby party she was hosting at her estate, and how she imported roses from the same hothouse in Louisville that would create the famous Garland of Roses. General Epstein looked ready to shoot himself out of boredom, but now that all five members were here, they could begin business. Between her own vote, Arlo, and Daisy, there was surely going to be no problem winning protection for the Roost.

Greg nodded to Alice to begin.

"I recently learned that the man designing the golf course at Tucker's Grove Country Club has taken up residence in the Roost," she said.

General Epstein had never heard of the Roost, and Alice provided a brief explanation.

"It was one of the original houses on the outskirts of Jamestown. We think it dates to around 1680 when the very first references to it showed up on some old maps. At the time it was called 'Reid's Roost,' but after the Tuckers bought the property its name got shortened to 'the Roost.' Nobody knows who Reid was."

"There aren't any property records with his full name?" General Epstein asked, and Alice shook her head.

"A terrible fire in 1698 destroyed so many of the early records for this part of Virginia," she said. "We're lucky that Virginia was still a colony in 1698, so there are some surviving records at the British Library in London. An old survey record from 1680 named the plot of land 'Reid's Roost.' We don't know if 'Reid' was an old Native American reference or an itinerant trapper or a settler. It could even be a misspelling for the reedy grasses that grow in the area. The first record we have of someone actually living in Reid's Roost dates to 1705 when it was bought by the Tuckers. After the Tuckers moved in, the name 'Reid' was eventually dropped, and most people just call it the Roost."

Daisy perked up at the mention of her family. "The Roost was the first house the Tuckers owned after they arrived from England," Daisy added. She'd only married into the Tucker family three years earlier, but latched onto the family's celebrated history like a barnacle and adopted it as her own. "After the Tuckers started getting rich, they bought more land and moved into bigger homes over the next hundred years or so, but they leased Reid's Roost to other people. I think it became a tavern at some point, then a whiskey distillery. During the Civil War it was a hospital, then it was a house again. I think it's been vacant for a long time."

"Not so vacant," Arlo said with a guilty smile. "When I was in college, the students dared each other to spend Halloween night at the Roost. Rumor had it that the ghost of Saint Helga was likely to show up."

Alice straightened. The legend of Saint Helga had been linked with Reid's Roost for centuries, although the origin of the story was lost to time. Most people thought the legend was pure myth. After all, there was no Saint Helga in any Christian denomination, nor was there any trace of a woman named Helga associated with Virginia at the time the Roost was built.

And yet, sometime in the earliest years of the colony of Virginia, legends of Saint Helga began to be associated with the Roost. The gorgeous stretch of water behind the Roost had been called Saint Helga's Spring as far back as anyone could remember. Even a census map from 1720 labeled the body of water after the mysterious Helga.

"Did you ever take the dare and spend the night at the Roost?" Greg McGarity asked.

"Once," Arlo admitted. "No Saint Helga or any other ghosts. We got nothing but mosquito bites, a stiff back, and a hangover. It was a thoroughly miserable experience from start to finish."

"Lightweight," General Epstein muttered beneath his breath, then began to describe what it was like to bivouac in the swamps of Vietnam.

"Please," Alice said before the conversation went completely off-kilter. "I'd like to talk about how we can save the Roost."

She sent an uneasy glance at Daisy. Did she even know what her husband had done? Daisy filed her nails with an emery board and didn't appear to be listening, so Alice continued.

"The man who is developing the golf course wants to demolish the Roost, an irreplaceable cultural treasure, to build an amphitheater. I'd like your help saving it."

Arlo's eyes widened as he looked at Daisy. "Did you know about this?"

"That's my husband's business, darlin'. I have enough on my hands managing the hotel in town to bother myself with sweaty golf courses."

"If the Tuckers want to sell the place, it's within their right to do so," Greg said. "I saw Kyle Tucker out at the yacht club last week, and he's gangbusters about building that amphitheater. He says it will make a fortune."

Alice squared her shoulders and met his gaze. "Yes, but they'll have to demolish the Roost to make it happen. I'd like the board to grant a permanent stay on development."

"That's a tall order," General Epstein said. "I don't like barging onto private property and telling owners what they can't do with their land. Maybe we can get a brief stay on development to give the historians time to make their case, but any longer could throw the construction schedule into a tailspin."

"A temporary stay, then." At the very least, she needed a few weeks to get inside the house and solve the historical mystery she suspected still lurked somewhere on that property.

"Daisy?" Arlo asked. "What do you think?"

Daisy lowered the emery board. "I think Kyle ought to be able to do whatever he wants with that house."

"But there is history on that land that pre-dates the Tuckers," Alice said. "I need time to study it."

Greg remained unmoved. "Historians and archaeologists have already combed over every square inch of the Roost. Anything of historic interest has already been discovered and documented. It's not right to stand in the way of progress to save a decrepit building that probably should have been condemned decades ago. It's unfit for occupancy and a public menace."

The tide was turning against her, and she was ready to play her trump card.

"I've learned something new in England that proves that Saint Helga may be more than just a legend," Alice said. "When I was in London, I combed through old records, looking for things of interest in this part of Virginia. I found a letter from 1672 that alludes to a woman named Helga. Take a look."

She had copies of the letter and distributed them to the others in the room. The spidery, cursive handwriting from the seventeenth century was notoriously difficult to decipher, so Alice read the important passage aloud:

Helga has sailed for Jamestown as she still has hope to conceive a child. The woman is a saint, but I fear we will never see her again. Virginia is a dangerous land.

Alice remembered the afternoon in the British Library when she first saw this letter. It was two weeks after she'd gotten fired from the *Emma* movie set and she'd been anxious, depressed, and desperate to save her failing academic career. Hoping to uncover some overlooked detail from Virginia's early history, she stayed glued to the chair, spending hours trolling through old records in their early American history collections. The holdings consisted of a mishmash of official dispatches, property surveys, land grants, court cases, and letters. Each day she nearly went cross-eyed while squinting at the hazy microfilm screen and struggling to read the spindly handwriting from long ago.

The name Helga jumped out at her. The Nordic name was not completely unknown in England, where the northern counties had been heavily settled by Vikings in the ninth century. Nordic names such as Helga, Erik, or Garth still popped up among the Norse descendants, so she couldn't automatically assume this Helga on her way to Virginia had any association with the lovely body of water behind Reid's Roost.

But there was a tiny clue on the letter that clinched it for Alice. She held back a smile as she watched the others in the room read the letter, their faces unimpressed.

"This is all you have?" Greg asked, holding up the piece of paper.

"Look at the mark at the end of the sentence," Alice said. The mark looked a little like a circle of palm fronds and was about the size of a thumbnail. Apparently it didn't resonate with anyone except Arlo. He put on his reading glasses and held the paper close, squinting at the mark.

"I've seen this before," he said.

Alice nodded. "That's the mark carved into the lintel stone over the hearth at the Roost."

"What's a lintel stone?" Greg asked, a clue that maybe he shouldn't be president of a historic preservation board.

Alice supplied the answer. "The lintel stone is a long slab of rock that spans the top of the fireplace in the main room out at the Roost. It supports the chimney above it."

"And this same squiggly mark is carved into the stone at the Roost?" Greg asked.

"*Exactly* the same!" Alice said. "It's a little doodle at the top right of the stone. Most people think it was a simple decoration or a bit of graffiti. I think the Helga referenced in this letter somehow made her way to Virginia and may have even lived at the Roost. I think she is the source of the legend of Saint Helga's Spring."

General Epstein tossed the paper onto the coffee table. "Women don't really believe that nonsense, do they?"

According to the legend, women who had difficulty conceiving a child should head down to the spring located behind the Roost at dawn. They were to stand on the rickety old pier that stretched into the water, and recite the Lord's Prayer five times while facing the sunrise. Over the years, hundreds of women claimed to have conceived a child after visiting the spring.

"I have a cousin who tried for years to have a baby and nothing worked," Daisy said. "She went to see the sunrise over Saint Helga's Spring, and sure enough, she got pregnant the next month."

The men in the room all looked mildly amused, but this was serious business for Alice . . . not because she believed the legend, but because her career could depend on discovering its origin. Her best chance of winning tenure had ended disastrously in London, but finding the source behind the legend of Saint Helga could be her salvation. It meant she could publish her findings in an academic journal and prove her scholarly merit to the college.

"This letter was written in 1672," Alice said. "That's thirty-three years before the Tuckers bought the Roost in 1705. I think that building is older than any of us know, and Helga was a real person. I need time to study the Roost with new eyes, and without Jack Latimer ruining the property. He's left trash all over the place that's attracting rodents and pests. I'd like him evicted until I can complete my study."

Daisy pursed her lips, looking interested for the first time. "It's private property, Alice. Jack and my husband have a business arrangement to let him stay there for free. We don't have any grounds to meddle with that."

Alice's salvation came from an unlikely source. Greg McGarity's knowledge of real estate law was deep, and his voice was laden with concern. "I'm not sure the Tuckers have the authority to let anyone live there. The Roost isn't fit for habitation and it's a lawsuit waiting to happen. According to Arlo, college kids dare each other to break into the place every Halloween. What if one of them tries to light a fire and burns the place down? The Roost is a temptation to vagrants and college kids, and the county could get sued for ignoring the danger it represents."

Arlo straightened in his chair, adjusting his spectacles. "I suppose we could use the condition of the building as a means of getting him out in the short term. That will give us time to complete an inspection and search for anything of historic interest."

Relief threaded through Alice's spine. Reason and respect for history had won the day, at least in the short term. "So are we agreed?" she asked. "We'll apply for emergency protection and keep the structure safe until I can determine if the building warrants landmark status."

"We need to have a vote," Daisy pointed out. She had gone back to filing her nails, and her expression was inscrutable.

Greg called for a vote. "All in favor of applying for an eviction while Professor Chadwick investigates the Roost for historic landmark status, raise their hand."

Alice shot her hand into the air. So did the three men. Daisy continued filing her nails, the rasp a little louder than before. It was the only sound of her displeasure, and Alice feared their friendship might take a hit.

And yet, she'd won a chance to solve a mystery and hopefully save her career.

Chapter Five

"Are you sure you have nobody?" the lawyer asked. "No family? No close friends?"

Heat crawled up Jack's neck, but he kept his face impassive. He hadn't come to this swanky lawyer's office to bare his soul to Ms. Lancaster, the estate attorney he picked out of an internet search. All he wanted was to get his will revised and signed.

He shot out of the chair to pace around the glass-and-steel office. A bank of windows overlooked the leafy greenspace of the town square below, but inside everything was as sleek and modern as the iMac sitting on the attorney's tempered-glass desk.

"I don't trust anyone to manage my affairs except someone I'm paying," he said, hoping Ms. Lancaster would quit poking into his personal life.

Not too long ago, Jack was legitimately filthy rich after twelve years of building golf courses all over the world. Now he was gambling it all to complete the Tucker's Grove Golf Course, the jewel in his crown. The Tucker family's ailing finances offered Jack the once-in-a-lifetime opportunity to actually *own* part of a spectacular golf course instead of merely designing it. Rather than accepting a final payment and walking away, Jack would collect revenue from Tucker's Grove in perpetuity. He'd have the freedom to continue his nomadic lifestyle designing golf courses to whoever paid him the most, but income from Tucker's Grove would provide a financial safety net for the rest of his life.

Owning a partial stake in the golf course meant he needed to revise his will and appoint someone to manage the business in the event of his death. Teresa Gutierrez, the woman who would inherit everything, wasn't the sort of person who could manage a golf course.

"Paying for long-term management will be costly and eat into your principal," Ms. Lancaster cautioned.

"I want to designate my lawyer in New York to serve as the estate executor."

Ms. Lancaster shifted uneasily. "Attorneys don't always make the best executors," she said. "Given that your estate will have an ongoing interest in a golf course, I think you'd be better served by having a trusted family member involved to ensure its viability."

Why did she have to keep pushing this? He didn't have any family and he never stayed in one place long enough to make lasting friendships. Cancer killed his mother when he was eleven, and an alcoholic father abandoned Jack into the foster care system a few years later. None of those foster homes worked out so well, and he ran away for good when he was fifteen, so no ... there wasn't anyone he trusted to administer an estate.

"No friends, no family," he said tersely. "If this isn't the sort of work you can handle, tell me now and I'll find another attorney."

Ms. Lancaster's face soured even more. "I've already completed the revisions and I'm perfectly capable of completing this will, but it is my fiduciary responsibility to let you know that your chosen executor is problematic."

That schoolmarm voice grated on his nerves. He wasn't proud that at the age of thirty-seven he had collected exactly zero close friends, but that wasn't any of her business. He had hundreds of golfing buddies. Dozens of business alliances. He dated more women than he could shake a stick at. He liked women and they liked him back, but at the end of every golf course he completed, he was always ready to move on. No loose ends, and no woman slung around his neck to slow him down.

He stared down at the courthouse square below. So many people moving in and out, most wearing business suits, all of them hurrying somewhere important ... but one woman in a flowy blue skirt was riveting. It was the same lady who had nagged him about messing up the Roost, and he squinted to see her better. In a world where everyone was rushing about, Alice Chadwick trailed her fingers along a planter filled with blooming flowers. It looked like she didn't have a care in the world as she leaned in to inhale.

"I'll need the name and address of your beneficiary," Ms. Lancaster said.

The spell was broken and he turned away from the window. Teresa Gutierrez was often a challenge to track down. She used to manage a laundromat in Baltimore and looked the other way when a homeless kid snuck in the back to sleep after the place closed for the night. She started leaving him a meal each night, and when she noticed he didn't have a decent winter coat, one of those appeared, too.

Over the years Teresa tried to get Jack back into foster care, but he was a stubborn idiot and wouldn't listen, so she helped him as best she could. She left him tokens for the machines so he could wash his clothes and quit being so stinky when he went to school. It was Teresa who encouraged him to apply for scholarships to get into college. In hindsight, she'd probably been risking her job if the laundromat's owner ever found out what she was doing.

That brand of kindness was rare, and he never forgot it. After Jack got rich, he started sending her gift cards at Christmas, but she moved around a lot, and sometimes the cards were returned to the post office box he used as his permanent address. He'd pay someone to track her down and send a few thousand dollars in gift cards to her.

Teresa didn't know he'd made her his beneficiary. If she outlived him, Teresa would be an instant millionaire, but she didn't have the financial experience to understand a golf course, and he didn't trust the Tuckers not to take advantage of her. That meant Jack would appoint Mueller, Mueller, and Kraft, paying them a hefty retainer to ensure whatever fortune he managed to save would go to the only person who ever sacrificed anything for him.

Dwelling on the fact that he had no real friends and no family was possibly his least favorite thing in the world. He turned his attention outside, grateful to see Alice still down there, sitting on the side of a planter to admire the morning glories.

He was going to be in Williamsburg at least five more months and perhaps she would be a wonderful female diversion that would make his stay in town more interesting.

The morning glories in the planters outside the courthouse blossomed with a riot of color on this lovely morning in early May. Alice couldn't resist admiring the impressive flowers, their velvety petals looking too heavy for their delicate stems.

She leaned in to pinch a few faded blooms. Deadheading helped the plant grow lush and thick instead of leggy and weak. She doubted the courthouse had gardeners to keep on top of tasks like this, but was there anything more lovely than a profusion of morning glories? It was impossible not to smile while looking at them.

"Hello, Professor Chadwick."

She startled at the man's approach. Had she met him before? It would be hard to forget those piercing blue eyes or the way his smile was a tiny bit lopsided. It made him look charming and naughty at the same time. Sunlight glinted on his chestnut hair that could use a good trim, but she always appreciated a man who could carry off a dark blue blazer with a pair of chinos.

His knowing grin indicated he knew she was scrambling to place him.

"Chocolate pudding," he prompted with a wink. "Jack Latimer. We met out at Tucker's Grove last week."

Oh heavens, this was the man she was about to file eviction papers against. The Historic Preservation Board delivered on their promise to draft an emergency order of protection for the Roost. It was tucked into her woven tote bag, ready to be hand-delivered to the clerk of court.

"I'm sorry, I didn't recognize you," she stammered. How different he looked from the grubby man she met last week, yet just because he cleaned up nicely wouldn't dissuade her from filing this order. "You look so different."

"Yeah, I put on a sports jacket approximately once a week when I need to do business," he said. He nodded to the raised planter. "You like flowers?"

"Morning glories are hard to resist," she said.

Jack's blue gaze remained locked on her. "They certainly are," he said. "Hey, I saw a flyer outside the grocery store about an annual garden tour. Can I convince you to go with me?"

Was he asking her on a date? She wasn't used to sweaty jocks showing interest in her. Alice had never been va-va-voom attractive. She was pretty, but most men preferred sexy, and she was too prim to be sexy.

The papers of eviction were burning a hole in her tote bag, and she scrambled for a way to gracefully decline. "You don't seem like the kind of person who goes on garden tours."

That slow grin spread across his face again. "Ma'am, I build golf courses, and an important part of course management is knowing what ornamental plants can stand up to people tromping through them in search of golf balls. Virginia's tidewater is a unique climate and I need to know what kind of flowers can withstand the heat, won't be tempting to hungry deer, and how much color they'll give."

Alice brightened. "You can't go wrong with morning glories."

"Yeah, no," he laughed. "I'm not going to pay someone to dead-head the morning glories. Azaleas give more color and less fuss. I need to educate myself on what other flowers can stand up to the climate here, and I'd like you to go with me."

Alice fiddled with the pearls at her throat. Jack Latimer was the antithesis of what she looked for in a man, but she couldn't deny his raw, masculine appeal. If she wasn't about to get him evicted from the Roost she might consider going with him on the garden tour ... only for the intellectual curiosity, of course.

"It never occurred to me that flowers are part of golf course design," she said.

"A lot of designers farm it out, but my first job was helping a golf course groundskeeper. I spent my high school years pruning, composting, and mulching. It didn't pay much, but I got to golf for free. By the time I finished high school I was good enough to win a golf scholarship to college."

"You went to college?" She hadn't meant to sound so surprised, and there was a slight stiffening in his demeanor.

"University of Maryland," he said. "I got a bachelor of science in landscape architecture. So how about it, lady? Want a date to the garden show?"

He was staring at her décolleté, and she hated being called "lady."

"I don't think we are a good match," she said, heat flushing her face.

"Come on, Professor," he urged. "You're sexy, smart, and you know flowers. And I've always had a thing for ladylike Southern belles."

Was he making fun of her? She was *not* a sexy woman. Pretty, yes, but hyper-masculine jocks like Jack Latimer usually wanted only one thing at the end of a date. Besides, once she got him evicted from the Roost, he wouldn't be so eager to escort her on a garden tour.

"I'm sorry, no," she said, pulling up the edges of her shrug to cover more of her neckline. "We're not a good match."

"Not a good match?" he said in surprise. "I respect you, Alice. When we met at the clubhouse, you never yelled or swore to make your point, even though I could tell I was driving you up a wall. I like a woman who understands that gentleness isn't a weakness, it's a choice. You strike me as the sort who can host a tea party with perfect manners but still hold your own in a debate without breaking a sweat or losing your class. And I'll tell you something else. I may be shooting myself in the foot here, but I like the challenge of getting to know you. The *real* you. I like the lace and the pearls and the perfume ... but underneath it all I think there's a woman I'd like to know. And Professor . . . I'd like to take you on a tour of the best gardens in Williamsburg."

His words were flattering, and the sheer masculine appreciation in his gaze was melting her resolve. If she wasn't about to get him kicked out of the Roost, she might have taken the chance.

"I'm afraid my answer has to remain no," she said with a gentle smile. "But for what it's worth, you make saying no an awfully difficult task."

She walked into the courthouse, wishing she could free herself from this strange, irrational flare of attraction.

Jack needed to buy a new sports jacket for the Kentucky Derby party out at Kyle Tucker's estate. While most of his career was spent wearing a polo shirt out on development sites or playing a round of golf with business associates, sometimes more formal events required a suit, and this was one of them.

"I'm not sure what I'm supposed to wear to a Derby party," he confided in the menswear sales associate.

"You'll need a lightweight silk jacket, or perhaps a seersucker blazer."

"So a business suit won't work?"

"Not unless you want to look overdressed," the sales associate said.

It was important to look like he belonged because Jack was always on the hunt for the next job. In the twelve years Jack had been designing golf courses, his contracts almost always began at social events.

The jacket the sales associate recommended was spot-on—lightweight, polished yet effortlessly relaxed. It exuded a timeless, gentleman-of-leisure vibe, perfect for the outdoor Derby party Kyle and Daisy Tucker were hosting. Showing up in his business suit would have been a disaster, so he felt a surge of gratitude for this find—until he caught sight of the price tag.

"Eight hundred bucks?"

The sales associate nodded. "The fabric was made in Italy," he explained. "It has reinforced stitching and a tighter weave. It drapes perfectly and has clean lines with a natural fall."

Great, but Jack still didn't want to pay eight hundred dollars for a jacket he might only wear once, even though he wasn't poor anymore. The Kentucky Derby bash at the Tucker estate was the most-sought-after invitation in the county. Jack would be rubbing shoulders with congressmen, celebrities, and all manner of rich people who spent too much time and money at country clubs. They were precisely the kind of people who thought nothing of splashing twenty grand a year on a golf membership, so it was a good opportunity to glad-hand his future customers.

Customers, not friends. Blurring the line between the two was a dangerous and expensive mistake.

He decided the overpriced jacket was a business investment, and he pulled out his credit card. He was still smarting over the cost as he drove home. It had been a long day and exhaustion tugged as he parked the truck and headed toward the Roost.

A note tacked to the front door fluttered in the weak breeze. He laid the garment bag with his pricy jacket over the porch railing to unpin the note and read:

We regret to inform you that this structure, commonly known as "the Roost," has been deemed unsafe for habitation due to significant structural deficiencies, as well as the lack of running water and electricity. Your continued occupancy poses serious safety risks and may hinder efforts toward potential historic preservation.

You are hereby notified that you must vacate the premises within 48 hours. Failure to comply with this eviction notice may result in legal action, financial penalties, and risks to your personal safety.

A haze of red clouded Jack's vision. There was nothing unsafe about living at the Roost. It was uncomfortable, but it wasn't unsafe.

This was Alice Chadwick's doing, and she was about to learn that he wasn't the sort of man to take something like this lying down . . . especially when it involved defending an investment that represented his entire life savings.

Chapter Six

Alice almost didn't attend the annual Kentucky Derby party at Cherrywood, the name of Daisy and Kyle's grand old plantation. It would be her first major outing since returning from England, and she wasn't quite ready for a high-society bash. She would have skipped the party if she hadn't promised to arrive a few hours early to help Daisy put the finishing touches on the canapés and decorations.

Thank heavens she didn't cancel, because Daisy was frantic when Alice arrived. Cherrywood's oversized gourmet kitchen was large enough to fit a small skating rink. High ceilings lined with exposed beams, a massive center island, and a vintage chandelier had the grandeur of old Virginia, while state-of-the-art appliances ensured effortless hospitality. Caterers in crisp uniforms bustled about, preparing most of the food. Yet Daisy insisted on contributing a few of her signature dishes, including her legendary corn fritters.

"I burned the corn fritters," Daisy said, her face white with mortification. "They were perfect when they came off the griddle, then I put them in the oven to keep warm, but it was too hot and now *look* at the horror."

Alice winced at the sight of the blackened crusts. There would be no saving them, but it wasn't worth ruining the party over some burned hors d'oeuvres. "That's all right. I can make more."

"How?" Daisy asked, the edge of hysteria creeping closer. "I spent all last night slow-roasting the corn over hickory chips. It's the only way to give the kernels the right smoky flavor, and now they're completely *ruined*."

Daisy was famous for her hickory-smoked corn fritters, but this wasn't the end of the world and Alice could fix this.

"Get me a couple cans of corn, some smoked paprika, black cardamom, and some good, sharp cheese. We can fake it."

Daisy set a hand over her heart. "Fake it? We can't!"

"Yes, we can," Alice said. "Nobody will know, and I'll use a little extra seasoning in the batter so nobody will know the corn isn't fresh. We can do this."

In short order, Alice mixed up the batter and Daisy shredded plenty of cheese. Alice commandeered the Tuckers' antique cast-iron skillet to begin frying. She never passed up an opportunity to use this skillet with its layers of seasoning built up through decades of splendid Southern cooking. It added a gentle infusion of depth and flavor impossible to duplicate any other way.

Once the crisis of the fritters was resolved, Alice set about doing what she'd come here early for: arranging mountains of hors d'oeuvres on antique platters with an artistic flair. Her problems melted away as she created little pyramids of cucumber sandwiches, deviled eggs, and mini crab cakes. She clipped sprigs of fresh dill and parsley to embellish the trays.

"Oh, Alice, you should come over every day," Daisy said. "We could have such fun! Nobody else understands the importance of a perfect cucumber sandwich."

Alice leaned in close to whisper, "Darling, some things are too important to leave to amateurs."

The Kentucky Derby was a pointless horse race with tacky betting, but she and Daisy would carve out a place for the ladies to enjoy the day indulging in a perfectly hosted celebration of feminine grace and charm.

Jack eyed himself in the mirror as he adjusted his cuffs beneath his pricey new blazer. He even added one of those silly pocket squares. Rule number one about going into battle was to put your enemy at ease, and he didn't mind showing up to the snazzy Kentucky Derby party looking like he was born with a silver spoon in his mouth. He'd given himself a close shave, slicked his hair back, and on the outside, Jack looked spiffier than he had in months.

Inside, he was furious.

He had liked living out at the Roost. After years of living in cold, impersonal hotel rooms, sharing the rustic digs with Doc had been surprisingly wonderful. That place had character in every square inch, with rough-hewn timber and raw simplicity. He even liked the birds that swarmed around the place. He'd started setting out bits of food to attract them and those silly birds were coming to know him, and he liked feeding them.

Alice Chadwick had put an end to that. The notice of eviction had been signed by the county housing authority, but he knew Alice was behind it. That day outside the courthouse when he offered to take her to the flower show? That was the day she filed the paperwork to get him kicked out of the Roost.

No wonder she'd been skittish. That woman radiated sweet gentility like fragrance wafting from a summer rose, but it was an illusion. She had her claws so deeply entrenched in Virginia's social elite that she could sweep him aside with the flick of her hand. He had underestimated her, but that wouldn't happen again.

What really drove him nuts—the extra bit of arsenic to make this sting even worse—was that he found her attractive. Knock-down, over-the-top, bombshell attractive. He'd always had a thing for ultra-feminine women, the kind whose handbags matched their shoes; who wore softly muted makeup and kept their long hair simply arranged. Alice had it all, along with a magnolia-soft, buttery Southern accent that triggered a tug deep in his gut. Everything about her was gentle, feminine, and sweet.

Except that sweet women didn't get people evicted with forty-eight hours' notice. He had to buy himself a hotel room, and since he didn't want Doc back on the streets, that meant shelling out for two rooms, so no, he wasn't in the mood to play nice today.

Jack ran his pickup through a carwash before heading out to Cherrywood, the country estate belonging to Kyle and Daisy Tucker. The Georgian-style plantation house sat on thirty-five acres and had been in the Tucker family since the Great Depression. While other families among Virginia's aristocracy had floundered, the Depression seemed to have magically bypassed the Tuckers, who continued drawing revenue from their wineries and a bourbon distillery in the western part of the state. They made a killing in wine and spirits during Prohibition, which meant they'd had connections with bootleggers and law officers willing to look the other way.

His Ford F-150 looked a little out of place beside the BMWs, Jaguars, and Range Rovers parked on the grassy lawn beside the winding drive up to the house. Who cared? Half these people probably inherited their money, and the others earned it through professions in law or business. Nine times out of ten when Jack mingled with the country club set, he was the only man who worked outdoors with his hands, his brain, and a clawing desire to climb out of the back alley where he'd been raised. No matter how rich he became, his vehicle of choice would always be an American pickup truck. No imported car could match the rugged practicality of a pickup that could withstand mudslides, haul tools, tow heavy loads, and take a man wherever he needed to go. The pickup truck represented the soul of hardworking Americans whose grit and determination built this country.

The Cherrywood mansion sprawled before the circular driveway like a Southern belle who knew she was the most gorgeous thing in view. The estate was rumored to have an award-winning botanical garden that he'd been hankering to tour ever since he got here. He intended to kill two birds with one stone today. One, he'd rub shoulders with the people who'd soon be members of his golf club. Two, he'd get a good look at the gardens. And somewhere along the way he intended to read Alice Chadwick the riot act for stabbing him in the back.

Men with bow ties and women wearing hats that looked like works of art already mingled on the front porch.

Greg McGarity recognized him. "Jack! When are we going to play a round of golf out at that snazzy new course?"

"The first weekend in September," he confidently asserted, and started chatting with others on the patio. He liked socializing with rich people and was good at it. Most of his experience rubbing shoulders with the one percent was at country clubs overlooking the 18th green, but a Kentucky Derby party was a nice change of pace.

Kyle Tucker soon joined him. "Thanks for coming," he said as he shook Jack's hand and gave him a clap on the shoulder like they were old buddies. He led Jack through the crush of people on the front porch and into the cool of the house.

Crossing through the front doors felt like entering Tara or some other fabled Southern plantation. A double staircase graced the foyer and led to a second-floor landing. Hand-painted wallpaper depicting rolling green hills provided relief from the white balustrades, white marble floor, and carved white paneling.

Kyle's wife was busy greeting guests in the front hall. Daisy looked like her name, poised and feminine but a smidge on the preppy side. "Jack!" she called out, and he leaned in so she could deliver the perfect set of air kisses. He glanced over Daisy's shoulder in search of his prey but realized instantly Alice wasn't here. From the moment he laid eyes on Alice Chadwick, it was as if a sixth sense immediately sparked to life whenever she was in the vicinity.

"Come on inside and help yourself to something to eat," Daisy said.

Jack was hungry enough to gnaw off his own arm, but the table displayed platters of miniature watercress and cucumber sandwiches. Women cooed over the tiny raspberry tarts cut to look like roses, but the corn fritters grabbed Jack's attention. Amid the dainty offerings that wouldn't feed a mosquito, he reached across the table to grab a wholesome, hearty corn fritter and groaned in pleasure at the first bite. It had the perfect crumbling crust, the smoky flavor, and rich, buttery corn. These would be great to serve at the golf course once it opened. Most men liked classic Southern cooking that didn't pay too much attention to carbs or looking like it came out of Martha Stewart's kitchen. These were *perfect*.

He was reaching for his third corn fritter when a blond woman wearing too much shiny red lipstick dinged a fork against a crystal glass.

"I've got an announcement," she said in a voice brimming with excitement. "Come Thanksgiving, there's going to be a little bundle of joy in the Conway household."

The chorus of feminine screaming was loud enough to be heard in the neighboring county. Jack grabbed another corn fritter and tried to back out of the room, but the stampede of women rushing toward the expectant mother blocked his retreat. They bombarded her with questions. They wanted to know the baby's due date, if it was a boy or a girl, what Skip said when he learned he was finally going to be a father.

The expectant mother managed to answer all their questions, giving thanks to Saint Helga for making the long-awaited conception finally happen.

A hefty arm landed around his shoulders. "Come on out back," Greg McGarity said. "They've got steaks and barbecue ribs outside."

Thank the good Lord! The female squawking showed no sign of letting up, and he gladly followed Greg down the center hallway. It was flanked on either side by rooms filled with fancy antiques and more silver than Jack had ever seen in one place. He accepted an ice-cold silver cup filled with a mint julep. An outdoor television mounted on the wall of the summer kitchen showed the Churchill Downs racetrack, where trainers walked their horses prior to the start of the races.

The hickory-smoked ribs and bourbon meatballs smelled like heaven itself. Jack wolfed down a barbecue slider and gazed at the gardens, chewing quickly because he'd just spotted his prey.

Alice strolled through the rose garden, casually admiring the blooms. Her pale blue and white gown flowed with grace, and the little white disk of a hat perched on the side of her head was perfection.

He grabbed another sandwich, not taking his eyes off her as he chewed. She might look soft and genteel, but she'd fired the first shot in this war between them. He'd staked his fortune and his future on the successful completion of this golf course, and he wouldn't take his foot off the gas pedal just because Alice Chadwick looked pretty while strolling in a garden. He knew her type and doubted that she would stop with his eviction from the Roost. Her next step would be to win historic preservation status for the derelict old house, which would ruin the prime location for his amphitheater.

He swallowed the last of his second sandwich and reached for the mint julep. It was pure summer in a silver cup, the minty bourbon and sugary syrup cut with plenty of ice. He smacked his lips at the tangy zing, still staring at Alice. He crunched some of the ice, savoring the bite of the bourbon and the sight of Alice Chadwick, who had no clue what was about to hit her.

He strolled down the steps set into the terraced hillside, mimicking the casual ease of others gathered on the lawn.

She saw him coming. For a moment she simply gazed at him, then recognition dawned and uncertainty clouded her wide, seemingly innocent eyes.

"Jack! I almost didn't recognize you," she said. "It's a lovely afternoon, isn't it?"

"I got your love letter tacked to my front door on Wednesday."

She knew exactly what he was referring to because her tone and expression were the perfect blend of empathy and anxiety. "I'm sorry if it was inconvenient, but I had to protect the Roost."

"They gave me forty-eight hours to clear out and move to a hotel."

Her expression brightened a little. "I'm sure you'll be more comfortable at the hotel."

"At two hundred dollars a night, I darn well ought to be."

"I truly *am* sorry," she said, and her voice had an achy quality that made it sound like she meant it. "The Roost isn't fit for human habitation."

"Yeah, that's what the note said, but I'm telling you it's fine. Get the decision reversed."

"It's what the county decided, not me," Alice said, the picture of innocence. "Surely the Tuckers can put you up at their hotel in town. It's their golf course, after all."

This woman was unbelievable. "You still don't realize they're flat broke?" There were always rich people walking on the edge of financial ruin, and the Tuckers were among them. Jack lifted his silver cup, condensation beginning to bead on the outside but the Tucker family crest still visible.

"It wouldn't surprise me if these cups go on the auction block soon. Kyle can probably get about five hundred apiece, which would pay the hefty bill I just got for seeding the greens."

"Why are they pouring money into a golf course if they're so poor?" she challenged.

Because they offered him thirty-percent ownership if he'd forgo his salary and take over paying the bills until the job was completed. Once the course went into business it would clear close to a million dollars a year, more if they could attract a PGA tournament. More still if he built that amphitheater and it could host summer festivals and concerts. Jack himself would bank a cool five thousand dollars a month. For a man with expensive medical insurance and whose health could take a nosedive at any time, it was a godsend.

But until then, Jack was living close to the bone and the interest on his loans accumulated by the day. He needed the course to open on time, not to argue with Alice about what the Tuckers did or didn't have in the bank. He wasn't going to let his inconvenient attraction to her interfere with business. It was time to defang her and scare her away from messing with his investment. He stepped closer so he could speak in a low voice without risk of being over-heard.

"I don't want to play hardball with you, but I'm good at it," he said. "You want to kick me out of my house? You claim it's a safety hazard? If it's such a hazard, I'll tear the Roost down on Monday morning."

"You can't!" The color drained from her cheeks and her eyes widened into blue pools of fear. It felt like he'd just stepped on a bunny. Threatening her pricked his conscience, but he wouldn't back down when everything he'd worked for was on the line.

"I can and I will," he asserted. "I was being nice by giving you permission to poke around the place and do whatever research you wanted to finish before I tore it down, but make no mistake ...

the Roost is private property, and I've already got permission from Kyle Tucker to tear it down and build an amphitheater."

Demolishing the Roost wouldn't feel good, nor did he like threatening Alice, but his life savings were invested in that golf course, and he understood how these activists worked. Nothing short of total capitulation would be good enough, and he needed her to back off.

"I want you to get the county to reverse its decision and get me back into the Roost. I wasn't hurting it. A pizza box? An uncovered trash can?"

"There's a porta-potty in the back," she said with a wrinkle on her nose.

"Would you rather we used the bushes? Hey . . . I get it. You think anything historic should be preserved behind glass and on display in a museum. That house has been through three hundred years of bad weather, wars, and a couple of hurricanes. A pizza box won't hurt it."

"The Roost needs to be studied. It's one of the oldest buildings in this area. There's a lot more to that place than historians have ever learned, and I want to know what it is. You can't tear it down! It would destroy a part of history forever."

His cell phone vibrated. He yanked it out as an excuse to slow the conversation down and jockey for position.

It was Sophie. *Again*.

He smothered the anguish that threatened to clobber him and sent the call to voicemail. Sophie had been trying to reach him for months, and so far she hadn't left a message, so whatever she wanted must not be that important.

He pocketed the phone and looked at Alice. Why was this so important to her? There wasn't any money to be made off whatever trivia she learned there.

And yet . . . he admired people who were passionate about unusual things. He once knew a guy who made models of real cathedrals out of toothpicks. They were built to scale and took years to complete, and then he donated them to local museums. There wasn't any money in it, but people loved those toothpick models. Alice apparently had the same sort of nonsensical commitment to the Roost.

"Get me back into the Roost by Monday. In return, I'll let you poke around and take pictures or samples or whatever you need to do, until I carry out the demolition later in the summer."

"Will you promise not to tear it down?"

"Of course not. I'll give you a month or two. That's all I can afford, since I'll need to break ground on the amphitheater as soon as the permits are ready."

"But what if I find something really important?"

Historians thought an old horseshoe or a bullet from the Civil War were worth grinding a million-dollar construction project to a halt. They lived in ivory towers where they didn't have to make payroll or float loans or build things that actually paid for themselves.

"If you discover something really important, I'll help you find a qualified contractor to relocate the Roost to a new location. On *your* dime."

She probably wasn't used to paying for anything. College professors lived in ivory towers where the university or the government wrote fat checks so she could sit around reading Jane Austen or whatever it was someone with a PhD did all day.

"It's a deal," she said and reached out to shake his hand.

An electric zing raced up his arm from where she touched him. Alice turned and walked toward the house, the fall of her skirt gently swaying with each step, and to the bottom of his soul he wished she wasn't the most intriguing thing he'd ever seen.

How was she going to reverse the eviction so Jack could get back into the Roost by Monday? Nervous energy coiled in her gut as Alice headed toward the Cherrywood mansion, avoiding everyone's gaze. She had to find Arlo Whitworth. He was her best bet among members of the Historic Preservation Board to ask for advice.

As for how to explain her about-face? The truth would work. Maybe she'd exaggerated the dangers of living in the Roost, but she hadn't exaggerated its historic importance. It was among the oldest surviving buildings in Virginia, and if her theory proved correct, it was far older than anyone realized. The Roost had a story to tell, and she needed to save it from being torn down on Monday.

Arlo stood with Daisy and a cluster of others inside the gazebo overlooking the terraced backyard. Towering oaks that had stood for decades shaded the lawn, and she trudged up the steps, wondering how to extricate Arlo from the women because this conversation should be handled privately.

Unfortunately, Daisy spotted her and sent an eager wave. "Alice! Just the person we've been looking for. Come and tell us about Sebastian Bell."

Alice forced the pleasant expression to remain in place. Her association with Sebastian and the Jane Austen movie was bound to come up again and again, and she couldn't avoid it forever. Sebastian was now in a pricey drug rehabilitation program, but his agent, an oily man named Graham Garfield, was still sending her threatening letters. Graham repeatedly warned that if she breathed a word about Sebastian that deviated from her confidentiality agreement, he would destroy her.

"I'm not authorized to talk about anything related to the *Emma* production," she began, which was true enough. Cast and crew on all major movie productions were required to keep mum about details of the filming.

"Not that," Daisy said. "Arlo was just telling us about the new Charles II miniseries. The one airing on Netflix? Have you been watching it?"

Sebastian had filmed *The King's Redemption* the year before she met him, and it was another of his historical smash hits. He played the dashing young King Charles II of England. The miniseries focused on the years of Charles's exile after his father lost his head on the chopping block during the Puritan Revolution. The young king lived on the run for two years, moving from one safe house to another, trying to rally enough support among the royalists that would allow him to retake the throne from Oliver Cromwell. He eventually fled to France, where he remained in exile for almost a decade.

It was the perfect role for Sebastian. With his smoldering good looks, he could play the warrior king with a perfect dash of wounded vulnerability. Sebastian privately told her that he hoped the role would bring him the longed-for respectability instead of his current heartthrob status. Alice had foolishly daydreamed of someday curling up with Sebastian before the fireplace, watching the miniseries together.

Now she would rather rinse her eyes with bleach than watch *The King's Redemption*.

"No, I'm afraid I haven't been watching," she said.

"You need to," Arlo replied. His bow tie today featured tiny embroidered roses in honor of the Kentucky Derby, but his expression was serious. "We're only three episodes in, but what strikes me is the similarity between the English Civil War and the American Civil War. The causes were completely different, but the parallels between Abraham Lincoln and Charles II are remarkable."

"Ha!" Daisy said. "Charles II was a rampant womanizer and Abe Lincoln was practically a monk."

"No, no, hear me out," Arlo said. "Both men wanted to extend forgiveness to their enemies. Charles II lived through years of sheer horror while he was on the run, yet after he regained the throne, he knew the only way to stabilize the country was by granting amnesty to the people who waged war against him. Abraham Lincoln wanted the same, but never got the chance to see it through. After he was assassinated, the North wanted to punish the South, and the country sank into years of revenge rather than reconciliation."

Daisy waved her fan. "Must we speak of the North?"

"Arlo, may I talk with you?" Alice sent an apologetic look to Daisy and the others. "It's just a little business. Nothing as exciting as resurrecting the war between the North and South, but quite important."

Arlo offered his arm as any gentleman would do as he escorted her down the gazebo steps. Sun pounded down and everything seemed glaringly hot and oppressive as she tackled the thorny subject of the Roost. Her gaze roamed the sprawling expanse of the Tucker estate and she wished people could simply get along with each other. Why couldn't Jack try to understand the people of Williamsburg? Respect for history was woven into their DNA.

"Jack Latimer is fighting his eviction from the Roost," she said. "He says if we don't let him back in by Monday, he'll tear it down. He claims to have the authority to do so."

Arlo's eyes widened in understanding. "If the Tuckers give him permission, he's right."

"What can we do? I think it's just a threat to make us reverse the eviction notice, but I don't know how to stop it."

Dismay morphed across Arlo's face as he understood her quandary. The two of them retreated to the far end of the garden to discuss their options. The county's primary concern was lack of power and water to a residential structure, but there were ways around that. A person could live in a pup tent provided it was on their own land and no rent was being paid in a landlord-tenant relationship. Since Jack wasn't paying rent to the Tuckers, the county could classify his occupancy as a non-commercial private arrangement rather than a formal tenancy. It would let the county reverse their decision without setting a troublesome precedent.

"I know the county commissioner, and he'll push this through," Arlo assured her. "It ought to be enough to get Jack off your back long enough to do your research."

Alice nodded, clinging to the hope that the plan would succeed. If it failed, her chances of uncovering the wonderful old secrets still hidden at the Roost would vanish forever.

Chapter Seven

Yoga always calmed Alice. Twice a week she took classes at a nearby gym where the instructor's soothing voice led her through the long, languid stretches. As always, she wore black leggings, ballet slippers, and a gauzy floral wrap to stay decently covered. She would have preferred a female-only gym where there weren't so many sweaty men ogling the women, but the yoga studio in the back was quite private. It had a ballet bar and hardwood floors reminiscent of the studio where she'd practiced ballet in France. She shouldered her gym bag, tucked the yoga mat beneath her arm, and walked inside the gym.

It wasn't overly crowded today. As always, the music was too loud and a bank of televisions mounted to the walls were tuned to sports channels. Over by the weight racks, a handful of muscle-bound men grunted while she weaved through the floor equipment on her way to the yoga studio. An obnoxious man in the middle of the walkway pressed out pushups with a giggling woman sitting cross-legged on his back.

The giggly blond urged him to move faster.

"Lady, I'm going as fast as I can," the jock groaned.

Lady.

She turned to gawk, and the chestnut hair damp with sweat was familiar, but it was the use of the term *lady* that Alice recognized. Commandeering the middle of the gym floor to carry on a flirtation was the sort of crass exhibitionism corroding modern society.

The giggling girl in shiny pink Lycra fell off his back and rolled onto the floor. Jack flipped onto his back, arms flung up and grinning as he panted in exhaustion.

He was looking at her. "You wanna hop on next, Professor?"

The muscles of his biceps and shoulders were sculpted and the leer on his face annoyed her. "No, thank you."

He sat up. "Don't run away so fast. Hey! I thought you'd like to know that Doc and me moved back into the Roost."

Doc and I, she silently amended. "Good," she said.

She and Arlo spent all of Sunday and a frantic Monday pounding on doors and humbling themselves before city employees until they lifted the eviction. Jack was now free to remain at the Roost so long as there was no tenancy agreement with the Tuckers.

Jack stood up, dragging a hand through his sweaty hair. "Thanks for holding up your end of the deal. I'm usually working during the days, but you can come by the Roost any time to do your research. Don't wait too long, though. As soon as the permits for the amphitheater come through, we'll break ground and tear down the building."

Exasperation spilled over. "Doesn't it bother you that a priceless piece of history is going to be destroyed so a few pampered rich people can play golf?"

Jack snorted. "Not everyone who plays golf is pampered."

"Oh? How much will it cost to play a round of golf once your course is open?"

He nodded to her rolled-up mat. "How much do your fancy yoga classes cost? Or the membership at this gym?"

"At least yoga serves a purpose. The benefits of strength and flexibility are priceless. Golf isn't a sport, it's a game."

"Golf serves a purpose," he retorted. "And there will be scholarships for kids who want to play but can't afford it."

"What a clever technique to encourage underprivileged kids to become lifelong consumers of a useless game."

He braced his hands on his hips, his jaw tight and voice hard. "Lady, golf is a sport, not a game. Not all of life's lessons come out of a book."

She took a step back. "Golf is an extravagant waste of natural resources practiced only by the privileged class and serves no health or moral purpose beyond sheer self-indulgence."

She whirled around to escape his sweaty, over-exposed body and scurried as fast as possible into the yoga room.

Jack glared at Alice's back as she retreated, itching to call her back and defend the sport that saved his life. His background was the opposite of privilege, but she couldn't know that. With her healthy, limber body and expensive yoga classes, she probably couldn't know what it was like to grow up spending more time in wheelchairs, leg braces, and hospital beds than outdoors playing like normal kids.

He headed toward the free weights, one of the few activities aside from golf his doctor allowed. He grabbed a pair of dumbbells and began cranking out curls, still steaming over Alice's ridiculous assertion about privilege. Sure, most people who played golf were rich. So? Most kids who went to college were rich, but he didn't attack her entire profession or suggest it shouldn't exist.

Golf demanded stamina, concentration, and muscular control. The first time Jack picked up a golf club he had been wearing leg braces but was so eager to try his hand at the sport that his dad drove him out to a public driving range to give it a whirl. He'd been stiff and clumsy, but it didn't matter. He was hooked.

His fascination for golf started when he was in the hospital after playing flag football during school recess. His parents had forbid him from participating in sports, but what ten-year-old obeyed his parents' rules once he was free of their eagle-eyed supervision? There wasn't any tackling in flag football, and it gave him a chance to test his speed and agility against the other kids. He wasn't as fast or coordinated as most of them, and he fell down a couple of times, but it didn't hurt and *it was exhilarating*. For once it felt like he was part of a team, running and chasing until he was breathless. He caught a pass and almost made a touchdown. He still remembered the scent of the grass and the dusty tang of dirt in the air. He was alive and free and kids cheered when he almost made that touchdown. Those ten seconds of pure joy powered him through the rest of the day at school.

It wasn't until that evening when the swelling started. His hip took the brunt of a fall, and the swelling turned serious quickly. His parents rushed him to the hospital, but there were tests and forms to fill out before Dr. Jensen, the staff hematologist, was summoned to the hospital. By the time the doctor ordered a delivery of frozen plasma, the swelling in Jack's hip was so bad he sobbed like a baby, rocking in agony even as his parents tried to hold him immobilized against the mattress. He tried to stifle it when Dr. Jensen was in the room, but it didn't work, and his humiliation was complete when the doctor rolled him over to examine his other hip and Jack screamed.

Once the plasma was ready, Dr. Jensen threaded a needle into a vein and Jack watched through a blur of tears, waiting for the clotting factor to start infiltrating his blood. It took hours for the swelling to stabilize, but he was trapped in a hospital bed for another week. His hip joint had been savagely damaged by the swelling, and any rapid movement could trigger another episode.

The day after the accident, Dr. Jensen came for a checkup, a clipboard tucked beneath his arm and a stethoscope dangling over his shoulder. He was fit and good-looking, and Jack instinctively tried to straighten up on the bed to prove that he wasn't a loser like the blubbering weakling of the day before.

"Well, kid, I think you're old enough to know that football isn't the right sport for you."

Jack looked away. "It was flag football," he mumbled.

"Yeah, you still can fall down and trigger a bleed," the doctor said. "You're going to have to learn the limitations of your body, even if your parents aren't there to keep you in line, okay?"

Was he supposed to lie in bed or sit in a wheelchair his entire life? Those ten minutes of flag football, the thrill of running, the grass a blur beneath his feet, reaching upward to catch a ball flying through the air—they were the best ten seconds of his life.

A sheen of tears prickled and he hunched over, defeated.

The doctor dragged a chair closer to the bed, the scrape of metal loud as he plopped the chair down and sat. "Hey, just because you can't play football doesn't mean there aren't other things you can do."

Jack snorted. "Like what?" The only thing his mother let him do was walk, always holding her hand and never letting him stray off the sidewalk. Other kids ran in the woods, climbed trees, played on monkey bars.

"There's lots of things you can do," Dr. Jensen said. "You can go swimming or play golf or maybe archery."

Jack didn't know what "archery" was, and there weren't any swimming pools where he lived. Golf looked boring and didn't seem fun like football or soccer or any of the other sports at school.

"Yeah, okay," he mumbled.

Like most times he was trapped in the hospital, there was little to do but watch the television mounted on the wall. That afternoon, while his father dozed in the chair beside him, Jack scrolled through the channels and paused when he landed on a game of golf. The television was on mute so it wouldn't wake his dad, and the game still looked boring . . . but at least it was outside.

Rolling green hills with patches of sparkling water stretched out in an endless expanse, so different from the stark hospital room with beeping machines and clinical smells. He lay on the mattress, letting the calming glimpse of nature carry him beyond the bleak hospital room. It was hypnotizing. The golf course looked like paradise, and the men on the course were tanned and fit as they positioned themselves before the golf ball with fierce concentration. What were they thinking about?

The television was on mute, but he didn't need sound to understand what was happening. For the first time, Jack could picture a future for himself. He could be one of those men, casually leaning on a club while watching other competitors. Or conferring with his caddy as he walked to the next tee box. Best of all was watching the men as they shaded their eyes to stare into the distance, thinking majestic things.

His dad eventually woke up and they turned the volume up, and then golf got even better. The announcers spoke in quietly reverent tones as they narrated the game, and Jack was swept along with the action. Hope and anticipation collided because the future was suddenly opening up before him. It would be filled with rolling green hills and comradery and challenge in a world flooded with sunshine.

In the months and years that followed, he did everything the doctors ordered to achieve that dream. Even after his mother died and his dad fell off the wagon, Jack learned to look out for himself. He avoided unnecessary risks and took his injections. Instead of tearing headlong down hallways and up staircases, he taught himself to stroll and be mindful, alert and aware. The doctors recommended stretching exercises for hemophiliacs to develop balance and stay limber, and guess what? Stretching was good training for golf, too.

Jack watched every PGA tournament on TV. He studied the golfers the way a microbiologist studied life forms under a microscope, gradually understanding their swings and techniques. He saved his allowance to buy a used set of clubs from a thrift shop, and mimicked what he saw on TV. While in high school, he volunteered to pull weeds at a golf course in exchange for free lessons. He soaked up golf lore and wisdom as he tended the greens and loved it all. Hard work, practice, and love of the sport won him a scholarship to college.

Sometimes it didn't matter how badly a person longed for a dream. Training, hope, and prayers could only go so far in making childhood wishes come true. Over the years, Jack's health improved, but there were still spells that landed him back in leg braces and sometimes a wheelchair. No matter how cautious he was, a simple sprained ankle or bruised knee could spark internal bleeding, with swelling so severe it risked joint damage. Those were the times he relied on crutches or a brace, sidelined from training until his joints could bear weight again.

The hope of a life as a professional golfer slipped further away with each passing year, not in one crushing blow but in a slow, relentless drift. Eventually, he accepted that dreams sometimes need to change. His early days tending the grounds at a golf course offered him a glimpse of a different future, one where he could still draw on his love for the game as a business, not as a player.

Jack's muscles burned as he powered through another set with the dumbbells, his mind growing more annoyed at Alice Chadwick with every rep. What an irony that college professors, who were so vocal about the plight of the working class, had such preconceived notions about them. She thought blue-collar guys didn't belong on a golf course? Alice was book-smart, but she didn't understand men or the world outside her elite ivory tower.

And for some unknown reason, it bothered him. She radiated smooth femininity and artful, quick wit. Her soft, cognac-brown eyes stirred something in him he couldn't shake, and that annoyed him, too.

Before he left Williamsburg, he intended to earn her respect.

Chapter Eight

Alice took Jack up on his offer to let her prowl around the Roost while he worked on the golf course. The less they saw of each other, the better.

She invited Professor Brandon Tilney to accompany her. Brandon was a plant biologist and he shared her love of history. His ability to estimate the age of wood would be priceless in determining when the Roost was built, but when she picked him up for the drive over, she hadn't realized he wanted to make a stop at the cemetery.

"Do you mind?" he asked as he squeezed into her Prius, holding a gorgeous bouquet of flowers for his wife's final resting place. "The cemetery is on the way."

Of course she didn't mind. The care Brandon gave in selecting each blossom for the weekly bouquet he set on his wife's grave was a symphony of symbolism. Clara had passed away three years earlier, yet he carried on a conversation with her through the figurative language of each bloom. Every flower that went into Brandon's arrangements were chosen to tell Clara a story about his week living without her. He used lilies of the valley when he was feeling low, and crocus blooms when his mood turned cheerful again. The leaves of a fern symbolized confidence, while ivy affirmed his hope for meeting her again in eternal life.

"What are those lovely orange flowers?" Alice asked once she turned her car onto the road.

"Nasturtium blossoms," Brandon replied, one of his fingers touching a ruffled petal. "They represent triumph after a long battle."

She raised a brow. "You've had a triumph?"

"I learned yesterday that my grant application to continue the dendrochronology lab has been funded for an additional two years. I intend to celebrate the victory with Clara."

"Congratulations!" Alice said, for winning a federal grant was indeed cause to celebrate. It was especially good news for Alice since dendrochronology, the study of tree rings to learn about the past, might pin down the exact age of the Roost. The fire in 1698 that destroyed the Jamestown statehouse wiped out so much history. The assumption was that the Roost was built shortly before the fire, but Alice had found a few scraps of information in the British archives that made her suspect it was much older.

The cemetery was five miles outside of town, and she parked the car near the front gate. The thick, leaden clouds hovering in the sky were gloomy and wistfully beautiful—the perfect backdrop for a graveside visit.

"I shall only be a few minutes," Brandon said as he left the car with the lovely bouquet.

Brandon's tall, elegant frame carefully wended through the headstones toward the well-tended grave near the center. Her friendship with Brandon had always been platonic, although if he'd been twenty years younger, she would certainly have been attracted to him.

Actually, *most* women were attracted to Brandon Tilney. He was fifty-two years old with a lean, angular face offset by intelligent eyes that always glinted with curiosity. There was an air of refinement about him as he sank to one knee and placed the flowers near Clara's headstone. As always, he wore flawlessly tailored linen slacks and a blazer, but his attire didn't stop him from plucking a few weeds to tidy Clara's resting place.

Such gentlemen were rare in today's era of loose morality and crass humor. When he bowed his head in silent prayer, she glanced away. The moment seemed too intimate to continue staring at him.

"Thank you, Alice," Brandon said as he squeezed back into the passenger seat of her compact car. His knees barely fit in front of the dashboard, but that didn't stop his good-natured smile. "Onward to the Roost and untangling your mystery."

Anxiety took hold as she turned onto the county road that would take them to the Roost. Hopefully, Jack wouldn't be there. He scared her. There was a raw, masculine edge underlying everything he did and it felt off-putting. He was too loud, too crass, too confident. He'd flash one of his good ol' boy grins and let fly a tacky joke with no other goal than to attack the foundation of her carefully curated world.

"A shame about these broken limbs," Brandon said as she drove through the tunnel of apple and pear trees leading to the Roost. Part of her wanted to point out how the damage was compliments of Jack Latimer's obnoxious service vehicles, but it wouldn't be ladylike to cast blame. Brandon was always so polished, so genteel, and she wouldn't sink into the muck to throw dirt on Jack's character, no matter how satisfying it would be.

"Jack said he'd be out in the field today, so we ought to have the Roost to ourselves."

Thankfully, there was no sign of Jack's pickup truck or the vagrant man who lived with him. Tension unknotted from her neck, and she reached into the back seat for her satchel. By the time she retrieved it, Brandon had come around to open her car door. He even offered his hand to help her out. Alice was perfectly capable of getting out of a car on her own, but she still appreciated Brandon's old-school manners.

The view of the Roost was completely spoiled by ugly pieces of construction equipment scattered about the woods. The bright yellow tractors were a blight and an ominous warning that the Roost's days were numbered unless Alice could find something extraordinary here.

By the time she and Brandon carried his equipment indoors, fat droplets had begun spattering the ground. Heavier rain would be here soon, and Alice hurried inside the darkened interior of the Roost. She set her satchel beside Brandon's tools, then twisted the dial on a battery-operated lantern to light up the room.

It looked like Jack and Doc had cleaned up some. No food had been left out, and the lid on the front-porch trash can was secured by a bungee cord. A sleeping bag had been rolled and stored in the corner along with pillows and a blanket.

Brandon opened a large tool case to reveal wicked-looking implements inside. Drills, augers, and a variety of measuring devices.

She set the lantern on the ledge above the massive stone fireplace. "How can I help you get started?"

"Allow me a few minutes to assess each room," he replied. "This place has had a lot of modifications and additions over the years, so first I need to find the original timber."

Alice began taking pictures of the interior while Brandon began his survey. The lintel stone over the fireplace drew her, and she pressed her fingers into the curious leafy mark carved into the top corner of the stone. It was the same marking on the old letter from 1672 she'd found in the British archives. She'd reread that letter so many times it was engraved on her heart:

Helga has sailed for Jamestown as she still has hope to conceive a child. The woman is a saint, but I fear we will never see her again. Virginia is a dangerous land.

The letter ended with the curving fronds, exactly like this one carved onto the lintel stone. She centered her camera on the mark and took a picture, hoping the symbol meant something and wasn't a coincidence.

She continued scanning the room for more things to photograph. Plaster had been added to cover the walls in the early nineteenth century, but the heavy beams supporting the ceiling were probably original wood. Some of Jack's belongings were stacked on the windowsill. A well-thumbed paperback about the history of golf lay atop the latest issue of *Sports Illustrated*. The kitchen was tidy, even though the contents of the cupboards could give her heart disease merely by looking inside. Boxes of sugary cereal, fluorescent-orange cheese crackers wrapped in cellophane, bags of potato chips. The mini-refrigerator operated on generator power, and she couldn't resist a peek inside. A jug of full-fat milk, cans of beer, and a plastic basket filled with small glass vials.

Medicinal vials.

The vials weren't any of her business and she ought to close the door, but couldn't stop herself from investigating. Most of the vials were clear liquid, but others looked cloudy. Some had purple caps, some had red. The prescription label had Jack Latimer's name on each vial, but the names of the drugs were unfamiliar to her.

She closed the refrigerator door. Jack's medical condition wasn't any of her business, though whatever he suffered from would surely benefit from a diet besides cheese crackers and beer.

She headed upstairs to take more photos. On either side of the staircase were two large matching square rooms, mostly empty. A cheap patio recliner with another sleeping bag was serving as a bed, and it looked like Jack was living out of his suitcases. The other room was identical in its square layout, but he had it set up as a study. A card table held a laptop and a printer. Rain spattered the slate roof, and an eerie sensation descended. This was the same sound of rain patter the early settlers would have heard. Outside, everything looked distorted through the wavy glass, but the view out the back was thickly wooded with silver maples and sycamore trees. Again, the same view they would have seen.

She touched the cool glass, marveling that hundreds of years ago, some woman probably stood at this window as water rolled off the eaves to pool on the ground below. This glass was original, and over the centuries a number of people had scratched graffiti onto its wavy surface. Elizabeth and William Tucker scratched their names and wedding date in 1771. In subsequent years they wrote the birthdates of their three children. A curious, disjointed snake was etched into the bottom of the window glass. Historians identified it as the "Join, or Die" snake, a symbol calling for unity leading up to the American Revolution. Other symbols were harder to understand . . . stray scratch marks, doodles, and random initials. Once upon a time, people not so different from her stood on this exact spot as they etched these markings into the glass.

Falling under the spell of this old place was an occupational hazard. Most people who studied the past probably had similar feelings, but Alice needed to quit daydreaming and find out the real age of the Roost if she had any hope of figuring out the source of the Saint Helga legend.

Her best shot was downstairs in the front room as Brandon prepared to take samples of the original wood ceiling beams. The old staircase creaked as she headed downstairs to join him.

"Before you drill, I'd like to take some close-up photos of the ceiling beams," Alice said. Brandon moved a card table below the center beam and helped her clamber onto the wobbly table. The ceiling was lower than in homes constructed today, letting her get close enough to an exposed beam to lay her hand on the wood. What secrets this old beam could spill! She took a few photographs, wondering if it was oak or maple. It was so darkened with age she couldn't tell.

"Nice legs," a male voice said.

Alice startled and turned to see Jack Latimer standing in the open doorway. He held a dripping umbrella in one hand and a bucket of fried chicken in the other.

She hopped down so that her knees wouldn't be eye-level with him anymore. She shouldn't have worn a miniskirt, but it was warm and he wasn't supposed to be here.

"What were you doing up there?" Jack asked.

"You said I could look around," she defended, and he flashed one of those annoying smiles.

"I said *you* could, but who's he?" Jack asked with a glance at Brandon, who held a boring tool. Jack had better not utter one rude comment about the kindest gentleman in all of Virginia.

"This is Professor Brandon Tilney," she said. "He's an expert in dating old structures by studying the tree rings in the wood."

"Cool," Jack said with a grin and clapped Brandon on the back, who looked a little taken aback by the vigor of the greeting. Brandon wasn't the backslapping type. He was more likely to execute a courtly bow than be a backslapper. The skinny man named Doc came into the room as well, dragging mud in with each step.

"So how do tree rings help you date a building?" Jack asked, and Brandon supplied the well-practiced answer.

"I'll compare the tree rings from this beam to other samples from the area. The core samples I'll be taking today won't hurt the structural integrity of the Roost."

"I thought you were going to be out on the golf course today," Alice said. Their work would be more challenging with Jack hovering over them.

"Yeah, I did too, but as you can see, the weather isn't cooperating." He set the bucket of chicken on the table. "Hungry?" he asked.

Her mouth watered. Deep-fried food was an insult to her arteries, her complexion, and her waistline, but fried chicken had always been her weakness. Doc set out paper plates and plastic utensils while Jack brought over two more folding chairs for the table.

Everyone else dug in, so Alice picked up a drumstick and discreetly nibbled.

"How long is it going to take before you get that tree-ring data analyzed?" Jack asked, then ripped off a huge section of chicken breast with his teeth and chewed with vigor. At least he seemed curious as Brandon replied that with luck, it could be within the week.

"It all depends on if I can find any wood with bark still on it," Brandon said. "That outside layer is the last year the tree was alive, so if I can pair those final few rings to one of our reference samples, I will be able to pinpoint the exact date."

To his credit, Jack fired off plenty of intelligent questions about everything from native trees to water quality in the tide-water. Jack and Brandon talked like old friends as the conversation skipped from trees to climate to invasive plant species.

The rain continued unabated all through lunch, and Brandon didn't want to get his equipment wet lugging it out to the car.

"Who is the chess player?" Brandon asked with a nod to the chess board on the hearth.

"That would be me," Doc said. "Can I tempt you into a game? I'm tired of beating Jack."

"Absolutely," Brandon said agreeably. Jack cleared away the remnants of the chicken while Doc set up the chessboard on the card table. Soon they had launched into a game Alice had never bothered to learn.

"I couldn't help noticing the feller machine you've got parked out back," Brandon said to Jack as he moved a pawn forward.

Jack grunted. "Yeah, that thing is costing me four thousand dollars a week, and I can't use it when it's raining this hard."

"Why didn't you clear the trees when you initially cleared the golf course   land?" Brandon's question provoked one of those dashing grins from Jack.

"That was before we got the idea for the amphitheater," he said. "It's going to have a view of the waterfall on one side, with Saint Helga's Spring behind it. A gorgeous venue like that can attract PGA tours and television rights, so I'm not sparing any expense. The quicker I can clear the trees, the quicker I can break ground."

"The local students are going to have a lot to say about that," Alice said. "If the integrity of the spring is in danger, they'll go into full eco-warrior mode. That means protests and petitions and even breaking equipment."

"Sabotage?" Jack asked.

She nodded. "It's happened before. They're already mad about the golf course, and will go into overdrive if they learn Saint Helga's Spring is going to have a tacky amphitheater plopped in front of it."

Given Jack's darkening expression, it looked like her words were starting to have the intended effect. "Yeah, well, the students aren't here. By the time they get back from their summer vacations in Saint-Tropez or wherever rich kids spend their summers, the amphitheater will be a done deal. Right now, they're not here and they don't know about it."

"Oh, they'll know about it. Trust me."

Brandon, ever the gentleman, deliberately changed the subject. "What are you going to charge for a round of golf?" he asked Jack.

Alice nearly choked on her own breath when she learned a round of golf would cost two hundred dollars on a typical day, and more on weekends. "Why would anyone squander that much money to broil in the sun all day?"

"Why would anyone squander their day reading a novel about made-up people?" Jack countered. He didn't sound mad, he sounded amused. "Pardon me, Professor, but I don't see Jane

Austen as being any more valuable to society than a decent round of golf."

Alice drew a breath and straightened her spine. "Jane Austen belongs in the pantheon alongside Shakespeare and Dante, and the only reason she's not there is because the male guardians of the canon won't let a woman past the gates. Jane Austen didn't need to create improbable plots about war or carnage or revenge. Her characters are the stuff of legend. Her novels are masterpieces of sparkling wit and social observation that celebrate the triumph of human reason over baser instincts."

She shouldn't have rambled on so much, but Jack was listening to every word, his expression rapt. Then he had to spoil everything by opening his mouth. "Jane Austen writes long-winded novels filled with boring tea parties and women wearing ugly nighties."

"The dresses *were* rather frumpy," Brandon said, but Alice would not concede.

"Regency gowns weren't flashy, but they were feminine and graceful without putting half a woman's body on public display. Our world would be a better place if people had the self-control to abide by the civilized norms in a Jane Austen novel. Meanwhile, golf is a mindless waste of time and money."

Instead of being insulted, Jack warmed to the subject. "You may not appreciate sweaty games of sportsmanship, but competing is hardwired into every red-blooded man's DNA. As soon as cavemen started walking on two feet, they competed. Who could run faster, throw a rock farther, drag home a bigger antelope. Look at Professor Tilney. Within ten minutes of spotting that chessboard, he rolled up his sleeves and wanted a match. Competition is normal human nature."

"Maybe it's a *man's* nature," she pointed out, and once again, Brandon sided with the barbarians.

"Are men not human?" he asked. "If you prick us, do we not bleed? If you poison us, do we not die?"

Referencing Shakespeare's *The Merchant of Venice* wasn't going to make Alice see value in golf. It was three men against one woman, and she was losing.

"Face it, Alice," Jack said. "Sports and competition are bred into us, and that's a good thing. Instead of going to war with the Russians, we go to the Olympics and fight it out on ski slopes and race tracks. Sports let mankind blow off steam. If I didn't have golf when I was growing up, I'd have landed in jail a million times."

The statement made her pause. She'd never known anyone who'd gone to jail or was even at risk of such a fate. What sort of man was Jack Latimer? It didn't really matter. He was simply wrong about the value of sports.

"The way to rescue America's at-risk youth is through academics, not sweaty   locker rooms and pointless contests of strength."

Jack remained cheerfully unconvinced. "That may have worked for *you*, but guys like me need an outlet to compete and conquer. Not everyone's salvation will be found in a library. I think you need to open your mind, Professor."

Did she? Alice had three brothers, and all of them would probably agree with Jack.

And to her mortification, she had to consider that he might be right about the value of sports.

The rain lasted all afternoon, but Brandon eventually got his samples, and Alice got an unexpected lesson in opening her mind.

Chapter Nine

Trying to teach a man wearing a monocle how to peer through a land surveyor's telescope was a challenge, but Jack needed Kyle Tucker to understand where the amphitheater would be situated. Once the Roost and surrounding trees were removed, the amphitheater would have spectacular views of both the golf course and Saint Helga's Spring.

"Looking good," Kyle said as he stepped away from the tripod, allowing reporter Micky Hayes to take his place. Micky was a great guy who covered local stories for the Williamsburg television news station, and had been giving favorable coverage of ongoing developments at the golf course. In a college town where the students were a built-in army to raise the alarm over the environmental issues associated with golf, Jack was grateful for Micky's practical understanding of the jobs and diversified streams of revenue the golf course would bring to the local economy. Positive news coverage was free publicity for the amphitheater, and Jack needed every bit of it.

"Our marketing consultant believes the amphitheater can attract events most weekends of the year," Jack said. "I see it hosting up-and-coming bands or maybe classical music performances from the college."

Kyle held his hands out as though framing a picture. "Shakespeare under the stars! Maybe some musical theater or even stand-up comedians. Anything to get folks outdoors and away from their glowing screens at home."

Micky scrutinized the lay of the land. "What sort of concession stand are you planning?"

Kyle jumped in before Jack could answer. "Wine and cheese. Maybe some cocktails, but we want high-end stuff. This won't be a greasy burger joint."

Kyle misunderstood the reporter's question, and Jack intervened. "A formal concession stand will be built later. It will be air-conditioned and have indoor seating, plus an outdoor patio overlooking the amphitheater. Everything will meet or surpass local building codes. The restroom facilities will support an audience of up to five thousand people. The parking lot will have spaces for automobiles and charging stations, plus an alley for food trucks or vendor displays. We're hoping art festivals will find the space appealing."

Most of all, Jack hoped the PGA would find the space appealing. Television rights to broadcast a PGA tournament could earn more in one weekend than most golf courses could earn in six months.

"We've got to get rid of the Roost, though," Kyle said, and Jack nearly choked. Today's mission was to drum up free publicity, not shine a spotlight on the most controversial aspect of the plan.

"The Roost isn't part of this discussion," Jack rushed to add. "We're not sure exactly what we're going to do with it."

"I'll bet that old building holds a lot of stories," Micky said, his voice unexpectedly wistful. "I heard it was a hospital during the Civil War, and that before that it was a tavern that turned out some of the best whiskey anywhere in America."

"Now it's just an eyesore," Kyle said. "It's blocking the view of Saint Helga's Spring and serves no purpose other than—"

Jack cut Kyle off before he could continue his rant. "Micky, can I give you a tour of the course? We've seeded the greens and started installing the shrubs and trees." There wasn't much to see yet, but Jack needed to get the reporter away from Kyle's babbling about demolishing the Roost. Kyle was an idiot. He'd come to Jack for more money last week, even though the ink was barely dry on the latest check Jack had written for someone to draft architectural plans for the amphitheater.

Micky started heading toward the course and Jack lifted a hand. "It's been good seeing you again, Kyle. Give Daisy my best."

Kyle Tucker might be an idiot, but he heard the dismissal in Jack's tone and gave a stiff smile, sunlight glinting on the gold rim of his monocle. People born with a silver spoon in their mouth rubbed him the wrong way. Not *all* rich people, just the ones who carelessly blathered confidential business plans because their livelihood never depended on making payroll or accurate long-term projections for the viability of a golf course that consumed most of their life savings.

Once Kyle was out of earshot it was easier to relax.

"The fairways look great," Micky said with a nod to the bright green seedlings of grass beginning to take root.

They ought to look great. Twelve thousand dollars of organic fertilizer spread over 160 acres took a bite out of Jack's budget, but proper soil nutrition would pay off in the long run if the grass could establish a healthy root system throughout the course.

"Let me show you the 7th hole," Jack said as he headed down the gentle slope. "It's a par 3 but I left a group of old willow trees standing in the middle of the fairway. They're pretty, but I can already hear the golfers howl in anguish at the fantastic obstacle they're going to create."

Micky laughed as they reached the bottom of the slope, the graceful willow trees arranged as if God himself had planted them here.

A *squelch* sounded as he planted a foot, then another.

That was odd. The sprinklers hadn't gone off last night, nor had it rained. He hunkered down, feeling the ground sink a little beneath his weight.

Everything was wet.

"Is it supposed to be this soggy?" Micky asked.

No, and something is wrong. Jack blocked any hint of concern from his face as he stood. Only a fool would let a reporter see a sign of trouble.

"Our guys are still calibrating the irrigation system," he said. "Maybe we should put this tour off. The landscaping will look better in a month and I'll give you a personal tour."

"Sounds great," Micky said.

Jack tried not to panic as he walked across the fairway, the gentle pull of spongy soil clinging to his shoes with each step. The sloshing noise from each footfall ratcheted his nerves tighter. Several acres were water-logged, which meant the irrigation system was going completely haywire.

He paused to survey the landscape. The slope of the land meant the water was draining toward Saint Helga's Spring, where it was washing thousands of dollars of fertilizer into the preserved wetland.

He cursed under his breath. If the environmentalists got wind of this, they'd want his head on a platter. Everything he used was organic, yet even organic fertilizer could trigger algae blooms that would deplete oxygen in the water. It would turn the water green, cloudy, and suffocate the fish. Turtles, frogs, and insects would all take a hit.

He jogged toward the clubhouse, praying he could find a quick solution to mitigate this disaster.

Alice clicked on the oven's light to check the progress of her chicken pot pie for the third time. Baking a flaky, golden crust without burning the delicate pastry leaves decorating the rim of the pie was always a challenge, but if Martha Stewart could do it, so could Alice.

Five more minutes? She set the timer, then lifted the lid on the pot of bone broth simmering from the roasted chicken carcass. She always used leftover bones to make broth that captured a depth and richness no store-bought brand could deliver. The aroma of savory meat and baking pastry filled the kitchen, stirring a deep sense of pride within her. Aside from the chicken, every ingredient she used today came from the farmers market or her own herb garden. She bought the carrots, onions, and peas this morning, and snipped parsley and thyme from her windowsill. Some people might settle for a frozen block of packaged vegetables, but creating a meal from scratch was a rewarding experience . . . even if she only cooked for one.

She'd use the last few minutes of baking time to make a bouquet garni for tomorrow's soup. It required clipping a bit of thyme and basil from her windowsill herb garden, which she did while smiling at the chirp of a wren nesting in a tree outside the open window. Evening sounds were always so soothing, a relaxing end to the day.

The slam of a car door from the parking lot startled the wren into flight. Why did people have to be so obnoxious? Most of the residents in this quiet row of townhouses probably had their windows open to savor the one of the last cool evenings of spring, and there was no call to slam that door so aggressively.

She focused on the calming scent of herbs as she wrapped them in cheesecloth, then reached for a bit of twine to tie it together.

A pounding on her front door startled her, but she didn't look up from the half-assembled bouquet garni. She wasn't expecting anyone, and they could wait while she finished the bouquet.

The pounding continued. "Open up, Professor," a voice growled on the other side of the door. "I know you're in there because your pansy car is sitting in the parking lot."

Jack Latimer. He had a lot of nerve to insult her responsible vehicle when he drove a monstrous, carbon-emitting pickup that looked like it was designed to transport Darth Vader around the known universe.

She tied off the bouquet and set it on the windowsill before strolling to the front door while the pounding continued. Did he think acting like a caveman was going to earn her cooperation with anything?

She opened the door to see Jack's face flushed with perspiration and annoyance. He had one hand braced on the frame of her door and held an official-looking document with the other.

"Would you care to explain this?" he demanded, holding the document before her face. She took a step back from the fury in his voice, which he mistook for an invitation to enter her home. He took a giant step inside and slammed the door.

She flinched. "I didn't invite you inside and have no intention of discussing anything if you can't speak in a respectful tone of voice."

"That's right; you don't discuss. You run to the government to fight your battles for you. I just got a warning letter for polluting Saint Helga's Spring, and it's got your fingerprints all over it."

She had no idea what he was talking about, but the ding of the kitchen timer gave her the perfect excuse to retreat. She hurried to the kitchen and grabbed a pair of mitts. A quick glance through the oven window confirmed the pot pie had achieved the perfect golden shade, with the pastry leaves a tiny bit darker. Satisfaction filled her as she lifted the fragrant pot pie from the oven and set it on a trivet.

"A fancy meal for one?" Jack taunted. "Why does this not surprise me?"

That was a nasty thing to say, but perfectly in keeping with Jack's boorish nature. She ran a cloth over the kitchen counters to hide her nerves. "Why do you think I had anything to do with that letter?"

"Because someone tampered with the irrigation lines on my golf course, and it magically happened the day after you told me to expect eco-warriors to interfere with the amphitheater. I also just laid a ton of fertilizer on the course, and the laws of gravity means it was all washed into Saint Helga's wetland. The request for an environmental inspection was filed the day *before* I noticed the problem. Somebody tipped them off."

She folded her arms. "It wasn't me, if that's what you're thinking."

"You were the one mouthing off the other day because I plan to cut down some trees on your sacred land. Now my irrigation lines are cracked in three places and it's washing fertilizer into protected wetlands."

The anger in his voice seemed too big for her cozy front room with its antiques and lace doilies. The kitchen counter served as a barrier between the kitchen and the living room, and she stood behind it as if it were a protective shield. "Is it so unthinkable to believe you may have made a mistake? Or that your irrigation guys were sloppy? Accidents happen all the time."

"Yeah, they do, except that last month the pump on the waterfall also broke and started dumping water toward the spring. It's not a coincidence. All my troubles started right after you got back to the United States."

His implication that she'd resort to sabotage to stop his project was ridiculous. She couldn't even change the oil on her own car;

she certainly wouldn't know how to rig an irrigation system to cause an ecological crisis.

"How bad is the runoff at the spring going to be?"

"Bad," he bluntly stated. "The nitrogen and phosphorus levels are twice the acceptable level. Algae blooms will start taking hold unless something can be done. The state is going to charge me a fortune to hire aquatic specialists to get things under control. They'll probably set up some aeration pumps and maybe break out some aerobic bacteria strains to get things in balance again. I'll be setting up security cameras to watch the course around the clock. All your wannabe mothers will need to go somewhere else to cast their witchy spells."

"You are so disrespectful."

"What else would you call sunrise appeals to mythological Saint Helga?"

"You've tracked mud into my home."

"Don't change the subject. The Roost and the Spring are on private property. I was being nice letting you stuffy academics poke around, but that's all over."

Her jaw dropped. "I need to do my research."

"Too bad, and don't ask me to feel sorry for you. You get paid to sit around talking to students about old novels. You couldn't run a hot dog stand out in the real world, and don't know how to build anything people actually want."

Anger gathered. Maybe she'd never managed a hot dog stand, but that didn't mean she couldn't if it was necessary. Jack Latimer was ill-mannered and ignorant about fine literature, but he held the keys to the kingdom. She needed to find common ground with him if there was any hope of saving the Roost—and the first step was changing the subject.

"Have you had dinner yet? I've just made a pot pie." And it was magnificent. She might not be the world's best history professor, but nobody could fault her ability to turn out a perfectly prepared meal.

"I'm too mad to eat." A sheen of sweat glistened on his face, throat, and on the muscles of his forearms. She filled a glass with ice from the freezer door.

"Water or iced tea?" she asked.

"Beer."

"I don't have any beer. Water or tea. And if you want tea, your choices are sweet tea, raspberry tea, or plain."

"What kind of person bothers to make three types of tea?"

"You must have a very low opinion of me to think I'd resort to illegal tampering to stab you in the back."

He opened his mouth to say something, but nothing came out. He simply gaped at her, all corded muscles and sweaty masculine intensity. For once, it appeared she had rendered him speechless.

"You're right," he finally said. "You don't strike me as the sort of person who'd stoop to something underhanded or illegal. So maybe I owe you an apology, Professor." He cleared his throat and a hint of humor lightened his face. "I hardly ever do this, so I'm probably lousy at it, but you didn't deserve that broadside I just flung at you. I've got a lot riding on this golf course, but that's no excuse for taking it out on you. I owe you an apology and hope you can forgive me."

For someone who claimed not to know how to apologize, he'd just done a bang-up job of it.

"Water or tea?"

"Whatever you're having. And for the record, that thing you just took out of the oven smells so good that the caveman inside me just woke up and is dying to attack it."

"Would you like to join me for dinner?"

He grinned. "Yes, ma'am." That drawl was both sexy and wholesome at the same time. The tanned skin on his neck and throat made him look healthy and strong, but the scarred, mottled skin on his arms spoke of something else. Diabetes?

"Are you . . . do you have any allergies or food sensitivities I should know about?"

He chuckled. "I like red meat, red wine, and anything with frosting on it. More often than not I settle for a microwaved burrito and a Twinkie."

He must have noticed the way she glanced at the track marks on his left arm and he sobered. "It's hemophilia."

He said the word lightly, as though it was no big deal. Hadn't hemophilia been the disease that afflicted the Russian czar's only son? The boy suffered so terribly his mother turned to an insane monk in a desperate attempt to assuage the child's agony, but that was the extent of Alice's knowledge about the disease.

"Is it true that you can bleed to death from a papercut?"

He shook his head. "Not really. If I get hurt, I take an injection of the missing blood factor to give my clotting ability a boost."

She nodded to the mottled skin on his arms. "It looks like you've taken a lot of injections."

"Three times a week ever since I was eight years old. Those injections mean that run-of-the-mill bumps and bruises won't send me to the hospital like they did when I was a kid. Things were a lot worse back then. I was a normal kid who always wanted to jump on the mattress or slide down a banister. It drove my mother nuts. A bumped elbow that wouldn't hurt normal kids could send me to the hospital for a week. Anyway, that chicken pot pie smells mighty good, and I'm up to date on my injections, so there's no worry of any traumatic bleeding emergency tonight."

It was a relief he could joke about his condition. From the outside, he looked extraordinarily healthy, but looks could be deceiving.

She filled his glass with sweet tea, then watched as he tilted his head back to drink, the cords in his throat moving as he drained the glass, then he slammed it down on the counter. She winced, grateful the glass didn't shatter because that was a hand-blown Murano tumbler brought back from Italy.

She set out her less valuable Staffordshire plates while Jack glanced around her home. It was hard to read his expression as he scanned the dried flowers on the mantel and the live herbs on her windowsill. Lace from France covered the end tables and Meissen figurines decorated the fireplace mantel. She braced herself for a snide comment. The porcelain sculptures were ridiculously feminine. She'd bought them for their idealized image of women from centuries past, ranging from the milkmaid wearing an apron to the grand lady with her tiny waist, piles of hair, and elegant hat perched atop her head. Each figurine was a masterwork of grace, their facial features delicately sculpted in perfect tranquility. She loved them. If he insulted them . . .

"I kind of like this place," he said.

It was the last thing she'd expected him to say. "You do?"

"Yeah, I do. It feels like I just stepped back in time, but I like it. This place suits you."

Her spine relaxed another notch. "What kind of style does your home have?"

He gave an amused snort. "I've got a PO box and a storage unit in Baltimore. The rest of the time I live in hotels around the world."

Such a thing seemed inconceivable. "Why do you live in hotels?"

"Because I don't like being tied down," he said. "My job keeps me on the road. I've been in Virginia longer than usual because I bought a stake in the golf course. I'm heading to Japan next."

She sat at the dining table and gestured for him to do the same. When he took a bite of chicken pot pie, his face transformed and he actually groaned. "Lady, this is a lot better than anything my microwave can make."

A smile spread across her face. "At last we are in perfect agreement! Tell me, why did you become a golf course architect?"

"Because I wasn't good enough to qualify for the PGA tour. I went to college on a golf scholarship but soon learned I wasn't good enough to turn pro."

"I didn't realize they gave scholarships for golf."

She must have said something wrong because he set his fork down and stared at her wall filled with hundreds of books.

"You know how some kids in high school are smart or good-looking or great at sports? I was the kid in the wheelchair who wasn't good at anything. I missed most of the third grade, and never caught up. Golf was an escape. I wasn't good enough to turn pro, but I knew what a gorgeous golf course should look like, so in college I majored in landscape architecture. I found my calling and won't ever look back. What about you? I heard in town you specialize in Jane Austen."

"Actually, it's the history of feminine domesticity in the nineteenth century, and Jane Austen is a big part of that. I still have to teach all manner of history classes. Everything from eighteenth to twentieth-century European and American history. I'm going up for tenure next year, and—"

"What's tenure?"

Alice blinked. In her world of academia, everyone knew what tenure was, but laypeople like Jack had no reason to understand the arcane and somewhat brutal process. "It's how we prove our academic merit through a record of publication and accomplishments in our field. If we pass, we get a lifetime contract."

"And if you fail?"

Alice gave a helpless shrug. "Then you go back on the job market. The odds of getting a position after failing to get tenure aren't good."

Jack nodded. "And you're hoping to bolster your tenure case by finding out who Saint Helga was?"

"Bingo," Alice said. "Solving that mystery will guarantee at least two journal articles and perhaps a few conference presentations. The topic appeals to historians, folklorists, and anyone interested in women's history. If I can trace the origin of the legend, I'll get tenure—and save my job."

Jack scrutinized her so long she grew uncomfortable. "You like being a college professor?"

"I like teaching."

"That isn't what I asked."

"I like my job," she said, hoping she didn't sound too defensive. "And I love living in Williamsburg. The place is brimming with culture and history and natural beauty. I want to stay here forever. It's my home."

And that meant she had to do something to bolster her thin academic record before her tenure hearing next spring. Her work on the *Emma* movie set was intended to secure her case for tenure, but that had clearly failed. Solving the puzzle behind the legend of Saint Helga was her last shot at proving her academic worth, and for that, she needed Jack's cooperation. Inviting him to dinner was a first step to finding common ground with him. It was a universal truth that even the staunchest of adversaries could find common ground over a well-appointed table.

Over the next hour they formed a cautious rapport. They still didn't trust each other, had nothing in common, and didn't even value each other's chosen occupation, but they found something perhaps more valuable.

They found a tiny glimmer of mutual respect.

Chapter Ten

Jack was tired and grubby as he arrived back at the Roost, but replete with satisfaction because he'd just had the world's best chicken pot pie.

Alice was getting to him. He'd stormed over to her house like a stampeding bull, but within two minutes she had completely tamed him. She was impossible to rattle. He came at her sweaty, mad, and mean, but she stood up to him with cool, unruffled class. Something about that soft, buttery accent was like a tonic, and he even liked her townhouse despite all the flowery stuff and lace doilies.

He parked his truck and looked through the windshield at the Roost, trying to see it through her eyes. Instead of seeing only a derelict money pit, he searched for the history and meaning contained in these massive old logs and the stone chimney anchored to the side of the house. What clues could shed light on the people who lived here long ago?

First of all, the site for the house had been carefully selected. It was close to a source for water and sat on a natural ledge. That would have been good for defensive purposes in a world where relations with the Native Americans were probably dicey. The windows on the ground floor were expensive. Diamond-paned glass would have been imported from England at great expense, but the windows upstairs were plain glass. Whoever built this house was used to the finer things in life . . . but if so, why leave England and venture into the wilds of an unsettled land? What sort of person set off into the unknown in search of something better? Whoever he was, Jack respected the guy's ambition.

He left the truck and headed to the front door. His footsteps thudded on the steps that were machine-milled, probably added in the early twentieth century, but the front door seemed original. The opening was low, and he instinctively ducked whenever he entered. People were shorter back then. Even the ceiling in the front room was low.

Doc was already stretched out on a plastic lounge chair in the front room, reading a paperback he'd picked up at a thrift store. He used the front room as a bedroom because he liked the view from the front window. He set the book aside and looked up, curious.

Did the professor own up to busting the irrigation pipes?" he asked.

"Nah, I don't think she did it."

"Told you so," Doc said, then went back to reading while Jack continued to scan the room, looking for clues. The fireplace was huge, tall and wide enough for cooking. He'd taken a tour at Colonial Williamsburg shortly after he arrived in town, where the guide said fireplaces like this were made to cook a number of things simultaneously. The small notch-alcove cut into the back was probably for baking bread. Holes in the brick probably once held rungs on which water could be heated and stews simmered on cold winter days.

It would have been hard to turn out a perfectly baked chicken pot pie like Alice just made. He hadn't even told her how good it was. He just shoveled it down like a barbarian and then asked for seconds.

"I'm heading up for bed," he said. Doc gave him a little salute but didn't tear his eyes off his book.

It was too early for bed, but his laptop had plenty of power and he could write a request to Kyle to see if the security cameras mounted at the club house spotted something suspicious. Maybe some drunk college students broke the irrigation lines, or angry environmentalists, or even one of his ex-girlfriends. He'd dated plenty of women, but backed away the moment anything got serious, so he doubted any of them would care enough to look him up and haunt him at this point in his life.

The bedroom window caught his attention. That seventeenth-century window filled with old graffiti scratched into it was suddenly a lot more interesting than security cameras. He smiled a little at the spot where Elizabeth and William Tucker scratched their names in 1771. Someone had carved a snake and some palm fronds. They didn't look like the kind of palm fronds from here in Virginia. Were they native to England? Or some kind of biblical or ancient Egyptian thing? They looked very stylized.

Although some of the scratchings had been done in spindly, somewhat sloppy lettering, the mark at the top of the window was different. In the upper left corner the letters were carved with purpose and clarity: SVOTZ∞

Could it be a date in Roman numerals? He checked his phone, but aside from the V, none of the letters were used in the Roman number system.

What about a town? Or somebody's last name? And what about that sideways figure 8? In calculus, it was the symbol for infinity, but maybe there were other meanings for it.

He'd never had much interest in history, but he liked solving puzzles. He scrolled through his phone, searching the internet for various meanings for the letters.

According to Google, there were no towns or villages named SVOTZ. The translator app didn't reveal any meaningful translations of the word. Could it be an acronym? If so, it opened up a whole world of possibilities that were too numerous to count.

Frustration drove him downstairs. "Hey, Doc, can you come up here for a minute?"

Doc tossed his book aside and the chair creaked as he got out of it. The old vet followed Jack back up the stairs and listened as Jack pointed to the strange markings.

"It could be a code for something," Doc said, rubbing the stubble on his leathery face as he peered at the letters carved on the glass. "In *The Da Vinci Code*, the guy in the book uses the Atbash cipher to decode old references. All you have to do is substitute each letter with its corresponding letter on the other side of the alphabet. The letter S is eight from the end of the alphabet, so you'd start from the beginning and count to the eighth letter, which is—"

"H," Jack said.

He jotted it down on the back of a Pop-Tart wrapper. The V corresponded with E. A smile tilted his mouth as he continued decoding the letters:

HELGA

He stood, his heart pounding. Doc stared at the word, equally entranced.

"Someone went to a lot of trouble to hide her name," Doc said. "What do you suppose that sideways 8 means?"

Jack stared at the markings but could come up with no ideas. Maybe Alice would know, and he looked forward to telling her about how the name *HELGA* was hidden in plain sight.

Jack was embarrassed by the way he accused Alice of vandalizing his golf course. After acting like an impulsive brute, Alice not only accepted his apology, but was pure class as she invited him to the best dinner he'd had in years.

He still needed to get to the bottom of who broke the irrigation pipes, and the following morning he headed to the police department to file a report. A clerk named Pricilla with brassy red hair and a syrupy drawl cut him off before he could even finish telling her what happened.

"Yeah, we're already on that one," she said, her fingernails thick with chipped polish tapping against the keyboard as she called up a record. "Last night a couple of local college kids were drunk and bragging about tearing up a golf course," Pricilla said. "A bartender overheard and pressed them for details. They called him a stupid townie who probably couldn't understand the importance of saving the environment, then bragged about how they dug up some pipes and then used their fraternity paddle to bust the irrigation lines. The bartender called the cops, and Lieutenant Sparks hauled them in last night."

"Is Lieutenant Sparks still on duty?"

He was, and ten minutes later Jack sat across from the night shift officer hearing the rest of the story. The two vandals were fraternity brothers who were staying in town throughout the summer for a special tutoring program, and this was their first brush with the law. Their story ratcheted Jack's resentment even higher. He struggled with his grades in college as well, but his summers were spent working a full-time job instead of getting into a special tutoring program.

"What kind of charges are they looking at?" he asked Lieutenant Sparks.

"Trespassing and destruction of property. Both are misdemeanors, unless the property is worth more than a thousand dollars, in which case the D.A. will bump it up to a felony."

The broken irrigation lines were going to cost *a lot* more than a thousand dollars to fix. Those college kids probably never held down a real job or knew anything about the backbreaking labor of laying irrigation lines. He wanted to teach them a lesson, not ruin their future by saddling them with a felony.

"Are there any diversion programs?"

The lieutenant nodded. "If you're willing, you could have them work it off on your golf course. That could be a win-win."

"Forget it," Jack said. "I can't trust anyone on an environmental crusade near my course."

After a few minutes discussing other types of diversion programs in the area, Jack liked the sound of making them help bring in the strawberry harvest. It was grueling work. Jack had picked strawberries every June when he was in college. He spent each day stooped low, knees locked, and his back screaming. It was dirty, itchy work, and it was the reason he disliked strawberries to this day.

Jack signed a form indicating his willingness to let the brats go into a diversion program, but as he prepared to leave, Lieutenant Sparks had a word of advice.

"There may be more trouble once the rest of the students return in the fall. Let me show you the various online groups to keep an eye on where the students post their protests."

It was all good insight, and Jack noted the names of the various activist groups that had been protesting the golf course for years. Some were on the college website, while others were Facebook groups. As soon as he got back to the Roost, he fired up his laptop to bookmark the sites.

He did a cursory scan of the social media sites associated with Williamsburg and was surprised to see Alice Chadwick's name pop up. There was a picture, too. He straightened his spine and leaned forward to look at the startling photograph.

Alice looked tragic and embarrassed as she was walked between two security officers, her wrists locked together in a pair of handcuffs. His jaw dropped as he read the headline:

Local College Professor Implicated in Celebrity Stalking Scandal

The photo was from earlier in the year in England. He skimmed the first few lines of the story, noting the name Sebastian Bell, one of those British heartthrobs who starred in a bunch of historical dramas Jack never wasted his time or money on.

Never in a million years would he have suspected Alice of something like this. She seemed too refined, too controlled, but the story was breaking out all over social media, and where there was smoke there was usually fire.

He was tempted to rush over to her place and warn her about what had been posted, but she probably already knew about it, and this wasn't his problem. He had his hands full with golf course business, and his life motto was to look out for Number One. He shouldn't worry about Alice.

It was still hard to imagine someone as classy as Alice Chadwick getting involved in a seedy celebrity scandal . . . and he already worried that something terribly unfair had happened to her.

Chapter Eleven

Alice arrived at the William & Mary library first thing in the morning to sink back into the joys of foraging through a world-class library on the hunt to solve a mystery. She needed to find something that might relate to the snippet in that old letter about a woman named Helga who had sailed to America in the hope of a child . . . and the strange botanical symbol doodled on the letter that matched the one carved onto the lintel stone at the Roost.

With her laptop open and stacks of books mounded on her favorite table, she was ready to start hunting the meaning of the leafy doodle mark. Could it have a symbolic meaning from long ago?

Her attention kept straying to memories of last night's dinner with Jack. He was her complete opposite in every way, and yet . . .

his rugged appeal attracted her like metal filings to a magnet. She'd never dated anyone like him, but he seemed to return her interest.

And yet, she could be wrong about that. Less than a year ago she believed Sebastian Bell was infatuated with her. He certainly gave her good reason to think so after their brief encounter on a train in Germany. She returned to Virginia, where Sebastian began bombarding her with gorgeous bouquets of flowers. He had his agent call her, beckoning her to the *Emma* film set. Her first day in London, he met her at the Heathrow Airport with a helicopter and whisked her away for a   bird's-eye tour of London's iconic landmarks. They flew past Big Ben, the Tower Bridge, and Hyde Park, all while sipping champagne.

It couldn't all have been her imagination, could it?

Maybe she needed to get back on the horse that threw her, as the saying went. Sebastian's betrayal wouldn't be so searing if she had another man in her life. The problem was that almost all the men she worked with at the college were either married or held no appeal for her.

For the millionth time she wished Brandon Tilney wasn't twenty years older than she, but was fifty-two really too old for her to date? Pierce Brosnan was forty-nine when he made his last James Bond movie, and any right-minded woman would be attracted to him.

Her cell phone vibrated with an incoming email, but she ignored it.

Brandon Tilney was everything she dreamed of in a man. He was intelligent and cultured and thoughtful. He always wore a collared shirt, even the time he came over to help her dig a trench to improve the drainage in her yard. Brandon Tilney would never eat chocolate pudding with his fingers.

Her cell phone vibrated with another incoming text and her attention was already fractured so she checked it.

Actually, there were five messages that had built up in the last hour. Most were from old friends, but she clicked on the one from

Arlo Whitworth from the Historic Preservation Board because it might be important.

It had nothing to do with the Roost; he wanted to know if she had checked Twitter.

Twitter? She had an account she rarely logged into, but the online conversation hub was noted in the subject line of several other messages.

A weight lodged in the bottom of her stomach. Why did so many people suddenly urge her to check Twitter? Her fingers shook so badly it took three tries to successfully log in. She went to her homepage, horrified to see that her name was trending.

Alongside Sebastian Bell's name.

And a photograph.

It was the photo taken by Sebastian's ruthless agent. Graham Garfield had been there that awful day when she was led away from the movie set by two police officers. She looked a wreck, her face tearstained and handcuffs on her wrists. The hashtag attached to the photo was damning: #SebastianStalker.

Her eyes drifted closed. She wasn't a stalker, but she'd signed a nondisclosure agreement to keep silent about anything having to do with Sebastian Bell. That NDA meant she wasn't even free to comment on this photo.

Could she break the NDA? Doing so would cost a fortune in legal fees and she'd probably lose anyway. Sebastian was rich, powerful, and universally adored. He had the power of the studios protecting him. He had his ruthless agent protecting him. Anything she tried to say in her own defense would be like shouting into the wind.

How many other photos did Graham Garfield have in his arsenal? The police officers who escorted her off the set that day took her to a trailer where she'd been finger-printed and photographed. Did they have any of those humiliating pictures?

Wait . . . Sebastian had signed his own NDA regarding this incident. Whoever leaked this photo, it probably wasn't Sebastian. It was almost certainly his agent.

Everything felt very cold. Goose pimples raised on her arms as she hugged them to herself. Why did they have to blast the air-conditioning in here? She glanced around the reference room. A summer student on the other end of the room was scrolling through his phone. Was he reading about her? What if paparazzi were waiting outside her home? She probably shouldn't even drive a car in this frazzled condition. All she could do was sit at the table and listen to her phone vibrate with an endless series of texts and emails.

Each vibration felt like the sting of a dart. Whatever hope she had of discovering something amazing at the Roost would be over-shadowed by the scandal currently sending shockwaves through social media. Soon it would hit Instagram, and the traditional media wouldn't be far behind.

Fear kept her paralyzed as she sat at the table, watching more texts and emails flood her phone, some from people she knew, others from strangers. She didn't have the strength to open any of them.

Until Brandon's name popped up in a text message. He would be safe.

She clicked on the message and read: *I'm sorry this is happening to you. Is there anything I can do to help?*

She sagged, then focused on calming her nerves so that her fingers would stop shaking long enough for her to send a text.

I could use a shoulder, she keyed in and sent. His response arrived quickly:

Where are you?

The library.

On my way. It was a Tuesday, and since Brandon practically lived in his campus office during the workweek, he ought to be here within minutes.

Sure enough, Brandon's lean, lanky form soon crossed into the library. He wore a sport coat, a loosely knotted tie, and a concerned expression as he spotted her on the far side of the reference room. His half-pained smile of compassion completely sapped the last of her strength as he walked toward her.

He lifted a brow and cast a dubious expression at her cell phone as it continued to vibrate. "That's impressive."

"It's a torture device."

"Then turn it off," he gently suggested. "Let's get out of here and go somewhere we can talk." The silence of the library meant their voices could be overheard, and she stood to follow wherever he led.

The William & Mary campus during summer might be among the most beautiful thousand acres on earth. Red-brick walkways meandered across the greens where stately colonial buildings exuded symmetry, tradition, and understated elegance. Walled gardens and courtyards abounded, and the sparse student population meant it was easy to find a place far from prying eyes.

Brandon chose a bench beneath the impressive limbs of an ancient white mulberry tree. Every muscle felt heavy as she sat on the opposite side of the bench, reluctant to meet his eyes, but he would be a safe person on whom to unburden these roiling emotions.

"Am I right that this was the reason you returned early from England?"

She nodded. "I had to sign a nondisclosure agreement, but that only stops me from letting any of this leak to the press. I can tell you what happened, but do you promise not to let it go further? I can be accused of breaking the agreement if word leaks, and these people are vicious."

"You can trust me, Alice."

"I met Sebastian Bell two years ago on a train from Strasbourg to Berlin," she began.

It all seemed so innocent. She'd been in Strasbourg because her father was delivering a speech to the European Union. Afterward,

she wanted to spend a few days in Amsterdam before heading back
to Virginia. She rode the train with an embroidery project on her
lap—a re-creation of Monet's garden brought to life in colorful
threads. Intricate stitches formed clusters of lilacs and daffodils
beside a pond, all beneath an azure sky. She didn't even look up as
the train jolted lightly and a man wearing sunglasses took the seat
opposite her.

It was a cloudy day with no need for sunglasses, so she mostly
ignored him as she continued plying her needle to finish the cluster
of tulips.

"I don't know how you have the patience for it," the man said.
His voice was a combination of wry admiration and pure, smooth
masculine appeal. She met his gaze as he peered at her over the top
of his sunglasses, and that was when she recognized him. Sebastian
Bell, England's foremost romantic lead actor in a dozen historical
movies and miniseries.

"I find it calming," she said. He asked to see the project better,
and she handed the embroidery hoop to him. When he asked her
to teach him, she did, and he stitched the world's sloppiest daffodil
nestled beside the pond.

"He'd been cast as Mr. Knightley in a new production of
Emma," she told Brandon. "When he learned I wrote my dissertation on how Jane Austen's writing influenced nineteenth-century
domestic trends, he started picking my brain for insight into Jane
Austen's world. He wanted my business card and I gave it to him.
I didn't expect to ever hear from him, but two days later he con-
tacted me, offering a chance to be the historical consultant on the
film."

The job of the historical consultant was to read the script, looking for historical missteps or anything that didn't belong in an
1815 setting. She would be expected to work with the crew to
make recommendations on details like what sort of card games the
characters should play, what the chime of a clock would sound like,
and the proper way to hold a teapot.

"I suggested that while I knew Jane Austen quite well, surely there were others somewhere in the United Kingdom that were more fluent in such details."

Brandon nodded. "I confess, I always thought hiring an American seemed a bit odd since the British are sticklers for excruciating accuracy in everything relating to Jane Austen."

"It should have been my first clue," Alice admitted. "The costume and set designers rarely needed my help. There wasn't much for me to do on the set. I later learned that historical consultants usually only show up for specific scenes or to work with the set and costume designers ahead of production. Sebastian wanted me on the set all the time. Every day. In theory I was supposed to be on hand to advise Sebastian and the other actors on historically accurate mannerisms and behavior. In actuality I drank coffee and scrolled on my cell phone."

She and Sebastian began dating the day after she arrived in London. There was an immense amount of downtime on a production set, and Sebastian consistently asked her to join him. He once pulled her down onto his lap to flirt, causing a seam to split on his trousers. It took an hour for the seamstress to arrive on the set and mend the tear before filming could begin again. After that morning, the director and everyone else on the set began looking at her askance, but Sebastian always defended her.

"Professor Chadwick is nonnegotiable," she overheard him saying to the assistant director, who'd been trying to get her ousted from the set. To her shame, she found the way Sebastian defended her to be flattering. He even called his agent to revise Sebastian's contract to make her his personal consultant.

"At first it was wonderful," she said to Brandon. "Sebastian was the most gallant, funny, and gleefully joyous person I'd ever met. It was like standing next to a meteorite: fast and dazzling and fun. Except sometimes he just seemed . . . off. Sometimes he couldn't concentrate, and his mood would swing from euphoria to anxiety.

After a few months I never knew which Sebastian Bell would show up on set."

One morning she rapped on his trailer door and entered, catching him in the act of sweeping something off the dinette table. He sniffled and brushed at his nose.

Alice had no experience with drugs, but she didn't need to be an expert to recognize the trace of white powder on his nose as cocaine.

She had known Sebastian had addiction issues in his past. His rehab stint a few years earlier had been widely covered in gossip magazines, but he'd told her he was clean and sober ever since. Yet here he was, twitchy, wiping powder from his nose.

"Don't tell anyone," Sebastian urged. "It's not a big deal, okay?"

She didn't know what to do. A more sophisticated person might understand all the implications of cocaine addiction and the paranoia it could cause. They were in love and she wanted to protect him, but did that mean keeping his secret or revealing it to someone who could help control it?

The cast and crew all stayed at the same hotel, and one night Sebastian had some sort of overdose. He stripped off his clothes and headed to the pool. She ran after him, trying to drag him back toward his room, which triggered a huge fight. The assistant director overheard and came to her aid. They got Sebastian into bed while she called a doctor, and the assistant director called Sebastian's agent.

The next day, Sebastian's agent reframed the incident so that *she* lured Sebastian to the pool. *She* showed up in his room to tempt him. The hideous Graham obtained a restraining order and called the police to arrest her when she showed up on the set. Then the movie company fired her and rumors started flying throughout the set.

Alice turned to her brother Adam for help. Adam wasn't a lawyer, nor was he familiar with the British legal system, but Colonel Adam Chadwick in full dress uniform was intimidating no matter where he was. Adam could stare through a person with those glassy blue eyes and make soldiers wilt. Normally Adam was busy negotiating Pentagon contracts with the Saudis or NASA, but he dropped everything the moment she reached out to him for help. He arrived in London with a lawyer in tow and ordered her to stand up and fight for herself. He demanded that Sebastian and his slimy agent sign equally binding nondisclosure agreements to protect Alice's reputation.

It worked. She never saw Sebastian again, and she escaped England with her reputation intact, although she had been informed that her name would be stricken from the movie credits and she had nothing to show for five months in England.

And now it was all coming out. Graham Garfield was ruthless in protecting his client from bad publicity. She was certain Graham was the one who originally started rumors that she was a stalker, and that she'd thrown herself at Sebastian.

And the worst part of it was, she *had* thrown herself at Sebastian. Even after his erratic behavior became concerning, she overlooked it because she was flattered to have attracted such an amazing man.

"I feel like this is my fault," she whispered to Brandon. "I was so blind. All the signs were there and I looked right past them. I only saw the parts of Sebastian I wanted to see."

"Why didn't the nondisclosure agreement stop this from happening?" Brandon asked.

"I don't know," she said, although she couldn't blame her brother. Adam had flown halfway across the world, hired the best solicitor money could buy, and somehow strong-armed the tabloids into silence—at least for a while. Even the English solicitor acknowledged that Adam had negotiated a surprisingly tight NDA, but warned her it could be difficult to enforce. Unless Alice could produce a smoking gun proving that Graham or Sebastian were the source of the photo, a lawsuit would take years and the outcome uncertain. It wasn't worth it.

Brandon's sigh was both sad and comforting. "There will always be times when we must walk through shadows, but it is in these dark moments that we find our strength. Keep moving forward, and soon the light will break through the clouds."

"I don't think I can ever recover from this. I'll probably be fired from the college. Everything I've worked for is collapsing, and tenure seems impossible."

"I've got something that might help with that," Brandon said, reaching into his satchel to retrieve a slim manila folder, then offering it to her like it was the crown jewels.

"What is it?"

"Proof of the date the Roost was built. I think you'll be pleased."

Her gaze locked with his. Brandon wouldn't tease about this. He knew how important it was for her to find proof that the Roost was somehow connected to the mysterious Saint Helga and her 1672 departure for Virginia.

She held her breath and flipped the file open. Inside was a single page with charts, cross sections of tree rings, and mathematical formulas, but her eye was drawn to the single line highlighted in yellow.

Construction on Reid's Roost began in 1661.

"Good heavens," she murmured. Never in her wildest dreams could she have imagined it was that old. Everyone in Virginia assumed it was built shortly before 1705 when the Tuckers first bought the place. Her mysterious letter said that   Helga sailed for Virginia in 1672, and by then the Roost had been here for eleven years. A world of possibilities had just opened up.

"Oh, Brandon, no wonder I haven't been able to find much on who built the Roost. I was looking in the wrong decade."

This finding was a lifeline. It would take some unconventional methods to research what went on in this area in the 1660s because most of the records had been destroyed in the 1698 fire, but now at least she knew where to focus her search.

Chapter Twelve

Alice longed to bury her head in the sand to hide from the biggest humiliation of her life, but she needed to warn her parents of the scandal before they heard it from anyone else.

Maude and Grayson Chadwick were supposed to be retired, but their illustrious lives remained packed with prestigious engagements and commitments, leaving them no time for unscheduled phone calls—even from their own children. Alice sent a text message requesting an appointment at their earliest convenience. Her mother replied they would clear space in their calendar at two o'clock.

Alice sighed at the brief reprieve, as if the Sword of Damocles had been lifted from her neck. Her parents were demanding, accomplished, and hyper-competitive. Her father had been the secretary of state for two presidents, and now gave high-priced lectures at symposia around the world. Her mother was a retired economics professor but had spent the past year teaching at Harvard. Each of them had reached the pinnacle of their respective careers, and demanded their children strive for the same.

Growing up, Alice and her brothers had followed her father's itinerate career in the foreign service all over the world, which meant she never went to a traditional school but got to study literature with scholars at Oxford. She spent a semester in Paris to learn French and studied art at the Vatican Museum. Ballerinas from the Bolshoi ballet taught her dance.

In the summers Alice returned to the family estate on the Potomac River, where her father insisted his children develop their physical stamina. Each morning he loaded Alice and her brothers into the motorboat and drove them a mile upstream, then dropped them into the river and required they swim home.

She hated that daily swim. She was the only girl and her brothers always left her far behind while Grayson punted along in the motorboat beside her, barking orders at her to swim faster. After their morning swim, the rest of her days were filled with sailing and tennis classes. Then lessons in French and German. To this day, her parents insisted on speaking a foreign language at dinner so their skills didn't fall into disuse.

Alice used to dream about having a mother like Marmee from *Little Women*, whose gentle voice could ease any heartache, or Caroline Ingalls, who could soothe a child's fevered brow with the touch of her soft, cool hand. Alice would gladly live in a little house on the prairie if she could have a mother to whom she could run with every small victory or disappointment.

But no. Her mother was Maude Chadwick, who co-authored a paper on the economic benefits of parental discipline.

At one minute before two o'clock, Alice initiated a face-to-face call with her parents. It was summer, so they were both back at the River House, working from the spacious home library. Her thumbs trembled as she entered the numbers on her cell phone, then began pacing as the connection was made.

Her call was accepted, and her father's face took up most of the screen on the other end of the FaceTime call. With his chiseled features and piercing eyes that could freeze a room with a single glance, he looked like a scarier version of Charlton Heston. Her mother was in the background, still typing on a laptop.

"Alice, what do you need?" her father asked. No greeting. No warm and cuddly inquiry about how her life was going.

"Hey, Dad. Mom, those pearls look amazing."

Maude looked up from her laptop to touch her necklace. "They belonged to your grandmother. What do you need, Alice?"

She swallowed hard and dove in. "Did Adam ever tell you about why he visited me in London back in April?"

"No," Grayson said. "I didn't realize he'd been gone."

"So you don't know anything about the bit of trouble I had on the *Emma* set?"

Grayson frowned. "Get to the point, Alice."

Her tongue froze and mortification crept up her spine, freezing her carefully-thought-out ways of softening the blow ... but really, was there any way to put a good spin on this? Maude and Grayson would weather the blow.

"Just Google my name," she finally said. By now, the story had leaked beyond social media to pollute websites all over the world. Clicking from her mother's laptop sounded like a hail of distant machine-gun fire. Her father rotated in his chair to look over Maude's shoulder. There was no change in his expression as he leaned forward to scrutinize the screen, but Maude's face iced over like she'd experienced a blast from Antarctica.

Grayson flicked his eyes back to Alice. "Explain yourself."

He didn't sound angry, or supportive, or curious. His poker-faced command had all the passion of a robot.

Alice drew a shuddering breath and told him everything: her misjudgment of Sebastian, the restraining order, and how Adam dropped everything when he flew to London and helped her navigate the avalanche of legal charges.

"Adam was so helpful," she said. "I don't know what I would have done without him."

"Grow a spine, Buttercup," her father growled. "You don't need a man to defend yourself. And you're better off without that Sebastian cad. Your misguided pursuit of that man has done nothing but knock you off course for over a year."

She sighed. "Is it so wrong to fall in love? To want a partner in life?"

"Alice," her mother reproached, "we didn't raise you to mope and lunge for a fainting couch over a broken heart. What is this going to do to your tenure case?"

Tenure seemed impossible now; she'd be lucky if they didn't fire her immediately. No college wanted a woman accused of stalking to be in the classroom. "Tenure is probably off the table," she admitted. "Colleges always give professors who don't get tenure a year to search for another position, so I should probably start looking for another job."

If anyone would even look at her application without laughing. Unless a miracle occurred, her future in academia looked increasingly bleak.

"I want you to demand a meeting with the head of the History Department," Grayson said. "Insist on a hearing, open a lawsuit against the people in England who violated the nondisclosure agreement, and fight for your career."

Anxiety began roping around her chest, forcing her to take shallow breaths. The only thing that could make this day worse was marching back onto campus to demand an audience with the head of her department. "That's not going to happen," she said. "I'm not cut out for it."

"We've been very patient with you, young lady," her father warned. "Your professorship pays peanuts, but at least it's prestigious. If you can't keep that job, you need to find another one, pronto. You think lying around and reading books is a job? The rest of the world gets up and puts in blood, sweat, and tears to earn their daily bread. I expect at least as much from you. Stand up for yourself, Buttercup."

The call came to a quick end after that, and Alice collapsed onto her sofa, gazing around the soft, muted tones of her living room and trying not to cry. She loved this place, with her collection of books and potted herbs on the windowsill. In a perfect world, she would teach history classes, read books, defend Jane Austen, and tend her gardens. Maybe do a little embroidery and entertaining.

She didn't want to fight for tenure or force herself to belong in a History Department where her colleagues merely tolerated her. They would never respect any historian who specialized in Jane Austen, and once they saw the gossip coming out of England, their condescension toward her would turn into gleeful disdain.

There were really only two options. The longer, harder option would be to follow her father's advice, march onto campus, and demand a public hearing. She'd have to hire a lawyer, break her nondisclosure agreement, and open a can of ugly worms, all merely to fight for the opportunity to continue pursuing tenure. Her only chance to earn tenure hinged on uncovering the truth about Saint Helga's existence. She would have to solve the mystery soon in order to get an academic paper written and accepted for publication before her tenure review. Even with the new date of the Roost that Brandon discovered, finding the origin of Saint Helga felt more like chasing a ghost than solid history.

Her other option was to give up. Turn her back on all the heartache and stress and simply walk away to start her life over somewhere else.

Neither path seemed appealing, but deep in her heart . . . she was tempted to give up.

Chapter Thirteen

Jack spent the day overseeing the emergency repair of the irrigation lines, but Alice was never far from his thoughts. She was bound to be wilting under the blast of derision coming at her via social media, and he instinctively wanted to help. He was an expert at surviving scorn, bullying, and just about anything else meant to humiliate a person. No kid who moved to three different junior high schools while wobbling on forearm crutches could avoid bullies, but he survived it and Alice could too. The trick was having something else to focus on, and he could offer her another clue in her search for Saint Helga.

After a quick shower in the clubhouse locker room, he headed to her townhouse. There was no answer despite ringing her doorbell three times. She was here . . . her car was parked out front, but he couldn't blame her if she wanted to hide out while licking her wounds. Still, she'd want to know about the Helga clue he found last night.

He'd bet his new set of pricey golf clubs she was out in the backyard, putzing around with her fancy herbs or heirloom tomatoes.

He was right. He braced an arm along the top rail of the fence rimming her garden to watch her pruning the herb garden. Being Alice, she knelt on a pretty gingham blanket with her skirt pooled around her, looking like a fancy picture that belonged in a museum.

"Hey there, pretty lady."

Her shoulders sagged. "Not today, Jack."

Her voice was sapped of energy. She hadn't even glanced up at him, just kept tugging weeds and looking miserable.

"You sure?" he asked. "I found some cool stuff out at the Roost that might interest you."

This time she didn't say anything at all, just shook her head while tugging at a bull thistle weed. "Ouch!" she said, because the pricklers on those things could be fierce. It must have bled, because she wrapped her finger in the blanket and squeezed.

Then she started crying.

Not loud or sloppy . . . but her lip wobbled and her face scrunched up and a piddly little gulp escaped from her throat.

It got to him. He planted a hand on the fence post and vaulted over. "Hey, now," he soothed. There was nothing worse than a pretty woman crying, even though she had good cause. She sniffled and regained her composure quickly.

"Not today, Jack," she said, a little more firmly this time. "I've had a really lousy day, all right?"

"I know. I saw."

She winced, and he kicked himself. He could have pretended he didn't know and just presented her with the stuff about Helga and retreated, but he'd never been good at deception.

"Look, I'm sure it's embarrassing, but it's not that bad," he said. "You'll survive it."

"How am I going to survive it? This is going to ruin my reputation. It's not even true, but I can't fight back. My life is over."

He grabbed one of her wicker chairs, plopped it a few yards away from her, and sat. "Alice, you've got a healthy body, a sound mind, and can bake the world's best chicken pot pie. You have more class in your pinky finger than most people have in their entire body. Don't tell me that your life is over."

Her mouth twisted. "You just don't get it."

"Maybe," he said with a shrug. "Alice, I'm one bad accident away from landing back in a wheelchair. Or in traction for weeks in a hospital, hooked up to tubes, trying to stay alive. Right now I'm healthy, but every day that I have the ability to roll out of bed and stand on my own two feet is a win. You've got your health. You've got a good brain. I don't care how dark today looks, you've got everything it takes to build a great future."

The cell phone beside her vibrated. Every muscle in Alice's body stiffened as she sent a worried glance at the phone. He knew exactly what that pop-up message meant. It was the top of the hour and she'd set her alerts for a regular update. Her body cringed as she scrolled through whatever garbage had just been posted about her.

"What would happen if you quit reading that?" he asked. "Cancelled the alert? Deleted the social media apps?"

She shook her head and continued scrolling. "I need to know what is being said about me."

"Oh yeah? What would Jane Austen say about someone so obsessed with what strangers thought?"

For the first time since he arrived, the corner of her mouth lifted in a bit of humor. "She'd whap me with a parasol and tell me to snap out of it."

They shared a momentary laugh, but she sobered quickly. "I don't think I'm ever going to get over this," she whispered. "It's really, really bad."

She looked like a broken flower as she sagged in the garden. There was no magic cure for what had happened to her, but that didn't stop him from wanting to prop her up.

"Some scars last a long time," he said. "You might not ever get over it, but trust me . . . there'll come a time when it won't hurt anymore."

She turned a curious look at him. "Are you speaking from experience?"

If sharing a bit of his rotten childhood would help, he'd do it.

"Growing up, I spent a lot of time in foster care," he said, and he immediately had Alice's attention. She probably never knew a kid who was raised by the state. She probably had no understanding of how most foster parents were in it for a monthly paycheck rather than any genuine love for damaged and abandoned kids. Jack ran away from three lousy foster placements before he got lucky.

"My mom died when I was eleven, and my dad did his best. He took me golfing and tried to keep on top of my infusions, but he was a pretty bad alcoholic. Things spiraled down quickly after my mom died. I cycled through a bunch of lousy placements, but I finally landed with a really great foster family when I was thirteen," he said. "Mrs. Shipley had three kids of her own, but I still got my own bedroom and she promised I could stay until I graduated from high school if I wanted. That's unusual in foster care."

Jack desperately wanted to stay with the Shipleys forever. They lived in a clean neighborhood. There wasn't yelling or swearing and he didn't have to worry about anyone stealing the spending money he got from the state. They went to church on Sunday, had family dinners every night, and everyone treated each other with respect.

School was still rotten because he tended to get bullied at any new school, but it didn't matter because each day he got to go home to the Shipleys. Besides, the only time things were really horrible at school was between class when hundreds of kids poured out of classrooms and hustled through narrow hallways. He was using forearm crutches in those days. That, plus the backpack filled with books, made him slow in the hallways, which drew bullies like sharks sensing blood in the water.

"Kids could be pretty brutal to someone who is different," he said. "One time a bunch of kids had me cornered and shoved me into a hallway locker."

To this day he hated the sound of a slamming metal locker door. Alice's golden-brown eyes widened in horror. Not that he liked seeing it, but at least she wasn't dwelling on her own problems, so he continued. "It was three against one, and I couldn't even resist because fighting them might have started a bleed."

The lock on the door automatically engaged as soon as the door slammed shut, and he was trapped. It was pitch-black and stank like gym shoes. He yelled and kicked, but all he heard was laughter as the boys ran away.

He started crying because the side of his head throbbed from slamming against the back of the locker, and throbbing was a sign of big trouble. If he didn't get an infusion immediately he'd end up back in the hospital. It felt like forever, but it was probably only a few minutes before someone heard his pleas for help and got him out.

"I ended up in the hospital for a month after that," Jack said. By now Alice had quit weeding and put her phone down. "Brain bleeds are life-threatening for a hemophiliac, so they kept me in the hospital for around-the-clock monitoring. Mrs. Shipley seemed to handle things pretty well. She visited me almost every day. Brought me cookies and comic books. One time she brought me a little medallion of Saint Jude, the patron saint who was supposed to look out for sick kids like me. What I didn't know was that during that time I was in the hospital she had asked the social workers to find me a different foster home. The accident freaked her out. She was okay with managing my disease if it only meant helping administer my shots a couple times a week, but the accident was another layer of responsibility and she didn't think she was cut out for it."

Jack tried to pretend like he didn't care when Mrs. Shipley drove him back to the foster agency, but inside he'd decided that he was through with foster care. The foster parents were either in it for the money, or people he couldn't trust. When he saw her the following year at junior high graduation, he turned and walked the other way. He never spoke to Mrs. Shipley again.

"Why are you telling me all this?" Alice asked.

"Because I want you to know that no matter how bad it gets, you can get up and face another day. I didn't have what it takes to be a professional golfer. That dream died and I had to shore myself up and figure out what to do with my life. It was better than crying into my soup and telling myself that life wasn't fair. If this stupid scandal stops you from getting tenure, you've got a good head, and good health, and a whole wide world of opportunities out there."

Alice breathed a heavy sigh. "I've trained all my life to be a college professor. If that's closed, I don't know what to do."

"What about that Saint Helga lady? Can't you still make some hay out of her?"

Alice shrugged. "Maybe," she said, but not very convincingly. "It turns out the Roost is a lot older than anyone thought, but searching for the real Helga seems impossible. So far all I've been turning up are dead ends. All the court records got burned up in the 1698 fire, and I don't know how to prove she even existed."

Maybe the graffiti on the window would be a dead end, too, but he'd let Alice make that call.

"I found something about Helga in the Roost. I thought you'd like to see it."

That got her attention. Her posture straightened, and a flicker of curiosity softened the weight of her expression. "I'd like that."

And he liked seeing her cheer up. "Good! I've got meetings with the Tuckers for the rest of the day, and it will be too dark to see at night, but come by tomorrow morning. I think you'll be impressed."

Alice was skeptical Jack could have found anything at the Roost. She and dozens of trained historians had combed through it for decades, but he'd looked so pleased with himself yesterday and it couldn't hurt to look.

She arrived at the Roost early the next morning, resolved to embrace Jack's perspective. He was right: Some things in life were undeniably unfair and beyond anyone's control. Yet, even in the face of hardship, the world brimmed with possibilities—if only she had the courage to look for them.

Jack grinned when he answered the door. "It's upstairs," he said as he ushered her inside the Roost.

There wasn't much upstairs, and she suspected he was taking her to the north-facing window with centuries of graffiti scratched into its old, rippled glass. Unlike the elegant diamond-paned windows on the first floor, the upstairs windows were made of ordinary glass, the panes each about five inches wide. Historians had already milked the random doodles scratched into the glass. A few people had scratched their names and dates, and there was some political graffiti during the American Revolution. Other random doodles and sketches were impossible to understand.

"Have you ever seen all these scratchings?" Jack pointed to the window with pride, beaming as if he'd just discovered the Rosetta Stone.

Half the historians in Williamsburg had already marveled over this window, but it was rather sweet of him to present it to her.

"I've seen them," she said, hoping he wouldn't be disappointed.

"But did you see Helga's name?"

Alice blinked. "There's nothing about Helga on the window."

"Look again," Jack prompted. It felt foolish to keep staring at this strange collection of scribbles because Helga's name wasn't here. The only word that had baffled historians over the years was a small, careful etching near the top: *SVOTZ*. It was followed by a mark that looked like an 8 lying on its side. The carefully printed letters were the only thing previous historians had given up hope of interpreting.

It was also what Jack pointed to. "It's right here," he said. "The guy in *The Da Vinci Code* uses the Atbash cipher to decode old references. That code dates back to Hebrew times. All you have to do is substitute each letter with its corresponding letter on the other side of the alphabet. Using the Atbash cipher, *SVOTZ* translates to *HELGA*."

She stared blankly at the word, mentally counting backward and forward across the alphabet. Her heart pounded as she stared at the letters. Jack was right. *Helga's name was right here!*

"How did you figure this out?" she asked, still marveling at the discovery.

He grinned again. "Doc gets all the credit. There's not much to do out at this old place after the sun goes down and he'd been reading *The Da Vinci Code.* He figured it out. And that sideways 8? In calculus, that symbol represents infinity. So in contemporary terms, I think the message means something like 'Helga into eternity,' or maybe 'Helga always.'"

Alice's heart thumped so hard she feared he could hear it, but she couldn't help smiling. "How do you know calculus?" she asked.

Jack cocked a brow. "Calculus is how I measure slope and gradient changes over distance on the golf course. Even dumb jocks can learn a little math."

She held up her hands. "I didn't mean to insult you, I just need to understand all the possible angles. I confess to being impressed. People have been staring at this window for a long time and never connected it to Helga."

Her fingers trembled as she set them against the marking on the window. Once, long ago and across eons of time, someone cared enough about a mysterious woman named Helga to carve her name into glass . . . but he hid it. A shiver raced through her, almost as if she could feel that unknown person beckoning her to solve the puzzle, to bring their story out of the shadows and into the daylight.

"What happens if you can figure out who she was?" Jack asked.

"I'll get an academic paper out if it," she said. "Maybe even a book. This story will have interdisciplinary interest. Folklorists want to know about the legend of Saint Helga's Spring. Historians will want to know about a woman in early America. But it's more than that. I'm simply . . . I'm simply *dying* of curiosity!"

She met his gaze, and it felt like an electric spark zinged between them. He was now as eager and curious as she.

He rubbed his jaw and glanced around the room. "You said the Roost is a part of local history," he stated. "You said college kids dare each other to haunt the place on Halloween and society ladies think there's some kind of fertility legend here. Who else is interested in this place? And why?"

"I think it appeals to people because it's one of the few remaining buildings from those earliest years of the English in America," she said. "Colonial Williamsburg reflects life in the mid-eighteenth century, but the English were here for over a hundred years before that. There's almost nothing left of those first settlers. The Roost is one of the few buildings representing those very first years."

"So there's value in the Roost," he said.

Wasn't that what she'd been telling him for weeks? "It's priceless. There's an aura here that resonates with people. The sound of footsteps on the old wood, the marshy scent from the spring, and the breeze rustling the leaves are exactly what the people hundreds of years ago would have seen and felt. It is as if I can reach back in time and experience a fleeting moment of exactly what a woman hundreds of years ago would have known."

Jack had a calculating look to his gaze. "What do you need to figure out who Helga was?"

"Time. These things take years to gather funding, then travel to libraries and archives for research."

"I haven't got years. Can you speed it up?"

Alice took a step back. "You still want to tear down the Roost?"

"Not if you can prove it's worth saving. If you can dig up something cool about Helga, it will put this place on the map beyond just the golfing world, and I can capitalize on that."

It sounded rather mercenary to Alice, but if finding the real Helga would save the Roost, she would do it.

Chapter Fourteen

Jack had finally obtained all the necessary permits to break ground on the amphitheater, but first, he needed to make a decision about the fate of the Roost.

There were only three options: tear it down, move it, or renovate it. The cheapest, easiest, and fastest would be to tear it down, but it would stir up bad will in the community.

Plus, it might be nice to save the place for Alice. When he showed her the etching in the window, they shared a brief, magnetic connection, both of them nearly on fire with curiosity about Helga and the Roost. It had been fun. She had looked at him with new-found respect, and nothing gave a red-blooded man a charge like earning a beautiful woman's admiration.

It would be monumentally stupid to take on more debt by trying to salvage the Roost, but the place was starting to grow on him. He'd never admit it, but when he decoded that strange word and revealed the name HELGA, he felt like cheering. He'd never been much for history, but the longer he stayed at the Roost, the more curious he got about the people who'd once lived in it. An odd sensation began to take root, like there was an invisible bond stretching forward and backward in time, making him a part of the old building's storied history and the people who once lived there.

He could save the Roost if he really wanted to, but it needed to be an investment, not a present for Alice. Letting foolish sentimentality interfere with his decision-making could drive him into bankruptcy.

It would be essential to take all the necessary precautions before proceeding with his plan. He needed to turn a profit on the derelict building, which was why he carefully chose this morning's golfing companions. Ever since arriving in Williamsburg, an invitation to play a round of golf with him had been an eagerly sought invitation. It was a win-win situation. Avid golfers wanted a photograph standing beside a famous golf course architect, and Jack was always on the lookout for networking opportunities. It never hurt to have a cordial acquaintance with the local fire marshal or the president of the Historic Preservation Board.

Greg McGarity was not only the president of the Historic Preservation Board, but a retired realtor who knew plenty about the local community and land regulations. Terry Holbrook was the fire marshal, and the Roost was going to run into a raft of safety challenges if Jack decided to save it. The cost of bringing the place up to code was enough to give him an ulcer, but it was time to learn what he was up against.

Jack watched as Greg stepped up to the third tee of the nearby golf course where Jack had been playing ever since arriving in Virginia. Greg was an old-school golfer, wearing bright green slacks and a plaid golf shirt. His club made a perfect *whoosh* as it sliced through the air, sending the ball soaring across the fairway.

"Nice," Jack said, for anytime a man could land a ball onto the green on a Par 3 was impressive.

Greg muttered a comment about how he used to get it twenty yards farther "back in the day." It was the frustration of all aging golfers. Their skill and accuracy improved, but their distance on a tee shot was often a victim of time.

Jack hopped into the golf cart to drive to the center of the fairway, preparing to open the conversation about the Roost. Once the three of them arrived, he parked and strolled to his ball, Greg and the fire marshal following.

"I've been thinking about renovating the Roost," he said, trying to sound casual as he lined up the next putt. He tapped the ball, watching it roll toward the hole, where it made a satisfying *clunk* as it landed in the cup.

"I thought the plan was to tear it down," Terry said.

"I did too, but I've been toying with the idea of turning the place into a high-end tavern. It has great potential: authentic old plank flooring, the exposed rockwork in the fireplace, the wooden beam ceilings."

Terry let out a whistle and shook his head. "That place is a firetrap!"

"Not the way I'm envisioning it." Another nervous rush of energy flooded Jack's gut as he thought of the expense, but if he executed his plan correctly, the Roost might be a gold mine. "I'm thinking of a complete renovation. I'll take off the roof and the second story so I can raise the ceiling on the ground floor. We'll number each stone and board as we take it down so it can be reassembled as close to the original as possible. Most of the building will be new, but I'll save as much of the original Roost as possible. I'll design the addition in the same spirit as the original, but with larger windows and plenty of space to host special events. I'll add a modern kitchen, bathrooms, and a porch out the back overlooking Saint Helga's Spring. No expense spared. The heart of the tavern will be the original Roost. I'll install a custom-built bar with a tap system serving craft beer and fine wines. The place is steeped in authentic old Virginia history, and that's worth a lot."

This time Terry's whistle sounded impressed. "I'd love to see it happen, but you're looking at millions in renovation costs, and a permitting nightmare."

Jack nodded. "I'm ready to pay, provided I can get the necessary permits and financing. What I need to know is if you think there's a market for this kind of thing."

Greg smothered a laugh. "Are you kidding? The local folks will fall over themselves to find a seat at that bar. You'll have a constant influx of tourists from Colonial Williamsburg looking to spend their money. Would you have a gift shop?"

Jack hadn't thought of it, but yeah, the markup on fancy antique reproductions was strong. Heck, a gift shop might make the most profit of the entire operation. "I can add a gift shop. What I need to know is if something like this would offend the history purists."

Greg gave a dismissive wave. "Some of those folks want history stored under lock and key so that only the academics can see it. Pay them no mind. Saving history for future generations means compromise. I think the popularity of a high-end tavern like you describe is a celebration of history, not a degradation."

They set off for the next hole, where Greg sank his putt, but Jack double-bogeyed because nervous excitement began swelling inside. Two potential and influential critics of his plan had just given him a hearty endorsement, and Jack wasn't sure if he should be ecstatic or terrified.

Talk of how to capitalize on the tavern continued as they played the next three holes. The tavern could offer exclusive events and tastings. Virginia had a stellar wine and craft beer industry that would be eager to strike deals and help promote the tavern. As long as Jack intended to expand the building, he could add a conference room that could host seminars, educational workshops, and VIP experiences.

Ideas crystalized out of thin air and everything was going gang-busters until they got to the 15th hole and Greg casually asked a question that left Jack flat-footed.

"How are you going to handle the lien on the Roost?" he asked.

"*A lien?*" Jack asked. The word hit him like a punch between his eyes.

"The bank has a lien on the Roost and the land it sits on," Greg said. "Kingsley Tucker took out a mortgage on the place late last year. The Roost has no value, but the land it sits on is worth a lot. Rumor has it he isn't paying on the mortgage, and the bank is threatening to seize it soon."

Jack kept his face carefully neutral as he lined up for the next putt. After surviving a childhood of frailty, bullying, and abandonment, he had mastered the art of appearing nonchalant.

"I'll work it out with Kingsley." He spoke in an offhand voice, but inside he seethed.

***

Jack cursed himself for being an idiot as he drove out to Kingsley Tucker's farm after finishing the round of golf. He'd known the Tuckers had money troubles and did plenty of due diligence before agreeing to build their golf course. He used an accountant, a lawyer, and a title company to protect himself before striking the deal for partial ownership of the golf course. The property survey clearly included the Roost, and somehow the Tuckers played a shell game after their deal to score a mortgage on the land where the Roost sat.

Jack turned his pickup onto the gravel drive leading to Kingsley Tucker's farm. Unlike his son Kyle, who lived at the ostentatious Cherrywood mansion, the family's patriarch lived in a newly renovated 1890s farmhouse. After thirty-five years in the banking industry, Kingsley reinvented himself as a gentleman farmer. His four-acre property featured a white clapboard farmhouse, a barn, and a dozen goats. Staff milked the goats and made artisanal cheese and goat milk soap. As far as Jack could tell, Kingsley's job was confined to walking about the grounds in work boots and tweedy clothes while sampling the cheese and petting a goat or two.

He was out at one of the goat pens tossing kitchen scraps into a trough when Jack arrived, still sweaty from his round of golf.

"Good afternoon, Jack," Kingsley said with a friendly wave.

"How much is the lien on the Roost, and why didn't you tell me about it?" he demanded.

Kingsley looked so shocked he almost dropped the bucket of scraps. A young man who did the actual work on the farm was busy at a milking stool, and Kingsley glanced nervously over. The Tuckers were good at hiding their genteel poverty, and the farm worker likely had no idea how precarious their financial situation really was.

Kingsley frowned and unceremoniously dumped the rest of the bucket into the trough. "Come on, let's head inside to talk. We can have something cold to drink."

"Is your wife inside?"

"Yes."

"Then we'll stay outside." Tearing a man to shreds while his wife could overhear wasn't Jack's style, but he needed to get to the bottom of this. Kingsley gestured him to a bench beneath the shade of a cottonwood tree. The old man suddenly seemed more stooped and tired than he had two minutes earlier. Kingsley sat, but Jack remained standing.

"Well?" he demanded. "How much is the lien and who owns it?"

"Sixty thousand. A bank in Richmond is holding it."

"Did you tell them that I had an interest in the property?"

A bead of sweat trickled down the side of Kingsley's face. "I don't remember."

"You went all the way to Richmond so they wouldn't know about me," Jack bit out. "You went to a lot of trouble to pull the wool over my eyes and scam the bank out of sixty thousand dollars."

Kingsley stood. "Now hold on. We intend to repay the bank. It's no skin off anybody's nose."

"It was fraud against the bank and against me. A felony."

Kingsley held out his hands in supplication. "Hold on. We can work something out."

The temptation to walk away from the entire deal clawed. Suing the Tuckers would mean a nasty lawsuit, and Jack was an outsider in Virginia. He'd be in Japan, busting his tail to earn a buck to compensate for this financial sinkhole while the Tuckers would be glad-handing the locals who admired and respected them.

Jack hated the situation, but he needed to avoid a lawsuit. He was already four million dollars in debt over his third of the golf course. He couldn't walk away over sixty thousand dollars, but he wasn't going to make this easy on Kingsley.

"I'll pay off the mortgage, but you're going to sign the Roost over to me. All of it. The building, the land, and Saint Helga's Spring. I'll have a lawyer write up an agreement, and we can conclude the deal tonight."

Kingsley sputtered. "The land alone is worth a quarter of a million!"

"That's the price of fraud, and those are my terms. Otherwise, I'll see you in court about the mortgage and seek criminal charges for the fraud."

Kingsley fanned himself with his straw hat, frowning as he surveyed his goat farm. As the patriarch of the Tucker dynasty, he probably believed he was worth so much more than these four acres and modest farmhouse. He'd been gambling for decades to resurrect the family fortune, and had staked it all on that golf course and country club.

Neither one of them was happy over this deal. Jack needed to find an additional sixty thousand he hadn't budgeted for, and Kingsley would lose a valuable plot of land.

And yet, by the end of the day Jack had the title to the Roost and the surrounding five acres in exchange for paying off the lien. He now had the freedom to develop it however he wanted. It would either be the best investment of his life, or lead him straight into bankruptcy.

Chapter Fifteen

Alice drove out to the Roost, curious as to what had Jack so all-fired impatient to see her. He'd texted a message to her last night a little before midnight:

Meet me at the Roost at 5:00 tomorrow afternoon. I've got something you will want to see.

Had he found another clue? She had spent the past two days searching online British archives for anything about a mysterious woman named Helga who left England for Virginia in 1672. She refused to be discouraged by her lack of progress. This would take weeks or months, and might require another trip to England, but if Jack found another clue, it might help.

Jack sat on the Roost's front-porch rocking chair, a muddy boot planted on the railing and a devilish grin on his face as she parked her car, then approached.

"Did you find something?" she asked, desperately trying to rein in her expectations.

He got to his feet and braced his hands on the railing to grin down at her. "I didn't find anything, but I won something."

She tried not to let her disappointment show since he seemed so pleased with himself. She pasted a polite smile on her face. "What did you win?"

He held up a document. "The Roost. As of ten o'clock last night, the Roost, the spring, and the five acres they sit on belongs to me."

She gasped. Why hadn't the Tuckers announced they were selling the place? The college might have offered a better price if they'd known. This seemed . . . well, this was simply awful.

"Why would you buy the Roost?" she asked, dreading the answer. It would be easier to tear it down if he owned it outright.

"I've got plans for this place," he said. He pointed to the barren area beside the Roost where he'd already ripped out trees and leveled the ground. "A modern kitchen and outdoor dining area could be built on that spot and attached to the original structure. I can take off the roof and dismantle the walls, then lay plumbing and electrical behind it. I'll be able to raise the ceiling, get the place up to code, and turn it into the most expensive tavern in Virginia. Top of the line!"

He continued rambling on about his vision for the Roost, but her brain quit processing the moment he said *tavern*. He might as well have said "fast food joint." Or "convenience store." The Roost was a time capsule of immense value, not a tacky bar for golf course customers.

"I'll still build the amphitheater a few acres farther north, but the Roost can be a one-of-kind tavern. It'll draw folks who appreciate historic character blended with modern conveniences. What do you think? It's brilliant, right?"

He actually looked pleased, like a little boy presenting a frog he found to his mother and expecting hugs and kisses.

"I don't think it's brilliant," she said. "It's an abomination. A cheap way to earn a buck—"

"Trust me, there won't be anything cheap about this tavern."

Everything he proposed was appalling. Take off the roof? Tear down the walls? "You can't contaminate the Roost with modern technology. It would destroy the historic integrity of the building."

He folded his arms and scowled. "Tons of old buildings in America have been renovated. Last week I toured Mount Vernon. Do you think it had electricity and air-conditioning back when George Washington lived there? The place was completely gutted and reconstructed, but they still boast about being one of the best representations of eighteenth-century architecture in America. By spiffing it up, people can actually visit the place and appreciate it. That's what I want for the Roost."

She couldn't even look at him. "The whole idea of capitalizing on a piece of history is tacky."

"Why?"

Her mouth dropped open, ready to launch a firestorm to defend the Roost, but no words came out. What was so awful about what he proposed?

"Give me a moment," she said, gathering her thoughts. He had a good point about the renovations at Mount Vernon, but it was a far larger building than the Roost. And what Jack proposed sounded so . . . so mercenary. Like he was trying to cash in on a piece of history. When she said as much, he fired back.

"I paid thirty bucks to tour Mount Vernon," he said. "I paid when I toured houses in Colonial Williamsburg and the Old North Church in Boston. And guess what, Professor . . . all those places were renovated with water and electric and brought up to code. Why is it wrong to do the same with the Roost?"

The derelict building loomed before her. The roof was beginning to slant and the porch had a three-inch gap where it was pulling away from the building. That porch was probably a nineteenth-century addition, anyway. Could the building survive being taken apart and reassembled?

Of course it can. Last year her father had an operation that required taking his kidney out to remove a tumor, then they put the kidney back in his body and patched him up. She'd been terrified during the eight-hour procedure, but now her father was in better shape than before.

Maybe this could happen after all.

She gazed at the Roost with new eyes. Her impulse had always been to preserve things rather than gutting and rebuilding them. Such an act was so much riskier, but potentially better.

"Well?" Jack prompted. He stood on the porch with hands propped on his hips. He looked tanned and strong, excitement beaming from his eyes. The boldness of his dream made Jack irresistibly attractive, and his excitement was contagious.

"Can I help?"

He did a double-take and looked stunned at her quick capitulation. "I can't pay you anything. Fixing this place up will probably take my last dollar."

"I don't need to be paid; I just want to help."

Jack bounded down the steps in a giant leap and tugged her into his arms, lifting her feet off the ground and hoisting her into the air. "Yes, you can help, you insane woman."

His laughter was warm and rich, sending a thrill through her even as he twirled her in a circle. She giggled, bracing her hands on his shoulders as she gazed down at him. Who could have imagined this annoying man could ever envision such a fabulous and innovative project?

"You should probably put me down," she said, a little breathless from the sudden wave of attraction that clobbered her.

"I probably should," Jack said, and his wholesome grin turned a little heated as he slowly lowered her to the ground, their bodies in full contact all the way down.

He didn't let go of her even after her feet landed back on the ground. His shoulders were well-muscled, and she let her hands roam over them, her gaze locked with his. He cupped her face in his hands and locked gazes with her, his nose almost touching hers.

"Do you still have a crush on that British guy?" he asked.

Sebastian Bell was on the other side of the world, and nowhere in her mind at the moment. "No," she whispered. "He's history."

The air crackled with electricity, and Jack gave a slow, barely noticeable nod of his head. "Good." He lowered his head and kissed her.

She wound her arms around his neck and returned the kiss. Jack was entirely wrong for her. He was a jock. He was too bold, too aggressive, too cocky, but he was also strong and visionary and fabulous. This was a kiss to get lost in and she did.

She smoothed her palms over his muscular biceps but their kiss remained unbroken, even though both of them began to smile. Her heart pounded by the time he lifted his head.

There couldn't possibly be anything lasting with Jack, but his attraction to her was a balm to her wounded spirit.

After learning of Jack's plan to transform the Roost into a first-class attraction, Alice was on fire to make progress on discovering the source of the Saint Helga legend.

The 1698 fire had destroyed most of Virginia's earliest records, but as a colony of England at the time, the British Library held important Virginia records, too. Alice had mined those records earlier in the year, but she'd been looking in the wrong decade. Her best shot for finding something new about who built the Roost was to ask the archivist at the British Library to search all the way back to the 1660s.

Unfortunately, the archivist for early American records was Margo Davis, a woman who despised and resented Alice. Even after all this time, Alice had never been able to figure out why Margo resented her. Alice had been in a radiant good mood when she first arrived at the archives last February. At the time, she was madly in love with Sebastian, work on the film was going well, and Alice had two entire days of vacation time to browse through the archives. Margo returned Alice's sunny smile with an eye roll and stark refusal to help, always claiming she was too busy with other patrons to help a pushy American.

First of all, Alice wasn't pushy. She was polite and curious and excited to delve into the British archives. All she asked for was a little professional assistance, and that seemed to annoy Margo to no end.

All that was in the past. Today was a new day, and Alice would let bygones be bygones. Margo would be more likely to help if Alice caught her early in the day before other patrons competed for attention.

The five-hour time difference meant Alice needed to get up at three o'clock in the morning. She splashed cold water on her face, brewed a cup of coffee, and turned on every lamp in her townhouse to help wake herself up.

Before placing the call, she arranged the scanty details she knew about the Roost so she'd have them ready for Margo:

One: Tree ring data indicated that construction of the Roost began in 1661.

Two: In 1705, a sale was recorded in the newly built statehouse in Jamestown with a single line: *Reid's Roost, once owned by the late Widow Santos, had been sold at auction to Archibald Tucker.*

Three: The archives at the British Library had a 1680 license from the Crown to "R. Santos" to operate a ferry on the James River.

Alice ran her finger along the paperwork. "R. Santos" was likely the husband of the Widow Santos. Was his full name Reid Santos?

It was an unusual name for an English settler, but perhaps Margo would use her powers to hunt through the dusty archives in search of additional information to identify this person. It couldn't hurt to ask, could it? Perhaps Margo was in a better frame of mind these days.

Still, Alice's fingers trembled as she keyed in the numbers for the British Library. The call was connected and rang only a single time before a cheerful voice from three thousand miles away answered.

"Margo Davis, how can I help you?"

Well! Margo's voice sounded remarkably bright and perky. Alice determined to be equally cheerful. "Hi, Margo! This is Alice Chadwick from Williamsburg, Virginia. I was in the archives last February looking at old records from Jamestown."

Alice held her breath and waited, a long pause growing uncomfortable. Alice cleared her throat and continued. "I was looking at records about a piece of property named Reid's Roost outside of Jamestown. Do you remember me?"

A muffled snort sounded on the other end of the connection. "I'm not likely to forget the only stalker I've ever met."

Alice shot to her feet and began pacing. "You saw Sebastian and me together. Did it look like I needed to stalk him?"

"No, he was too busy hanging on to your every word and scattering rose petals in your path. Drug addicts so often show poor judgement."

"Sebastian wasn't on drugs when we were at the library." Sebastian was clean and sober and wonderful during that golden time. It wasn't until two months later that everything careened into disaster.

"What do you need, Alice? You're wasting my time."

"I'd like your help looking through records from the 1660s. I hadn't realized I needed to search that far back when I was there in February."

Another snort laden with contempt reached all the way across the ocean. "Then I suppose you'll need to get your pampered rear end onto a plane and come over here to do your own research."

The connection was severed before Alice could even draw a breath.

Alice diverted her frustration into making Jack a magnificent home-cooked Southern dinner. It began with a pecan-crusted goat cheese salad before a main course of blackened catfish, roasted okra, and golden-brown hush puppies. She served everything on her patio overlooking the backyard. The table was set with flickering votive candles and a pitcher of raspberry iced tea. It was a lovely meal, even though her blood pressure rose while relaying her frustrating telephone call with Margo.

"'Your pampered rear end'?" Jack asked in amazement. "She actually used those words?"

"She did."

"It sounds personal," Jack said as he filled his glass with more tea. "What did you do to tick her off?"

"Nothing! She just hates me, and has since day one. Now that I know the Roost dates to 1661, I am completely at her mercy to get at those records. Margo and the British Library are my only hope."

"Then I guess you'll need to get your pampered rear end on a plane and go to England."

Alice threw a hush puppy at him. Jack caught it mid-flight, popped it into his mouth, and they both laughed. Their relationship was still new and fragile—and yet, she had loved every minute of it.

It had been a week since their first kiss, and they'd had dinner together every evening since. She either cooked for him or they went to a local restaurant, but the evening always ended the same way. They returned to the Roost and Saint Helga's Spring, where they sat on the pier to watch the sunset. Sometimes they kissed. Other times, Jack laid his head in her lap and told her stories about his travels around the world, building golf courses.

"Maybe this Margo woman is simply a bitter person," Jack said once the laughter faded.

"She's not," Alice said. "There was one time Sebastian Bell accompanied me to the library because it was too rainy to film. You should have seen how Margo fawned over him. She was all smiles and friendliness. All it took was a 'pretty please' from Sebastian, and she fell over herself to help. That was the day she found a license from the Crown to someone named R. Santos to operate a ferry on the James River."

Jack made a timeout gesture with his hands. "Hold on. What does a 'license from the Crown' mean?"

"During the 1600s, Williamsburg and Jamestown were a royal colony under direct control of the king. Operating a ferry was a plum job, and the king awarded positions like that to whoever could pay the fee. I've always suspected that whoever built the Roost was wealthy. The windows on the first floor probably cost a fortune."

"And this Margo woman found the license?"

Alice nodded. "That was the first time I'd heard the name R. Santos. He's probably the husband of the Widow Santos. I went back to the British Library the next day to see if I could find anything more about R. Santos, but Sebastian wasn't with me, and Margo was back to being surly and mean."

If Alice was to discover the Roost's origins, and Helga's relationship to it, she might indeed need to get her pampered rear end on a plane to England.

And yet . . . at the moment she didn't really care. She was happy. For the first time since her career began imploding, she was simply *happy*. Jack had taught her to celebrate the gift of what she'd been given rather than enumerate her difficulties. Even if she lost her job and never worked as a historian again, she had so many blessings.

The odds of keeping her job seemed to dwindle with each passing week, but the wait for an answer was almost over. At last, her long-anticipated summons from the head of the History Department had arrived. It would be the first time she'd come face-to-face with Tom Dolan since the awful stalking scandal had tarnished her name.

Tomorrow morning, she would return to campus and learn her fate.

Chapter Sixteen

Alice parked on the far side of campus, hoping the ten-minute walk beneath the leafy oak and maple trees would help her relax before her meeting with Tom Dolan, the chair of the History Department. Soon she would learn if she was going to be teaching classes in the fall or abruptly fired.

The July air was thick and heavy, motionless, as if it was too tired to summon a breeze. The last of the magnolia blossoms still emitted a weak scent, but most of the other blooming flowers and shrubbery were beginning to fade, as though the heat of summer had sapped their strength. A few daylilies and coneflowers still clung to life. Soon the groundskeepers would descend on the flowerbeds to replace them so the campus would be blooming once again when students and their parents arrived.

She squared her shoulders and drew a sobering breath as she opened the heavy door of James Blair Hall. The clicking of her heels in the vacant hallway ratcheted her tension higher. The departmental secretary wasn't in, but Professor Dolan's door was cracked open and the office lights were on.

"Tom?" she called out in the empty foyer. They were always on a first-name basis when students weren't around.

Tom soon appeared in the doorway and opened it wider. He wore only a white polo shirt and sloppy beige cargo shorts. Why did so many academics treat their appearance this carelessly? He hadn't even worn a pair of socks with his loafers.

"Alice," he said with a polite smile, his face noncommittal, "please join us."

Us? She scanned the office as she entered, her stomach plummeting at the sight of Anita Gebhardt from HR and Brent Bowers, the college's attorney. They were both dressed like they belonged in a corporate law office. Anita's bowl-shaped hair was paired with a floppy bow tie and boxy beige suit.

There was no need to panic yet, but she should have brought a lawyer. This suddenly seemed about as bad as it could get as she sank into the empty chair at the small conference table. Tom closed the door and offered a sad smile as he took a seat opposite her.

"How are you doing, Alice?" he asked, giving a good impression of compassion behind his round spectacles.

"Okay," she said, and it was more or less true. Her life got remarkably easier after she quit obsessing over what was said about her on social media each hour.

"Good, good," Tom said. He shifted uneasily and fiddled with a pen. "Well, we might as well get straight to it," he said. "There have been a lot of concerns ever since this latest news about cocaine hit the press."

Alice blinked. "Cocaine?"

Tom nodded. "Things were dicey even before, but, Alice, we can't have a professor who has been accused of distributing cocaine. I'm sure you understand."

Her jaw fell open as she swiveled to gape at Anita from HR and the college lawyer. "I have no idea what this is all about."

Anita's beige suit matched her beige hair and wan complexion. Her mouth thinned and it looked like she was smelling something bad as she met Alice's gaze. "There have been credible assertions that you were the one who supplied Sebastian Bell with cocaine on the set of *Emma*. Cocaine is illegal in the United Kingdom, as it is here. Not only does possession of cocaine show poor judgment, it is especially egregious in light of Mr. Bell's well-known attempt to stay clean and sober."

The assertion was so ridiculous she didn't know where to start. Alice had never done an illegal drug in her life! She wouldn't even know where to get cocaine, let alone expose Sebastian to it. She'd been proud of the way he kicked a debilitating cocaine habit four years earlier, and thought it was well behind him.

"I don't know where you heard this rumor, but it isn't true," she stammered.

"It's all over social media," the college lawyer said. "Sebastian Bell's agent confirmed that you were the source of his client's access to cocaine, and it was the primary reason Sebastian wanted you to be on set at all times. I'm sure you can understand there is no way the college can risk having you teach students, many of whom will be away from home and their parents' protection for the first time."

"Are you firing me?"

"We're putting you on indefinite suspension," the lawyer said, opening a file and handing her a stack of papers. "We'd like your signature acknowledging the terms of your suspension."

She turned her gaze back to Tom, whose incessant jiggling of his knee betrayed his unease. They'd known each other for five years. He used to call her "Goody Two Shoes."

"Tom, you don't believe this, do you?"

Tom shifted in his chair, then went back to jiggling his knee. "It doesn't really matter what I believe," he said. "From the outside, it looks pretty bad, so I've got to follow what the lawyers say. Sorry, Alice."

Mr. Bowers slid the stack of papers closer to her. "Your signature, please."

There was nothing worse than confrontation, but if she didn't stand up for herself, nobody else would. "I won't sign anything until a lawyer looks over this," she said.

"That's your right," Mr. Bowers replied. "I am notifying you in person and in writing that you will not be teaching in the fall, nor may you enter the college campus. You may use the college library databases, but only from a remote computer connection off campus. Any attempt to enter the college grounds will subject you to arrest for trespass."

Arrest? Alice hadn't so much as jaywalked in her entire life. She wasn't the sort of person who needed to be threatened with arrest to obey the rules, but the threat awakened terrible memories. The humiliation of cold, steel handcuffs clamped around her wrists when security guards escorted her off the *Emma* set haunted her to this day.

"You will still be paid while HR convenes a Faculty Conduct Review," Tom said.

That was a relief, but this was still a perfectly horrible and humiliating situation. "How long will the review take?"

"At least through the fall semester," Tom replied. "You may want to use the time searching for another position." His expression was the picture of sympathy even though he always resented having a Jane Austen specialist foisted on his department. "I'll be able to write you a positive letter of recommendation, although if there is a threat of a lawsuit, I'll need to refrain from any form of recommendation on your behalf until things are settled."

It was a nice way of warning her not to make trouble. "I'll let you know soon," she said as she took the fat stack of legal paperwork and left the office.

How long had they been preparing these documents? Her palms sweat as she cradled the horrible stack of documents in her arms and left the building. Normally she loved strolling beneath the tree-shaded paths through campus, but this might be the last time she would ever walk along these herringbone brick pathways. They could arrest her if she dared set foot on campus.

Maybe it had been foolish to stop monitoring social media. This wouldn't have caught her unawares if she'd been paying attention. She took a deep breath, savoring the scent of freshly mowed grass.

No, she hadn't been a fool. Ignoring what the trolls were saying about her was the only way to keep her sanity, and she needed to focus on her blessings. Jack had helped her understand that. He could let problems roll off his back and bounced back with good humor and optimism.

Jack could help her cope with this. She didn't want to wallow in the muck of social media by re-downloading those poisonous apps onto her phone, but she needed to know exactly what was being said about her, and who was saying it.

She set off for the country club, praying she could find Jack before her fragile hold on sanity slipped away.

Jack sat on the front steps of the country club, binoculars held to his eyes as he watched a group of golfers on the third hole. The foursome were all avid golfers he asked to play a test round and evaluate the course for playability and identify last-minute issues for improvement. Hosting test rounds was a routine part of launching a new golf course, but he'd never been this nervous before. This was the first time he had an ownership stake in a golf course he designed. Its success meant the difference between working until his dying day or having a safety net to pay his bills in case his health took a nosedive.

A movement in the distance caught his eye, and he trained his binoculars to zoom in on Alice. It was impossible not to smile. She wore those high-heeled wedge sandals she looked so good in. Espadrilles, she called them. They made her legs look fantastic even though her floaty skirt covered her knees. Her hair was blowing in long, soft billows and looked pretty enough to be in a shampoo commercial.

Something was wrong. Her entire body looked tense and her face looked like she was trying not to cry. He dumped the binoculars, then strode across the fairway to meet her.

"Hey, pretty lady," he called out as he drew near. She managed a half-smile.

"Hey, Jack. I need a favor."

"Anything."

"I've heard that another round of really bad gossip is circulating about me on the web. I don't have the heart to look. Can you do it and tell me what's out there? It has something to do with cocaine."

A spark of anger flared. Alice and cocaine didn't even belong in the same sentence, but he didn't comment as he yanked his cell phone from his back pocket, opened an app, and searched for her name.

It didn't take long to land on a story.

The comments were savage. Sebastian Bell was a widely respected actor, and Alice was the nobody who dangled cocaine before him to attract his attention. The story claimed that when Sebastian tried to distance himself from her and the cocaine, Alice began stalking him. By the time Sebastian sought help, he was hooked again and Alice had to be served with a restraining order.

"Well?" she asked.

Jack continued clicking around because there were countless posts on the topic. One of them had a photo of a young, bleary-eyed Sebastian Bell staggering out of a nightclub with smears of white powder on his dark sweater. It was probably an old photo from the worst years of Sebastian's early addiction. Most of the posts also included the infamous photo of Alice in handcuffs being led off the movie set.

Jack wished he could lie and downplay this, but she needed to know. He tried to soften his words. "It's pretty bad," he acknowledged. "They're blaming you for supplying Sebastian Bell with coke and getting him hooked again."

She gazed at the sky as though looking for answers. "It's ridiculous. I don't even smoke cigarettes, let alone smoke cocaine."

People *snorted* cocaine, they didn't smoke it, but her error just went to prove how naive she was when it came to drugs. He continued skimming posts. One man was quoted over and over in the posts.

"Who's Graham Garfield?"

"He's Sebastian's agent," Alice said. "He's part creepy lawyer, part Lord Voldemort. Even Sebastian doesn't like him, but he's the best in the business."

Part of an agent's job was to defend his client's reputation. If the client took a financial hit, so did the agent. Jack knew enough sports agents from men on the PGA tour to know that their job went well beyond negotiating contracts and managing publicity. Product endorsements were a huge part of a celebrity's earning power, and Sebastian Bell had endorsements from Rolex and Dior. No wonder his agent was eager to foist the blame somewhere else.

"The college released me from teaching in the fall semester," Alice said. "They put me on indefinite suspension while they conduct an investigation. From the way my department head spoke, it sounds like a foregone conclusion that they're going to fire me for cause unless I go quietly."

He looked away from the phone to draw her into a hug. "Oh, Alice, I wish I could stand in front of this craziness and take the brunt of it for you."

His phone beeped with an incoming text, and he instinctively reached for it.

Sophie's name appeared on the screen. He clicked it off and stuffed it in his back pocket, but not before Alice saw.

"Who's Sophie?" she asked, pulling away from him.

"Nobody."

Alice let out an exasperated breath. "She keeps texting you, and you keep saying she's nobody, but your entire body tensed up the moment you saw her name."

Sophie truly was nobody ... at least, nobody he wanted to discuss. He'd never even met the woman, and owed her nothing. In the distance, the foursome was moving on to the 9th hole, and he hadn't been paying attention.

"Let's not do this here. She's nothing for you to worry about."

"The only thing that could make this day worse is for my boyfriend to be flirting with another woman behind my back."

He shifted uneasily. The word *boyfriend* made him uneasy. It had all sorts of connotations he didn't like. Japan beckoned, and even if it didn't, he would never stay in Williamsburg or anywhere else for very long.

He reached for the binoculars. "I'll come over to your place tonight and I can tell you about Sophie. Deal?"

She looked a little mollified. "What do you want for dinner?"

"Whatever is easiest for you." Anything Alice made was terrific, and he managed a genuine smile before pulling her into a farewell hug, but inside, he dreaded the coming conversation about Sophie.

Chapter Seventeen

Jack walked toward Alice's townhouse like a condemned man facing an executioner. He'd delayed this meeting as long as possible. After sweltering on the course all afternoon, he lingered in the country club's locker room for a long, cool shower.

At least he was clean now, but he was still sick at heart. He didn't *need* to tell Alice about Sophie. He didn't owe Alice anything, and opening up about his past violated a lifelong resolution: look out for Number One. There was no way to discuss Sophie without cracking the door to the dungeon where he'd locked away his worst childhood memories. Why should he subject himself to that?

Because Alice was hurting. She'd just been accused and humiliated, and he added to her misery by being a jerk about Sophie. This was one area where he might be able to put her mind at ease, even if it was likely to cost him a bundle.

Besides, he was hungry. He hadn't eaten since breakfast and tempting aromas surrounded him the moment Alice welcomed him inside her townhouse.

"I think I've died and gone to heaven," he said after giving her a quick kiss. "What smells so good?"

She wore one of those charming aprons over her dress, her hair in a long braid draped over her shoulder as she lifted a crock from the oven.

"Lobster mac and cheese," she said, setting the crockery bowl on a trivet. "Are you hungry?"

She hadn't changed since he saw her this afternoon. Knowing Alice, she probably went straight to the grocery store to buy everything fresh, then swung into high gear to prepare a meal from scratch. On one of the worst days of her life, she was cooking for him.

It would be easier to enjoy dinner if he could get the hard part out of the way.

"Sophie is my stepmother," he said quietly.

Alice glanced up and froze. "I thought you said you didn't have any family?"

He had a father he hadn't seen in twenty-two years, plus a stepmother and two half-sisters he'd never met. He gestured to the sofa so he could unload the story, then they could eat.

"My mother died of cancer when I was eleven," he said. "She had been the one who looked out for me and made sure I took my infusions, made sure I didn't do stupid stuff like slide down the bannisters or jump off balconies. After she died, everything was left up to my dad, and he wasn't cut out for it."

For a start, his father was an alcoholic. Social workers said he had been a "functioning alcoholic" while his mom was alive, meaning he could hold down a job and pick up Jack's clotting factor from the pharmacy. Things got a lot worse after his mother got sick. The stress of caring for two invalids broke Frank Latimer, who was so drunk he wasn't able to attend his wife's funeral. He started drinking during the day and missing work. He'd forget to pick up Jack's prescriptions or buy groceries.

Jack would walk to a convenience store at the end of the street to get whatever he could carry home, usually junk food or boxes of pasta with the bright orange powder. He'd take money out of his dad's wallet to buy food, but there wasn't always enough, and Jack didn't always pay. A couple times he shoplifted easy stuff like beef jerky or candy bars. When he was thirteen, a clerk noticed him shoplifting and Jack dropped everything to run out of the store. He tripped over a curb and got a bad asphalt burn. He hadn't been taking his injections, so the bleed landed him in the hospital.

"That was when the state got involved," he told Alice. "A social worker came to our apartment to investigate. There wasn't any food in the fridge and my prescriptions hadn't been filled. They wanted to work with my dad to set up a plan for my care, but it didn't go so well. My dad thought I'd be better off in foster care."

His dad broke down and sobbed when he told Jack. It was December, and they were alone in the apartment. For once, his dad was sober, but he was trembling and pathetic. It was dark in their apartment, but Christmas lights from the other side of the parking lot sent red and green blinking lights into the darkness. It was too hard to watch his dad blubber; all Jack could do was look outside at the blinking lights, waiting for it to be over.

"My dad finally dried out while I was in college," he said. "He married a lady named Sophie. I've never met her, but she sent me an invitation to the wedding. Dad even wrote a note on the back of the invitation, saying he was sorry for letting me down. He swore he was sober for good and hoped I could forgive him."

Alice looked stunned, her eyes wide and a little hopeful. "What happened?"

"Oh, I forgave him," he said, taking care to keep his voice nonchalant. "I don't want to ever see him again, but I forgave him. I'm glad he got better."

"You didn't go to the wedding?"

"Nope. I was still pretty bitter at that point, and was finally getting my life together. Everything was perfect. I had a scholarship for college. Friends. My health was mostly okay, and I had a part-time job doing landscape at a golf course. That had to be my priority. I wasn't going to waste the money to fly across the country for Dad's wedding. I used to look at Sophie's Facebook page. They've got two kids now. Girls. I guess they're teenagers by now."

His father spent longer with those girls than he ever spent with Jack. He wasn't jealous, but he still had no interest in getting looped into that family.

"Why is she contacting you now?"

"My dad has emphysema. Sophie has been texting me about it, nagging me to go for a visit. They live in Baltimore, and that's a long drive just so my dad can tell me he's sorry. Anyway, that's who Sophie is. You don't have any cause for jealousy, and dinner really smells great. Let's eat, okay?"

He said it pretty definitively, and mercifully, she agreed.

Alice was still processing what she'd just heard as she set the bowl of lobster mac and cheese in the center of the table. She had selected the perfect bottle of pinot grigio to pair with the lobster. It had a light and crisp zest to complement the lobster, but after what she'd just heard about Jack's father? The bottle of wine sat in the ice bucket and she hoped he wouldn't notice.

Her career as an academic was likely over. Her idealized plan of sharing Jane Austen with a new generation of students was smoldering on the ash heap of her failed romance with Sebastian Bell. The life she'd planned was gone, but Jack was still here, and he was a good man even though he suffered from a howling void in his life.

She approached the subject with caution. "I don't think you'll ever regret it if you drive to Baltimore to see your dad."

Jack swallowed and wiped his mouth. "Alice, this is the best mac and cheese I've had in my life. You should get a medal for this." He flashed her a wink before taking another healthy forkful.

He didn't intend to go. Maybe she shouldn't be surprised he didn't understand the value of family. A plant raised without sunlight or fertilizer was going to be frail and easily burned. Jack spent his whole adult life fleeing from commitment, but she could help.

"Jack, someday you might have kids of your own. Don't you think they'd like to have a connection with your family?"

Jack set his fork down. He wasn't angry. He just seemed . . . defeated. "I'm not ever going to have any kids, Alice."

She tried not to flinch. "Are you sure?"

"I live my life on the road. As soon as I finish one golf course, I'll move on to the next. No kid should have to put up with that. I'm telling you all this because . . . Well, because you need to know why I won't ever get married or settle down. Most women want kids, don't they?"

Alice had looked forward to having children all her life. "Yeah, most women do," she admitted. "Where will you go next?"

"Japan. They've offered me a great opportunity, and they're paying me a fortune. The food is good, too. Not good like this," he said with a forced laugh while nodding to the center of the table.

Her heart squeezed a bit. She probably would never be a college professor again, but nobody could say she didn't know how to cook and style a fine meal. For a centerpiece, she'd chosen crimson-colored zinnias to contrast with the muted tones of the mac and cheese. In a subtle nod to the lobster, she'd placed a few seashells and beads of sea glass around the vase of the zinnias.

"Alice, can we just take things day by day?" Jack asked. "I'll be here another three months. I like you more than I've ever liked any other woman, but come   October, I'll be leaving. Is that okay with you? Or should we wrap things up now?"

It wasn't okay with her, but she wanted more time with Jack. She was falling for him . . . and each new day enjoying his company was proof that she was going to recover from Sebastian Bell.

"It's okay with me," she said, trying to convince herself it was true.

Chapter Eighteen

Jack sat in the glass and steel office of his lawyer in Williamsburg as Ms. Lancaster helped revise his contract with the Nakamura Golf Course in Japan. His growing investment in the Roost and Tucker's Grove Golf Course meant he needed to remain here until October, which put him behind schedule in Japan.

Mr. Nakamura agreed to waive the late penalty, which was a godsend, and Jack needed to express proper appreciation in this flurry of contract renegotiations. He would have preferred to sign these forms online, but Mr. Nakamura was old school and wanted things on actual paper.

Ms. Lancaster set the revised timetable on the glass table before him, and Jack skimmed it quickly. "This is fine," he said, signing his name with a flourish.

"I'll have my secretary fax this over," the lawyer said. "As soon as the revised timetable is signed by Mr. Nakamura, it will be official."

Jack glanced at his watch. Alice was making Beef Wellington with a mushroom risotto tonight. When a woman like Alice Chadwick was pulling out all the stops on an intimate dinner for two, he didn't want to be late.

"Can you send the signed documents to my hotel?" Jack asked. "I'm staying at the Tucker Inn."

He had to move out of the Roost and into a hotel so the structural engineers could get inside to do their thing. The Tuckers were still trying to keep Jack mollified, and had offered him a discount to stay at their fancy hotel in town. Jack had been prepared to put Doc up too, but the old guy had finally patched things up with his wife and moved back home. Alice couldn't bear the thought of Jack eating fast food, so he went to her place every night for dinner.

They had now been dating for a month, and it was the best relationship of his life.

It was shameful the way he let her fuss over him. She cooked his meals and set everything out on lace tablecloths adorned with flickering candles and antique dishes. She preloaded television shows for them to watch in the evenings, then snuggled beside him on the couch, tracing little patterns on the back of his hand. She laughed at his bad jokes, kept a stash of his favorite coffee blend in her pristine kitchen, and even taught him to waltz one evening—twirling him around her living room to the soft strains of a classical melody. Jack couldn't remember the last time he'd felt so completely cared for, or so utterly charmed.

He loved walking beside her when out in public. In the hot humidity of Virginia in the summer, most people wore cut-off jeans and flip-flops, but not Alice. Her flowing skirts and lacy blouses were poetry in motion. She wore makeup and earrings and her hair styled beautifully.

And yet, she never nagged him about his rough edges anymore and seemed to genuinely appreciate a little rowdy humor. The first time she came over to the clubhouse, where he was watching a baseball game with the crew, she was wearing a sundress with a wide straw bonnet. He set down his beer, stood up, and hollered across the bar. "Hey, Alice! Do you think I can burp the Star-Spangled Banner? Let's see!" He wrapped an arm around her neck, pulled her in close, and started belching. By the time he got to "at the twilight's last gleaming," she was laughing so hard she had to wipe away happy tears.

Every few days they went to the Roost to check on progress. The architectural plans for the new addition had moved on to the permitting stage. The sloping land behind the Roost couldn't accommodate the expansion, so they were going to move the old building to flatter ground two acres away where it would have the perfect view of Saint Helga's Spring. Grading specialists and a foundation contractor were prepping the land for the addition. All of it required Jack to take out a million-dollar construction loan, but the enthusiastic endorsement of the bank confirmed Jack's hunch that this was going to be a great investment.

Best of all was having fun with Alice. Her suspension from the college held, but she shook it off to throw herself into planning the Roost. She took delight in *everything* as they prowled around the Roost.

"Look at this old nail," she marveled while rolling the bit of iron with its square shank and crudely forged head. She found the nail while crawling in the attic and brought it down for him to admire. "I'll bet the blacksmith who forged this never imagined we'd be admiring his work three hundred years later."

That was the sort of daffy idealism he loved about Alice. She found everything fascinating and insightful. Heck, she even got *him* excited about the history of this place. When she wasn't at the Roost, she was on her computer looking through scanned archive files for any hint of a woman named Helga or the Widow Santos. They both suspected she might be the same woman, but without proof, she couldn't make much progress on solving the mystery.

The day the foundation was poured for the new Roost promised to be a long one. Wooden frames and trenches outlined the perimeter of where the building would sit. Stubby pipes jutted up from the ground for plumbing. By the time Jack finished his work at the golf course, the mixer truck had already deposited the concrete into the waiting forms and workers used long-handled brushes to push it into every corner of the frame.

Alice sat on a wobbly wooden bench to watch, her elegant back perfectly erect, and he simply had to stop and stare. Her profile was so perfect, so quietly feminine and serene she looked like she ought to be on a cameo. How could she be this happy? Her career was in the toilet and people in town still whispered behind cupped hands wherever she went.

"Hey, pretty lady," he called as he drew near, and a wide smile blossomed as she stood to welcome him with a kiss.

"Isn't it fabulous?" she said with a nod toward the foundation.

"Fabulous," he agreed, gazing at her instead of the construction site. He loved the feel of her in his arms, and drifted his hands gently across her back. "You want to go into town and get something decent to eat? I hear there's a new Italian place."

She shook her head. "I'm going to stick around for a few hours. I'm worried about birds who might land on the wet concrete."

He choked back a laugh. "The birds aren't going to hurt the concrete. They're too light."

"I'd still rather stick around to warn them away. And look, I've brought a picnic for both of us. Want to stay and help me play scarecrow?"

That was how he spent a perfect summer evening on a blanket with the most beautiful woman in Virginia. They ate pimento cheese sandwiches, freshly cut chunks of pineapple, and almonds, olives, and squares of smoked gouda cheese. She set out homemade blueberry tarts and arranged everything so perfectly the spread ought to be featured in a magazine.

Every so often she sprang up to wave away birds that flittered around the foundation, which was completely ridiculous, but he enjoyed watching her. He was too gentlemanly to point out that the only real danger to the foundation would come overnight if a deer got curious and walked onto it. Heck, Alice would probably camp out all night to be sure Bambi didn't get into trouble.

Alice was scampering after a pair of bluebirds that were swooping through the air when her cell phone rang. He tilted the phone to glance at the screen, which simply read *Adam*.

She had a brother named Adam. There were three brothers in the Chadwick family: a nice one, a scary one, and one who'd joined the French Foreign Legion and hadn't been seen in years. Adam was the scary one. He was a lot older than Alice and a colonel in the Air Force.

"Yo, Alice!" Jack bellowed, his voice echoing across the rolling hills. It was far more effective in scaring the bluebirds away than Alice's gentle hand flutters. "Adam is on the phone."

Alice seemed a little spooked as she darted back to the blanket to accept the call. "Hey, Adam," she said, still breathless from her mad dash to save the bird population.

"Who's the new guy?" a voice demanded.

She had answered the call on speaker, but Adam couldn't see them and she looked confused. "What are you talking about?"

"Mom was in Washington for a consultation about Federal Reserve policy and heard through the grapevine that you've been seen hanging out with a new guy in Williamsburg. Who is he?"

Alice shot a wide-eyed, panicked glance at Jack, her mouth contorted in a pained grimace, but her voice strove for calm. "Oh, Jack is a super-nice guy. Really funny and supportive."

That might be the first time anyone described him so harmlessly, and Adam wasn't settling for it.

"Yeah, fine. Mom and Dad want to meet him."

"They do? Why?"

Adam cleared his throat. "Possibly because the last person you cavorted with turned out to be a drug addict who ruined your reputation. And they don't think you're serious about searching for another academic job. They want to know what's going on."

Alice stood and began pacing. "Adam, it's impossible to search for a college position this late in the summer. New academic postings don't get listed until later in the year."

"Don't change the subject. Mom and Dad want you to bring your new guy out to the River House this weekend. I'll be there, and so will Quentin. We all want to meet him."

Alice mugged another panicked face Jack's way. "Oh, you know . . . Jack is very busy," she dissembled. "He doesn't have time for that sort of thing."

"Look, Alice, Mom and Dad are already upset with you. Keeping this new guy a secret isn't doing you any favors. You need to come down here, bring Jack along, and sort this out. Sooner rather than later, okay?"

The phone disconnected, and Alice sighed as she plopped down on the blanket beside him. "I'm sorry," she said. "Adam's bark is worse than his bite . . . well, actually that's not true. He can be pretty scary. So can my parents. You don't have to answer their summons."

It sounded like she didn't want her illustrious family to meet him. "Are you embarrassed to be seen with me?"

"No!" Alice rushed to say. "It's just that command performances out at the River House can be pretty intimidating, and you are under no obligation to them for anything."

First of all, what kind of family actually gave their house a name? She'd told him that the River House was their "country estate." It was close enough to Washington for weekend getaways, but still countrified enough for sailing, horseback riding, and other rich-people sports. If her parents intended to give her grief for dating a guy like him, he wanted to be there.

"I'll come with you to the River House."

Surprise widened her pretty eyes. "You will?"

"Yeah, I will." It was a test. If she balked, if she was ashamed of him because he didn't have a cultured Southern accent or the sort of pedigree to impress her parents, he'd walk away from her right now. It would hurt, but he'd survived   worse.

She sagged in relief. "Oh, Jack. Thank you. I would really love for you to come."

"You would?" He tried not to let his surprise show. "Why?"

"Because I feel stronger when I'm with you, and you're a great man to have in my corner. I'd be eternally grateful if you'd come with me."

Her confidence filled him with a surge of electricity that lit his every nerve ending, and a strange sort of happiness descended. When she looked at him like that, it made him want to go to the ends of the earth for her. "Sure, Alice. I'll come with you."

Chapter Nineteen

Alice shouldn't have agreed to let Jack come with her to the River House. Jack wanted to drive since he didn't trust her electric vehicle to last the distance, and he was already an hour late picking her up because he was waiting on the delivery of two dozen golf carts. When he finally replied to her barrage of text messages, the easygoing reply was so typically Jack.

Don't worry. I'll be at your place with plenty of time to make the two-hour drive.

But not plenty of time to arrive before dinner. Her parents were sticklers for punctuality, and she was already arriving with the stain of public scandal slung around her neck. The least she could do was be on time for dinner. She sat on the front porch of her townhouse, checking her watch every five minutes and dreading the weekend.

She adored Jack's rollicking-good fun, but her parents would disapprove. Jack drank milk straight from the jug, took pride in how loud he could belch, and wiped his greasy hands on her embroidered tea towels. Last week she ran into him coming out of the fitness club. 'Hey Alice, come smell my gym bag. It's *rank!*' She squealed and hurried toward the lady's locker room, his laughter echoing after her, and she couldn't stop laughing either. She accepted him totally, and would never dream of trying to change him, but her parents wouldn't understand. She finally heard the gas-guzzling growl of his monster truck at three o'clock when he rolled into her parking lot.

Alice tossed her overnight bag in the back seat, then climbed into the passenger seat of the ridiculously jacked-up pickup truck. "Did the golf carts arrive?"

"Finally," Jack replied. "I wasn't going to accept delivery until they'd all been tested for noise and vibration. Don't worry. I can see that dent between your eyes. We'll get to your parents' house in plenty of time for dinner."

He merged on to I-64 heading north to Ashborough County. "Tell me more about your parents," he said once they were safely on the highway.

She sighed, dreading the coming confrontation with her parents. "My dad is pretty tough, and my mother is worse. I know parents are supposed to set high standards for their kids, but they've always leaned into that pretty hard."

"Give me an example," Jack said, his eyes still on the road.

Reliving her long and tortuous history of letting her hyper-competitive parents down was among her least favorite topics, so she reached for an example of how they treated her older brother.

"When he was twenty-two, Adam qualified for the Summer Olympics in the Pentathlon. It's the contest where you compete in swimming, fencing, horseback riding, pistol shooting, and running. Adam won the silver medal, and my parents were disappointed. He messed up the fencing with too many penalties. It's been sixteen years, and they *still* give Adam a hard time for losing out on the gold medal because of those penalties. That's what I mean about my parents being tough. They raised us all to excel in athletics, although it didn't take with me. Obviously."

She glanced at the map on her phone and sighed. According to the app, they'd arrive at the River House five minutes ahead of the six o'clock dinner. Way too tight to feel comfortable.

"Do you read the newspaper?" she asked Jack.

"Nope. Just the sports page sometimes."

Her parents had the *Washington Post*, the *New York Times*, and the *Wall Street Journal* delivered daily. Growing up, they'd drill their children about world events at the dinner table, and that continued to this day.

"Be prepared for a quiz about current events," she said. "It's another of their quirks. Dinner wasn't a chance to relax and celebrate the day when I was a kid, it was just another opportunity for instruction. My parents wanted us to learn about government and international law, so they held mock trials for offenses. Crimes could be anything from who ate the last donut to what should happen if one of us refused a direct order . . . like when my brother Quentin couldn't bring himself to help gut and clean the turkey my dad shot for Thanksgiving dinner. The trials were supposed to educate us in legal principles. Poor Quentin! He's always been such an animal lover, but my mother charged him with dereliction of duty, so we had to have a mock trial. I was appointed defense attorney, and Adam was the prosecution."

Jack hid a smile as he stared at the road ahead of him. "Who won?"

"I was only fourteen and my mom was judge and jury. Of course, Adam won. Quentin was sentenced to reading a book about the Bataan Death March to teach him the value of a hearty meal."

She could have added more, but the muscles in Jack's forearms were oddly attractive. They flexed beneath his tanned skin each time he adjusted the steering. His hands casually held the wheel.

Those hands could swing a golf club with perfect finesse or caress her until she was breathless. She'd never been trapped in such a small space with Jack like this, and it stirred something inside.

Soon they were in the rural tidewater area and speeding past marshlands filled with tall, whispering grasses. Great blue herons stalked through the waters with their elegant gait, searching for fish. Despite the warmth, she and Jack both liked to drive with the windows down, and the earthy scent of sun-warmed grass was soothing.

It took almost two hours to reach Ashborough County and the two-lane route leading toward the River House. The narrow lane wound through towering white oaks and red maples, their canopies intertwining to create a lush, green-tinted world. Glimpses of the Potomac occasionally peeped through the forest wherever the understory was sparse.

They arrived at the lengthy driveway leading to the River House with eight minutes to spare. The drive had been so delightful she'd forgotten to provide Jack with last-minute instructions, and prayed he wouldn't do something like eat pudding with his fingers or display his talent for singing through a burp.

"Did you bring a pack of chewing gum?"

Jack nodded. "Everywhere I go."

"Could you maybe only chew it when they aren't around? My mother thinks it's tacky."

Jack grinned as he continued chomping down on his stick of spearmint gum. "They really have you spooked."

She knew them and he didn't. "Maude and Grayson Chadwick could spook General Patton." Alice handed Jack a wad of tissues. "Here, spit out your gum, please."

He obliged, wadded up the tissues around the gum, and slapped them back into her palm. She shoved the wad in her pocket without complaint, because Maude had already emerged onto the front porch, and the show was about to begin.

Jack gaped at Alice's family home. The River House didn't look like a home, it was more like a country club. It was a sprawling stone-and-timber affair with a helicopter pad in the front yard and a pier, boathouse, and lawn next to the Potomac River in the back. A terraced garden unfolded before the house, held in place by slate retaining walls artfully arrayed to look natural, but they were clearly installed by a master landscape architect.

Alice's mother looked as imposing as her home. Wearing an indigo cashmere sweater and a strand of steel pearls, she looked like a cross between Jackie Onassis and Cruella de Vil.

"You must be Jack," she said in a skeptical voice as she greeted them on the porch leading to the house.

He dipped his head in a little bow. "Thank you for inviting me, Mrs. Chadwick. This place is spectacular."

Not a dent of softening as the older woman locked a laser beam on Alice.

"Hi, Mom," Alice said, exchanging air kisses with her mother. "Jack was nice enough to drive me up since my car isn't the best for long drives."

"Well, don't just stand there. Come inside; dinner is waiting." Maude gestured them into the foyer and through the family room rimmed with loaded bookshelves and a baby grand piano in the corner. Dozens of photographs in silver frames covered the lid of the piano.

A dark-haired man about Jack's age stepped forward to shake his hand. "Adam Chadwick," he introduced himself. "Golf? Tomorrow morning? I've got reservations for an eight o'clock tee time."

"Sounds great," Jack said. Alice's older brother had a tall, athletic build, but none of her beauty. His face had the ruggedness of something carved with an axe—sharp cheekbones and a nose that looked like it had been broken a few times.

"Please ring the dinner bell," Maude ordered Adam, who gave his mother a little salute before heading outside.

"Brace yourself," Alice whispered to him. "The dinner bell is an air raid siren from World War II."

The piercing wail began before she even finished speaking. It escalated in volume, the spine-tingling wail setting his nerves on edge. Alice cupped her hands over her ears, but Maude remained unfazed.

"We started using the siren to call the children in from sailing on the river," she explained once the siren began winding down. "Now we use it to let Quentin know it's time to leave his hovel and join the civilized world for a meal."

Alice had already told him about Quentin, her younger brother who was the only genuinely kind person in her family. He was a wildlife biologist and lived about a mile away "in a little shack out in the swamps" where he studied turtles.

The dining room reflected a blend of classic East Coast style and rustic Virginia heritage. The long dining table was polished to a soft sheen beneath a set of antler chandeliers. French doors opened onto a veranda overlooking the Potomac.

Alice walked him over to an older man with silver hair and a military bearing who stood at the head of the table. "Jack, this is my father, Grayson Chadwick." It would be easy to be intimidated by a man who once served as secretary of state under two different presidents, but Jack was used to dealing with big shots at   country clubs and met the man with a firm handshake.

"You must have robbed the entire county of slate to build that fantastic retaining wall out front. Is it Buckingham slate?"

Grayson gave a growl of appreciation. "Vermont slate. I wanted that smoky gray tone that wouldn't crack in the winter. It cost a fortune to import."

"Good slate is worth it," Jack replied.

"Tell that to my wife. That wall has been standing there for thirty years, and she still gripes about the cost."

A household helper named Sharon wheeled a dinner cart into the dining room, and everyone took their seats. During the drive, Alice had told him that Sharon had been with the family "forever." Maude didn't cook, and some of Alice's earliest memories were standing at Sharon's elbow, watching and learning and dreaming of the day she too could cook.

Grayson sat at the head of the table, while Jack and Alice sat beside each other, Maude and Adam opposite them. Sharon quickly filled each of the plates, but when she came to the empty place setting, the maid cleared it.

"We aren't waiting for Quentin?" Jack asked, and a chill came over Maude's face.

"He heard the siren. If he can't arrive on time, he won't perish from missing a meal."

Grayson gave a brief blessing, then silverware clattered as everyone began cutting into the chicken Florentine.

Before Alice took a single bite, her father pierced her with a pointed look. "What's this nonsense about renovating some old house?"

Alice cleared her throat before answering. "It's not nonsense," she said. "It's where we think the Saint Helga legend originated, and if I can prove it, I'll have the makings for a really great academic paper."

"That will be a first," Grayson said, and Alice visibly wilted for a moment before rallying.

"The Roost has the potential to be a learning center. Half of it will be modeled after an old tavern, serving high-end drinks and food. The other half will be a learning center where we can host small classes or conference talks or can rent out for special events."

Maude frowned. "But what is the use of that sort of arcane education?" she asked. "Why don't you put your efforts into something useful?"

"History can be useful," Adam began, but Maude interrupted him.

"Bah! You waste time on a golf field."

"Golf *course*," Jack corrected.

"Golf *course*," Maude conceded with a stiff nod. "None of those things deserve public funding. Next week the county is voting to cut Physical Education programs in the schools, and the proposal has my full support. Schools should focus on reading, writing, and critical-thinking skills rather than squandering money on football or track. Look at Adam. All that money we dumped into fencing and riding lessons, and he had to settle for a silver medal."

Adam dropped his fork to glare at his mother, who sent him a tight smile. "I'm just teasing, darling," but it didn't sound like teasing to Jack.

Alice's father took up where Maude left off. "Gym class is a distraction from serious learning," Grayson said. "Most of the students playing high school football turn in substandard grades. Their time would be better spent with a rigorous tutor, not in gym class."

The dining room reeked of elitism, and Jack couldn't remain silent. "I was one of those dumb kids in the back row who teachers never thought would amount to anything," he said.

Beside him, Alice stiffened and sent him a panicked glance, but Jack wasn't ashamed of the struggles he'd endured, and met Grayson's critical glare squarely as he spoke.

"I had my share of problems and hated being trapped at a desk while a teacher droned on. School wasn't my thing—academics just didn't click for me. But gym class, that one hour each day, showed me what kids like me could gain from moving, even if I couldn't always join in. Watching others push through challenges, or trying small exercises when I could, taught me resilience and how to keep going despite life's hard knocks."

"Plenty of studies indicate that an accomplished tutor could have achieved better results," Maude said.

Jack folded his arms, ignoring Alice's pleading look to let the subject drop. "Sorry to disagree, but sports can teach some of the most important lessons in life. Seasoned athletes know that real competition never comes from your opponent. It comes from learning your own pain threshold and developing your ability to persevere. An hour of gym class can let a kid test himself against hard, objective demands. Those kids may not be able to memorize the Constitution or love a Jane Austen novel, but someday those dumb jocks are going to climb telephone poles and build your houses and serve in your military. They need to learn to read and write and all that other good stuff you teach them in school . . . but a lot of them need that one hour of gym class where they can be successful and blow off some steam and learn the value of team-work. People who say that sports is a distraction from academics have it backwards. Success in sports sets kids up for success in other areas of life. At least, that's how it was for me."

He leaned back in his chair, satisfied that he'd made his case. Maude and Grayson both scowled and Alice looked like a doe caught in the headlights, but a gleam of respect showed in Adam's face.

Jack was glad Alice suggested he bring his golf clubs, because he was going to be tested this morning. It wouldn't be a contest of skill, but whether he could keep his sanity while playing with these men. After hearing each man's golf handicap, it was obvious he was the best golfer, but the raw competitiveness between Adam and Grayson Chadwick was astounding. Throughout breakfast and the ten-minute drive to the golf course, father and son engaged in a relentless needling match like two gladiators fighting for domi-nance. How someone as soft and gentle as Alice managed to sur-vive in the competitive maelstrom of her family was miraculous.

By the time they arrived at the golf course, Quentin was already waiting for them.

"Very thoughtful of you to skip dinner last night," Grayson barked at his youngest son. Quentin had a poet's face with dark hair and soft brown eyes. Unlike Alice, who quivered in trepidation near her parents, Quentin let the insult roll off him without a ripple of concern.

"I found a nest of bobwhites that are in trouble and have been caring for them."

Grayson rolled his eyes, but Jack was curious. "What's a bobwhite?"

"They're a type of quail that nests on the ground and their habitats are getting wiped out by all the development around here. There are four chicks, and they need to be fed every couple of hours, so I'll head back home after nine holes."

Grayson muttered something under his breath about quitters, but Jack instantly liked a man who cared for someone in need, even if it was only an abandoned nest of chicks. Anyone who'd been helpless at some point in their life understood the value of open-handed compassion.

Quentin's look was as serene as a cat napping in the sunshine while they headed to the first tee box. That was when Jack noticed Quentin was barefoot.

"I like to feel the grass and soil beneath my feet," he said. "Studies prove that contact with soil leads to a healthier microbiome and triggers the release of serotonin. I never wear shoes unless I have to."

The elder Chadwick continued taking subtle digs at Quentin during the first three holes. He critiqued Quentin's lackluster golf swing, his sloppy board shorts, even his bad taste in music. Watching a bully in action was infuriating, but Quentin was thirty-one and perfectly capable of standing up for himself if he chose to. The remarkable thing was, he didn't seem to care. Nothing fazed his easygoing demeanor, so Jack bit his tongue and silently vowed to let his game do the talking, determined to wipe the floor with Grayson on the course.

By the fourth tee, the elder Chadwick quit belittling Quentin and turned his ire toward Alice. "Why isn't that woman suing the college to get her job back?" he groused after they all arrived at the next tee box.

"She signed a nondisclosure agreement," Adam said.

"In *England*," Grayson pointed out. "The cat is out of the bag all over the world, so why isn't she fighting for her job?"

Jack had often wondered the same. When attacked, his instinct was to go on the offensive, but Alice retreated. He'd carry a lance into battle for her if she asked, but the world of academia was a foreign land to him. It was up to Alice to decide if she wanted to wade back into the quagmire of fighting to win tenure.

Grayson set the ball onto a tee, positioned himself, then took a hearty swing that launched the ball cleanly, rising high and true—one of those outstanding hits that was impressive for a man of any age, let alone one in his late seventies.

The instant the ball stopped rolling, Grayson went back to attacking Alice. "She ought to drop all that folklore nonsense about ancient legends and put her nose to the grindstone by writing a scholarly paper of actual merit. Maybe then the academics will take her seriously. That woman needs to get off the fainting couch and *do* something with her brain."

Jack stepped up to the tee and placed his ball. "Maybe she defines success differently than you. I rather like Alice's nose exactly as it is."

"You didn't have to pay for eight years of college so she could read a bunch of Jane Austen novels," Grayson retorted.

"You didn't *have* to pay for it," Quentin said. "She could have gone to a public college on scholarship; you were the one who insisted she go to Princeton."

The statement didn't go over well with Grayson, who went on the attack. "I was right to push her into Princeton. A degree from Princeton is a pedigree, a lifetime pass, not some flimsy certificate from a third-rate state school. Jack! You're up."

Jack stepped forward with a cocky grin as he placed his ball on a tee. "Are you sure you want to play with a guy from a third-rate state school? The stink might rub off."

Grayson merely growled, though the other two men smiled at the comment. Jack took his swing, easily sending the ball past Grayson's hit and landing a mere two yards from the hole. Both of the younger men congratulated him, but he was getting tired of this mind game. It looked like Grayson was gearing up to continue badmouthing Alice, and Jack didn't want to hear it. He turned his attention to Adam.

"You're two strokes below par," he said in a complimentary tone. "How long have you been playing on this course?"

"Ever since I picked up a golf club when I was about twelve," Adam replied.

"I only wish Alice and Quentin had a fraction of Adam's talent," Grayson said.

Quentin helped turn the conversation away from assassinating Alice's character. "Tell us about your golf course, Jack."

Over the next few holes they spoke only of golf course design and famous clubs where they'd played. Then Adam said something interesting.

"The golf course at Camp Lejeune is a wreck," he said. "Rumor has it that it's going to get a complete renovation in the next year."

Jack stilled. He typically focused on designing new courses rather than handling renovations, but he was always on the lookout for future contracts to bid on. "Have they hired a designer yet?"

"I don't think so," Adam said.

Jack filed away the information for future reference. As always, the best business leads usually came during situations like these. Soon he would be moving on, leaving Alice and her family behind. What an irony that the most meaningful relationship he made among the Chadwick family might be networking with her brother for a lead on landing a new golf course contract.

Chapter Twenty

The next three weeks were too busy for Alice to dwell on Jack's looming departure for Japan. She couldn't change his decision to live like a nomad; all she could control was how she saw her own life—and it was a good one. She was still drawing a salary, which meant she had the freedom to do exactly what she wanted. She'd lost the future she'd always envisioned for herself, but that curveball led her to a new and exciting mission. She was completely committed to saving and restoring the Roost so it could be shared with generations to come. And with luck, she might still solve the mystery of Saint Helga . . . not because she needed an academic publication, but simply for her insatiable love of history.

August arrived, and along with it the annual influx of students back into town. Alice hid out at the Roost. For the first time in six years, her August had no flurry of faculty meetings or appointments with students. There were no classes to prepare for, no assignments to grade. She didn't even have to rush to complete her research about Saint Helga because she no longer worried about tenure; it was only curiosity and love for history that drove her.

It wouldn't be long before the Roost would be moved to its new location. The foundation for the building was poured. Lines for electrical and plumbing were installed. The permits had been signed, and the next step was the actual disassembly of the Roost. A contractor named Zeke Mackenzie had been hired to oversee the move. Each log, windowpane, and roof slate had been numbered so that it could be reassembled in its original position.

Alice spent her days designing the interior of the Roost. Jack trusted her to search out deals and select pieces to enhance the seventeenth-century vibe of the tavern. She drove to Lancaster, Pennsylvania, to buy reclaimed wood from a nineteenth-century barn and made arrangements for it to be cleaned, sanded, and stained to match the original Roost. It would be used as the exterior cladding of the brand-new kitchen and conference room. From the outside it would be a perfect match with the rest of the Roost.

She haunted antique malls in search of old lanterns and chandeliers that could be wired to supply light. The refurbished antiques would add an air of authenticity to the Roost, but most of the furnishings needed to be new. Tables, chairs, drinking glasses, and crockery would be getting heavy use. She bought slightly mismatched wooden tables and chairs, then she and Jack spent their weekends distressing them. They attacked the wood with great joy, laughing while smacking it with mallets and heavy chains. She even used an awl to create the look of a few wormholes and insect damage. Once the wood was sufficiently beat up, she finished the job with a layer of dark antiquing wax to make the tables appear to have endured centuries of use.

The most fun was shopping for artwork for the tavern. A large replica of a seventeenth-century map of Virginia was perfect to hang on the wall of the original building. Someday soon, their patrons would enjoy gazing at the map with its crudely drawn coast, rivers, and a few scattered towns, while land east of the Blue Ridge mountains remained unexplored territory.

She hoped to find some genuine eighteenth-century artwork to hang in the new conference room. A trip to the Tuckers' antique art gallery proved those pieces too expensive for her budget, but Arlo Whitworth, the bow-tie-wearing graduate of William & Mary, came to her rescue. Arlo worked as a curator at the Colonial Art Museum and had a good head for artwork from the era.

"Don't pay Kyle's inflated prices," he advised. "The museum has hundreds of paintings kept in storage. We can offer some to display on permanent loan, provided you give the museum credit in the nameplate."

It was a brilliant idea. The Colonial Art Museum only had space to display a fraction of their collection, so finding a use for artwork in their overflow collection would be a win-win. One afternoon in early September she and Jack headed out to the museum's warehouse to peruse the available pieces.

"I'd love for some of these old paintings to finally see the light of day," Arlo said as their feet crunched along an oyster-shell path toward the climate-controlled warehouse behind the museum.

Jack, being Jack and concerned with the bottom line, wanted to know why the museum didn't simply sell the overflow.

"Most of these old artworks came from donations," Arlo said, keys jangling as he opened the locks. "The donors usually ask us to agree to preserve them for posterity, rather than sell them."

It was dark and cool inside the warehouse. Chest-high metal cabinets featured slim drawers, each containing an original painting. Arlo pulled the switch for the overhead fluorescent lighting, the click echoing off the cinderblock walls. Everything looked so cold and hard, but excitement gathered at the prospect of picking out free art.

"Our oldest works are this way," he said, leading them down an aisle. A drawer rattled as he opened it to reveal a fine painting of a mahogany brown stallion, painted in the Rococo style, standing before a classical landscape with Grecian columns in the distance. It was unframed, but of exceptional quality.

"I think the tavern needs something a bit more rustic," Alice said. "Something that speaks of America. Those Greek columns are too formal."

Arlo nodded and moved deeper into the warehouse. What a treasure trove it was! Drawer after drawer displayed portraits, landscapes, and religious subjects. Genre scenes depicted everyday domestic activities like dancing and bringing in crops. Those would be good. Some of the subjects looked too European, but she felt like they were getting closer.

Jack nodded toward the back wall, where many of the paintings were simply laid on open shelving. "Why aren't these in drawers?"

"They're less valuable," Arlo said and led them over. Most were paintings of people in various poses and groupings. Some of the subjects were single men staring stiffly out of the frame, but some were children or couples. None were very appealing.

"These were probably done by itinerate portrait painters," Arlo explained and pointed to one of two children standing beside a pet dog. "Traveling artists in early America often pre-painted the body and background of a portrait. They'd hit the road with dozens of these canvases, then painted the subject's facial likeness onto the pre-painted canvas. It made portrait painting quicker and more affordable, though it rarely yielded exceptional results."

Alice agreed. All the paintings looked generic and stiff, but one seemed exceptionally odd. A stern-looking man sat beside his wife, both of them wearing lavish satin clothes dripping with lace and pearls. Their solemn expressions seemed a mismatch for the garish clothes.

Jack nodded to the stern-looking man. "I'd be annoyed too if someone painted me wearing a pink suit. He looks like a pansy."

"I'd say it's more of a peach shade than pink," Arlo replied. "Some of the earliest settlers in Jamestown were the second sons of English aristocrats. Impractical colors and fabrics were a sign of wealth. My guess is that the portrait painter had lots of pre-painted canvases with lavish clothing so people could look like the upper-class."

Alice definitely wouldn't include any of these awkward portraits in the tavern. There was a bounty of paintings that better reflected the rustic beauty of early Virginia, and by the end of the afternoon, Alice had selected a landscape of the James River and another showing a woman gathering apples into a basket. Both reflected what the people who lived at the Roost might have seen and experienced.

Her only regret was that when she finally hung these paintings in the Roost, Jack wouldn't be there to see them.

Alice battled the strangest feelings the night before the Roost was to be disassembled. The workmen had left for the day, leaving her and Jack to wander the rooms alone. She ran her hand along the cool lintel stone above the empty fireplace and touched her fingers into the little frond leaves someone carved into the stone centuries ago. That unknown artist etched that mark more than 350 years ago.

"I feel like I should apologize to this old place," she said. "It seems as calm and solid as ever, and yet, this time tomorrow it's going to be pulled apart. I'm terrified on behalf of this old building. I want to apologize to it for what's about to happen."

Jack's expression was part sympathy, part humor as he gazed at her. Not long ago he would have made fun of her; now he was the rock she leaned on for support.

"It's going to be okay, Alice," Jack said, his voice tender. "Taking a building apart isn't rocket science. It's normal to be nervous, but we've got to do this if we're going to save the Roost."

The confidence in his voice released the knot of tension in her neck. She was so lucky to have him in her life. He tugged her against him for a hug and her trembling eased, slowed, and then fully stopped.

She pulled back to gaze up into his face. "You're the strongest man I know. To suffer what you've endured, to rise above it and still embrace life with such a good attitude, is inspiring."

He tucked a tendril of hair behind her ear. "You have no idea what that means to me."

"Tell me."

He kissed her, a hint of desperation in his manner. He deepened the kiss, his mouth twisting against hers, then he looked away to hug her fiercely.

"Oh, Alice! I love this rickety old building. I love knowing we're a part of its history, and that we're going to save it. You and I aren't going to end up sailing into the sunset together, but I want you to know that I kind of love you."

Her eyes widened. With her face pressed into the slab of muscle on his shoulder, she couldn't see his expression, but his voice was heavy with emotion as he continued.

"I love your kindness and compassion. I adore the way you care about history and tradition. I don't think I'll ever be able to look at a lace doily and not remember you."

She choked on a laugh. "Good!"

He pulled back so she could finally see his expression, alive with happiness and affection. "Thank you, Alice. I don't know what's ahead for me, but these last few months . . ." His voice choked up and he cleared his throat. "All I can say is thank you."

It was enough. She and Jack were as different as chalk and cheese. She wanted children, he didn't. She loved history and antiques; he liked shiny and new. She wanted roots and stability, and he never saw a horizon he didn't want to venture toward.

They were both exhausted but too wound up to sleep. Jack came back to her townhouse, which was stuffed with the artwork and a couple of old lamps she'd use in the new Roost. She'd bought an old grandfather clock from the 1790s for the corner of the tavern, but it needed a lot of work and Jack wanted to help cleaning it up.

"I didn't know this thing would have so many pieces," he said. The pulleys, cogwheels, and the pendulum were made of brass, but age had dulled them with a layer of grime that would interfere with the functioning of the clock. Alice had already disassembled the pieces and laid them on her dining table.

"I buffed away the worst of the dirt," she said. "I don't want to completely destroy the patina, but I could use your help with the polishing."

They both pulled on latex gloves and set to work. "I've got a pressure-washer that would blast these parts clean a lot faster."

"Bite your tongue," she said with a laugh. "This clock is two hundred years old."

"And I'm thirty-seven and have red blood in my veins and think you're the sweetest thing I've ever seen."

She leaned in for a kiss, but her gloved hands were gunky with brass polish and she held them out to her sides. His hands were just as bad, so they touched nowhere except their lips. When she tried to retreat, he followed with his lips still locked on hers. Even when they started laughing, he continued kissing her, pressing a trail of kisses along her jaw and down her neck.

The ring of the doorbell startled them. It gave her the excuse to finally pull away.

"Are you expecting anyone?" Jack asked.

"No," she said as she pulled the rubber gloves off to lay them on the newspaper. "With everything going on at the Roost tomorrow, I'd better answer it."

She headed down the hall to look through the peephole. A man holding a bouquet of red peonies stood on her porch. His handsome face was carved with emotion, and her heart began to thud. She looked away, gathering her thoughts.

It couldn't be, but the doorbell rang a second time, and when she looked through the peephole again, there could be no doubt.

"Who is it?" Jack called out from the dining area.

She gathered a breath and tried to sound normal. "It's Sebastian Bell."

Chapter Twenty-One

Alice couldn't believe Sebastian was actually here on her front porch. She flung the door open and stared, taking in his dark, tousled hair. He looked healthy and vibrant, with high cheekbones and a nose that was a little too big for his face but somehow made him seem even more handsome. His white dress shirt was open at the collar, exposing the strong column of his neck, and his soulful eyes looked at her as if he wanted to lay the world at her feet.

"Alice," he said, a world of emotion packed into that single word. He said it as though in prayer, with hope and yearning and regret. Longing was carved into every line of his expression, and his dark eyes were like a window straight into his soul. He extended the bouquet of peonies, and when she didn't reach for them, he lifted her hand to wrap her fingers around the stems of the bouquet. She took them, too stunned to move, to speak, to jumpstart her brain that had stopped functioning.

Flowers weren't the only thing he'd brought. A Louis Vuitton suitcase sat at his feet. "Can I come in?"

Was this a dream? It could *not* be happening, but when she tried to speak, her tongue wouldn't move; all she could do was gape at him.

"Alice? What's going on?" Jack had come to stand beside her and stared at Sebastian with surprise and a healthy dose of contempt.

Of all the ways she'd imagined running into Sebastian again, not once had she pictured Jack striding forward to speak for her because she was too dumbfounded to form a single sentence.

"You can take that bag and crawl back beneath whatever rock you've been living beneath," Jack said in an oddly calm voice.

Sebastian acted as if he hadn't heard. "Alice, it's starting to rain. Let me inside and we can talk."

It *was* starting to rain. She couldn't leave him standing outside. Mrs. Wieland, the nosy neighbor next door, might snap a photograph and stir up the hornet's nest of publicity again.

She stepped back and gestured him inside. Sebastian smiled in relief and lifted his suitcase, while Jack sputtered in outrage.

"Why don't you tell him to jump off a cliff?" Jack bit out.

"I can't leave him outside in the rain."

"He left you outside to get arrested and hauled to jail," Jack said in a tight voice.

"Hey, I didn't know anything about that," Sebastian said, already walking down the corridor into the main room of her townhouse. He set his bag down and craned his neck to look all around the interior, his admiring gaze taking in the wall of books, the mantel with its collection of Meissen figurines, the lace, the dried flowers.

"I *love* this place," he said. "It suits you." Then he saw the mess of the disassembled grandfather clock on the table. "Am I interrupting something?"

"Yes," Jack said at the same moment Alice said, "No."

Sebastian heard only Alice. "Good," he said as he smiled into her eyes. "I've been traveling since daybreak . . . English time. It's good to finally arrive."

"Seb, what are you doing here?" she finally managed to choke out. "I thought you were in rehab."

His shoulders sagged, and a world of hurt bloomed in those soulful eyes. "I got out yesterday. Alice, I didn't know anything about what was happening to you until I got my phone back. They took it from me while I was in rehab, and the first thing I did was start looking for you. Alice, I am *so* sorry."

He reached for her, but she stepped back, holding the flowers before her like a shield. She'd seen that soulful Sebastian Bell expression a million times . . . in every movie he ever starred in. It's what had made him famous. Her blood began flowing again, her brain unlocked. Anger began to replace her shock.

"I got suspended from the college because of you," she said, beginning to rally.

"I know and I'm sorry," Sebastian said, one hand extended palm up as though begging her to take it. "I'll make it up to you."

"How?" Jack demanded. "She was less than a year away from tenure, and that stunt in the UK has ruined her chances in academia forever."

Sebastian glanced between Jack and Alice. "Who is this guy?" he asked.

"He's my friend," Alice said.

"Boyfriend," Jack corrected.

The news seemed to hit Sebastian like a physical blow. He recoiled at first, then swallowed hard, nodded a few times, then geared back up. "It's nothing less than I deserve, I suppose. Alice, I messed up. Please give me another chance. Give *us* another chance."

He sounded so desperate. It ought to be pathetic, but the earnest appeal in his upper-crust British accent sounded exactly like the climactic groveling scene in a million romance movies and she was only human. It got to her.

"It shouldn't end this way," Sebastian continued, his voice breaking with anguish. "All I'm asking for is a few minutes alone with you."

Jack bristled. "I'm not leaving her alone with a coke head."

The spell broke and Sebastian shot him an annoyed glare. "I haven't done cocaine in 145 days," he defended. "Or 144, if we take the time change into account. I am determined to be brutally honest in all things. Alice, I want to be a better man. You did that for me. From the day we met on that train to Berlin, I knew you were the right woman for me. When you're near, I feel like I can conquer the world. I can certainly conquer drugs."

Jack scoffed. "Didn't look like it from what I saw on Twitter."

Sebastian didn't take his eyes off her. "I stumbled and I fell. I messed up, but I'm back. If you'll have me, I will lay the world at your feet. You are my North Star, and together there's nothing we can't do."

Anger began to unfurl, because it was a direct quote from one of his movies. She threw the flowers against his chest. Petals scattered, and Sebastian flinched.

"You messed up your life and got to do a stint in a luxury rehab center in the south of France; I got slapped with a restraining order," Alice said. "There are pictures of me in handcuffs all over the web. Strangers all over the world have accused me of doing horrible things. The people at my college want to fire me. Do you know how humiliating that is?"

"Guilty," Sebastian said, holding up his hands in supplication. "It won't happen again."

She bit off a cynical laugh. "It won't happen again because nobody in the world will hire me."

"I would," Sebastian said. "You could be my wife."

The sentence knocked the breath from her lungs, but she recovered quickly. "Is that a marriage proposal?"

Sebastian muttered a curse under his breath, then leaned over to pick up the abused peonies. "I hadn't meant to spring it on you like this," he said. Sebastian sank onto one knee. "Alice, I love—"

"Oh, get up!" she shouted. "Do you seriously think I would consider any kind of proposal from you? I could get arrested for even being in the same room with you."

Sebastian stood, looking sick at heart. "Really? I didn't realize. Maybe British law doesn't apply over here?"

"She shouldn't have to risk it," Jack ground out. "Why are you here? Is this some kind of trick? A scheme to fix your reputation?"

Once again, Sebastian didn't look at Jack, just kept his gaze locked on her as he spoke. "Alice, it's not a trick, I swear it. All that stuff that got leaked to the press, that was Graham's fault. Please give me another chance to prove that I love you."

He kept talking but it was as if his voice came from far away. Months of humiliation. Having her career yanked out from beneath her, enduring the snide looks and delighted whispers. The first issue of the student newspaper this semester had editorial cartoons about her, and student essays were exploring themes of female enablers and female stalkers.

"Seb, for the past few months I have been hanging on to my sanity by a thread. I've finally found a new purpose, and I won't let you waltz in here and drag me back into the whirlwind."

"Alice, please—"

"You heard her," Jack said. "You can walk out of here on your own two feet, or I can throw you out."

"Jack, don't!" The only thing that could make this worse was if Jack got into a fight and landed in a hospital, bleeding uncontrollably from a hemophiliac crisis and it would all be her fault. "I'll be okay. Sebastian knows what we had is over, and my life is here in Virginia."

"Does he?" Jack asked. "Then why did he bring a suitcase, prepared to spend the night with you?"

It was a good question. She turned to Sebastian for an explanation, and once again he smoothly put her at ease.

"Alice, I would never presume such a thing. I checked into a hotel in town an hour ago. The suitcase has a script and study materials for my next movie. I didn't want to leave it unprotected in a hotel and brought it with me."

"Prove it," Jack said.

Sebastian scoffed. Even his scoffing seemed elegant and refined. "Really?" he drawled in that lofty, upper-crust tone.

"Yeah, really," Jack replied. "I think it's a bogus story and you came here with your roses and groveling apology, planning on sliding right back into Alice's life."

"First of all, they're peonies, not roses. Peonies are Alice's favorite flower, and I went to three different florists to find them."

"Along with your overnight bag," Jack pointed out.

"Look," Sebastian said a little more firmly. "Maybe you don't understand how scripts for upcoming movies can be big business. I am contractually obligated to keep the script in a secure location, and the hotel isn't secure. Everyone behind the check-in desk at the hotel recognized me and wanted an autograph. I've had hotel staff riffle through my belongings on more than one occasion and can't risk letting this script out of my sight. It's the second season for *The King's Redemption,* and yes . . . those can be worth a lot."

Jack gave a fake smile. "If what you say is true, it will be the easiest thing in the world to prove."

Alice began to fidget. She wouldn't trust Sebastian if he told her the sun rose in the east, but a part of her needed to believe he was still a decent man. Despite all that he'd put her through, she prayed he really was on his way to recovery and what they'd once had wasn't all a lie.

Sebastian sauntered toward the suitcase, fixing Jack with a mocking gaze as he hefted the gorgeously trimmed, leather case onto the sofa. It had a brass combination lock, and Sebastian's elegant fingers casually rolled through the numbers. In England, Seb had weekly manicures to keep his hands in flawless perfection, and it looked like that habit had continued. In England, she'd loved Sebastian's hands. Now, Jack's callused, blunt workingman's hands had more appeal.

Please, please, please don't be lying, she silently prayed. Sebastian couldn't be a complete scoundrel, could he?

At last, the fastening clicked open. He lifted the lid, then twisted the suitcase for her to see.

The script for the second season of *The King's Redemption* sat atop a mound of history books and a couple of biographies of Charles II. No clothes or toiletries.

"Happy?" Sebastian asked. "The hotel promised me they'll deliver a safe to my room first thing in the morning, but until then, this script goes with me everywhere. Have you been watching it? *The King's Redemption?*"

She shook her head. "I took a pass." When she first met Sebastian, he'd already filmed the first season of *The King's Redemption*, and he boasted that it was the best performance of his career. For once he wasn't playing a romantic lead, but the role of a seventeenth-century English prince whose father had just been executed. The moment the axe beheaded his father, Charles II was a young king in exile, on the run and trying to rally troops to retake the throne.

Sebastian slanted her a reproving glance, which was entirely spoiled by his charming wink. "Watch it," he urged. "It's the best work I've ever done. People have been saying I'm a shoo-in for an Emmy."

"So why are you really here?" she asked.

"I wanted to do you a favor," he said with one of those lopsided smiles that melted women's hearts across the globe. "I remember how hard you were working finding out something about that Saint Helga lady, and I nagged Margo at the British Library to get cracking on it. She's turned up some interesting stuff."

She sucked in a quick breath. "Margo Davis? I asked her too, and she refused to help."

"Ah, but I'm Sebastian Bell," he said in a voice laden with enough charm to make her toes curl. "Sometimes people work harder for me."

"Your name is Sam Bartholomew," Jack said in a flat voice, and Alice flinched a little. Yes, Sebastian took a stage name on the advice of his agent, but he never used his real name anymore.

"Regardless, I'm a man who knows how to get things done," Sebastian said. "I knew Alice ran into a dead end with Margo because she's overworked and underpaid. I personally appealed to her and she was willing to burn the midnight oil. Margo turned up some genealogy information, and there's a woman named Helga in it. Plus, the name Reid is in there. I'll bet my bottom dollar they are the people we were looking for back in January."

Jack folded his arms and adopted a mocking stance. "Here's what I don't get, *Sam*," he said, suspicion heavy in his voice. "If you only got out of rehab yesterday, and didn't have access to a phone or the internet . . . how did you and Margo make so much progress on this?"

Sebastian froze, and a guilty flush stained his cheeks, but he recovered quickly. "Okay, maybe I exaggerated," he conceded. "I've been out for a few weeks, but I really do feel lousy about what happened, and I didn't want to come empty-handed. Alice, you know I adore you. Even if you aren't ready to forgive me, I was hoping we could mend fences. Let me take you out to dinner. Or to one of those theaters beneath the stars I saw advertised all over the airport. Let me help repair your reputation."

It might work. The best way to prove she wasn't a stalker would be to let Sebastian publicly shower her with affection. It wouldn't even have to be real . . . they could merely stroll around the artsy streets of Williamsburg to start restoring her reputation. Perhaps he would even grant an interview with the press to exonerate her. What happened in London could be attributed to an unfortunate misunderstanding caused by Sebastian's relapse into drugs, and her reputation could be restored.

Sanity hit her like a fist. She mustn't let Sebastian suck her into the whirlwind again. "Seb, I think you should leave."

He didn't move as he stared at her and waited. After a moment, he started cracking every knuckle on his right hand, the way he always did when nerves were getting the better of him.

"It's not going to end like this," he said.

"Maybe not, but I still need you to leave," she said, proud of how steady she managed to sound.

Sebastian closed the lid on his suitcase and secured the lock. "I still want to deliver Margo's research to you. We'll take this up again after you've had time to think," he said gently before heading to the door and closing it softly behind him.

"You're not seriously thinking of having anything to do with that guy, are you?" Anger made Jack's voice tight.

"No," she whispered. "Of course not." She shook herself and cleared her throat. "We should get back to working on the clock."

Jack gave a terse nod, but it occurred to her . . . tonight was the first time she'd seen Jack jealous on her behalf, and she cared enough about him to find that oddly wonderful.

Chapter Twenty-Two

Jack arrived at the Roost early. The nip of autumn was in the air, and dew on the grass glittered like diamonds as the sun rose. He stood before the Roost, its sagging lines and dark wood looking bedraggled and derelict, and he couldn't help but smile.

This was its last day located on this patch of land where it had sat for more than three centuries. Within the hour, a crane would lift the roof and carry it to a new location. Every board, window, and stone would be taken apart. Alice's sentimentality must be getting to him, because it was hard not to mourn just a bit for the old Roost.

"You've had quite a run," he whispered to the building. Soon it would be better than ever, positioned atop a solid foundation, wired for electricity, reinforced, and spiffed up, but it was still sad to see it taken apart. Nothing would ever be quite the same.

He was still staring at the Roost like a sentimental fool when Alice joined him. She looked unbelievably sexy in a slim-fitting suede jacket and tall leather boots. He slid an arm around her, and she was trembling. It was chilly, but not that cold.

He pulled her in front of him and wrapped her in his arms. "How are you doing, pretty lady?"

She shrugged. "I've been better. I know this is the right thing to do to save this place, but it will be hard to see it taken apart."

"Heard anything else from that fancy actor?"

She laughed a little. "Not a word. My head is screwed on a little tighter this morning."

He smoothed a strand of hair behind the shell of her ear. "Good," he said gently, relieved she had found her equilibrium.

Over the next hour, the heavy construction equipment arrived, the crane rumbling and moving toward the Roost like a vulture. Construction workers scrambled across the roof, securing cables and preparing for the lift. A few members of the press had arrived because dismantling the historic landmark was going to make the evening news.

Alice seemed determined to put a good face on things. "At least the Baltimore Ravens flag is gone, never to be seen again."

"I'll fly it outside my hotel room," he teased. He had been staying in the classy historic hotel owned by the Tuckers. Daisy Tucker gave him a good rate since she was still trying to curry his favor over the spat about the Roost.

Soon the construction crew had secured the cables to the roof, then they climbed down and the lifting was ready to begin. The engine of the crane rumbled, the driver pulled levers, and the cables went taut. The rumbling from the crane grew louder.

Alice rotated in his arms, burying her face in the crook of his neck. Every muscle in her body was tense, and she trembled even more.

"You're going to be okay," he murmured against her hair.

"I know, but I can't watch."

She didn't sound okay, and even he flinched a little as the roof began to lift a few inches. Bystanders began cheering, cameras were rolling, and the roof swayed as it was lifted higher.

Alice hugged him tighter. She was hating this, and the cheers from the crowd probably made it worse.

"Soon, the Roost will be put back together and welcoming thousands of people every month," he murmured against her hair. "It will be bigger and safer. You will have done your magic on the inside, and Reid's Roost will be the most popular gathering spot in all of Virginia. Once, this place was a home for people struggling to survive in the wilderness. It was a gristmill, a brewery, a hospital during the Civil War. It was a place where a lonely golf course designer and a drunk once camped out."

She smothered a laugh against his shoulder, but the creaking of the roof as it swayed in the air was nerve-racking. The crane rotated, carrying the roof clear of the building. The Roost looked strangely decapitated without the steeply pitched roof atop it, and he squeezed Alice tighter.

"Alice, this place has a new lease on life because *you* made it happen. No matter how long either of us lives, the Roost is going to outlast us both and be here for generations to come."

"Thanks, Jack," she whispered against his neck, the tears in her voice making his heart squeeze.

Jack waited until the roof was safely deposited onto the structural support that had been built to hold it. Over the next few hours, a dozen construction workers scrambled over the house to begin dismantling the second floor. Old nails were pulled, hammers banged, and mortar knocked to the ground. All they could do was watch as the professionals took over.

Alice, being Alice, came prepared with a picnic lunch for them. There was fried chicken, pasta salad with artichokes, and a peach pie with a lattice crust. All of it was packed in a wicker basket lined with a blue-and-white-checkered fabric. No paper plates for Alice. Her basket came with china plates and silverware strapped to the inside lid, and real wine glasses. She spread a blanket across the lumpy grass, and once all the food had been taken from the basket, she spread another cloth atop the flat basket lid to serve as a table.

"We're attracting attention." He smiled. "This is probably the fanciest picnic anyone has ever seen."

"Nonsense," Alice said as she raised her glass of white wine in a toast. "You're in Virginia. Picnics are an artform here."

They toasted and watched from a distance as work continued on the Roost. Everything was unfolding according to plan, but Jack kept a wary eye as more members of the press continued to arrive.

Alice was pleased with how her picnic was the perfect accompaniment to watch as work began on the Roost. Who could be anxious on a perfect autumn day with a picnic basket worthy of a *Better Homes & Gardens* magazine spread? The glass of pinot grigio had helped, and now she successfully adopted Jack's confidence as she watched the crane lift one log after another from the second story of the Roost.

It was going to be okay. The decaying Roost had been on its last legs, and now a team of experts was here to rebuild it better than before. Jack would be working on a golf course in Japan by the time the renovation was complete, but she would send him photos and invite him to return for its grand opening next year.

Jack elbowed her. "Do you recognize those guys?" he asked, nodding to some photographers standing near Micky Hayes and the rest of the local news crew.

They didn't look familiar. Instead of a shoulder-mount television camera, these guys had cameras with long zoom lenses.

And one of them was pointing it at *her*. She scrambled to her feet and reached for her basket, preparing to leave. Jack got up, too.

"You don't know them?" he asked, his voice grim.

"I don't, but Sebastian Bell is in town, and I have a very bad feeling about this." Tension gathered tighter as the other two men pointed those awful zoom lenses at her. Now even the local news guy had trained the video on her.

"I'll take care of this," Jack said. "This is private property, and I'll get them to back off."

Alice turned her back to the photographers and scrambled to clean up the remnants of lunch. She tossed the remainder of the wine and dumped the glasses into the basket. A wine stem broke, but it didn't slow her down because the reporters were strolling toward her. All of them!

She flung the plates and the chicken bones into the basket. It would make a greasy mess but she needed to get out of here, and no, she couldn't abandon the basket. Littering would add fuel to the social media hail of condemnation. Gingham fabric could be washed, but another round of intrusive photos would haunt her forever.

"Miss Chadwick?" one of them asked.

"*Professor* Chadwick," Jack corrected, and she winced. He meant well, but could she still consider herself a professor after being fired? It was one more thing the paparazzi could skewer her for.

"*Professor* Chadwick," the skinny guy corrected. "Do you have any comment on what Sebastian Bell posted about you this morning?"

Her stomach dropped. She'd uninstalled every social media app from her phone, so how could she possibly know what Sebastian said?

"I haven't read anything," she murmured, wadding up the picnic blanket and avoiding their eyes.

"It was a video," the skinny guy said. "He couldn't have been nicer. You really haven't seen it?"

Micky got his cell phone out and started scrolling. "Here it is," he said, turning the phone to her. There was Sebastian, looking remarkably casual in an open-collared white shirt, hair perfectly tousled, with a half-pained, sheepish look of charm as he spoke with a female reporter.

"Falling in love with Alice Chadwick is the best thing that ever happened to me. She didn't deserve any of the garbage that happened to her while I was in rehab. When I go to my grave, my biggest regret on this earth will have been letting Alice down."

The breath left her in a whoosh. Sebastian could always turn an elegant phrase, but this statement and apology were pitch perfect. *Sebastian* was perfect.

Well, he was still a rogue and a scoundrel and possibly battling a drug addiction, but he was as smoothly elegant as ever. It hurt to see.

The reporters kept their cameras trained on her, ready to record anything she said. What could she say? Sebastian had left her speechless.

"She doesn't have anything to say," Jack said. "This is private property, and I need you folks to leave."

"Professor Chadwick, if Sebastian was here, what would you like to say to him?"

She still stood mute, helpless to express the tangle of emotions roiling inside, and Jack stepped up to the plate.

"Alice is too polite to say anything, but she'd like to punch him in the jaw," Jack said bluntly. "Sebastian Bell hung her out to dry while he lounged in the south of France. A few pretty words can't blot that out."

"Professor Chadwick?" the skinny reporter asked.

Her tongue became unstuck. Jack couldn't begin to imagine the pressure Sebastian had been under, repeatedly carrying the weight of blockbuster movies on his shoulders. Seb wasn't perfect, but who among them was?

"I wish Sebastian nothing but the best," she said, and it was true. His good side far outweighed the bad, even if his weaknesses left her open to becoming a punching bag in the press and academia.

Far from pacifying them, her statement triggered a flurry of additional questions. Had she and Sebastian mended fences? How did they meet? Why was Sebastian in Williamsburg and were they seeing each other again?

Jack stepped in to deflect the firestorm. "Alice is way too classy for any of this, and all of you are standing on private property. *My* private property, and I'm asking you to leave immediately. You can go quietly, or I can call a couple of those cops our taxes pay for each year. Your choice."

Was there anything better than having a strong man defend her? She didn't need Jack's protection, but it felt good anyway. The journalists soon drifted away, and Alice reassembled the remnants of their picnic. She set out a basket of homemade strawberry shortcake cookies while Jack stretched out on the gingham blanket again.

"Thanks for taking the lead on that," she said with a nod to the last of the journalists leaving the site. "Sebastian is still difficult for me to talk about, and those cameras in my face made me freeze, so thanks."

"Anytime, Professor," he murmured as he settled his head into her lap for an after-lunch nap. He said it with such easy confidence, and yet, it wouldn't be anytime. Soon Jack would be gone, and she would be alone again. She smoothed his hair with gentle strokes, wishing it were otherwise.

Chapter Twenty-Three

Alice spent the evening creating a hand-crafted autumnal wreath, an annual tradition she always enjoyed, even though weaving the assortment of fresh greenery into the wires was a challenge. Her hands were full when her cell phone beeped. She ignored the incoming call to finish weaving the strands of grapevine through the dried herbs and eucalyptus leaves. The green and gold leaves were perfectly offset by miniature pinecones and bright red berries.

The phone rang again and she reached for a towel to wipe the grit from her hands before picking it up.

Sebastian's name lit up the screen, and she sighed. Jack would tell her to block the call, or maybe answer it and tell Sebastian to take a flying leap.

But she was a weakling and took the call. "Hi, Sebastian."

"Hello, gorgeous! Did you see the statement I released to the press this morning?"

Once again, he wanted to talk about himself, which shouldn't be a surprise. "I did. Thank you. It was very generous of you."

"Good! Can I come over?"

"No!" At last, she found a backbone and could sense Jack fist-pumping his approval.

"Are you sure? I never got around to showing you the research Margo found about that Helga lady. I brought it all the way from England."

She couldn't help herself. "What is it?"

"It's hard to describe, but she made an oversized photograph of an old tombstone that's crammed with information. I didn't want to send something like that through the mail. I came all the way from England to deliver it in person. You'll like it. Can I come over? Pretty please?"

She didn't trust herself alone with Sebastian, but Saint Helga was her Achilles heel and she desperately wanted to know what Sebastian had. She let out a ragged sigh.

"What's that sigh supposed to mean?" Sebastian asked, and for once he sounded uncertain.

"It means I want to know what Margo found, but I don't want to be alone with you."

"Then invite the golf guy over. Alice, I threw a major wrench into your life, and I'm glad you found someone to move ahead with. I'm happy for you."

"That was bad acting, Seb."

His laughter came through the phone, warm and self-deprecating. "Cut me a break. What happened to us was entirely my fault, and I've been bending over backwards to make it up to you. Nagging Margo to take another look at the Saint Helga case was the only way I knew to make amends."

Her hand tightened on the cell phone as her heart started thumping. "Let me call Jack first, and then you can come over."

Jack's presence would ensure Alice wouldn't do something stupid like fall under Sebastian's spell again. She called Jack, who was up to his knees fiddling with the waterfall basin. He was busy, but instantly vowed to come straight over once he heard what she wanted.

Jack must have broken every speed limit in the county, because he arrived less than ten minutes later. She was hanging the autumnal wreath on the front door when the tires on his obnoxious truck squealed as he turned into the parking lot. The engine cut off, his truck door slammed, and she turned to greet him.

His expression looked like a Viking intent on pillage as he stalked toward her. Dirt and sweat streaked his face, mud caked his boots, and a glint lit his steely eyes. "Nice wreath," he said. "Where is he?"

"He'll be over in a few minutes."

She led him inside, and Jack kicked the door closed, cupped her face between his palms, and kissed her. He tasted like coffee and smelled like perspiration mixed with a hint of Irish Spring soap. She didn't mind. Jack was a real man and smelled like one.

He went on and on kissing her, his breathing growing deeper until he grabbed her shoulders and pushed her back. "I like that you called me for help," he said. "I won't ever let that pompous creep take advantage of you again."

Jack's expression was so grim that she needed to lighten the mood. "My knight in shining armor?"

He laughed a bit and flashed her a wink. "It's how every man secretly thinks of himself. Alice, you don't need anyone to save you. You've taken some hits lately but survived it all without losing an ounce of dignity. You are pure class and can outshine all the Tuckers and those tired old professors on campus. Alice, you're the kind of woman Jane Austen only dreamed about writing."

A rush of happiness bloomed inside. It was the nicest compliment she'd ever had, and it was delivered by a man dirty from the golf course, who lacked all appreciation for fine literature or cultured manners, but she adored him all the same.

Even though he just tracked mud across her hardwood floors. She handed him a damp towel to clean his hands while she took care of the floor.

"I was mucking with the fountain," he grumbled while taking his work boots off. "I've had problems with it since the beginning and am sick of wading in to fix that pump."

Alice listened to his woes while swiping a bit of dirt that got smeared on her gauzy floral skirt, but it was easy enough to get off. She'd just finished the job when Sebastian knocked.

Jack bounded in front of her in his stocking feet to answer the door. "Hey there, Sam," he greeted.

Sebastian ignored the use of his real name and only had eyes for Alice as he stepped inside, holding a slim cardboard tube beneath his arm. His gaze flicked down her wrap dress with butterfly sleeves and a floaty skirt.

"I love a vintage chintz pattern," he said, his voice warm with appreciation as he nodded to the pastel tones of her dress. "There's nothing quite so feminine as a cottagecore wrap dress. I hope they stay in style forever."

"What did Margo give you?" Jack demanded.

Sebastian ignored him and proudly extended the skinny tube toward Alice, as if presenting her with the sword freshly pulled from the stone. "For you, my dear. I don't know what to make of it, but Margo swears you'll like it."

Alice grabbed the tube and wiggled a large roll of paper from its interior. It was a photograph, big enough to cover her entire dining table.

"It's a life-sized photograph of a tombstone from Yorkshire," Sebastian said, grabbing a candlestick to anchor a corner of the curling photograph. Jack placed additional candlesticks on the other three corners. "Margo hired a commercial photographer to go out to the cemetery and make a life-sized image of the Denby family tombstone. She thinks it might prove something."

This was the first Alice had heard of the name Denby. "Why does she think this would have anything to do with Reid's Roost?"

Sebastian retrieved a slip of paper from his pocket. "Margo cross-referenced the names Reid and Helga from archival records of the 1660s and was able to come up with this tombstone, the only documentation of the two names in such close proximity. She thinks this might relate to your settler."

The photograph showed a ledger tombstone, the sort of large flat stone used for family plots with room for plenty of inscriptions. Scaley white lichen marred the surface. Centuries of wind and rain eroded much of the slate, and the inscriptions were blurry but still legible:

Beneath this stone lays the body of Lord William Reid Denby,
who departed this life on 18 Dec 1668, aged 82.
Also his wife Mary Elizabeth Denby, died 12 Feb 1648.
Also his son William George, aged 2 years.
Also his son William James, aged 4 months.
Also his son William Reid Denby, who departed this earth in
1659 in his 36th year, beloved husband of Helga.

Alice folded her arms and stared hard at the stone. This was no smoking gun; it was merely a record of a family with too many dead children and a single reference to someone named Helga.

"The etchings are in different styles of fonts," Alice said. "That's surely because people's names were added over the decades by new engravers."

She started to pace and kept thinking aloud. "There's no record of Helga's death here, and the letter I found written in 1672 indicated that she sailed for Virginia because she still hoped for a child. Somebody named R. Santos built the Roost a decade earlier and carried quite a torch for Helga. He possibly scratched her name in the window and made an infinity symbol."

Jack pointed to the last line on the tombstone. "The guy she was married to in England died in 1659, but why did she wait thirteen years to sail to America? What was holding her back?"

It was impossible to guess the motives for people who died hundreds of years ago. Could it have been a forbidden love affair? Lack of money to make the journey? Reid Santos seemed rich enough to build a fine house with expensive diamond-paned windows. He was able to get a license to operate the ferry in Jamestown, so he would have been one of the wealthiest men in the village. Money should have been no obstacle.

Alice turned to Sebastian. "Was Margo able to find any evidence of someone named Reid Santos? When I looked in February, I couldn't find anything, but I was searching in the wrong decade."

"She looked and came up empty," Sebastian said. "It's like the guy came out of nowhere."

Alice nodded. "The name Santos seems a mismatch for the early settlers of Jamestown. It sounds Spanish. Could he have been one of the survivors of the Spanish Armada who washed ashore in England? I heard there were quite a few who made it ashore and had to live their lives on the run."

Sebastian smirked. "The Spanish Armada was wiped out in 1588. You're a hundred years off, darling."

"Don't call her darling," Jack said.

"No chest-thumping, please," Alice said, still staring hard at the old tombstone. The Denby family patriarch and his only surviving son both shared the middle name of Reid. Could the Reid Santos who built the Roost have been an illegitimate son of the Denby patriarch? Could that account for a forbidden romance with Helga and why he hid Helga's name in code? Falling in love with his brother's wife would certainly be a reason to hide his love for Helga.

"Well?" Sebastian asked. "Do you think you can make anything out of this?"

"I don't know, but thank you for bringing this to me. The Denby family is new to me, and now I've got another lead to follow."

"Anytime," Sebastian tossed off. "You look great, Alice."

"So do you," she instinctively replied, and Sebastian preened.

"It's from three months baking under the Mediterranean skies," he said. "The production company had me in total lockdown at the rehab place. They paid for a fitness coach and an esthetician to get my skin in shape. It's not easy being this gorgeous."

"It's not easy stopping myself from punching you in the throat," Jack muttered, but Alice waved the comment away.

"I'm serious, Sebastian. Are you okay? Really?"

Sebastian dropped the cocksure grin. "Going through detox was the worst nine days of my life. They kept me there for three months to make sure it stuck. Now it's up to me to walk the straight and narrow. I'm clean now. I've got endless regrets, but what happened to you is at the top of the list. It's why I hounded Margo to come up with something about your mysterious Helga, but maybe it won't lead to anything after all. Tell me what you want, Alice. Order me to go fetch you pearls from the east or a bit of moondust from outer space. If it's within my power, I'll get it for you."

Alice had a ready answer. "I want my name back on the movie credits for *Emma*."

Sebastian grinned. "Already done."

"It is?" Hope bloomed inside, triggering a burst of joy so powerful it felt like she could float. Sebastian gave a smug smile.

"I told Graham to get your name added back to the credits or I was going to bail on season two of *The King's Redemption*."

"Can you do that? I thought you were under contract."

Sebastian gave a nonchalant shrug. "It wouldn't be easy, but the studio would rather keep me happy than hire lawyers to fight over small potatoes. Not that you're small potatoes!" he rushed to say. "Anyway, your name is back in the movie credits, and I'll do whatever humanly possible to restore your reputation."

Jack didn't seem impressed. "I'd be more impressed if you fired Graham for leaking Alice's photo to the press."

Alice drew in a sharp breath. From the moment she'd arrived in England, Graham Garfield had slithered around Sebastian like a shadow—always watching, always pulling strings. She would love nothing more than to see him face consequences for ruining her career. She turned to Sebastian, hope rising.

But he only gave an exaggerated sigh and waved a hand. "Darling, don't ask me to do that. Sacking Graham would be an absolute nightmare. He's a bit of a snake, but he gets things done. Finding a new agent now would be such a headache."

Alice blinked. The words stung, even if they weren't a surprise. Sebastian's charm had always masked a certain laziness when it came to taking responsibility.

Jack didn't bother with diplomacy. "The man torched her reputation while you were off snorting coke. And you're still letting him run your career?" His voice was low but fierce. "Grow a spine."

Sebastian wrinkled his nose as he glanced at her. "Honestly, Alice—what do you see in this guy?"

He sounded genuinely baffled, but Alice locked gazes with Jack. She saw a *man*. His shirt was filthy from a long day at the worksite and his arms were scarred with years of needle marks from treating his hemophilia, but he never let adversity blot out his dreams. He was a man who worked hard, planned ahead, created jobs, and could laugh at himself as easily as he conquered every obstacle in his path.

"I see a man I've been very lucky to meet," she said, never looking away from Jack's gaze.

The corners of his eyes crinkled as affection lit a fire in them. "Right back at you, Professor."

She basked in that affection shining in his eyes. He would be leaving soon, and even as she dreaded losing him, memories of their golden, bittersweet summer would linger forever.

Chapter Twenty-Four

Alice arrived at the construction site first thing the following morning and was relieved to see that Jack had arranged for security to block the end of the rural lane leading to the Roost. A guard checked the identification of anyone who wanted to get through, which meant the construction zone was blessedly free of distractions, photographers, and onlookers.

A fresh autumn breeze greeted her as she stepped from her car into a glorious morning. Acorn caps crunched underfoot and her boots sliced through the long grass, still damp with dew. Everything had a rich, peaty smell. Was this what the settlers would have experienced three hundred years ago? The rustle of autumn leaves and the soft, damp give of the earth beneath her feet would have been the same. So too the chirping of birds in the sycamore trees and the musky-sweet scent of the field grass going dormant.

The Roost was halfway dismantled. Without its roof or second story, it looked naked and exposed. The stone chimney remained untouched, sticking up from the ground floor and encased in scaffolding from the ground to its top. Taking the chimney down stone by stone would be their first task today.

Jack looked cautious as he approached. "Any more trouble last night?"

He didn't even need to mention Sebastian's name. "No trouble," she said easily. "Why are you dressed like that?" Instead of chinos and a golf shirt, he wore jeans, work boots, and a pair of heavy-duty gloves.

"I'm going to help take the chimney apart," he said. "Nothing needs my attention at the golf course and this seems like more fun."

She eyed the scaffolding. A couple of workers wearing hard hats and goggles scrambled up the widely spaced bars, hand over hand, on their journey to the top of the chimney. Hammers and chisels dangled from their work belts, and it looked like a dangerous job. For someone like Jack, maybe even deadly.

"Are you sure?" she asked. "Chiseling the stones out of the mortar might cause a cut and then—"

He stopped her worries with a kiss. "I've been living with hemophilia all my life," he said. "I'm always careful, but I can't live my life wrapped in cotton and watching from the sidelines."

Jack gave her another quick kiss before putting on a hard hat and heading up the scaffolding. A cherry picker with a platform basket was positioned beside the top of the chimney to collect the stones.

The tapping of chisels and mallets filled the air. She shaded her eyes to watch Jack as he climbed to the top of the chimney. The flash of his white smile in his tanned face showed his delight as he jawboned with the other workers. Was he paying full attention? His skin glistened with sweat as he wiggled a metal shim beneath a stone, rocking it free of the mortar. A fellow worker lifted the rock free and passed it over to a man standing in the basket of the cherry picker. Bits of mortar rained down, pinging on the rungs of the scaffolding.

She couldn't look. Jack might want to risk his neck playing macho man, but standing mutely down here while he did it was torture.

Her cell phone vibrated, and Sebastian's name appeared on the screen. Accepting his call would be as reckless as Jack risking a catastrophic accident by dismantling the chimney, but she couldn't help herself and accepted the call.

"Yeah, Seb, what is it?"

She had to cover her other ear against the construction noise to hear him. "The security guards won't let me through," he said. "I'm trapped at the end of the drive. There are reporters here, and none of us can get through."

"That's why Jack hired security," she pointed out. Sebastian's presence was going to trigger a fresh round of publicity she didn't need.

"Can't you let me through? I came all the way from London to see the Roost in person."

She sighed. Back when she was in the depths of her infatuation with him, she told Sebastian all about the Roost and its layers of history. He seemed genuinely curious and asked insightful questions. He even offered his own speculation and got Margo to do some additional research.

She couldn't deny him the opportunity to see the place he had helped her research. "Pass the phone to the guard," she said, feeling like a pushover. All it took was a few words with the guard to grant Sebastian permission to enter the site.

Five minutes later he came strolling up the path, once again looking like a Ralph Lauren model, this time the safari version. He wore a white, open-collar shirt with its cuffs rolled up and khaki trousers, as though he was prepared to hunt a lion or pitch a tent on the African savanna.

"So that's Reid's Roost," he said with a nod to the halfway-pulled-down building.

"It *was* Reid's Roost," she replied. Without its roof, the chimney mostly dismantled, and the second floor laying in stacks of logs, the remnants of the building looked puny and sad. It was a little embarrassing to have painted such a grandiose picture of it for Sebastian when England was full of castles and manor houses far older and more impressive.

"The roof and the logs from the second story are in those tents," she said with a nod to the two oversized canvas tents erected near the golf course.

"Give me a tour," Sebastian wheedled, and she obliged. He was full of questions, and within minutes their old friendship was coming back to life. She spread a blanket well away from the falling bits of mortar to watch the dismantling of the chimney.

After an hour, the job was halfway complete, with only about eight more feet to go. At some point Jack spotted Sebastian and climbed down the scaffolding to approach them.

"What's *he* doing here?" Jack asked, swiping a grubby forearm across his sweaty face. Sebastian came dressed like a gorgeous outdoorsman, but Jack was the real deal, with sweat and soot covering his muscled arms.

"I'm curious about the Roost," Sebastian said.

"You scammed your way through security."

Alice bit her lip. "Actually, I let him in."

Instead of getting annoyed, Jack looked mildly amused. "You're way too tender-hearted and forgiving."

"Is that a flaw?"

He paused, tilting his head as if genuinely weighing the answer. "I'm not sure," he said at last. "It's either a glaring weakness or the purest form of selfless Christian compassion. But right now"—his smile deepened—"I'm not in the mood to argue about it." He tossed a pair of work gloves to her and she caught them. "Come on over and help us take down the rest of the chimney."

She instinctively recoiled. She'd just painted her nails last night and construction work wasn't really her thing. "The others are far more qualified," she hedged, but Jack wasn't having it.

"Maybe, but you need to trust me. The crane is going to lift the lintel stone, then pulling the rest of the rocks down will go quickly. Put the gloves on, get off your tush, and follow me."

"That's rather rude," Sebastian began, but once again, Jack ignored him.

"You're going to want to experience this," he told her. "I can't describe it, but the second you get near that fireplace you'll know what I mean."

Curiosity began to gnaw, not so much because of what he said, but from his expression. His eyes glinted in anticipation, as if a tremendous surprise awaited her.

"Okay," she said, tugging on the gloves. The battered leather gloves were laughably too big and the fingers had been permanently molded to a man's hand. They were dirty and grubby, but she needed them if she was to handle the heavy building stones. Jack plopped a hard hat on her head, and she felt a little silly as she approached the Roost.

How strange it felt to walk inside this once-familiar house. It had always been so dim inside, but now everything was open and exposed to the bright sky above. Jack stood beside the fireplace, one hand propped on the massive slab of the lintel stone stretching across the top opening of the fireplace. It probably weighed a thousand pounds.

"Come closer," Jack urged.

She drifted a few steps forward, then she caught it . . . the reason Jack beckoned her here. That smell! The smoky aroma of a thousand home-cooked meals emanated from the fireplace. Chipping away at the mortar had exposed pockets of soot and residue to the air. It smelled like bacon and bread and meaty stew.

It sent shivers down her arms, and she locked gazes with him. "You feel it too?"

"I feel it," he confirmed. "We could smell all those cooking aromas the second we lifted the capstone off the chimney. Probably thousands of meals were cooked in old cast-iron pots, pumping up smoke that smelled like bacon and homemade soup."

"Biscuits," she added.

"Warm bread and hot apple pies."

Alice leaned closer to inhale again, and it seemed she could smell every one of the foods they listed. How often had women through the centuries cooked at this exact spot? Dismantling the chimney released the scent molecules that had been trapped in the chimney mortar for centuries. The remnants of those former meals danced in the air, an echo from long ago. The thought triggered another shiver.

"Who invited you inside?" Jack said in a surly tone.

Alice whirled to see Sebastian, sporting his devil-may-care grin as he strolled inside.

"The lady out front gave me a hard hat and said it would be okay to come inside. You don't mind, do you, Alice?"

It was hard to resist Sebastian, but she needed to do a better job of it. "Jack owns this place," she said. "It's up to him."

Jack looked heavenward and muttered a string of salty curses, but it wasn't in his nature to be needlessly unkind. "Don't get into any trouble," he grumbled.

Sebastian strolled to the fireplace and ran the flat of his hand across the lintel. "I'll bet this old stone could tell a lot of interesting stories." He ran his hand across the surface, then zeroed in on the palm frond carved into the corner. It was the same doodle Alice had seen on the letter connecting Helga to this house.

"Look at that, a Commonwealth wreath," Sebastian murmured as he traced the palm fronds, then gave a little shudder. "Creepy."

Alice blinked in confusion. "Creepy? How so?"

"Commonwealth wreaths were used by followers of Oliver Cromwell during the Puritan Revolution."

She looked again, studying the pair of curved palm fronds more closely. "Is there some special meaning behind it?"

"Absolutely," Sebastian said cheerfully. "After they beheaded the king, the Puritans refused to use English coins because they had the king's face on them. They melted them down to mint new coins and wanted a Christian symbol instead of a monarch. They chose palm fronds, a symbol of Christ's triumph, to surround the outer rim of the coin. Come on, Alice, you should be watching my miniseries. It's all in there."

Alice gaped at the tiny emblem with new eyes. Could it really be a symbol of the Puritan Commonwealth? And if it was . . . did that make Helga and the man who built the Roost part of the Puritan Revolution?

If Reid Santos and Helga had been followers of Oliver Cromwell during the bloody English Civil War, it could have been an excellent reason a wealthy man would need to flee to the New World.

After a crane lifted the massive lintel stone and carried it to the staging area, Jack headed back inside the Roost to continue dismantling the fireplace. Now that the stone had been safely removed, it wouldn't take long to finish taking apart the rest of the fireplace. Most of the fireplace was made of local stone, but the lining of the fireplace was crude, handmade brick. He started chiseling at the line of bricks that had been directly beneath the lintel stone.

It was better here than outside, where he'd have to watch Alice lounging on the picnic blanket alongside Sebastian Bell.

Sam Bartholomew, he silently corrected himself. Everything about the man was a fraud, from his name to his surgically corrected nose. He tamped down his frustration and went back to chipping away at the mortar between the bricks. The interior of the cooking area was coated with creosote, the oily black sludge from years of wood-burning fires. Outside, Sebastian looked fresh as a daisy, while Jack was smudged with soot and sweat. It was tempting to flop down next to Alice on the blanket and draw her into a big, sweaty hug. A man was supposed to get dirty . . . not submit to facials, manicures, and wear everyday clothes that required dry-cleaning.

He focused on the next layer of bricks, angling his chisel carefully because this section had an extra-thick layer of mortar. Taps with the mallet slowly chipped the soot-blackened mortar away, revealing the smooth beige mortar that hadn't seen daylight in over three hundred years. He rocked the brick free of the mortar and carefully set it with the other bricks.

A chunk of the remaining mortar fell into a cavity beneath the brick he had just removed. That was odd. The bricks were uniform in size, so they should have been snug. A cavity like this made no sense, so it was probably deliberate. It was about the size of a deck of cards. He yanked off his gloves to scoop out crumbles of mortar from the hollow. It was brittle, dry, and grainy . . . but there was something smooth inside the cavity.

He stirred his fingers around until he grasped the cold and smooth object. He lifted it out and swiped away the grit.

In the palm of his hand lay a heavy gold signet ring.

Chapter Twenty-Five

Alice took the mysterious ring Jack found to an expert. Daisy Tucker had a fine eye for antique jewelry and managed the gift shop at the Tucker Inn located in downtown Williamsburg. The three-room gallery was much more than a mere "gift shop." One room specialized in authentic colonial antiques, another in high-end gifts and clothing, and the final room sold estate jewelry.

"It's clearly a signet ring," Daisy said from her position behind the jewelry counter.

Alice nodded. "It had to have been hidden in that fireplace since the Roost was first built. It was beneath the lintel stone, and whoever put it there never wanted it to be found."

Daisy scrutinized the heavy, masculine ring with a jeweler's loupe for a better view of the coat of arms pressed into the flat bezel of the ring. In olden days, a coat of arms identified the wearer's family lineage and their loyalty with tiny symbolic markings. The coat of arms on this ring featured six tiny acorns in a half-circle above the rearing stag. The shank of the ring was etched with a scalloped shell pattern.

"Do you know what the acorns mean?" Alice asked.

"I have no idea, but they keep track of these things in England," Daisy replied. "The College of Arms in London is the official authority for issuing coats of arms and tracking related symbols. It's our first place to check."

Alice hoped to find a quick answer at the College of Arms website, but quickly ran out of gas. According to the website, there were thousands of English family crests dating back to the twelfth century, and identifying a crest usually required the help of a specialist. A search could be initiated by submitting a series of photographs and paying a deposit.

Alice was used to leaning on specialists for research like this. She placed the ring on a velvet pad to take several photographs from all angles. After uploading them to the website, she paid a deposit with her credit card and hit send to initiate the search.

"Do you know how long it will take to get an answer?" Daisy asked once Alice returned the ring to her purse.

"About two weeks," she said. "Why are you looking so strange?"

Daisy bit her lip and paced before the case of Victorian cameo brooches. "Well," she said reluctantly, "I know Jack bought the Roost from Kingsley in some sort of underhanded deal, but I don't think it included the contents of the Roost, did it?"

Alice blanched at the implied audacity of the statement. The deal happened because the Tuckers hadn't been honest about their finances, and Jack kept them all out of court by agreeing to a quick settlement instead of seeking criminal charges. Alice was probably the least confrontational person in the state of Virginia, but she wasn't going to let Daisy claim this ring.

"It cost Jack sixty thousand dollars to pay off the mortgage Kingsley hid from him. He is entitled to everything on those five acres, including the ring. Jack plays hardball, and you'll poke a sleeping dragon if you push this."

Daisy giggled and gave Alice's shoulder a friendly nudge. "Don't mind me," Daisy said. "No respectable Southern woman can resist making a play for a bit of heirloom jewelry. Forget I said anything."

Alice was still thinking about the incident as she prepared dinner at her townhouse for Jack. She'd made chicken salad sandwiches with the crusts cut off because they were his favorite. The spinach salad came from her own backyard, with freshly picked spinach leaves, red onions, and a little raspberry vinaigrette dressing.

He probably wouldn't notice that the blue hobnail drinking glasses perfectly coordinated with the Spode dishes. What man would? She didn't care. This was going to be one of the last evening meals she would make for Jack, and she wanted it to be perfect. He would be leaving for Japan at the end of the week, and she'd probably never see him again.

The *rat-a-tat-tat* at the door banished her gloomy thoughts. She fairly skipped to the door and flung it open. Jack greeted her with one of those devilish smiles and a heart-stopping kiss. She was grinning by the time he lifted his head.

"What smells so good?"

"Blueberry pie, but I've got chicken salad sandwiches and a spinach salad first."

He kissed her again. "Sounds great."

As expected, he didn't comment on the table layout or compliment the linen napkins she took out of storage. He devoured the meal like a hungry wolf, but that was fine. She liked a man with a healthy appetite.

He was still shoveling down the blueberry pie when she set the gold signet ring on the table. "I've sent a request to London to ask for identification of this family crest," she said. "The answer might take a couple of weeks to get here."

When she warned Jack that Daisy suggested the ring might belong to the Tuckers, he shoved the ring onto his finger. "She'll have to pry it off me. That woman has a lot of nerve."

"Don't think badly of her," Alice said. "Antique jewelry brings out the worst in Southern belles, but I set her straight about who owns it."

"How much do you think it's worth?"

Alice straightened. "I have no idea, but you're not thinking of selling it, are you?"

"Not until I learn the story behind it. Once we can figure out who it belonged to, it will probably make it even more valuable."

She rocked back in her seat. "How can you even think about selling something this priceless?"

"Whoa . . . Hang on to your horses, Professor. You can do whatever research you want with it, but once we know where it came from and how it got into that fireplace, of course I'm going to sell it. I'm up to my eyeballs in debt and can't afford to overlook a windfall like this."

Not everyone valued the historic heritage of Virginia, but to sell an extraordinary relic was unthinkable. "Don't be hasty, Jack. Maybe I can find a buyer who will donate it to a museum. It shouldn't disappear into some rich person's private collection."

Jack shrugged. "So long as that rich person can pay the highest bid, I'll be happy to turn it over. Just get your research done before I go to Japan because I could use the cash."

"Don't you know how short-sighted and venal that sounds?"

His eyes narrowed. "I don't even know what 'venal' means, but I'm guessing it's not good."

"It means a seedy and self-interested desire to make money. Jack! Be patient. This ring is priceless and belongs right here in the Tidewater." She clasped the arms of her chair to stop her hands from shaking. Jack had that angry bulldog look that made her want to shrink.

"Well, princess . . . you and I grew up in different neighborhoods. I didn't have sailing lessons or summers in France. I grew up with foster care and food stamps and medical bills I couldn't pay, and hanging on to a useless gold ring doesn't fit into my portfolio. Got it?"

She shot to her feet, turning her back on him to head into the kitchen. A quick squirt of dishwashing liquid and a jet of hot water pouring from the spigot gave her an excuse not to look at him. If she did, she might cry, and she needed to gather her thoughts.

Why did she keep falling in love with inappropriate men? Jack didn't believe in setting down roots; he believed in building a bank account. Despite everything they'd shared over this magical summer and autumn, he was going to do exactly as he always said and pull up his stakes to leave.

She cut off the hot water but still couldn't face him. She braced her hands on the cool porcelain sink, staring at the kitchen window that normally overlooked her herb garden, but because it was night and the lights were on, it was like a mirror and all she could see was Jack's reflection standing behind her. He stood motionless with his arms folded; his face grim.

"Are you going to live the rest of your life like this?" she asked. "Never putting down roots, never making real friends or forming a family?"

Nothing but silence came from behind. She grabbed a sponge and began aimlessly sloshing soapy water over a salad bowl. "Falling in love and setting down roots is scary. I'm scared to death at this very moment because I know you're probably going to reject me, and that's going to hurt, but I'm willing to risk it."

She met his gaze in the window's reflection. He still hadn't moved a muscle, but his expression was pained.

"Alice, I need to get away from you."

She turned around to face him. "Do I make your life that miserable?"

"No, you've made it wonderful, and you know that. You also know that I live my life on the road and have no intention of ever settling down. I've always been honest about that."

"You don't have to live like a nomad forever," she choked out. "Stay here and run the golf course."

"And see you every day?" She flinched, and he softened his tone. "Alice, we're not going to get across the finish line together. You deserve someone better than me who will be happy to settle down and build a big, happy family with you. I don't want to stand on the sidelines and watch. Next week I'm leaving for Japan, and I won't come back."

The anguish in his voice was a dead giveaway that he was struggling. Maybe all he needed was the confidence that he could stay. "Do you really want to go through the rest of your life with no family? No roots?"

He nodded. "Just because I'm not like you doesn't make it wrong."

She sighed, debating whether she should bring up the heart of the problem. For all his self-confidence and bravado, Jack feared the emotional risk of forming ties, so he took pride in his itinerant lifestyle and never looked back.

She scrambled for the words to help him view the world through a different lens. "You went through a lot of rejection while growing up," she said, venturing cautiously into dangerous territory. "I can understand that the thought of forming lasting ties is a risk, but living like a nomad is a bigger one. Don't you want to be part of a family? Part of a community? The human race isn't meant to—"

"You know what, Alice? Shut up. Shut the heck up and quit nagging. Settling down isn't for everyone, and I don't see the world through rose-colored glasses."

"Maybe you should try it."

Her cell phone buzzed from its position on the kitchen counter, and Sebastian's name flashed on the screen.

"Don't answer it," Jack said.

She reached for a towel to dry her hands and strode toward the phone.

"Alice! Don't answer it."

Who was he to give her orders? He was on his way to Japan and out of her life. She picked up the phone, tapped the button, and held it to her ear. "Hey, Sebastian," she said, staring straight at Jack.

"Hello, gorgeous. Can I take you out to dinner?"

The phone wasn't on speaker, but given the furious look from Jack, he overheard.

"Sorry, I've already eaten."

Jack grabbed the phone and hung up the call.

"You had no right to do that," she sputtered.

"Yes, I did."

She stormed over to the globe in the corner and whirled it to show Japan. "There!" she said, landing her finger on the country that was literally on the other side of the world. "You just said you can't wait to go to Japan, so I don't see any reason I can't speak with a man whose friendship I value and who actually wants to be with me."

"He's a drug addict and always will be."

"He's an imperfect human being, and aren't we all."

Jack scoffed. "*You're* not," he taunted. "Look at this place. Jane Austen would feel right at home here with your lace doilies and homemade jam, all tied up with a neat little bow. Life isn't a Jane Austen novel, and I'm not one of her buttoned-up heroes. I'm a flesh-and-blood man, Alice, not some fantasy figure in a cravat."

Alice flinched. What was so wrong in striving to be perfect? Striving for a life above the crass behavior and loose morals of the day? Anger boiled over and she couldn't contain it any longer.

"Oh shut up! I'm done listening to your insults. The door is over there—you can leave."

Jack scooped up the signet ring and stormed from the room, slamming the door on his way out.

Chapter Twenty-Six

Jack arrived at the construction site before dawn. His flight to Japan was in five days and he couldn't wait to get out of town. The golf course was ready to go, and sticking around to oversee the resurrection of the Roost was the only thing holding him back from leaving immediately and putting Alice behind him forever.

The security guard at the base of the road was already in place. Jack slowed his truck and rolled down the window. "If Sebastian Bell shows up, tell him he can't get in."

"Got it," the guard said, and Jack felt a guilty thrill from giving the order. He owned the Roost and the land it sat on, which meant he got to set the rules. No Sebastian Bell. Heck, he could ban Alice if he wanted. After last night, he had zero desire to endure another round of her holier-than-thou pronouncements. He'd been nothing but honest with her, and now she was pecking him to death with a list of demands to fix himself.

He met with Zeke, the lead contractor, at the concrete foundation that would soon support the new addition to the Roost. The stub-out pipes stuck up from the concrete like sentinels, ready for the plumbing and electrical systems.

"Have we got all the electrical permits done?"

Zeke nodded. "The state guy came by yesterday and confirmed everything is in order."

"Good," Jack said. "I want to get everything squared away for the next stage of construction before I leave. With luck, I'll be out of here on Friday. Do you see any problems with that?"

"Nope," Zeke said. "So long as you answer your cell phone, I can keep you in the loop no matter where you are."

It was exactly what he wanted to hear. He spent the next twenty minutes walking through the construction site, inspecting the stakes for the future terraced gardens, the meandering walkways, and the wooden balcony that would someday overlook Saint Helga's Spring. At the Roost, the final stage of prying up the original floorboards was underway. The air was filled with the sounds of clattering hammers, squeaks of old wood, and pings from hand-forged nails being collected in a tin can. Those old nails couldn't be reused, but Alice planned to put them on display in clear glass jars in the tavern.

Alice's blue Prius slowly turned onto the parking lot. He turned away and sighed, wishing she hadn't come. Everything about seeing Alice hurt, but he owed her too much to let last night fester any longer. He rubbed the back of his neck, jaw tight. He wasn't good at this. Never had been. But he owed her something—maybe not an apology, but a clean ending. He squared his shoulders and walked to meet her.

"Hey, Jack," she said in her eternally soft and kind voice when she got out of her car.

He nodded but didn't look at her. "What's up, Alice? Is there anything you need my help with? I'm working over at the golf course today, so I don't have much time." The words came out colder than he intended, but he didn't take them back. Better to draw the line cleanly.

"I wanted to say I'm sorry about last night."

He kept his gaze focused on the line of trees in the distance. "Yeah, me too. It doesn't change anything, though. I'm leaving Virginia; you're staying; end of story."

"Have you thought any more about going to see your father?"

His cell phone buzzed in his pocket. The sound was sharp and sudden, and for once, he was grateful. Saved by the bell.

He pulled it out, answering without even glancing at her.

"Jack, we've got a big problem at the waterfall," the golf course manager said. "The water has stopped flowing and we can't get it working again. Should I call the engineers in?"

Jack bit back a curse. That pump had been wonky since the beginning, and he could only pray the entire waterfall wouldn't need dismantling to replace it with an entirely new system.

"Hold off on that; I'll be right there," he said, then did an about-face to stride toward the waterfall.

Naturally, Alice had overheard and started following him. She was probably worried water might spill over into the wetlands around Saint Helga's Spring, and if that happened, he'd end up with another environmental cleanup bill.

His annoyance ratcheted higher as he drew near the waterfall, his feet sinking into the soft soil of the fairway, leaving ugly footprints on the pristine grass. He plopped down onto one of the boulders lining the artificial pond to yank off his shoes and socks.

"Jack, time is growing short, and your father needs you," Alice said. "Are you going to keep running for the rest of your life?"

He yanked off his second sock, balled it up, and threw it to the side. "You and your happily-ever-afters," he groused. "How did that work out for you and Sebastian? Or your parents? Those two are drill sergeants, not husband and wife."

"*Your* parents were happy," she retorted. "You said your father idolized your mother."

"He did, and then he fell apart after she died and became a useless drunk. It taught me the value of self-reliance. I don't need anyone, with the exception of a good doctor and an occasional lawyer."

Alice rolled her eyes heavenward. "You are the most cynical man I know."

He braced his hand on the boulder as he stepped into the frigid water. "And you're the most naive woman in the solar system."

The pump was near the base of the waterfall a few yards away. He carefully moved toward it, water saturating his jeans as it covered his knees, then his thighs. Water sloshed and cold droplets spattered his face.

"Shouldn't someone else do this?" Alice said from the edge.

"I need to know what the problem is. If it's what I suspect, I'll be able to fix it." He didn't have a spare thousand bucks to call the fountain engineers again if it was a simple matter of a clogged intake valve.

He unhooked his watch, yanked his phone from his pocket, and handed them both to Alice. "Will you hold these, please?"

It would be better if he had a pair of goggles so he could go down and get a good look, but his arms were long enough to reach the intake valve.

Sure enough, the valve was blocked. If it was just silt or vegetation clogging the valve, it wouldn't be a big deal—but this was a major problem. The synthetic lining from the bottom of the pond somehow got sucked up and dragged into the valve, completely blocking it. He yanked at the liner but was unable to make progress. This would require the pond to be drained and the installation of a new liner if he couldn't get it out.

He tugged at the slippery lining so hard he fell backward, water reaching up to his shoulders.

"Jack, be careful," Alice called from the shore, but he almost had that liner out. The sucking noise proved it. A few more good tugs and the water would be flowing again.

He got a firmer grasp on the lining and cleared it all out, grinning in satisfaction as the trickling water percolated through the lines again.

"Watch out!" Alice screamed, but a blast of water hit him in the head from above, knocking him down hard.

Alice shivered on the edge of the waterfall, listening to the wail of the ambulance siren in the distance. She was soaking wet from head to toe. Once Jack unclogged the intake valve, a blast of water came shooting from a pipe and hit Jack so hard he fell, smacked his head against a boulder, and lost consciousness.

She'd jumped in the pond to hold his face out of the water so he could breathe, but she wasn't strong enough to lift him up the steep bank of the pond. Thankfully, a pair of men from the ground crew heard her scream and lugged him onto the grass.

Jack's blood was all over her. He'd been unconscious for several minutes after they dragged him onto the green, but he was starting to come around.

"You're going to be okay," she said to Jack. "The ambulance has just turned on to the road."

Jack stared at the clouds above, his face chalk white and eyes pained and frightened.

"M-my medical card," he said in a shaking voice. "In my wallet."

Someone grabbed the wallet and located the card.

She wasn't used to seeing him so scared. She'd learned an injury to the head was one of the worst things for a hemophiliac. She'd told the 911 operator about his condition, and they instructed her to keep him as still as possible. Even now blood could be pooling inside his skull, leading to unbearable pressure and compressing his brain tissue.

The ambulance rolled across the golf course and halted a few yards away. A medic hopped out of the front seat and strode toward them while two others unloaded a stretcher from the back.

The lead medic knelt down beside Jack. "Sir, can you hear me?"

"Yeah," Jack said.

"How many fingers am I holding up?"

"Three."

That had to be good. If his brain was in bad shape, he might be too confused to answer.

"We're going to take you straight to the hospital to get some clotting factor into you. Then a bunch of docs will do their thing, okay?"

"Yeah," Jack said again, this time his teeth beginning to chatter. Was it from the cold or from fright? She'd been shaking like a leaf ever since getting out of the pond.

One of the EMTs held Jack's head while another slipped a collar around his neck. Once it was secured, they slid a plastic backboard beneath him.

"Who's coming to the hospital with him?" an EMT asked.

"I am," Alice automatically said, and mercifully, Jack didn't countermand her. She didn't know what to expect, but Jack needed someone with him at the hospital, and she wanted to be that person.

Chapter Twenty-Seven

The next five days were the longest of Alice's life. Jack had been put into an induced coma because the neurologist said it would reduce the brain's metabolic demand and hopefully stabilize the bleeding. Jack's brain bleed was severe, and unless it could be controlled, it could lead to a seizure and permanent brain damage. Keeping him in a controlled, sedated state was his best chance of survival.

At least she was allowed to remain in his room, which was a major concession since the first thing the hospital staff wanted to know was Jack's next of kin. Aside from a father he hadn't seen in decades and a stepmother he never met, there was no one. She scrolled through his cell phone, looking for an emergency contact, but came up empty.

The hospital let her stay, but with the recommendation that Alice contact Jack's parents.

She did. A string of unanswered text messages from Jack's stepmother were still on his phone, and she sent a brief message alerting Sophie to Jack's condition.

She framed the message in the most positive terms possible, but as she looked at Jack in the center of the hospital bed, hooked up to monitors and beeping machines, it was hard to be optimistic. He looked awful, with dark shadows beneath his eyes and a bruised, swollen lump at his temple. The plastic neck brace kept his head immobile and a cannula was taped beneath his nose to supply supplemental oxygen. His ankle looked hideous. The fall had caused an ankle sprain and the swelling in the joint had reached monstrous proportions. The orthopedic surgeon warned this would cause cartilage damage and could ultimately require a joint replacement if it happened again. Both of Jack's arms were hooked up to IVs that dribbled drugs, nutrition, and most importantly, a steady supply of Factor VIII plasma to heal the internal damage to his brain.

The nurses said Jack might have some level of subconscious awareness and suggested Alice speak words of comfort to him. It was the reason she refused to leave his bedside.

"The greens look terrific," she said. "The club's new ground manager came by earlier today and said that three groups of golfers played a test round, and they all loved it." The waterfall was a mess and the ambulance left huge gouges in the greens that still needed repair, but Alice stuck to positive messages.

"The Roost is already being reassembled," she continued. "Zeke is sending me photographs. The fireplace and chimney are back in place, secured with brand-new mortar. They color-matched the mortar so it looks exactly like what was used before. The entire ground floor has been reassembled and the floors laid. They're working on the second floor now."

It was hard to believe how quickly it was coming together. Every board and stone had been numbered and erected exactly as before. Additional logs that had been cut and stained to look like the original were added to the top of the first floor to raise the ceiling. The second story would require new flooring to be up to code, and it would be finished this week.

When she ran out of things to say, she turned up the volume on the PGA tournament playing on the television mounted in the corner of his room. It was probably her imagination, but it seemed Jack rested a little easier with those calm, soothing voices of the golf announcers.

It was during those times when the golf announcers took over that Alice scrolled through Jack's cell phone. At first she felt horribly guilty, like she was snooping ... but that phone had been vibrating with incoming texts from his business partners in Japan. She sent noncommittal answers, saying a medical emergency would keep Jack unavailable for the following week, but he would return their messages as soon as possible.

Her own phone vibrated, and Daisy's name appeared on the screen. Things had been tense between them ever since Daisy suggested the signet ring found at the Roost might belong to the Tuckers. They also needed to discuss Jack's bill at the hotel. Alice didn't want him to overhear anything troublesome, and stepped into the hallway to take the call.

"How's he doing today?" Daisy asked.

"No change. The doctors are going to keep him under for at least another day. Daisy, I need to check him out of the hotel. It seems pointless to pay for a room when he's trapped here at the hospital."

"Of course," Daisy agreed. "I'll let the front desk staff know to let you in to collect his belongings."

"Thanks," Alice said. Now came the hard part. "Can you waive the fees for the past few days? He didn't use the room, and money has been tight for him."

"Bless his heart," Daisy said, and she sounded genuinely sympathetic. "I wish I could do it for him, but rules are rules. The room was in his name, his belongings were in there, and we've already billed his credit card."

"Then reverse the charges, please."

"Honey, you know we can't do that. If you'd cleared out his room the day of the accident we would have quit billing him and rented the room to someone else."

Jack didn't have anyone to fight for him but her, and Alice intended to win this battle. She channeled the steely tone her father used, the one that always sent a shiver down her back. "Daisy, unless you show me records indicating the inn was at full capacity for the past five days, I want you to reverse the charges on Jack's card. Is that understood?"

Daisy huffed. "There's no need to get nasty. I'll speak to my husband. I'm sure we can work something out."

"Thanks, Daisy," she said, aiming for a conciliatory tone. But as the words left her mouth, a flicker of doubt crept in. When it really mattered, would the Tuckers stand by her—or would they double-cross her?

A hotel bellhop walked Alice up to Jack's room at the Tucker Inn. Like all rooms at the hotel, it was tastefully decorated with a Colonial Williamsburg vibe, complete with a four-poster bed, dark wainscoting, and reproduction brass sconces affixed to the walls.

Her heart squeezed at the sight of Jack's golf clubs propped in the corner. Would he ever play again? The doctors assured her he ought to make a full recovery, but at the moment he looked so frail and broken it was hard to believe.

She dragged Jack's suitcase from beneath the bed when a discreet knock sounded. The bellhop had promised to bring a luggage trolley, and she opened the door without a second thought.

Instead of a hotel clerk, Sebastian Bell held the luggage trolley. "Hello, gorgeous. Daisy said you'd be coming by to empty out Jack's room." He flashed her a wink. "I'm here to help."

Alice snuck a peek down both sides of the hall to search for paparazzi. Once assured the coast was clear, she tugged him inside. Being alone in a hotel room with Sebastian probably wasn't the smartest thing in the world, but she didn't want to press her luck by carrying on a conversation in the hallway.

"Why are you still here?" she asked. "I assumed you'd already gone back to England."

"I needed to see you again. Alice, we need to talk."

She opened the top drawer of the highboy to begin clearing out Jack's things. "Seb, we don't really need to talk. It's over, okay? I'm glad you've made it through rehab and things are going well for you, but I've already moved on."

Sebastian watched her through somber eyes. "He'll never marry you, and I've been dreaming about it since the day we met."

It hurt because both things were true. That didn't mean Sebastian was the right match for her. She and Sebastian were hopeless romantics. Who else could fall head-over-heels in love with a perfect stranger in the space of a day? And yet, beneath all his charisma, Sebastian was impractical, irresponsible, and charmingly selfish. She had to learn it the hard way, but she would never regret knowing him.

Alice's future was uncertain, but she needed to face it on her own. "Can you lift Jack's clubs onto the cart? With luck we can get this done in one trip."

How sad that all of Jack's possessions could fit on a hotel cart. He admitted to having a storage locker somewhere, but for the most part, two suitcases of clothes, a laptop, and a set of golf clubs were his worldly possessions.

The closet held two business suits, two casual jackets, a rain coat, and a winter coat. She held the hanging garment bag as Sebastian helped fill it.

Her phone rang, and she reached for it. An unfamiliar number flashed on the screen.

"Hello?"

"Is this Alice Chadwick?"

"It is," she said, her eyes locked with Sebastian, praying it wasn't bad news about Jack.

"This is Sophie Latimer, Jack's stepmother," the other voice said. "The hospital said you're overseeing Jack's care. Can I ask how he's doing?"

She paused, then started to pace. Jack had been dodging Sophie's calls ever since Alice met him. Who was she to reveal his personal information to a complete stranger? And yet, it would be cruel to completely withhold information, since Jack's father was still alive and no doubt concerned.

"Can I speak to Jack's father?"

There was a long pause. "Frank is right beside me listening in. Say something, hon."

"I'm here," a raspy voice on the other end of the connection choked out.

"He's got emphysema, and speaking is difficult for him," Sophie said. "We've been so worried about Jack. Please tell us how he is. The hospital wouldn't tell us anything, except that you've been with him since he was admitted."

"That's right," she said. It still felt like a violation to reveal Jack's medical information to the people he'd been avoiding for years, but it wasn't in her to be unkind to desperate people. "He's in an induced coma, but the doctors plan on bringing him out of it tomorrow. They anticipate a full recovery."

"Thank you for looking out for him," Jack's father said, his raspy voice sounding painful. "Tell him that I love him. Proud of him."

Whatever else Frank Latimer intended to say was cut off by a series of gasping coughs. Sophie murmured some soothing words to her husband, urging him to sip something through a straw. There was more coughing and wheezing, then a long pause before Sophie came back on the line.

"I got my husband settled on the patio outside so he can't overhear," she said. "I want to thank you for letting us know how Jack is. We have been praying for him every day for years."

"I'll tell him." Not that it would make much difference.

"Alice, my husband is dying. We've both come to terms with that, but Frank wants to see Jack before he goes. I've been trying to get in touch with him ever since it became obvious that Frank didn't have long. The biggest regret of his life is losing contact with his son."

What could Alice say to that? For a man to abandon a seriously ill child was appalling, and it was up to Jack to decide about forgiveness or a reconciliation.

"I'll pass along what you've said but can't make any promises."

She ended the call and set the phone on the bedside table. Sebastian was his typical insouciant self. "That sounded uniquely awful. Care to tell me what it was all about?"

It wasn't her story to tell. If she hadn't been so surprised by Sophie's unexpected call, she would have taken it off speaker phone immediately. As it was, Sebastian heard everything.

"Not everyone has great relationships with their parents," she said simply, and mercifully, Sebastian seemed to accept it.

They finished packing up Jack's room in short order. Everything fit easily onto the cart, and Alice took a quick final inspection of each drawer, beneath the bed, and through the shelves in the closet.

Nothing left. "Seb ... did you see the signet ring anywhere?"

"No. Is it supposed to be here?"

She did a mental inventory. Jack took it with him after their argument at her townhouse. It hadn't been on him when the accident happened. The hospital put all his personal belongings in a sealed baggie, and there hadn't been much. His wallet, his watch, a pair of sunglasses, and a roll of mints. No ring.

"Let's go through his pockets," she said, opening the first suitcase.

Between the two of them, they searched every pocket and golf bag cubby. Sebastian dumped Jack's toiletries on the desk and unscrewed every lid, searching for a hiding place.

They found nothing. The room now looked like a disaster zone, with clothes strewn everywhere in their hunt for the ring.

"Maybe he has a safe-deposit box at a bank," Sebastian said.

She nodded. "I'll ask him when he wakes up."

It took another twenty minutes to fold and pack everything up again, but Sebastian never once complained. After reloading the cart, he met her gaze.

"Alice ... I need to know. Is there any hope for us? I've dated some of the world's most beautiful women, but you're the one. You're the last puzzle piece I need to make my life perfect. Say the word, and I'll buy a castle for us."

Dear Sebastian, charmingly self-centered and irresponsible as always. She blinked back a suspicious prickle in her eyes but told the truth, even though it was painful for them both. "I'm sorry, Seb. It's over."

Chapter Twenty-Eight

He should be grateful to be alive. This wasn't the first time Jack had been knocked unconscious and had to endure the protocol for head injuries, but this groggy, drugged feeling was never easy. He couldn't remember the details of what happened, only that there'd been an accident at the golf course and it was bad. His brain felt encased in sludge that made thinking a struggle.

And yet, here he lay, going through a series of questions with a neurologist. The flashing light measured eye response. The neck brace kept him immobile, but at least his eyes could follow that pinprick of light, which was a good sign. How long had he been under? His tongue felt coated in cotton as he mumbled the question.

"You've been out for six days," the doctor said. "Can you give me a thumbs-up with your hand?"

He managed to do so with both hands. "Excellent," the doctor said.

He'd missed his flight to Japan. There were so many people around his bed. Beeping monitors. IVs attached to both arms. Electrodes taped on his head fed data to a laptop monitoring his brain activity. A lady in scrubs watched the laptop data. Someone else stood behind his head.

"Alice?" he said.

"What was that?" the doctor asked.

"Is Alice here?" It was a long shot, but the room was crowded and the brace on his neck stopped him from looking around.

A nurse pulled aside, and suddenly Alice moved into view, her face radiant as she hunkered down where he could see her.

"I'm right here, Jack."

She wore his favorite yellow dress, the one that brought out the gold in her warm brown eyes, and he smiled back at her. "Hey, pretty lady."

The doctor gave a laugh. "Okay, I'll mark you down as being able to recognize faces," he said. Alice pulled back and the nurse watching the monitors took her place.

It was humiliating to have Alice see him like this, hooked up to machines and with the awful neck brace. There was even a tube and a bag so he could take a whiz without leaving the bed. No man wanted to be seen like this, and yet . . . he was so glad she was here.

"Alice," he slurred again.

"Yes, Jack?" This time she stood at the end of the bed where he could see her perfectly. So perfectly pretty, like a long-stemmed rose. "What is it, darling? What do you need?"

"Nothing. Just saying your name."

Alice stayed where he could see her for the duration of the tests, which drained what little energy was left in him. He didn't like needing her, but for today, he was grateful she was here.

Jack's mind was in better shape the next morning, which was a mixed blessing. The fogginess had cleared, which meant he could focus on his dire financial situation. The accident had postponed his trip to Japan and their patience was growing thin. Repairs to the waterfall would delay the opening of the golf course. The renovations at the Roost were going to be incredibly expensive.

Alice had been doing her best to set his mind at ease. "I already spoke with the contractor about the waterfall," she said. "He's going to fix the lining free of charge, so don't worry about a thing."

The contractor had to fix the lining because it was a shoddy installation from the beginning. They'd used the wrong grade of liner, which was why Jack had been having water problems from the beginning.

"I need to get in contact with the guy in Japan," he said. "I'm going to need you to read the latest emails to me." The plastic torture device encasing his neck made it impossible to look at his phone or even read a laptop.

"Jack, please don't worry about these things. You need to heal."

Easy for a rich person to say. "What else has been going on while I've been out? Are you seeing Sebastian?"

"Of course I've seen him," she said. "He helped me clean out your hotel room. Oh! And I got Daisy to waive the hotel fees from your time in the hospital. That's good news, isn't it?"

He would nod if the neck brace would permit it but had to settle for a thumbs-up instead.

"Jack, I wish I didn't have to bring this up . . ."

All senses went on alert. Her Pollyanna brightness had dimmed, so it must be bad. "Yeah, what's up?"

"I spoke with your stepmother," she said, and like clockwork his heart started pounding faster. "She knows about your accident and I had a long talk with her."

Sophie probably told Alice a sob story about his dad's health. People always took advantage of softies like Alice.

"Don't worry about it," he said. "I've known my dad has been sick for a long time." And yet, the panic was setting in again. He forced himself to breathe calmly, trying to release the tension that gathered in his muscles. It felt like bands constricting around his chest, making it hard to even drag in a decent lungful of air.

"There may not be much time," Alice said, her voice heavy with regret. "Sophie says that your dad's lungs are so bad that his heart is going to give out soon. She thinks he only has a few weeks left."

The words landed hard and he squeezed his eyes shut. *Oh, Dad.*

This shouldn't hurt so bad because it was his dad's fault for smoking two packs a day and being a lousy drunk all those years.

He opened his eyes to focus on a golf game on the TV. The first time Jack became interested in golf was from a hospital bed, and Frank Latimer explained the rules to him. No hospital stays were fun, but that one, in which he and his dad bonded over a PGA weekend, had been pretty good.

"Well, I'm sorry for that," Jack managed to choke out, because his heart still hadn't quit thumping like a freight train barreling down the tracks.

"Sophie says she would like to arrange a visit."

"Absolutely not."

Alice's face transformed from pity to pleading in the space of a few seconds. "Don't look at me like that," he said. "You have no idea what it's like to be sneaking into a laundromat every night to sleep because your dad would rather suck down a bottle of vodka than look after you."

Alice looked away and nodded, although he knew she still disapproved.

"Will you be okay if I leave for a few hours?" she asked. "Sebastian needs a ride to the airport, but he can call a cab if you'd rather I stay."

He narrowed his eyes. "Do you suppose he's going to make another go for you?"

She laughed a little. "You never know with Seb, but trust me ... I'm finally immune to Sebastian Bell."

It was the only spot of good news Jack had heard in a week.

Sebastian flirted with her the entire drive to the small regional airport at Newport News. He was back to being his devil-may-care self: charming, arrogant, and vain.

She parked in the lot before the drop-off zone, and Sebastian made no move to leave the car after she turned off the engine.

"You need to watch *The King's Redemption*," he said in a playfully castigating tone. "I'm telling you, it's the best work I've ever done. Filming on the second series starts next month."

"What's going to happen in the second series?" she asked. "I thought the story ends with Charles regaining the throne and his triumphal return to London."

"It does, but the second season is going to be about the wicked aftermath. It's going to be very *Game of Thrones* as he hunts down the men who killed his father. Charles was willing to forgive most people who fought for Oliver Cromwell, but the fifty-nine men who signed his dad's death warrant? They went on the run, and he went after them. You'll have to watch the next season to find out what he did, but it was *savage*," he said with a delicious leer.

Grisly executions never appealed to Alice, but the revenge plot would probably attract a lot of viewers. "So Charles had no forgiveness in his heart for the regicides?"

"None at all. There were hard limits to the king's clemency." Sebastian began fiddling with the clasp on his bag, his brow furrowed in concentration. His cocksure demeanor was gone, replaced with a contemplative look. "I admire how he led the country in the years following the civil war. He forgave almost everyone, even though they put him through pure hell. Heck, I was miserable even filming some of the scenes hiding out in haylofts or crouching in streams to hide from Cromwell's army, and I only had to deal with it for a few days. Charles spent years on the run, starving and searching for a safe place to lay his head for the night. Most of the roles I've played in my career are made-up characters, but Charles II was real. I admire him, and come up short in comparison."

He paused and looked down, clasping his hands together. She waited, sensing he had more to say.

"Alice, I treated you shamefully," he finally said. "Not many people are lucky enough to meet a woman so genuinely kind. I was the one who made a mess of my life, but you paid the price. Your career is in the toilet because of me, and I'm sorry."

"Seb, I'll survive."

He gave a bitter laugh. "You deserve more than just 'surviving.' I let them hustle me into rehab to save my own reputation and never gave a thought to you. Instead of being consumed by my own selfish needs, I should have let the world know you were blameless for my shortcomings. I will be forever sorry about that. Will you forgive me?"

A wave of fondness swelled inside. It had been easy to despise Sebastian while he'd been AWOL and she hadn't understood what happened or why. Now she understood. She still wished he had been strong enough to have defended her, but at least he understood the magnitude of what his weakness had cost her.

"Of course I forgive you, and wish you all the best. I'll even watch your movies." He choked back a laugh, and she opened her door. "Come on. You'll miss your plane unless we get moving."

This would be the last time they'd ever see each other. Maybe she would watch his movies in the years and decades to come, witnessing him grow older on film while she aged here in Virginia. If Sebastian's visit to Virginia brought her nothing else, it had restored memories of a fleeting courtship that would forever add a dash of glamour to her mild-mannered life.

She popped the trunk open, and he lifted out both bags. Sebastian turned to face her, then set down a bag. His expression mirrored her own: regret, affection, nostalgia. He cupped the back of her neck and leaned in to kiss her forehead.

"Take care, Alice."

She nodded. "You too, Seb."

She remained beside her car to watch him walk away. A part of her would always love Sebastian's charming, effervescent good humor, but they weren't the right match for each other. Sebastian looked amazing in a cravat and could recite a Shakespearean sonnet with ease, but those weren't the things she was looking for in a man.

She needed someone like Jack, who rolled up his sleeves to get a job done, rain or shine, good times or bad. Who defended her when she had no one else on her side. Jack would never have Mr. Darcy's polished manners or be able to recite Shakespeare from memory, but it was men like Jack who built the world. Men who weren't afraid to get their hands dirty and faced each challenge head-on, not with elegant words but with sturdy, unrelenting grit and know-how. They didn't just preserve what was good; they built it, protected it, made sure it would endure. Jack was no romanticized hero out of a novel—he was real, solid, and someone she would forever admire.

Jack taught her resilience through humor. With his rough hands and easy laughter, he had changed her in ways she couldn't fully grasp yet, building her up as surely as he built all else in his world. Even though he would leave soon, he would remain forever etched into the framework of her heart, a lesson in strength and joy she would carry forward always.

Chapter Twenty-Nine

"You cannot get on an airplane for at least three months," the neurologist told Jack first thing in the morning. "The changes in cabin pressure during a long flight can cause intracranial bleeding. Do you really want that to happen at thirty thousand feet over the middle of the Pacific Ocean?"

It meant Jack couldn't fulfill his obligations in Japan. He had never walked out on a contract in his life—a point of pride for him. The Japanese investors had been more than patient with him, but they couldn't wait forever, and he had to let them down.

Then the physical therapist arrived, delivering a boot for his bad ankle and a new set of forearm crutches he'd have to use for the next month. She had been prepared to teach him how to strap on the bulky plastic boot and use the crutches, but there was no need. Jack spent most of fifth and sixth grade in a plastic boot with geeky crutches. The aluminum poles with arm cuffs and wrist handles would make it easier to protect his ankle, but he'd always hated them. He walked like a praying mantis and felt like crippled.

Alice showed up at noon with lemon cookies and a sunny smile. "You got your neck brace off," she cheered, beaming.

"Yeah," he grumbled. "The neurologist gave with one hand and took away with the other. I can't get on a plane so I can't go to Japan." Would the wrenches thrown into his life by hemophilia never end?

Alice sat on the bedside chair. "I'm sorry about that. I know you were looking forward to seeing Japan."

He kept his face immobile, refusing to let Alice know that the real problem was that he needed the money.

"They're renovating a golf course at Camp Lejeune that I can make a bid for," he said. It would be a four-hour drive from here, but at least the plastic boot was on his left foot so he could still get himself to North Carolina to assess the golf course and submit a proposal ahead of the deadline.

He met Alice's gaze. "I'm supposed to be discharged tomorrow."

"You can stay at my place," she said. "Your suitcases are already in my guest bedroom. I didn't know where else to put them after I moved you out of the hotel. You'll be more comfortable at my place than there. I'll even cook for you."

He glanced away, even as temptation clawed. "I'll head back to the Tucker Inn," he said. It would be easier on them both. The convenient, impersonal touch of a hotel was exactly what he needed.

"Jack ... when I packed up your room from the Tucker Inn, I couldn't find the signet ring anywhere."

He blinked. "It's gone?"

"I'm not sure," she said. "I did a pretty thorough search, but maybe you have a hiding place? Like in a hidden compartment somewhere?"

"It was zipped up in my laptop case. It wasn't there?"

"No, we checked there. I worried one of the hotel staff stole it because of the gold. If it gets melted down ..."

Her phrase trickled off. They both knew the real value of the ring was its history, not its gold, but that wouldn't be obvious to someone unfamiliar with the ring.

"The good news is that we've got a lot of pictures of it," Alice continued. "I've sent them to the College of Arms in London."

"I remember. Any word back from them yet?"

She shook her head. "I gather that it can take several weeks. Are you sure it was in that laptop case?"

"Certain," he bit out, anger beginning to gather anew. A lot of people had access to his hotel room while he'd been laid up, so it could have been stolen by any of them. That ring meant a lot to Alice. The gold alone was worth a few thousand dollars, but it was the history of the ring that mattered more than anything.

A nurse tapped on the open door. "Are you up for a visitor?"

He sagged against the pillows. He was broke, sick, and now he'd disappointed Alice by failing to protect that ring. All he really wanted was to be alone, but it could be important. "Who is it?"

"He says he is your father. Frank Latimer?"

Jack recoiled. The last time he saw his dad had been in a Dairy Queen for a supervised visit when Jack was fourteen years old. Dad bought him a chocolate milkshake. It had been hard to drink while watching his dad battle tremors from alcohol withdrawal. Jack should have been grateful his dad sobered up enough for the visit, but all it did was disgust him.

"Mr. Latimer?" the nurse asked. "Shall I let him in?"

"No," Jack said. "My dad and I said our goodbyes a long time ago."

"Jack," Alice said. "I think perhaps—"

"It's a hard no, Alice." He met the nurse's eyes. "I don't care what you tell him. Tell him that I'm sleeping or too sick. Or that he's had twenty years to see me if he wanted, but just don't let him in here."

Alice stood. "Could you give us a few minutes?" she asked the nurse.

"Of course," she replied. Alice crossed the room to close the door, but not before shooting a quick glance down the hallway.

Jack folded his arms across his chest and slanted her a surly look. She was probably going to appeal to his softer side, as if he *had* one of those. "Don't waste your breath, Alice."

"I dropped Sebastian off at the airport yesterday."

"Yeah? He's finally gone, then?"

"Yeah," she said with a little laugh. "We had a nice talk in the parking lot. He feels really lousy about everything that happened and did his best to apologize."

"Kind of the least he could do, isn't it?"

"Jack, he asked for my forgiveness, and that was nice . . . but letting go of my hurt and anger at Sebastian was a gift to myself. Bitterness can corrode the good inside of a person. By mending fences with Sebastian, I've been able to let go of the resentment and reclaim the good memories I have of him."

The gentle compassion in her face moved him as she sank into the chair beside him and reached for his hand. Hers was cool and soft and felt perfect as he curled his big palm around it.

"Jack, you will never regret seeing him. Don't let a person's bad actions stop you from being a good person. Your dad is right outside. He's in a wheelchair with an oxygen tank, and he looks terrible. He's using a few of his last hours on this earth to come see you."

He turned his face to the wall and blinked at the pinpricks behind his eyes. The worst thing would be for Alice to see how hard this was.

Her voice was soft as she spoke. "Maybe your dad came here for selfish reasons, but he's also giving you the chance to speak your piece. Tell him whatever you've got festering inside that you've been wanting to tell him for years. Getting it off your chest might help. Or perhaps you can forgive him. I don't know what you're capable of on such short notice . . . but if you turn him away, I think it's going to be something you will regret for the rest of your life."

Cracking open the door into his past was terrifying. He barely survived it the first time and didn't want to risk opening up the avalanche of painful memories. It would be so much easier to keep on hating Frank Latimer.

He reached for the hospital bed's remote control, pressing the arrow to raise the back of his bed. He wanted to be sitting up for this, not lying down like an invalid.

"Yeah, you can let him in," he said.

The first sight of his dad was a shock. It had been twenty-two years, and Frank Latimer had shrunk into a little old man bundled in a nubby wool sweater with a scarf around his neck. He looked barely able to sit up in the wheelchair and was hooked up to an oxygen tank. A strong-jawed woman with chestnut hair pushed the wheelchair.

"I'm Sophie," she said, extending her hand. She was well-dressed in a sporty blazer and ankle boots. Jack felt underdressed in a hospital smock, but at least he didn't have to wear the plastic collar around his neck anymore.

He shook Sophie's hand, but merely looked at his dad.

"Thanks for this," Frank rasped out.

"Sure thing, Dad." The words weren't genuine, but it seemed to set the other two at ease. An awkward pause lengthened and grew.

Frank glanced at the bag of clotting factor hanging on the IV pole. "How are your numbers?"

"They're good. I'm getting out tomorrow."

Frank managed a smile. "Good!"

Then another long and torturous silence. Alice had stepped outside to grant them privacy, but he wished she'd stayed because she could always keep a conversation going. He scrambled for something to say.

"How long have you two been married?"

"Eighteen years," Sophie said.

"And I've been sober for nineteen," Frank added.

It made sense. That was around the time Frank and Sophie started bombarding him with Christmas cards and notes of congratulations each time one of his golf courses opened. They'd always been sent to his lawyer's office, and he never responded. Why had they kept sending them year after year?

"We've got two daughters," Sophie said. "Want to see? They're your half-sisters."

She started scrolling through her phone before he could answer. Jack managed a polite smile as he took the phone from Sophie.

"That was from last summer," she said. "Jessica is our oldest and volunteers at a rescue center for horses."

They were nice-looking girls, young women, really ... but looking at them made bitterness well up inside, threatening to choke him. Frank raised a second family and shed the problematic sick kid from his first marriage. Those girls had riding lessons and summer camp. When he was their age, he worked pulling weeds on a golf course and visited soup kitchens.

He clenched his fists as Sophie kept talking. It was easier to hate than forgive. Forgiving would crack the thin veneer of his strength and expose a world of hurt feelings underneath.

Frank drew a breath that sounded painful. "I love that you design golf courses," he said. "I'm so proud of you. I watched every one of them from afar."

"I know," Jack said. "I got the cards."

"Son, I let you down, and it's the biggest regret of my life. I held on to sobriety enough to walk your mother through her final years of cancer treatments, but it broke me. I wasn't able to take care of you after that. I figured the state could do a better job than I could."

Jack clenched his jaw and looked away. The state probably *did* do a better job. The fact that he was still alive was proof of that. He had survived. So had his dad. He ought to be happy, right?

A lump formed in his throat. Actually, he *was* happy. Alice was right. He'd been carrying the weight of resentment his entire life; letting it go would free him.

It was time to forgive his father. There was no need to pick apart every old scar or dig through the wreckage of all he'd endured. Jack could let go of it all, not to absolve his father, but to clear his own path forward without the baggage of the past.

He'd never been good at this sort of conversation and struggled to find a way to move forward.

"Do you still root for the Baltimore Ravens?" he asked his dad.

Frank's eyes widened in surprise. "They've had a great run. You?"

"Yeah. I thought of you when they won the Super Bowl a few years back."

Frank's face lit up, fragile but unmistakably pleased. "Maybe we'll be able to watch them win it again this year. Together, maybe."

"Yeah," Jack choked out. "That would be really great."

Over the next hour, as they carried on a stilted conversation, Jack silently vowed that no matter where he found himself—Japan, Scotland, North Carolina—if the Ravens made it to the Super Bowl this year, he would show up and watch the game with his dad. Heck, maybe he should just show up in Baltimore on any given Sunday to watch an ordinary game.

Win or lose, it would be the best game in the world.

Chapter Thirty

Alice was on her way to the hospital to help Jack check out when the email from the College of Arms in London arrived. Her phone dinged at a red light, and when she glimpsed the attachment icon, her heart leapt.

Finally—answers about the signet ring.

The ring itself was still missing, and Jack suspected one of the Tuckers had swiped it from his hotel room. At least this report might tell her where the ring came from—and who it had once belonged to.

At every stoplight, her fingers itched to tap the screen, to dive into the report, but she forced herself to wait. This was something she wanted to share with Jack. Her heart thudded as she pulled into the hospital's garage, parked the car, slung her laptop bag over her shoulder, and all but jogged into the hospital.

Jack was half-dozing when she burst into the room, golf murmuring softly from the wall-mounted TV. A few yogurt cups sat on the rolling table across his lap. He blinked awake as she swept in.

"Jack! The report's here—the one from London about the ring. I haven't opened it yet. I wanted to wait."

He sat up straight, instantly alert. "About time," he said with a grin. For a man who once had no appreciation of history, he'd certainly grown fascinated with the Roost and the signet ring. With an underhanded toss, he flung the yogurt containers toward the trashcan. They landed inside with a satisfying clatter.

"Let's get cracking," he said, slapping the tabletop with open palms. "I've been dying to read that thing."

She slid the laptop onto the table, angled the screen so they could both see, and opened her email.

The report was brief, but packed with insight:

> *The coat of arms on the signet ring you have submitted was granted by His Majesty Henry VIII in 1536 to the Denby family. The rearing stag was the traditional emblem of the Denby family. The scallop shell pattern on the ring's shank is a symbol of Christian faith.*
>
> *In keeping with the family's tradition, the number of acorns surrounding the stag signify one acorn for each generation. This ring has six acorns, meaning it belonged to the sixth Lord Denby since the granting of the title. Thus, the ring most likely belonged to William Reid Denby, 1615–1659.*
>
> *William Reid Denby was listed on the death warrant signed by Charles II following the king's restoration. His death in 1659 spared him arrest and execution for treason.*

"Good heavens," Alice whispered, rocking back in the chair in amazement. "The owner of our signet ring was a regicide."

Jack looked at her in confusion. "What are you talking about?"

The pieces were falling together. Sebastian had told her how Charles II granted amnesty to everyone who fought on the Puritan side except for the fifty-nine men who voted for his father's execution. For them there was no mercy.

"Charles II spent more than a decade in exile after his father was beheaded during the Puritan Revolution," she told Jack. "After he was restored to the throne in 1660, he wanted revenge against every man who signed his father's death warrant. Any regicide who was captured was put on trial, then they were hanged, drawn, and quartered."

Jack looked skeptical. "How did his signet ring get to Virginia? The guy died in 1659."

It was a good question. That ring went into the wall in 1661 when the house was built. "There must have been a relationship between Reid Santos and William Reid Denby," she said. "The name Reid is somewhat unusual for the time. He might have been an illegitimate child?"

"But why did the ring come *here*?" Jack pressed. "And why go to such trouble to hide it?"

Alice's heart began to pound and her palms tingled. "Santos means *saint* in Spanish. The Puritans called themselves 'the Saints' during the English Civil War, and William Reid Denby was a highly-placed Puritan, probably a member of the parliament."

If he was to escape the wrath of the king, he would have needed a new name. More pieces started falling into place in her brain and a slow smile spread across her face.

"Reid Santos and William Reid Denby were the same person," she said. "And he didn't die in 1659."

Jack nodded, his eyes alight. "He faked his death, and his family covered for him," Jack said. "They wrote a fake date of death on his tombstone when it became obvious that Charles was going to retake the throne and was out for blood. Helga probably backed the story and helped spread a story that William was dead . . . but in reality he fled to Virginia, still an unsettled and dangerous wilderness."

"Too dangerous to bring his wife," Alice said. The story seemed wildly dramatic and still had holes. She stood and began pacing. "If William Reid Denby was a Puritan, why wouldn't he have gone to New England? Massachusetts was settled by Puritans who would have been sympathetic to his cause. Virginia was settled by Royalists."

Jack clapped his hands together and flashed a roguish grin. "Nope! Virginia makes perfect sense. Nobody would be looking for him here. If William Denby was well known among the Puritans, all it would take was for a single person in Massachusetts to recognize him and turn him over to the Crown for a fat reward."

It was making sense to Alice. "So he came to a place nobody would recognize him," she continued. "He made up a fake name and lived happily ever after. It's why I couldn't find a birth or death record for Reid Santos in England, because there never *was* a Reid Santos . . . only William Reid Denby."

If anyone had good cause to disappear, it was a man the king of England wanted to see hanged, drawn, and quartered. Charles II vowed he would never call off the search until every person who signed his father's death warrant was made to pay the ultimate price.

Jack leaned over the laptop to study the photograph of the signet ring. "All those religious symbols show Denby's loyalty to the Puritan cause. It looks like our man was one of the bad guys. A regicide on the run."

She released a heavy sigh. A man who carved his wife's name into window glass? She didn't want to believe it. "There were a lot of good Puritans," she said. "Had the war turned out differently, William Reid Denby would have been considered a hero. The Puritans started out with noble intentions. They wanted a fair and representative government. They wanted to curb the abuses of wealth and believed in universal education, even for women! Once they got into power, they started implementing all those things. History is written by the winners, and the Royalists ensured that the Puritans were remembered not for their reforms, but for their most egregious abuses."

Jack leaned back against the pillows and looked at her with a speculative gaze. "So you think Helga was the Widow Santos?"

"Probably," Alice said. "The letter I found said Helga sailed to Virginia because she still had hope for a child. It's sad that it never happened for her."

"How can you be so sure about that?" Jack asked.

"Because the Roost and all its contents were sold at auction in 1705. Courthouse records indicate the Roost was owned by the Widow Santos, but she had no children so it was put up for auction after she died."

Jack continued to stare at the image of the ring on her laptop monitor, his expression growing darker. "I want to know who has that ring."

"I've already reported it to the police," she said. "Every pawn shop in a fifty-mile radius will be on the lookout for it."

"I don't think it's going to show up at a pawn shop," Jack said. "I think one of the Tuckers took it. They know its historic value and had access to my room. I'm going to get it back."

Right after he was released from the hospital, Jack asked Alice to drive him to Kyle Tucker's fancy art gallery. It was in the rich part of Williamsburg, crammed with snooty cafés and antique shops.

"Please be nice," Alice cautioned as she scanned the street for a parking spot.

"I'm not feeling nice," he replied. "I have a hunch Daisy's got her hands on my ring."

"She claimed not to know anything about it," Alice said, slowing down to ease her car into a tiny spot.

"And you believed her?"

"I suppose," she said with an uncertain shrug. Alice was too sweet to risk an ugly confrontation, but Jack wasn't. Somebody swiped a historic relic, and he wanted it back. Responsibility for the security of his hotel room began and ended with the Tuckers. He'd make Kyle launch a search to identify everyone who had access to his room.

The Tucker Gallery took up two storefronts, the display windows filled with Old World furniture, highboys, and elegant writing desks. Alice walked ahead to hold the heavy glass door for him as he navigated inside. It was hard to project an intimidating aura while tottering on forearm crutches, but he'd get the job done.

Inside, the gallery smelled like old leather, lemon polish, and a whole lot of money. Silver candlesticks and gilt-framed mirrors gleamed. Jack peeked at the tag on a spindly-looking chair. It was a Hepplewhite chair, circa 1760. Who would pay four thousand dollars for a chair that looked too fragile to sit on?

"Remember, don't accuse him," Alice whispered. "We don't want to offend them because they might be completely innocent."

"Can I help you find anything?" An elegant gentleman in a bow tie and with a priestly demeanor had materialized beside him.

Alice stepped in front of Jack before he could answer. "Hi, Winston. We're looking for Kyle. Is he in today?"

"Absolutely. I'll let him know you're here."

Winston disappeared behind a tapestry curtain covering a rear hallway. Jack made a beeline to a glass display case filled with vintage jewelry, scanning the velvet cushions quickly. Pearls, cameos, gold pocket watches, lots of jewelry ... but no seventeenth-century signet ring.

The tapestry flipped away from the back hall and Kyle came striding forward, monocle in place, his white teeth displaying perfect veneers as he smiled. "Alice! Oh, and Jack . . . it's good to see you up and about. Healing nicely?"

Jack's gaze slid down Kyle's sports jacket to land on his right hand. "You're wearing my ring," he said bluntly. On his pinky finger, too! The Denby signet ring had been polished and now gleamed in the dim of the shop. Kyle looked completely unruffled.

"If you check the paperwork of our agreement, you'll see that this ring actually belongs to the Tucker family."

"How do you figure?" he bit out. "That agreement stated that in exchange for paying your debts, I took ownership of the Roost, the five acres it sits on, and everything inside it."

Kyle gave a gentle laugh. "That's not the agreement I'm referring to. It's the hotel bill. The fine print on the hotel agreement says that any guest who walks out on their bill, leaving property in the room, is subject to having that property seized."

"But, but . . ." Alice sputtered. "But I worked out a deal with Daisy! Jack was unconscious and I checked him out of the hotel. He shouldn't have had to pay for those days he wasn't staying there, and she agreed."

Heat began to simmer beneath Jack's collar. He grasped the handles of the crutches, wishing he could punch the condescending look off Kyle's face.

Kyle gave a sad shake of his head. "Daisy's sympathetic gesture had no legal bearing on the contract. She cleared the bill, but that didn't void Jack's responsibility for paying it. But look! I'm happy to take the ring as compensation."

The self-righteous expression on Kyle's face made Jack clench and unclench the grips of his crutches. Physical fights were off-limits to a hemophiliac, but Jack was good at fighting with his intellect.

"I will gladly sue you to kingdom come," he said quietly. "I already own a third of your family's golf course, and if you challenge me, I'll go after you for the rest of it. I didn't sign any agreement with Daisy—"

"But you didn't contest it once you were conscious again," Kyle interrupted. "That's a token sign of consent."

"A jury of our peers will side with me ten times out of ten."

"There won't be a jury trial," Kyle said. "The fine print on the hotel contract you signed requires arbitration, to be decided by a judge. And the law is quite clearly on the hotel's side."

Jack faked a patient smile. "One of the things I've learned about the Tuckers since I've been here is that they don't like anything that puts the family in a bad light. I've never been burdened by that weakness. There were a couple dozen witnesses when I found that ring, and local news reporters love this kind of gossipy story—"

"You're not listening," Kyle said. "The terms of the hotel contract are quite clear, and we've won every time we've gone to arbitration. Don't waste your money hiring lawyers over an antique of piddly value."

The problem with people like Kyle was that he was used to hiding behind lawyers, fine print on contracts, and his family's reputation. Jack intended to render those defenses useless. He affected a congenial tone that still had a bite just beneath the surface.

"You're right, Kyle," he said. "This case doesn't belong in a judicial courtroom; let's take it to the court of public opinion. I'd love to hear what the local newspapers will think about how your wife stole a ring from a man who was fighting for his life in a hospital bed. In fact, why stop at the newspaper? I'll talk to the local radio stations, the TV news, the town halls and neighborhood associations. Heck, the college is back in session, so I'll sponsor a letter-writing campaign or maybe put some flyers up at the tourist hotspots."

It didn't take long for Kyle to cave like a house of cards. Ten minutes later, Jack walked out of the shop with the Denby signet ring back on his finger where it belonged.

Chapter Thirty-One

B y the time Alice helped Jack get checked in to a chain hotel, the day was almost over, but he wanted to see the Roost.

She worried about it, because the ground was lumpy and littered with construction waste, dangerous terrain for a hemophiliac who walked with the aid of forearm crutches, but he insisted. It had been ten days since his accident and he was anxious to see the progress on the Roost before leaving town. Although his trip to Japan was cancelled, he was heading off to Camp Lejeune in North Carolina in hopes of winning the golf course renovation contract. The deadline for proposals was next week, and Jack had already arranged to meet with the golf course manager and local contractors to discuss his bid.

It was nearing dusk as they arrived at the Roost. The chilly air carried hints of leaf decay and damp earth, as if the first frost was waiting quietly to arrive. Deep furrows left by tractors made the terrain uneven, and long shadows cast across the land made it even harder to navigate.

"Be careful," Alice cautioned as Jack maneuvered his crutches around a lumpy pile of churned-up grass.

"I'm an old pro at this," Jack said as he headed toward the blank patch where the original Roost had stood for hundreds of years. A line of boulders still demarcated the outline of the original building, but the rest of it had been dismantled. New shoots of weeds already peeked through the soil, exposed to sunlight for the first time in centuries.

"I'd like to do something special with this spot," she said. "The footprint of the original Roost is still of historic interest, and I'd like to plant a garden on the plot. Perhaps medicinal herbs, the kind that would have been used in the seventeenth century. It will be another opportunity to teach history."

"Good idea," Jack said, heading toward the site of the new Roost. Rough-hewn logs from the old building were already in place for the ground floor of the future tavern. Surrounding them, the massive foundation for the new kitchen, a sprawling conference room, and a patio designed to overlook the shimmering waters of Saint Helga's Spring hinted at the transformation to come.

When she'd first met Jack back in early May, she'd thought his boasts about attracting PGA tours and concerts and amphitheaters was an abomination, and yet, it wasn't boasting. It was going to happen and by saving the Roost, this historic treasure would someday be shared with thousands of people each year. Someday soon the tavern and the terrace overlooking Saint Helga's Spring would attract customers for elegant weddings, academic seminars, and even Jack's prized PGA tournament crowds. Many would simply knock back a few drinks, enjoying the charm and exclusivity without a second thought. But for others, entering the Roost would be like stepping back in time. They'd stroll along garden paths brimming with the same herbs and heirloom vegetables cultivated by hands from centuries past, feeling the whispers of history in the air. For those few, this place would be a touchstone to the past, a reminder that they were walking where stories had been lived and legends born.

Jack wouldn't be here to share all that with her. A weight of sadness descended, and prickles of sweat broke out across her body.

Jack's face was expressionless as he scanned the vista. What was he thinking? His entire fortune was invested in this building and the golf course. When finished, it was going to be magnificent. He had reason to be proud of what he'd accomplished here, but he looked anxious and uncomfortable.

"Are you okay?"

He nodded. "My ankle is throbbing. Don't worry . . . it's not a new bleed, it's just overheated from this stupid boot. Let's head down to the spring," he said with a nod toward the pier stretching into Saint Helga's Spring.

Alice walked ahead to scan the ground for obstacles as Jack followed. The pier was low enough that he'd be able to cool his feet in the soothing water. The old wooden planks creaked as they ventured forth. A soft, chilled mist hovered over the water, and a few midges hovered over the spring. Their translucent wings caught the last bits of twilight as they zigzagged just above the surface. Hundreds of years ago, Helga Denby probably watched midges just like this.

Jack unstrapped the plastic boot from his foot. He gingerly removed the sock, revealing shockingly white skin against the yellow and brown bruising around his still-swollen ankle.

"This is heaven," he sighed after sinking both feet into the water.

She pulled off her boots and socks to join him, the cooling water sloshing between her toes.

Jack chuckled. "It's been sixty seconds, and my hand to God, my ankle already feels better." He lifted his foot, the skin glistening in the fading light. Perhaps it was her imagination, but his ankle looked a smidge less swollen.

"Maybe there really is something to the healing legend of this spring," she said.

Jack lowered his ankle back into the water. "Maybe, but there's probably a rational explanation. The water is cool, so my ankle feels better and the swelling went down. Women desperate to get pregnant come out here because they won't leave any stone unturned, but I'll bet they're trying science, too."

She nudged him with her elbow. "That's so cynical."

He gazed into the distance, where the sun sank low in the sky, a blaze of burnt orange and streaks of purple. He remained silent and pensive, only the dry rustle of leaves and the call of a whip-poorwill somewhere in the distance breaking the quiet.

"I'm not cynical," he finally said. "I'm proud of people who never give up. No matter how often they get smacked down by fate, they'll figure out a way to change course and stand up again. For people like that, for people who refuse to quit . . . good things usually happen. So all those ladies who trek out here at the crack of dawn? They're not quitters. It doesn't surprise me that they get a baby sooner or later, some way or another. The trick is to never quit. They might have to adjust their sails. Heck, I wanted to be a pro golfer, but I wasn't good enough. And yet, all those years of studying and training helped me become a great golf course architect. It's not what I originally hoped for, but it worked out in the end."

She traced a finger along the weathered, silvery gray planks of the pier, trying to reconcile Jack's thoughts with her own faith. "I believe God answers our prayers, just not always in the way we hope. Helga came to America hoping for a child. It never happened for her, but she inspired women for hundreds of years. Perhaps Helga didn't get what she prayed for, but she played a role for a lot of women who conceived." She glanced back at the gap in the tall grass where the Roost once stood. "It's sad that it never happened for Helga. The records say she died without an heir, so the Roost and all its contents went up for auction."

"And the Tuckers bought everything?" Jack asked.

"Just the Roost and the land," she said. "Another family, the Dunstables, bought the contents of the house in 1705. The furniture, a couple of flintlocks, that sort of thing." She searched her mind. She'd read the inventory of the house back when she first started researching. It contained a number of well-to-do furnishings, such as silver spoons and a gilt mirror . . . and a portrait."

She straightened, excitement starting to brew as she turned to face Jack. "The estate inventory mentioned a portrait. A *marital* portrait."

"Do you suppose it could be them? Helga and her husband?"

"Maybe. Remember when we visited the Colonial Art Museum's archives? Rich people in the seventeenth century often had portraits painted when they got married. I could see that it might be something William Denby might have brought with him when he fled into exile. It could have been the only image he had of his wife."

"Are there any of those Dunstables still around? They might know what happened to it."

Dunstable was a distinctive name. They'd been one of the First Families of Virginia, but many of those early families died out or went back to England. "I don't think so. At least, I don't think there are any left in the area."

"I'd love to get a look at that portrait," Jack said, and she matched his smile. It felt like they were in this together. She grabbed his hand.

"Let's search for it! I'm good at genealogy, and we should be able to turn something up quickly. Tomorrow?"

He withdrew his hand. It felt like his entire body froze up as he inched back onto the pier and dragged his socks back on. "Alice, I can't. I was able to schedule some appointments at Camp Lejeune to evaluate the site and submit a bid for their golf course renovation. I'm leaving for North Carolina tomorrow."

She lifted her feet from the water, suddenly chilled. Of course he didn't have time to chase down a rabbit hole for historical curiosities, but she worried about him.

"Surely you can't drive all that way. I'll take you down."

Jack visibly stiffened again. "I'll be fine. The boot isn't on my driving foot."

And he didn't want her along. He didn't need to say it, and it hurt, but that was okay. She'd been preparing herself for Jack's departure for weeks now, even while she feared he wasn't yet healthy enough for the journey.

Chapter Thirty-Two

I t didn't take long before Jack reached open countryside on his drive to North Carolina. He rolled the windows down to smell the autumn scents of freshly mowed hay from the final cutting of the season. The radio played Garth Brooks, the wind rustled his hair, and the autumn day was perfect.

Too perfect, maybe. It felt like a betrayal of Alice and the summer they'd carved out of borrowed time. Moving forward to his next project didn't feel like liberation; it felt hollow. Every mile he put between himself and Alice pressed against his chest like a slow, steady weight.

The ache would pass. It always did. He'd left plenty of places before, but Alice and Williamsburg weren't just another dot on the map. For a while it felt like home, and she felt like a partner. She'd gotten under his skin in a way he hadn't anticipated, even though he wasn't made for gardens and porches and sleepy weekend mornings.

He gripped the steering wheel a little tighter, wondering how long this ache of regret was going to last. He'd just crossed the North Carolina border when his cell phone buzzed and he glanced at the screen.

Sophie.

His heart squeezed and he stared straight ahead, nothing but farmland on either side of him, the yellowing leaves of a late soybean crop looking withered and tired.

He didn't want to take this call, but a glance in the rearview mirror showed nobody behind him. He slowed the truck and pulled to the side of the road, then parked. He took a sobering breath before answering.

"Yeah, Sophie?" His voice was sad, gentle. So was hers.

"Jack, your dad passed away this morning."

The prickle of tears shouldn't have happened, but they did. He turned to gaze out over the shriveled crops, strangely beautiful beneath the vast autumn sky. Sophie continued talking. "It was very peaceful. The whole family was here, and he died in his own bed. It was what he wanted."

"Thanks for letting me know," he said, his gaze scanning the expanse of sky above. A few wispy clouds feathered across the blue horizon, a vast and boundless canvas that seemed to go on forever.

Oh, Dad. The pain in his chest widened and expanded. Frank Latimer hadn't been the best father, but Jack hadn't been the best son either. They both should have been better.

At least they made up at the very end.

"The funeral will be on Wednesday, here in Baltimore," Sophie said. "It's going to be a celebration of Frank's life rather than something somber and serious. He wanted to make sure you were invited. He wanted you to meet your sisters. I'd like that too."

Sophie's voice choked off, and regrets crashed down on him. If he had answered Sophie's calls a year ago, he would have had more time. He could have taken Frank to one of his golf courses. Maybe they could have even played a round together.

The funeral was scheduled right in the middle of his meetings with the Camp Lejeune folks. If he didn't win this contract, he would be staring at six months with no work, no income.

It didn't matter. If it was what his dad wanted, then Jack did too.

"Thanks, Sophie. I'll be there."

Jack's departure for North Carolina left Alice feeling alone and adrift, but nothing soothed a broken heart better than throwing herself into a thorny research challenge. The inventory of Reid's Roost when it was auctioned in 1705 mentioned a portrait, and the odds were good that it was a painting of either Helga or William Reid Denby. Maybe even *both* of them. Alice turned to Arlo Whitworth from the Colonial Art Museum for help locating it.

Arlo's office was nestled beneath the slanted ceiling of the history museum, and she gave him a wide smile in greeting. Something about a man wearing a polka-dotted bow tie made it impossible not to smile.

"I'll get you a cup of tea," Arlo said as he turned a chair out for her to sit. The long, narrow office was crowded with his desk and a massive work table. The sloping roof made it feel even more congested, but she'd always liked the cozy feel of the place.

Soon Arlo brought her a cup of Earl Grey tea in a Wedgwood teacup. The citrusy aroma immediately soothed her as she settled in on the opposite side of his desk.

"I've got a thorny research question for you," she began.

He lifted his teacup in a silent salute. "My favorite kind." Which made her smile all over again.

She showed him the copy from the courthouse records indicating that Samuel Dunstable bought the contents of the Roost, including a portrait, back in 1705.

"What are my odds of being able to find that portrait?"

"You came to the right place," Arlo said. "The last Dunstable married into the Hewitt family sometime in the early twentieth century. The decorative art wing of the museum is named after the Hewitts. They donated an art collection worth millions in the 1970s when taxes were high and the law granted huge write-offs to encourage philanthropic donations. All that fancy silver and porcelain in the Hewitt wing came from that collection. They gave us a complete collection of Sevres serving dishes that once belonged to Marie Antionette."

"Were there any portraits in the collection?"

"There were plenty of oil paintings, but we sold some and put the rest in storage. One of our interns keyed the inventory into an online database a few years ago." He flashed a toothy smile and wiggled his mouse to wake up his computer. "Let's have a look."

Arlo's fingers flew across the keyboard, the rattling sound tapering off as he scanned some pages. Then tapped another key. Then another. All she could see was the glow from his monitor reflected in his round spectacles. If she struck out here, there was almost no chance anyone else would have records of the Dunstable art.

"I'm glad the intern added a searchable field for date," Arlo said. He turned the monitor so she could see the archive record filled in. "The items purchased at the 1705 estate sale from the Widow Santos are right here. There's your portrait," he said. "It's in our remote storage building."

A rush of excitement was hard to quell. The portrait might not be of Helga or Reid, but *maybe it was!* She and her husband came from wealthy families, certainly affluent enough to commission portraits.

It was hard not to get her hopes up as Arlo led her out of the museum, down the oyster-shell path, and toward the climate-controlled warehouse. Keys rattled as he opened a series of locks, then turned on the lights.

"This way," he said as they walked down aisles of metal shelving and cabinets. Her heart began to sink as they approached the unappealing leftover paintings of little value. Her jaw dropped in disillusionment as Arlo brought her to the gaudy marital portrait propped on the back wall. It was the one she'd seen the last time she was here. The man wore a peach satin coat and the woman was swathed in pearls and gemstones.

"This is it," Arlo said. "We tried to sell it a while back, but there were no takers. It's simply not very appealing."

She studied the faces. The man's face was strong, his brows inky black slashes above piercing dark eyes. The woman stared straight out of the portrait, her flaxen hair parted in the middle and gathered smoothly at the nape of her neck. There was a quiet loveliness about her, but her hairstyle seemed so plain for her lavish wedding gown.

"I don't think this is them," she said. "They were Puritans. I can't imagine any Puritan man would be caught dead wearing a peach satin coat with gold ribbons on the sleeves."

"Remember, this may have been the work of a traveling portrait painter," Arlo said. "The clothing and background would have been stock paintings, and only the head and faces would reflect the sitter."

Alice crossed her arms as she scrutinized the portrait. It was still hard to believe a devout Puritan would consent to having his image attached to such an outlandish costume. The style was in keeping with the opulent court of the Royalists, the sort of people William Reid Denby risked his life to challenge.

"Frankly, it's badly done," Arlo said. "The best part of the portrait is their faces. The artistry is masterful, portraying character and pride. The countryside behind them is well done, too. Those clothes aren't in keeping with the rest of the painting. They are a mismatch, almost certainly done by a different artist."

She'd seen enough portraits of Puritans to know how they dressed. Their clothes were well-made, but austere. They favored black, indigo, and other dark colors, a deliberate rejection of the splashy extravagance found among the Royalists.

Maybe she was letting her imagination run away, but if a man was on the run, desperate to hide his identity, carrying a portrait of himself dressed like a Puritan could be a deadly mistake. And yet . . . he wanted to take a portrait of his wife into exile.

"I think the gaudy clothes were painted on later," she said, meeting the enigmatic gaze of the man in the portrait. It felt like he was staring out at her, reaching forward from three and a half centuries ago and urging her to find the truth.

Arlo whipped out a magnifying glass and leaned in to scrutinize the beribboned satin coat. "The brushstrokes are different," he said. "It appears to have been painted by a different artist, perhaps overlaying an earlier image. The only way we'll be able to tell if there's something else underneath these clothes is to use imaging spectroscopy."

"Do you know someone who could do that?" she asked, her heart pounding.

"It won't come cheap, but I know a fellow in Richmond who could do it for you."

Alice cupped her face in her hands, staring at the somber couple before her, almost certain she was looking at William Reid Denby and his wife, Helga. Three hundred and sixty years ago he escaped from England, changed his name to Reid Santos, and carved out a home in the dangerous new land. Once it was safe, his wife joined him.

Now all Alice had to do was prove it.

Chapter Thirty-Three

Jack spent the next two days walking every hole of the course at Camp Lejeune, making notes and taking mental snapshots. The greens were poorly contoured, the fairways flat and featureless, and the routing lacked any sense of rhythm or visual drama.

He could turn this into a fantastic course if he could only concentrate without regretting the way he left Alice or worrying about getting back to Baltimore for the funeral on Wednesday. Drafting a landscape plan was a major undertaking and finalizing an accurate budget was essential. Given enough time, he could transform the place into something exceptional: a course that honored its military roots while offering a memorable and dynamic playing experience.

The problem was timing. His proposal was due Friday, and attending the funeral on Wednesday meant he'd have to do a rushed job. Military timelines didn't bend, budgets had to be airtight, and the proposal format left no room for improvisation.

Jack managed to keep his meeting with the base's facilities engineer on Wednesday morning, then hopped in his truck for the seven-hour drive to Baltimore. He arrived at the chapel a few minutes after the celebration of life had begun and slipped into one of the open seats in the back pew, carefully propping his crutches beside him.

An older man was at the front of the chapel, recounting how Frank answered his call for help in the middle of a stormy night. The man's sump pump had failed and water was backing up into his basement.

"Frank didn't even know me. I'd just moved into town, but I'd heard good things about him at church, and that he was a plumber. He drove through the worst thunderstorm in memory to help a new guy out at two in the morning. When he learned my wife was expecting a baby, he didn't even accept payment for it. That's the kind of guy Frank Latimer was."

Heads nodded throughout the chapel. Another lady stood up to talk about how Frank used to play Santa Claus at Christmas parties, and how the kids would shriek with laughter when he "accidentally" pulled out carrots or broccoli instead of candy. He'd act confused, make a big show of checking his list twice, then make the kids bargain with him to swap the veggies for some candy.

The story triggered a round of warm laughter. Weren't services like this supposed to be sad and serious? He'd never been invited to a celebration of life, so maybe this was normal. A glance around the chapel showed happy faces. Happy! Maybe Frank's lingering illness had been so long in coming that his passing wasn't a shock, but this sort of sentimental fellowship was astonishing.

He glanced down at the memorial card, a photograph of his dad on the front. Jack never saw his dad look like this: clear-eyed and healthy with a grin that tilted up at one corner.

Jack had the exact same grin. The same hairline and shape of nose.

Odd. He'd never realized how much he and Frank looked alike. What else had he inherited from his dad? So much was lost. So much he would never know about the man who did an about-face in middle age and changed the entire trajectory of his life.

Sophie was in the front row with two blond young ladies beside her. They were his half-sisters. Those two girls were the only living relatives Jack had on this earth, and yet, they wouldn't know him if he passed them on the street.

Who would come to *his* funeral? Not that Jack cared, but it was a depressing thought.

Soon it was all over and the guests were funneling out of the chapel. To his surprise, Sophie intercepted him before he even reached the lobby. He managed an awkward hug despite his crutches.

"Thank you for coming," she said. "Please tell me that you'll stay with us. Courtney is bunking in with Jessica, so we've already freed a room for you."

Curiosity tugged. What sort of house had Frank managed to provide for his second family? What were his sisters like? Staying with Sophie would answer those questions.

"Thank you. I'd be grateful."

Following the reception, he headed out to the Latimer house. It was a modest, two-story home filled with family pictures, high school trophies, and two lumbering old mutts that left their dog beds to sniff Jack's fingers when he arrived.

Jessica and Courtney, his half-sisters, were curious and eager to spend time with him. Surprisingly, they knew all about him. They led him to a hallway crowded with family photographs on both walls. Frank had led a full life with his new family . . . horseback riding, sailing, and church picnics. Jack startled when he saw a photo of himself, probably five or six years old, sitting in the saddle of a fiberglass horse on a merry-go-round. His mom and dad stood on either side of him, holding him on the brightly painted horse. Even then, his foot was in a boot. A merry-go-round was one of the few rides at an amusement park safe for a hemophiliac.

"What's it like to have hemophilia?" Courtney asked. "Will you bleed to death if you get a papercut?"

He chuckled and answered the infamous question, grateful his sisters would never have to worry about the disease. It was passed down through the maternal line, so Jack got the gene from his mother, and neither Courtney nor Jessica would ever be touched by it. Still, they were curious and listened as he explained some of the challenges of the disease.

He continued walking down the hallway, letting the girls explain their life that was so alien to Jack.

Envy clawed. What would it have been like to have had summers on the beach? Building sandcastles and sailing and picnics by the sea?

"Jack, come sit down," Sophie urged. "Take the weight off your feet."

He nodded gratefully, and the girls followed. They sat on either side of him, plopping a photo album in his lap, showing him more glimpses into Frank's life over the past twenty years.

Photos of his dad looking tanned and healthy as he pushed the girls on a backyard swing. Christmas mornings and an Elf on the Shelf. One showed the girls when they were little tykes, gazing at Frank in adoration as he carved a pumpkin. Every page triggered a rush of painful joy.

His dad wasn't a failure. He built a happy family and had been a good husband and father to his second family. It was hard not to wonder how things would have turned out if Jack had accepted one of the million phone calls when Frank tried to mend fences. The fact that Jack never became a part of this new family was *his* fault, not his father's.

It was almost ten o'clock before the family turned in and Jack could retreat to Courtney's bedroom, where he tugged up the window. Alice's love of fresh air must have gotten to him, because he had a hankering for the soothing sounds of the crickets and evening breeze.

Except ... Mingled with the rustle of leaves came the sound of muffled sobs. He peered outside, into the backyard. Sophie sat on a bench beneath the trees, her face buried in a dish towel. Had there ever been a more heart-rending sight? It wasn't so much the sight of her alone in the garden, it was the keening wail of grief she struggled to hide. The dish towel covered her face, but the long, endless sobs leaked through it anyway.

Sophie had been brave all evening, but this sort of crippling grief ... it was hard to even hear, let alone offer her comfort.

He should go down to offer his shoulder, but what would he say?

It didn't matter. Comforting Sophie is what his father would have wanted of him. He shut the window quietly, shouldered his crutches, then made his way downstairs.

Once outside, he propelled himself across the lawn. Sophie startled and looked up, and he didn't look away. She stood as he approached, unsteady on her feet. He didn't say a word—just opened his arms. And that was all it took.

She collapsed into his arms, sobbing, her small frame shaking in his embrace. He held her tightly, letting her cry, letting himself cry, too. Quietly, but without shame.

He hadn't known he could feel this much. It was awful. And beautiful, too. He wouldn't abandon these people again. His sisters needed him. And so did Sophie.

Becoming a decent son was the one gift he had left to give his father.

And he meant to give it.

Jack left before dawn for Camp Lejeune the following morning. With luck, he'd be able to complete the budget and get the proposal turned in before the five o'clock deadline on Friday.

But first, he needed to give himself a regular infusion. Once the sun had risen, he pulled into a McDonald's parking lot. He bought a cup of black coffee and headed to the outside dining tables, glad they were empty so nobody would have to watch the distasteful medical procedure. Cars zoomed by and the parking lot smelled of crumbling asphalt, but it would suffice to take care of business. He spread a disposable pad on the picnic table, then opened his insulated bag of infusion supplies.

A note lay atop the vials of life-saving clotting factor. It was written in Sophie's handwriting. He opened the note and read.

Thank you for coming. I wasn't the best hostess for you, but I hope you can still become part of our family. Will you come for Christmas? You will be warmly welcomed.

He set the note aside, pensive as he opened a packet to disinfect his arm and the tops of the vials. The medicinal smell of alcohol floated in the air while he laid out the syringes, butterfly needle, double-ended needle, and the filter needle. Ironically, the longest part of the process was bringing the factor and solution up to room temperature.

He rolled both vials between his hands, urging them to warm faster as he thought about Sophie's invitation. Some people thrived in a family setting, others were best off on their own, and Jack always knew which camp he belonged in. For the past twenty years he spent Christmas in a hotel room binge-watching whatever football games were scheduled. The easiest thing would be to revert to his normal routine, but Sophie's note tugged at him. He should probably go, but first he had to win the contract at Camp Lejeune.

Once the vials were warm enough, he mixed the contents into a reconstituted solution, then tied a rubber strip around his bicep. He flexed his hands until a vein in his forearm rose into prominence beneath his skin, then held his breath as he inserted the needle and began the infusion.

Now all he had to do was sit and wait.

And think.

Alice had nudged him toward reconnecting with his father from the very beginning, and as with most things, she'd been right.

Alice. What a frumpy name for such a magnificent woman. Alice was beauty and humor and indefatigable resolve. She was gingham dresses and warm apple pie. Her daffy idealism was as delightful as it was frustrating. She was clever and funny and could deploy a battering ram of smooth Southern charm. He teased her for living in the past, for pretending she lived in a Jane Austen–inspired world.

Except it wasn't pretend. Alice created a world that embodied kindness and beauty and refinement. It was real, and it was who she was. She deserved so much more than he could give her.

The level of fluid in the vial slowly lowered as it drained into his arm. He wished it would drain faster so he could get back on the road and crank up the radio with a wall of hillbilly music to banish these memories about Alice.

Once the infusion was complete, he began packing up the supplies when a blue Toyota Prius swung into a parking space. He froze, not quite believing his eyes as the door opened and a woman with long dark hair stepped out.

Alice? Had she somehow followed him here? Put one of those tracking devices in his golf bag? A thrill ran through him, because all of a sudden the only person on the planet he wanted to see was Alice Chadwick and she was here and it was a miracle.

"Alice!" he called out across the parking lot.

The woman glanced his way but kept walking toward the restaurant.

A teenager. Not Alice.

The momentary flash of joy evaporated, and he was back in a bleak parking lot. Why was he always happy when Alice was around? He never should have let his guard down with her. Alice was his kryptonite, his Achilles heel. She was the one person on this earth who had slipped beneath his defenses and made him believe he could have something besides this life of loneliness and constant travel.

He would get over her eventually. Just like all the other times he pulled up stakes and moved on, he'd soon heal. The faster he could get to Camp Lejeune, the faster he could get back to work and the life he had chosen for himself.

Chapter Thirty-Four

The email Alice received from the specialist hired to perform the infrared scan of the portrait was cryptic. Professor Dreyfuss's email said his initial scan was "disappointing," and he was coming to Williamsburg to show her the results in person. The professor also suggested she would need to come up with additional funds if he was to proceed any further.

Alice wanted Arlo in on this conversation, and arrived at his office ahead of the appointed meeting time.

"It sounds like he didn't find anything," Alice grumbled as she dropped into the chair opposite Arlo's desk. "Do you think he just wants to gouge us for money?"

"Maybe not," Arlo replied. "He wouldn't drive all the way from Richmond if he came up completely empty."

Jack didn't have any more money for the Roost. She'd heard nothing from him since he left town last week, but he'd already taken on far more debt than he ever imagined. Fascination with Helga and William Reid Denby was *her* thing, not his. She couldn't ask him to fund expensive scientific tests that were likely to come up empty.

When he sauntered in the door, Professor Dreyfuss was nothing like she had imagined a distinguished optical engineer ought to look. Instead of a gray beard and thick glasses, the gangly kid wore a Coldplay T-shirt and flip-flops. He had a laptop bag slung over his shoulder and carried a large tube beneath his arm. There was no sign of the gaudy portrait.

"You have a PhD in Optical Engineering?" Alice asked, stunned.

"Yup," he said with a good-natured reply. "I thought I'd go into medical research, but the same technology that looks inside a human body can also look inside paintings. So here I am! Call me Jason."

Arlo offered to make them both a cup of tea before they started, but Alice declined, wanting to get straight to the results. Jason accepted the offer of tea, and the steeping process seemed to go on forever.

What was in the cardboard tube? She clenched the arms of her chair to stop herself from lunging for it. Maybe the results were disappointing, but he had *something* in that tube to show them, and she wished Arlo and Jason would gulp down their tea so they could get on with it.

"Did you find anything beneath our painting?" she finally blurted out, unable to wait any longer.

"Yeah, but it was a little disappointing." He reached for the tube to pop the plastic top from the end. "You were right. The fancy clothes were added later, but I haven't had much luck getting the details of what was underneath. I was able to come up with a shadowy image, but that's all."

Alice held her breath as Jason wiggled a large roll of paper from the tube. "This is a reproduction of the painting you gave me, but instead of the original clothes, I've located a different spectral band and overwrote the silk and satin clothes. This photo is as close to the original as I can get, and it's not very good."

Jason unrolled the photo paper and Arlo reached for wooden blocks to anchor the corners to the table.

Oh my! Instead of gaudy peach and aqua clothes, a hazy, X-ray-like image revealed a shadowy imprint of the original painting. Their clothes looked like a smudged charcoal drawing lacking all detail, but she could still see it. They were dressed like Puritans!

Their hazy, ghostly image blurred even more because tears were beginning to prick at her eyes. *She had found them.* William Reid Denby and his wife, Helga, were immortalized for all time in this painting.

"This image is the best my equipment can do," Jason said. "If you want a clear image of the original painting, you'll need to pay a restoration specialist to physically chip away the top layer of paint to get to the original, and that's expensive. Is there a budget for it?"

"I'll pay for it," Alice said. "I'll give anything if I can restore this portrait to the way they wanted the world to see them."

Once, centuries ago, a man backed the losing side in a long and bloody civil war. William Reid Denby fled to the wilds of Virginia to save his life. Like many of the well-to-do settlers, he brought window glass, slate roof tiles, and enough hardware to build a home.

He also brought a portrait so that during his lonely years in exile he was able to gaze at his wife's image. He arranged for someone to disguise their Puritan attire, just as he changed his name to escape his past. Reid was his middle name, and Santos? It was Spanish for *saints*. Reid Santos was the identity he created for himself, and which he carried for the rest of his life.

Back in England, Reid's family faked his death and added an engraved line to the family tombstone. When the king was restored to the throne in 1660, they presented it as proof that Reid had already died. Helga went into mourning but never forgot her husband overseas, and chose to join him in exile once Reid deemed it safe for her to come.

What did Reid and Helga think of the gaudy portrait? Did they hate having to hide beneath the bling, or did they secretly joke about it?

She'd probably never know. The answers to some questions would be forever lost to history. One thing she knew for sure was that Reid and Helga put their lives, their fortunes, and their futures on the line for a cause they believed in. Once Helga finally arrived in Virginia, they built a life for themselves at Reid's Roost, with Reid plying his trade as the owner of a ferry. And Helga? She was surely glad to be with her man again. They were two people of immense character who lived their faith steadfastly, enduring great personal loss to remain true to their beliefs. She admired them and couldn't wait to see what they would look like once their portrait was fully restored.

Alice spent her days out at the construction site. The reassembly of Reid's Roost was proceeding quickly, but the additions of the kitchen and conference room would take months to complete. Soon she would oversee the furnishing of the tavern, but for today she wanted Brandon Tilney's insight into her ideas for creating a seventeenth-century herb garden.

"Well?" she asked as they arrived at the foundation stones that outlined the Roost's original footprint. "Will this soil support the sort of medicinal herbs they would have used in the Colonial era?"

Brandon hunkered down and felt the soil. Pinched it between his thumb and forefingers, watched how it crumbled. Sniffed it.

"There's a lot of clay in the soil, but it could be amended to support herbs," he said as he stood back up. As always, he was impeccably dressed, with a tweed argyle coat and a hunter green scarf casually looped around his neck.

"Would you be interested in lending your name to the project?" she asked. "Jack won't be able to pay you anything, but serving as our consultant will be another line on your academic record."

And colleges loved that sort of thing. Any time professors donated their expertise to the local community, it helped strengthen town and gown relations.

"Sure, I can be a consultant," he said. "What are your plans for the future? I heard the college wants to reinstate you, now that the mess with Sebastian Bell has been cleared up."

Although her expulsion from academia had been brutal, she now felt liberated, as if granted a new lease on life. "I won't go back. I haven't applied for any other academic jobs and I'm not sure what I'll do. What I love most is working out here on the Roost."

The place had seeped into her blood. It had so much to offer the community in addition to being a high-end tavern. It could educate people. Inspire future historians, spark a curiosity about the past. She was uniquely qualified to create ties to the academic and social side of the local area, and this medicinal herb garden could be a part of that.

Jack owned this place lock, stock, and barrel. She'd probably overstepped even by speaking to Brandon about helping design a medicinal garden, but she couldn't help it. As her interest in reviving her academic career faded, hope for a new one as a historic preservation educator rose.

The problem was that it all depended on Jack. He'd made it clear their summer romance was over, and he would move on to whatever golf course hired him next. He would need someone here at the Roost to manage the place for him, but he might want a clean break with her. That would be okay. If she couldn't work at the Roost, Virginia was filled with historic sites where she might seek a job.

She found a smooth section of the foundation rocks to sit. Brandon joined her, both of them facing out toward Saint Helga's Spring in the distance. Hanging moss draped the gnarled branches of the oak trees and clusters of ironweed with their spiky purple flowers lined the bank of the spring. It was the last burst of autumn color before the woods would sink into winter hibernation. The cool air carried the scent of moss and ancient oaks. Did it look like this when Helga lived here? She outlived her husband and might have been terribly lonely out here.

"Have you ever thought of remarrying?" she asked Brandon.

His smile was sad as he tugged at some weeds growing along the foundation stones. "No. I've already had a great, magnificent love. For nine years, Clara and I lived in the firmament. When she died, I came crashing back down to earth. It took a long time to emerge from the shadows. I have no desire to head back to that dark place. I'm fine on my own. More or less."

It didn't sound like he was particularly happy. Brandon was a mature man his wife died, yet he still seemed too shell-shocked to risk another love affair. Jack was only a child when he lost his mother. Then his father. Then came a series of foster homes—one of which he had grown to love, only to have it taken away as well. Could she blame him for his reluctance to settle down? If a man as well-adjusted as Brandon Tilney hesitated to risk his heart again, she could hardly blame Jack for the same.

"I hear the sound of a dozen hearts breaking," she teased.

Brandon gave a good-natured chuckle, but sobered quickly. "We have to accept the good with the bad. Sometimes I think the good things in life wouldn't be so sweet unless we had the bitter to teach us the difference."

"Yeah, I feel like that, too," a different man's voice said.

Alice stood and whirled around, stunned by Jack's sudden arrival. He looked vibrant and alive, and carried a bouquet of wilted daisies.

"Jack! When did you get back in town?"

"Just now," he said and extended the wilted daisies to her. "I bought these when I stopped for gas a couple hours ago, but they didn't hold up so well. Sorry."

She took them, cradling their drooping blossoms. The fact that he brought her flowers was kind, but a little confusing, too.

"I thought you were gone for good," she said.

"Yeah, I kinda thought that for a while, too."

Brandon stood, startling Alice. She had completely forgotten he was there and she scrambled to include him. "You remember Brandon Tilney," she said to Jack. "His tree ring data pinpoint-ed the date of the Roost's construction."

The two men shook hands, then Brandon took a step back while adjusting his scarf. "I suddenly remember an important meeting in town. A support group for third wheels," he said with a wink at Alice.

She choked back a laugh as she watched him walk to his car, all while a seed of hope began blossoming inside her. This was the first time Jack ever brought her flowers, and it wasn't something he would have done casually.

"Did you submit a proposal for Camp Lejeune?"

"Nah. I ran out of time and decided to drop it. I was on my way to North Carolina when I got word that my dad died."

The daisies fell out of her hand and dropped on the ground. "Jack, I'm so sorry."

He nodded and stared out over the spring, where a pair of mallard ducks landed on the water, leaving ripples in their wake. Several more pairs came behind them. The flock was surely migrating to warmer climes, just taking a brief rest here. Maybe like Jack himself.

"I went to the funeral and stayed at Sophie's house. It confirmed everything I've always suspected about families. They mean heartache and baggage and worry and disappointments. But, Alice, I saw the really good stuff, too. I realized that I've been a coward because I spent the last twenty years running away from anything or anyone who tried to tie me down, and it almost cost me *you*."

He turned her shoulders to face him. "I don't want to keep running," he said with tired affection. "I had the best summer of my life here with you, and I want it to turn into the best autumn, the best winter . . . actually, the best rest of my life. Once the golf course is finished, I can stay here and run it. I'll probably still hit the road to design other courses if someone pays me enough, but I'm ready to settle down. Here."

She gazed up at him, this strong, tough man with such hidden depths of tenderness and vulnerabilities. She loved all of him, even the crude humor and rough edges.

"Good," she said simply.

He glanced over her shoulder back at the Roost, where construction workers were busy framing the new additions.

"I'll need someone to manage this place," he said. "I've been told it should be an academic who understands history and has fancy degrees, but they also have to have an eye for design and outreach. You interested?"

"Are you offering me a job?"

"Yeah, if you want it."

Instead of answering, she hugged him tightly. He returned the hug, and his heart thudded so hard she could feel it all the way through their clothes. It was the only sign of how nervous he'd been.

"Sorry about those miserable daisies," he said, and she brushed his apology away. She didn't care if the daisies were wilted and frail. She and Jack were both dinged-up too after a long, challenging year.

"I can save them," she said. "I'll press them between wax paper, then seal them in clear laminate sheets to make bookmarks. They'll last forever."

Jack put his hands on her shoulders, and pulled back enough to meet her gaze. That was when she noticed he was shaking. "I'm sorry it took me so long to figure it out," he choked out. "I love you. I love you, love you, *love you*. If I was a poet I would know better words, but all I can say is that I would be really grateful if you'd take me back. Alice, sometimes I can be a real idiot."

Tears prickled the backs of her eyes as she hugged and rocked him from side to side. Jack wasn't an idiot. His education came from the streets, from foster care, from the world of sports and locker rooms and hospital corridors. Very little of it came from a college classroom, but that made it no less valid, and she cringed that she ever dreamed that it was. She was grateful that Jack had overlooked her initial snobbish judgment of him. Now she'd have the chance to join his rollicking zest for life and couldn't wait to start spoiling him.

"I'm going to make you the world's best chicken pot pie. What do you want for dessert?"

"Blueberry pie," he said instantly.

Blueberries weren't in season, but she could use frozen and he'd probably like it just as well. Life didn't have to be perfect. It was better to appreciate the blessings they'd been given rather than nitpick at imperfections.

"I'll make you a pie," she said. "Then I'd like to hear about your father's funeral. We'll say a prayer for him and toast his memory to celebrate that you found each other again before the end."

Jack's eyes looked a little watery. "I don't know what I ever did to deserve you."

She laid a finger over his lips. "I'm grateful, too."

They were two imperfect people who would lift each other up, giving and receiving, the steady rhythm of two souls who would do the best they could with the gifts they'd been given. Jack propped her up last spring when she'd been humiliated on an international stage. And now, she would help him walk through the loss of his father and the unwieldy emotions that would come from forming lasting ties and settling down. These were the normal, terrible, and beautiful rhythms of life. She thanked God that Jack was ready to walk alongside her for that journey.

Chapter Thirty-Five

Two Years Later

Jack was reviewing ticket sales for the sold-out amphitheater when a disturbance near the parking lot caught his attention. He opened the office window in Reid's Roost Tavern and strained to hear. It sounded like *Alice* was having a run-in with someone.

He dropped the clipboard to hurry outside. Two dozen vendors were setting up for the county's Apple Blossom Festival that would begin in a few hours. Was one of them giving Alice a hard time? She'd been working her tush off for weeks to get this festival organized, and anyone who wanted to speak to her disrespectfully would have to go through Jack first.

He rounded the bend in front of the amphitheater, which would host thousands of people to watch tonight's country music concert. The parking lot was straight ahead, where vendors were setting up ice cream trucks, hot dog stands, and all manner of tents where locals would sell art and baked goods. Competition for a coveted vendor slot had been fierce this year, and it looked like someone without a vendor's badge had slipped in and was trying to set up a table. Alice faced the tall, silver-haired man, her cheeks flushed with frustration.

It was Grayson Chadwick, Alice's father. Ever since he and Alice married eighteen months ago, Jack had been trying to get along with Grayson, but it hadn't been easy.

"Dad, we've sold all the vendor slots, and you can't sell your book here."

"Why not?" Grayson barked. "You've got three thousand people showing up today, and I'm happy to sell autographed copies of my memoir."

Retirement didn't sit well with Grayson. He'd recently published a memoir reflecting on his years as a diplomat and was now setting out neat stacks of books on the table as Maude brought over a box of pens.

Jack stepped forward. "Vendor permits cost two hundred dollars for the day, and they sold out last month. You can't set up a table."

Grayson reached into his back pocket and thrust a form at Jack. "There's my permit."

A glance at the document showed the free pass Alice issued to her brother so Quentin could gather donations to create a waterfowl rescue center. It didn't seem right to charge Quentin a dime for setting up a table. First of all, Quentin was simply the nicest guy he'd ever met. Secondly, Jack and Alice owned the Roost and the amphitheater, so they got to set the rules and charge whatever they wanted.

He pulled Alice aside to speak in a low voice. "I don't suppose there's any harm in letting your dad piggyback on Quentin's table, but this is your call."

He would step in front of a speeding train to make Alice happy, but sometimes that meant yielding to her parents' quirks. In the last two years, Jack had established an excellent relationship with his stepmother and two half-sisters, but bonding with Alice's family was a lot tougher. Aside from Quentin, they were a fierce lot, but then again, he was nobody's pushover, so he was learning a reluctant respect for this unconventional family.

In the few moments since they'd taken their eyes off Grayson, Alice's parents had set finished setting up their card table and draped it with patriotic bunting. Maude wore a wide-brimmed straw hat trimmed with red, white, and blue flowers, but still managed to look like a hard-bitten general about to storm the beaches at Normandy. She set out baskets filled with branded bookmarks, mousepads, and candy meant to lure people to the table.

Jack and Alice headed to their table, where Alice handed the vendor form back to her dad. "It's okay if you want to share the table with Quentin, provided he doesn't mind. Where is he?"

"He didn't come," Maude said. "I set his donation box out if anyone wants to give something to his silly bird refuge."

"Why isn't he here?" Alice asked, bewilderment on her face, but Maude only scowled.

"He's back at home, prostrate with grief and wallowing in it like a tragic poet dying for love. He's barely eating; no wonder he looks so terrible."

"Oh dear," Alice said, her voice heavy with concern. "This is about a woman? I didn't realize he was seeing anyone again."

"He's not. It's the same old girl," Grayson said. "He should have gotten over her years ago, but no . . . like an animal that can't resist ripping a scab off its wound, he keeps watching out for her from afar."

"When did all this happen?" Alice asked Maude.

"Last week." Maude leaned forward and whispered quietly to Alice. "He blames your father. He says he's leaving the country and won't speak to us."

Alice grabbed a cheap paper fan from Maude's basket of freebies and began fanning herself as she met his gaze.

"Let's head to the Roost," she said, and Jack guided her toward the tavern. It was cool inside, thanks to the raised ceilings and artfully concealed air-conditioning ducts. In a few hours the festival would begin and the taproom would be standing-room only, but at the moment it was empty.

Reid's Roost had been open for a year now, and was wildly popular among people willing to pay top prices for the tavern's historic character. He had commissioned a master artisan to carve a custom bar from rich, dark oak that perfectly matched the timeworn hues of the original Roost. They served craft beer from local breweries and fine Virginia wines. The tavern still had the original diamond-paned windows and the immense fireplace that was almost large enough to stand in.

Their footsteps thudded on the old reclaimed floorboards as they headed to the bar. "What's going on with Quentin?" Jack asked once they were seated on two of the barstools.

Alice kept fanning herself. "He had a great, epic love affair while he was in college, but she left him and he's never gotten over her. Something must have happened to dredge it all up again. I'll send my parents home with a chicken pot pie for him. It's Quentin's favorite and maybe it will tempt him to eat."

Alice baked that pot pie this morning because it was Jack's favorite, too. He cradled her hand, knowing how spoiled he was to be showered with Alice's cooking, baking, and affection every day of his life. If the chicken pot pie might encourage Quentin to eat something, great. Wallowing in an old love affair ten years after the fact seemed a little extreme even for a man of Quentin's soft heart, but Jack wasn't in a position to judge. Alice had become the foundation of his life, his partner in all things, and the woman whose kindness and cleverness enriched every day of his life. He couldn't imagine a life without her in it.

His gaze strayed to the portrait of William Reid Denby and his wife that had been hung in a place of honor above the fireplace. Reid lived here at the Roost for a decade without Helga. He had nothing to remember her by except a disguised portrait and her name cleverly scratched into the upstairs window glass.

Alice had been able to give Reid and Helga the dignity of restoring their portrait to its original state. A specialist carefully chipped away the gaudy clothes to reveal magnificently tailored Puritan clothing beneath. Now the world would see Reid wearing a charcoal wool suit with a high-collared doublet and tall leather boots. Helga's gown was fashioned from silvery gray fabric softened by a crisp, intricate lace collar that framed her face like delicate frost, her sleeves puffed gently at the wrists. The gown was stark in its simplicity, yet lovely all the same.

One surprise the restoration expert found was the Denby signet ring on Reid's hand. It had been painted over to protect his identity, but now was proudly revealed once again.

Voices from outside indicated that the first of the festival goers had arrived. Most were headed straight to the row of vendors, but a woman with two teenaged children wandered into the tavern. Their T-shirts from Colonial Williamsburg were a sure sign they were tourists, but Jack gladly welcomed all-comers.

"Is this where they filmed *The King's Redemption*?" the mother asked.

Alice hopped down from the barstool and led them to one of the diamond-paned windows. "The outdoor scenes were filmed in the yard right outside this window. The inside scenes were done on a reproduction set over in England."

The King's Redemption had just aired its third season, and the flight of William Reid Denby had been incorporated into the plot. Alice had served as the historical consultant to the scriptwriters, and the production company filmed several of the outdoor scenes right here in Virginia, prominently featuring the exterior shots of Reid's Roost. He and Alice watched from a distance as they filmed a totally pointless scene of the bare-chested actor portraying Reid as he chopped wood outside the front door. "Stop drooling," Jack had whispered to Alice during the filming. It was a gratuitous scene to ratchet the actor into heartthrob status, and it had worked.

"Was Sebastian Bell ever here?" the teenaged daughter asked.

Alice shook her head. "Sebastian Bell's scenes were all filmed on location in England because Charles II never came to America." She leaned toward the girl with a conspiratorial whisper. "I hope that's not a spoiler."

"I don't know much about history, but I like Sebastian Bell."

"Who doesn't?" Alice teased as she flashed Jack a wink.

"I don't," he replied in a mock growl, even though he had no doubts about where Alice's heart lay. By all accounts, Sebastian had remained clean and sober, and still had lavishly kind words about Alice whenever people asked about the curious scandal a few years ago. Given the success of the third season of *The King's Redemption*, a fourth season looked likely, and this one would include the arrival of Helga in America.

The tourists wandered around the interior of the tavern and took a few pictures standing before the portrait. It was a reproduction painting because Alice insisted the original be kept in the museum, but this was a perfect replica and it seemed fitting to hang it in the house where Reid and Helga once lived.

Alice's plan to use the tavern to inspire a love of history had succeeded beyond all their expectations. So far, it had hosted eight weddings, three academic symposia, and thirty thousand tourists who learned the love story of two political refugees who found a new home in the early years of Virginia.

The group of tourists moved toward the bar. "Do you think they were happy here?" the mother asked Alice, who shrugged.

"We haven't been able to find anything they wrote, but I'd like to think they were. Helga gave up a lot to follow her husband here."

Jack gazed at the wedding portrait. Rather than the happy smiles typical of today's portraiture, Reid and Helga's expressions were solemn, a reflection of their staunch character in a time when it was dangerous to practice their faith. The year this portrait was painted marked the start of the long and bloody English Civil War and they could have no idea of the trials they would face in the years ahead. Marriage entailed sticking together for better or for worse. Reid and Helga had a whole lot of worse, and yet, they endured. Helga never got her child; Reid lost his inheritance and lived his final years in exile. Had they been happy? It was impossible to know, but Jack had found happiness here.

As for the legend of Saint Helga's Spring . . . Jack never believed in superstitious claptrap, but he couldn't entirely discount it, either. He was healthier and happier than he'd ever been. In October, he and Alice would welcome their first child—a boy they would name William Reid, in honor of the man who had built the Roost so many centuries ago. Without the Roost, he and Alice never would have met or fallen in love. The old place had held on through centuries of war and ruin, storms and abandonment. Now it stood strong once again—full of life and laughter. It was a haven for him and Alice, where the past was honored and the future was an adventure they would build together.

Author's Note

I was inspired to write this novel after reading about "the regicides," the fifty-nine men who signed King Charles I's execution warrant following the king's conviction for treason in 1649.

When Charles II was restored to the throne in 1660, the new king's first objective was to unify the nation, which he believed was the only way to stabilize his reign. He offered clemency to the Puritans who participated in the revolution in order to bring almost twenty years of strife and bloodshed to an end.

The only people excluded from the new king's clemency were the fifty-nine regicides. Although twenty of them died before the Restoration, the search for the surviving men was the greatest manhunt of the seventeenth century. Many fled to the Netherlands or the American colonies, where bounty hunters followed them in hope of winning the massive rewards. Most of the regicides who fled to America went to the Puritan colonies of New England, where sympathetic friends hid them. Many, however, were betrayed, handed over to the Crown, and met a predictably grisly fate.

One man, John Dixwell, had been inaccurately reported in England as already dead. Whether his relatives faked his death or it was a genuine mistake is unknown, but none of the bounty hunters came looking for him. John Dixwell lived out his days under a false name in New Haven, Connecticut, where he was a popular man assumed to be a wealthy, retired merchant. He lived with his wife and children, and only revealed his true identity shortly before he died peacefully at his home in 1689. His story inspired me to create the fictional William Reid Denby and the adventures of a man who went to great lengths to conceal his identity and be reunited with his wife.

Questions for Discussion

1. Alice and Sebastian Bell are both romantics, and believe that love at first sight is possible. Do you?

2. Jack's father reinvented himself after years of alcoholism, but Jack has difficulty forgiving him. How can a person who has transformed their life rebuild ties to those they have hurt? What obligation did Jack have (if any) to reconcile with his father?

3. Jack has firm ideas about the positive value of sport programs in school. What is your opinion?

4. It has been said that history is written by the winners, and the Puritans have suffered from bad publicity ever since Charles II was restored to the throne. Did this book teach you anything about them?

5. Alice and Jack are opposites in most things. Do you predict they will have a happy marriage? Why or why not?

6. Alice's self-perception was deeply shaped by the themes in Jane Austen's novels. Have you ever been similarly influ-

enced by an author's work? If so, how did it shape your perspective on life?

7. Some experts believe historical sites should be preserved and remain off-limits to visitors, while others want to renovate them so people can touch, see, and feel the historic artifact. What's your opinion?

8. How do you feel about the way Jack and Alice renovated and capitalized on the Roost? Did turning it into a tavern cheapen it or did the benefits outweigh the compromises?

Thank you for reading *Meet Me in Virginia*! It is the first novel in the Far & Away series, all of which will feature love stories about intelligent people with fascinating careers, daunting challenges, and a hint of a mystery to solve.

The best way to learn more about my upcoming books, recommended reading, and more cool news is to sign up for my monthly newsletter at https://elizabethcamden.com/official-elizabeth-camden-newsletter

Everyone who signs up for my newsletter will get a link to an exclusive short love story available nowhere else. *Hope on Heartbreak Mountain* is a one-hour read about a woman who climbed a mountain to find a reclusive botanist and stumbled into a love story rooted in hope, healing, and second chances.

Please read ahead for a preview of the next book in the Far & Away series, which is Quentin's love story . . .

Preview of The Top of the World

Princeton University

Holly knew something was off the moment three identical black Mercedes-Benz sedans rolled into her dormitory parking lot. Plenty of students at Princeton University drove expensive cars, but not in a convoy.

Quentin's father did. As the U.S. Secretary of State, he never traveled without a security detail—but why was he here? Quentin was in Costa Rica on a two-week seminar studying humpback whales, and campus was nearly deserted for winter break. Only a handful of students, including Holly, had stayed behind for tutoring—a desperate attempt to salvage her grades and keep her scholarship.

A shiver raced through her as she peeked through the blinds, eyeing the men in long wool coats as they left their cars. Sure enough, Quentin's father was in the middle of them. They looked like ravens walking across the snow-covered parking lot as they approached her dormitory.

Holly raced to the closet to pull on something respectable because her oversized flannel shirt came out of a charity bin. Her hair looked like it belonged to a wild woman, a mass of untamable red curls spilling down her back. She dragged on a Princeton sweatshirt, finger-combed her hair, then twisted it into a loose bun. She hadn't even bothered to brush it this morning because the snowstorm was going to keep her inside so why bother?

Quentin's father scared the willies out of her. He was always polite, but his disapproval seeped through anyway. Maybe it was only natural that someone as rich and worldly as Grayson Chadwick would be suspicious of how quickly she and Quentin fell in love. Within a week of meeting each other they had become inseparable and Quentin even brought her home last summer to meet his parents. It hadn't gone well. Quentin swore his parents would warm up to her eventually, but they'd been dating for more than a year and there was no sign of a thaw.

Footsteps crunching across the icy snow loomed closer, and Holly rushed to tidy the room. She straightened her rumpled bedspread and scooped up clothing draped over the chair when the brisk knock sounded on her door.

"Who is it?" she called out, stuffing the clothes beneath her bed.

"Grayson Chadwick."

She wilted a little at his commanding tone. Quentin used to joke that his father could convince the Goths get along with the Visigoths. She wasn't exactly sure who those people were, but she'd often seen Grayson Chadwick on television, standing resolute between presidents and ruthless dictators from every corner of the globe. If seasoned diplomats found him formidable, maybe this anxious feeling in her chest wasn't anything to be ashamed of.

"Okay, just a sec," she said, rummaging through her closet for better shoes. Quentin called her tattered slippers a health hazard, but he laughed when he said it. His father surely wouldn't laugh.

She raced across the room, pressed a hand over her chest to calm her breathing, then opened the door. "Hi," she said brightly. "What a surprise. Can I help you?"

Mr. Chadwick gave a grandfatherly laugh. "My dear, I've come here to help *you*."

"Well, come inside. It's freezing out there."

One of the dark-suited men came inside with Mr. Chadwick, scanning her room as though searching for hidden terrorists . . . which was probably what he was actually doing. She just hoped he wouldn't check beneath the bed to see a week's worth of laundry.

The inspection didn't take long. "Allow us some privacy, please," Mr. Chadwick said, and the security agent nodded and opened the door to leave. A freezing gust blew in, and it seemed cruel to make him and the others wait outside.

"If you get cold, there's a café at the other end of the dormitory that's open," Holly called out, but Mr. Chadwick had already closed the door behind the security officer. The dorm room felt suffocatingly cramped with him inside, and yet the older man seemed perfectly at ease as he pulled out the desk chair to sit. With his chiseled features and distinguished graying hair, he looked like a sharper, more refined version of Harrison Ford—if Harrison Ford wore tailored suits and commanded a room with a single glance. Beneath the wool coat he wore a business suit and a gold tie pin. She didn't even realize men still wore tie pins before she started dating Quentin, but the Chadwicks had all sorts of quirks common among old money.

"Quentin told me of your mother's difficulties," Mr. Chadwick began, which was the last thing Holly expected him to say. She'd been so busy studying it hadn't left much time for dwelling on her mother's worsening case of diabetes, but of course she had told Quentin. He was the world's best listener, and she'd been leaning on him for support ever since her mother's diagnosis.

The last thing Holly wanted to discuss with Mr. Chadwick was her parents or her unconventional upbringing. "My mom's doing okay," she said.

"My understanding is that this is going to require some expensive treatment, and I'd like to help with that."

Holly blinked, stunned by this turn of events. "That . . . that's very generous of you, but I'm sure I'll be able to figure something out."

Mr. Chadwick gave a kindly smile. "I gather your family prides itself on their self-sufficiency."

Self-sufficiency? That was one way of putting it. Another would be that her parents were too paranoid to trust the electrical grid, fluoridated water, or the American food supply. Her parents insisted their children learn to hunt, fish, raise chickens, and grow their own vegetables. They didn't go to the doctor, send their children to school, or trust anything from the government. If they needed something they couldn't hunt or grow, they traded their eggs or honey with a few of the other oddball hermits who lived on Casper Mountain. The Fermoy family didn't just live off the grid . . . it was like they built a wall against the entire world.

None of them had been vaccinated against anything, and when her father died two years ago because he refused to get a tetanus shot, the veil slowly started to lift from her mother's mind. She'd been in failing health for years and finally consented to start visiting a free clinic in the tiny town of Bartow deep in the mountains of Maine. That was when her mother first learned of the diabetes that was ravaging her body, slowly sapping her strength. The disease left her exhausted, her wounds slow to heal, and her vision blurred. Worst of all, it stole away her vitality bit by bit, like a tide eroding the shore.

"I'm trying to find some sort of government program that might help," Holly said, embarrassed to discuss such things.

"Quentin said there aren't any paved roads leading to your mother's house. And that she doesn't have a car. How will she get into town for treatment without a car?"

"I'll think of something," Holly said.

"How are your grades?"

She looked away. Her grades were awful but they weren't anyone else's business and she was under no obligation to reveal anything. "They're fine," she said with a shrug.

"Quentin said that you couldn't go to Costa Rica for the January seminar because you're taking a chemistry class, but it's not really a chemistry class, is it? It's a special tutoring program for students at risk for failing out of college. Am I right?"

Somehow the compassion in his voice made it even harder to take. It was mortifying that she was on the verge of losing her scholarship, and when the academic counselor suggested special tutoring over the January session, she nearly wept in gratitude. Princeton's outreach program for first-generation rural students was the only reason she'd been able to come here, but she had to maintain a C average to keep the scholarship. She and her sister had been homeschooled by their mom, and they never had math beyond the eighth-grade level. She'd never taken chemistry or physics at all. If it weren't for her natural aptitude in English and biology, she would have flunked out last year.

None of this was Mr. Chadwick's business. She already felt cowed and inadequate among Quentin's overachieving family, and this visit was cutting into her study time.

"I don't understand why you're here," Holly said.

"You may think my wife and I disapprove of you—"

She interrupted him with a cynical laugh. "You made that quite clear when I visited your home last summer."

"Nonsense," Mr. Chadwick said. "We admire your resourcefulness and ambition to make something of yourself. Nevertheless, it won't be possible for your mother to manage a complicated disease if she lacks a vehicle to get off that mountain and into town, let alone pay the medical bills. My wife and I would like to set up a trust to arrange for your mother's medical care. Would that be acceptable to you?"

A fine sheen of perspiration broke out across her skin despite the chilly air. She wasn't precisely sure what "a trust" was, but it was probably some sort of financial thing. She was at sea in a world she didn't understand. Every mistrustful hackle in her body was firing, but she needed to know more.

"How would it work?"

"To begin, I would provide your mother with a reliable four-wheel-drive vehicle and arrange for medical insurance. Going forward, I will ensure your mother's insurance and any other medical expenses are fully covered. I will also provide a substantial one-time payment to make some improvements to your family's home. There is no electricity or telephone service in the cabin, correct?"

All she could do was nod.

"We can't have that for a seriously ill woman," Mr. Chadwick said gently. "The payment would be enough to connect the cabin to the electrical grid, at least giving her the power to run a satellite dish for communication."

Now that her father had passed, her mother would probably be willing to wire the house. Most of the other people living on Casper Mountain now had electricity, but it would be expensive and her mother pretended not to want or need it.

"It would cost an awful lot," she said, her voice barely more than a whisper, but oh! What a blessing it would be not to worry about her mother and sister each time a bad storm descended on Casper Mountain.

Mr. Chadwick's smile was grandfatherly. "Never you mind about the expense. I will be happy to fund these improvements. In exchange for setting up the trust, I would require you to leave Princeton University and have no future contact with my son.

Ever. Holly, we respect you, but we both know you're not the right match for Quentin."

He spoke the words kindly, but they felt like a fist squeezing her heart. She'd sensed this might happen last summer when she lived with the Chadwicks for a month at their summer home in Virginia. They lived in a mansion, and always had visitors. Congressmen and business leaders and famous athletes. Quentin stuck to her side like glue and helped ease her in to the conversations. She'd just been gaining a little confidence when she made a stupid gaff in front of the whole family. Mr. Chadwick was reminiscing about the time he turned down an offer to become the ambassador to the Soviet Union because he didn't speak Russian. Holly blurted out, *"Why would you need Russian? Don't they speak Soviet in the Soviet Union?"*

She still flushed when she remembered their shocked faces. Quentin quickly changed the subject, but her embarrassment remained.

After that disastrous summer, she and Quentin decided on a different plan for their life, one that wouldn't require Holly to adapt to the rarefied air of the Chadwick family. They knew exactly what their future looked like. After all, it was charted out on the six-foot world map tacked on the wall above her bed.

That map meant everything to her. She and Quentin had made it together as their final project for Cartography 301. They analyzed topography charts, satellite imagery, and scientific journals to accurately depict geological features and climate zones. Combining traditional research with cutting-edge geographic software, they used the data to create a scientifically accurate and artistic map of the Earth's complex landscapes. In the process of making this map, Holly realized the immensity of the world and how limited her education had been before coming to Princeton. That map encapsulated a thousand dreams she and Quentin shared to see and save the world.

Mr. Chadwick noticed her gaze and leaned in to study the map. His gaze zeroed in on a line across the middle of the United States that had recently been added, and his lip curled in contempt.

She stiffened. She and Quentin drew that line together, the route of their future quest to hike across America. The pencil mark started at the tidewater of Virginia and headed west. It wended across the glory of the Blue Ridge Mountains and the horse country of Kentucky. It traversed through the large, square prairie states covered with amber fields of grain. At least, that's what was always said about them, and she'd longed to see it for herself. What would it sound like when the wind rippled across that grain? Would there be an aroma? A taste in the air?

The pencil line then turned south toward the sunbaked lands of New Mexico and Arizona and the Painted Desert. What exactly did that name mean? Quentin was determined to show it to her, and hiking across it would be one of the most challenging parts of their journey, but she'd been dreaming about it for months. The pencil line finally arrived at the promised land in California. By the time they reached it, she and Quentin would have trekked across America from sea to shining sea. It wasn't for any pressing academic need or mission. They wanted to do it because they were young and in love and Holly had seen so little of the world. Quentin persuaded her that they could do it. Holly knew survival skills like trapping and camping, while Quentin knew how to navigate and make his way in the world. They'd selected their route, their resting points, and the things they wanted to see along the way. The journey would take ten months, and at the end of it they planned to get married with the sun rising over the Pacific Ocean before them.

Quentin had told his parents about their plan to take a year off college for the hike. It was probably their epic hike and intention to get married when they reached the Pacific that spooked his parents.

Now here was Quentin's father, trying to split her apart from Quentin and using her mother's ailing health to do it. She felt like Eve being tempted by the apple.

A lump formed in her throat as she gazed at the line marking their grand trek across the country. What a silly, impractical dream. How could she skip off into the wilderness for ten months when her mother was ill?

The crinkling of paper sounded as Quentin's father removed a document from his briefcase. "Here are the terms of the agreement," he said. "It is quite generous, but nonnegotiable, and you will be required to sign it."

She averted her gaze and began to pace. It would be disloyal to even look at that piece of paper. Being trapped in this tiny dorm room with Grayson Chadwick's overwhelming presence felt suffocating. No wonder Quentin always warned her about his parents. He loved them, but they were tough and demanding, while Quentin was the kindest man she'd ever known. The first week she met him he tried to save a raccoon whose foot was trapped in a drainage grate. It bit him. Quentin actually apologized to the raccoon for frightening it and continued working until he set the little guy free. She accompanied him to the student clinic while he got the mandatory rabies shots, which were no picnic, but Quentin never balked. No matter how long Holly lived, she was certain she'd never meet a man who could rival Quentin Chadwick for gentle kindness.

"I don't know," she said.

Mr. Chadwick reached into his coat pocket and brought out a photograph. "This is Quentin at Thanksgiving dinner two months ago."

She froze, not wanting to look, but she couldn't resist. The photo showed the formal dining room at the River House, the grand estate on the Potomac River where the Chadwicks lived. Over a dozen people sat at the table that looked like it came out of a magazine, but her gaze homed in on Quentin and the young woman beside him. It was Sara Wetherford, the girl he took to his high school senior prom.

She swallowed hard. This picture didn't mean anything. The Chadwicks and the Wetherfords were close family friends, so this could be entirely innocent.

But why hadn't Quentin told her that he'd seen his high school girlfriend when he'd been home at Thanksgiving? She didn't doubt his faithfulness. They'd always been completely honest with each other and Holly wasn't the jealous type . . . and yet, Sara looked so perfect sitting beside Quentin. She wore pearls around her neck and her hair was in a perfect, shoulder-length bob. She looked like Jackie Kennedy; like she belonged at that table. Sara Wetherford probably didn't need special tutoring classes or to have Quentin secretly whisper what caviar was when the strange little blobs were served at cocktail hour.

Holly handed the photo back, unable to meet Mr. Chadwick's eyes. In return, he handed her a legal contract, and she took it. Unlike most contracts, the terms were plainly spelled out in simple language that fit onto a single page. In exchange for Holly leaving Princeton and severing contact with Quentin, Grayson Chadwick would provide Holly's mother with a brand-new four-wheel-drive pickup truck to get off the mountain and into town. He would also pay the monthly premium for top-of-the-line medical insurance for as long as Holly continued to abide by their agreement. He would ensure their house was wired for electricity.

She tried to read the document but was hyper-aware of Quentin's father sitting only a yard away as he nosed around her desk. He tilted her chemistry book to read the spine.

"You're still enrolled in General Chemistry?" There was a hint of surprise in his voice, even though she suspected he knew she had failed General Chemistry her freshman year, which was why she was taking it again.

"Yes," she admitted simply, as if there was no shame in having to take it again.

"Then you'll need to take Organic Chemistry, then Biochemistry, and Analytical Chemistry, right? At least, that's what Quentin took during his first two years for his biology degree."

Just hearing those class names was enough to trigger a rush of acid in her gut. Who was she trying to fool? Even with special tutoring, it was going to be a stretch to pass General Chemistry. How could she even dream of passing Analytical Chemistry? The odds were good that she was going to flunk out of college no matter how much tutoring she received. All those dreams she'd nurtured while growing up in that lonely cabin would come to nothing.

But she'd still have Quentin. They could still hike across the country together and see the world and get married. She didn't need a college degree to do that.

Except that her mother would die for want of treatment, and her sister would be condemned to living on Casper Mountain in a cabin without electricity. She should sign the paper and take the money. If she did, she could change the fortunes of her family.

"I don't want you to think badly of my mother," she said. "I know she's odd, but the Fermoys are a great family. My great-grandfather was Patrick Fermoy . . ."

Her voice trailed off. Nobody knew who Patrick Fermoy was anymore. He was a cartographer who died young, leaving only a few maps to document his amazing life. It was Patrick Fermoy's dashing, daredevil life that had inspired Holly to leave the mountain and reach for something better.

She stared at the map she and Quentin had made, and the line marking their future trek across the country. That line was a cruel joke now, just another dream that would never happen. She twisted her hands, cracking her knuckles and pausing for time.

"Don't feel bad," Mr. Chadwick said. "By signing this document, you will be helping your family, and giving Quentin the time he needs to make wiser decisions that are more in keeping with his life."

It was a delicate way of saying that Quentin deserved someone better than a girl who grew up in a cabin without running water or electricity. Who couldn't pass General Chemistry, and didn't know the difference between Russia and the Soviet Union.

For as long as she could remember, Holly wanted to be as daring and adventuresome as her great-grandfather. She gazed at the map and smiled a little at the dotted islands scattered across the Aegean Sea. It was where Patrick did his best work during the dangerous years of World War II. Patrick didn't have a college degree; he simply left the mountain and envisioned a daring future for himself. The world was a wide and wonderful place, and perhaps it was big enough for her to follow in Patrick's footsteps after all.

Hope mingled with defeat as she turned to look at Mr. Chadwick.

"Where do I sign?"

Look for *The Top of the World* in the Spring of 2026!